Subterfuge

A clever device or strategy used to evade a rule, escape a
consequence, or to hide something...

The Critics on *Celebration:*

"Reynolds's 'Soirée' is a bitterly ironic SF parable about space travellers reaching their destination at last, only to find others – friendly seeming others – have got there first, rather as in van Vogt's 'Far Centaurus', but with added bite.

Celebration is a highly readable book."

Nick Gevers, Locus *– April 2008*

"Jon Courtney Grimwood's 'The Crack Angel' is a *very* stylish sf-noir detective tale. What starts out like any other private eye story, with a beautiful blonde giving lots of money for a tricky job, unfolds into an altogether more unique story. It's an excellent piece.

This is a good collection featuring some strong stories by many of the biggest names in British SF… I commend it to you."

Mark Watson, Best SF *– 25th May 2008*

"'The Killing Fields' by **Kim Lakin-Smith** does exactly what its title implies. It's fast, brutal, and as nihilistic as anything written since Michael Moorcock introduced Jerry Cornelius.

Martin Sketchley's 'Deciduous Trees' is a closely observed slice-of-life full of details beautifully observed. Numinous and moving, it's a fine story by a writer who on this evidence deserves wider exposure."

Colin Harvey, the fix *– 21st July 2008*

"The concluding tale is Adam Roberts' 'The Man Of The Strong Arm', a story full of in-jokes and clever twists that will be appreciated by the SF buff…. There are some great satirical concepts, such as the silent robed women who even have to zip up their eyes, which make this a very satisfying conclusion to a wonderful collection. A fitting celebration of the BSFA? I certainly think so. The variety of stories is amazing, covering a huge swathe of the Science Fiction spectrum and beyond, but peppered with unmistakably British stories. A definite recommendation from me."

Gareth D. Jones, SF Crowsnest *– 1st September 2008*

And on *Myth-Understandings*.

"But the best tale on offer is certainly 'The Ecologist and the Avon Lady' by Tricia Sullivan. Here, in a crazy delirium-soaked landscape, an operative of a monster-extermination agency, who for some reason is also an Avon Lady equipped with all the appropriate stock in trade, battles a shape-shifting creature on a mountain, false seemings everywhere, identities and locations fluid, thematic implications richly multitudinous. Good stuff, brightly daft, daftly bright."

Nick Gevers, Locus – *April 2008*

"*Myth-Understandings* showcases women writers of the UK, and it features plenty of strong work. The best story is a reprint, Gwyneth Jones's 1996 World Fantasy Award winner "The Grass Princess", but I for one hadn't yet read the story and I'm glad I did – it's delightful. New writer Heather Bradshaw's "TouchMe™: Keeping in Touch" is a madcap thing about a customer service representative for the title device, a way for people – mainly lovers – to keep in constant touch – often a decidedly mixed blessing."

Rich Horton, Locus – *May 2008*

"Sperring weaves a beautiful, poetic tale of a creature as innocent as a flower bud, slowly blossoming into a more solid and perhaps more painful reality. I enjoyed the music of the words as much as the fascinating look inside the mind of an alien creature.

'Do You See?' by Sarah Pinborough is a wonderfully creepy story about missing children, shadows, monsters, and magic words. It was a pleasure to read."

Janice Clarke, the fix – *27th June 2008*

"The theme of 'communication' has produced some very interesting and enjoyable stories… Anyone who has ever worked in an office or call centre will be rooting for Bradshaw's main character in 'Touch Me', as she battles her way through her work day, dealing with irate customers, questing for a cup of coffee and avoiding the boss… the book greatly enlivened my bus journeys home."

Selina Lock, Prism – *Summer 2008*

And on disLOCATIONS:

"Chaz Brenchley's 'Terminal' is a rich, dense, highly textured story about the teleportation of consciousness and the nature of identity, set on an exotic planet, and which lingers long in the memory, and like the MacLeod story, is one of the best of the year, let alone in the book.

While 'Lighting Out', the Ken MacLeod story that ends the collection has none of the obvious glamour of the Brenchley story, its setting is equally exotic, and like the Brenchley, deals with the nature of consciousness. It has enough invention for a full length novel, and should, if there is any justice, be picked up by at least one of the *Year's Best* anthologies."

Colin Harvey, Suite 101 – *September 2007*

"The Cadigan, Brenchley and West, Macleod stories bookend the collection with particularly strong SF stories. It's another good collection from Whates/NewCon, available in a limited edition, signed by the authors.

Mark Lawson, Best SF – *11ᵗʰ October 2007*

"*disLOCATIONS* proves yet again that Ian Whates has the capacity to become an important force in raising the standard of independently produced anthologies. I hope that NewCon Press can maintain the momentum of their first two excellent works."

Paul Skevington, SF Crowsnest – *2ⁿᵈ February 2008*

"*DisLOCATIONS* is another short story collection in a run of 500 copies signed by contributors. Fortunately, this is a book worth reading as well as collecting.

Whates's theme for the book is 'displacement', and this is honoured by all the stories present even when a number of pieces would also fit into a book like Dozois and Strahan's recent anthology, *The New Space*

Opera. This might be less than astonishing when it comes to a writer like Ken MacLeod, but Pat Cadigan channelling Alastair Reynolds is rather more unusual. This is just one reason why Cadigan's 'Among Strangers' is a great opener."

Duncan Lawie, Strange Horizons – *8th February 2008*

Subterfuge

Edited by Ian Whates

NewCon Press,
England

First edition, published in the UK October 2008
by NewCon Press

NCP 006 (special edn. hardback)
NCP 007 (hardback)
NCP 008 (softback)

10 9 8 7 6 5 4 3 2 1

ISBN: 978-0-9555791-5-8 (special edn. hardback)
978-0-9555791-6-5 (hardback)
978-0-9555791-7-2 (softback)

Invaluable editorial assistance from Ian Watson

Cover illustration, layout and design by Andy Bigwood

Book layout by Storm Constantine

Printed in the UK by Biddles of Kings Lynn

Contents

The Subtle Art of Subterfuge
An Introduction

It was while in the Stravaigin – a quirky and welcoming restaurant-cum-bar in Glasgow's West End – that the theme for this anthology emerged. Meal finished, Neil Williamson and I were sitting back and nattering while Hal Duncan feverishly signed a stack of signature sheets for the *disLOCATIONS* anthology. The place was packed and Franz Ferdinand were at the table behind us, their meal interrupted by gushing female admirers.

I had recently read Neil's Elastic Press collection *The Ephemera*, an impressive set of elegant tales deftly told, and I was determined to have something from him in a forthcoming NewCon Press book. The problem being that the next planned volume was ladies only, so Neil would have to wait until the one after. This time, when the inevitable question arose, I was prepared. "What's the theme?" Neil duly asked.

I have always enjoyed stories with a twist. Such things can be annoying when done badly, leaving the reader with a sense of being cheated because the author withheld some vital detail, but when executed skilfully, the twist provides a piquant aftertaste rather than anything remotely bitter. Having read *The Ephemera*, I knew that Neil would be a master of the piquant. So, I responded to his question with the single word, "Subterfuge," and the theme was born. Now to find other authors who could do the theme justice.

John Meaney has been a favourite author since I read the first of his *Nulapeiron* series, and I've been badgering John for a story for some time. When I told him the theme for this one, he immediately became enthused and said he would love to write something for it. The resulting story proved more than worth the wait.

Jaine Fenn and I met at the 2008 Eastercon, when I moderated a panel which both she and her agent, the ebullient John Jarrold, were on. However, it was Jaine's friend, Kari Sperring (whose story "Seaborne" features in the *Myth-Understandings* anthology), who encouraged her to send me "Collateral Damage". I'm delighted she did. This is a wonderful piece of SF and totally appropriate to the theme.

Gary Couzens has appeared frequently in venues such as *Interzone* and *Fantasy and SF*, but his consistently high quality work has yet to translate into the level of wider acclaim he deserves. "Jubilee Summer" is another example of just how good Gary can be.

Juliet E. McKenna goes from strength to strength, producing unashamedly high fantasy with depth, texture and characters who demand to be cared about. She was one of the first authors I spoke to regarding this anthology and one of the first to submit. I remember thinking as I read her piece, "Wow, if all the stories are this good, I'm in for a treat!"

Pat Cadigan is not just a special person, she's a veritable force of nature – a larger-than-life character who also happens to be a damn fine writer. I was honoured to publish the first in a new series of tales from her in *disLOCATIONS*, delighted to publish the second in *Myth-Understandings*, and I'm grinning from ear-to-ear now that I can present the third. The first *Tale from the Big Dark* was deservedly selected by *Locus* as one of the best short stories of 2007, and you know what? I reckon *Lie of the Land* is even better.

Pat's story was the last to be submitted. With it came a note which read, "Hey, Ian, when's the next anthology due? I want to get a head start so I can be late earlier for that one!" Can't wait.

Neil Williamson did not let me down, by the way. Set in a wonderfully off-kilter world, his story "Moth" delivers in every sense, and is as well-crafted and satisfying as you would expect from Neil.

Tony Ballantyne is the dark horse of British SF, building a reputation quietly as others bask in the limelight. Two of his stories appeared in David G. Hartwell and Kathryn Cramer's 2008 *Year's Best SF 13*. There is a deliciously retro feel underpinning his story *Underbrain*, even though it is set on a bizarrely alien future world.

Tanith Lee is an author I have admired for years; capable of work which invites you to pause and reread, simply for the pleasure of experiencing again the richness of the narrative. Tanith is another who seemed to revel in the theme of *Subterfuge*, adding a further facet of interpretation to the anthology. You can almost feel the seafret on your brow!

Sarah Singleton contributed a wartime thriller noir to the first NewCon Press anthology, *Time Pieces*, a piece which subsequently made the shortlist for best short story of 2006 in the British Fantasy Awards. This time around she delves into Russian history, producing an eerie and harrowing tale as a woman flees into the unknown.

Una McCormack has been making quite a name for herself lately, with a story selected by Gardner Dozois for his most recent *Year's Best* anthology. Her submission was hard for me to resist, not least due to the familiar Cambridge setting and the great interaction between characters. Besides, any story which references Pink Floyd, Fairport Convention *and* the Strawbs has to be a winner.

Dave Hutchinson's "Multitude" significantly expands on the world first encountered in Lou Anders' 2003 anthology *Live Without a Net* and revisited earlier this year in the NewCon Press anthology *Celebration*. This is Dave's most ambitious tale yet in the setting, and reveals many new aspects of this cruel Elf-dominated future Britain.

Neal Asher is another author I have pestered for a story. Sadly, the 'Tourists on Spatterjay' tale briefly mooted for *disLOCATIONS* never happened, but I was delighted when this time around "The Rhine's World Incident" (set in the Polity Universe) did.

As with previous anthologies, I was keen to highlight some newer voices along with more familiar ones. **Steve Longworth**, a fellow member of the Northampton SF Writers Group, made his fiction debut earlier in 2008 with a story in the science journal *Nature*. His sharp wit and keen intelligence invariably delivers something special. **Nik Ravenscroft** is another newcomer with a definite gift for writing. Her story breathes fresh life into an established SF trope.

The third 'newer voice' is a little different. The British Science Fiction Association operates several internet-based writing groups, the Orbiters, and I ran a competition to choose one story from their recent output to appear in *Subterfuge*. Six stories were selected by myself and Orbiter organiser Terry Jackman, stripped of anything identifying the writer and sent to established author (and this book's co-editor) Ian Watson, who subsequently picked the one he considered to be best.

I had already been impressed by **Nick Wood**'s "Thirstlands" when workshopping it within the Orbiters, so I was delighted to include it in *Subterfuge*. Of course, as I write this, Nick has no idea that his story has won; nor will he until the book is launched on October 11th, 2008, during the NewCon 4 SF convention which **Ian Watson** and I are organising. To commemorate this event, there is also a special edition of the anthology featuring three additional stories; one each from Ian and myself, plus a cracking tale from one of our Guests of Honour, the inimitable **Storm Constantine**.

There you have it: *Subterfuge*. Not every story here necessarily has a twist, but all contain a sleight of hand, a deliberate deceit or misrepresentation, and all are the kind of story that I particularly enjoy. I hope that you do too.

Ian Whates, August 2008

Emptier Than Void

John Meaney

Precognition isn't part of my curse, thank God. But when I first met Anne-Marie's gaze, not yet knowing her name, her eyes were like polished oak beneath glass, and what resonated went beyond attraction, carrying a premonition of importance. She looked over from across the aeroplane aisle, and nodded towards the window beside me.

"Your first time here?"

Gallic tonality, observant eyes, a definite sense of focus.

"I've never even been in Asia before."

And already I knew the place was going to be different – not just from the manner of the Singapore Airlines staff, but from the shining silver-turquoise sea below, the clumps of dark islands veiled with the invisible mist of hot sea-saturated air, and the myriad lines of slow-moving cargo vessels webbing the waters around the archipelago.

"You'll enjoy it."

"Yes."

I wanted to say more, because I was finding her attractive as I'm sure you realized, but if the hunger hadn't been growing inside me then Ferguson and Reilly would have kept me home and given the assignment to someone else, because that was the whole bloody point, so the only thing to do was disengage.

"Excuse me," I said, looking at my watch then pulling my half-read *Cognitive Neurophysics* from the seat pocket. She might have been about to speak, but I looked down as I opened up the pages, and pretended to lose myself in a paper that listed *K. Tan, University of Singapore* as one of the authors, which was a nasty coincidence because he was my target.

The plane dipped left, commencing a downward arc towards the airport at Changi, a place with historical associations to Japanese occupation and British captives that surely did not fit the resurgent, vibrant 21st century East. Soon enough, we were down.

She was ahead of me at the immigration gates, and an officer –

perhaps with Vietnamese family – was taking the opportunity to practice his French.

"*Docteur Catillon? Vous resterez ici pendant deux semaines?*"

"*Une quinzaine, oui.*"

"*D'accord, et bienvenue, Madame Docteur.*"

So she had a doctorate, but then I'd already guessed she was bright. And I liked the way she walked, but by the time I got through the gate myself she was gone from sight, and that was a good thing. Maybe afterwards, when the thing was done... but I'd be suffering by then, hardly in the mood for holiday romance.

Shit and damn it.

"You need a taxi, sir?"

I'd gone left because of the ATMs, while the sign marked *Taxis* had pointed the other way along the spotless white concourse.

"We have the luxury cars," the man continued. "Air-conditioned."

"Sounds good. Give me a moment."

After getting plastic-feeling Singaporean dollars from the machine, I allowed the guy to take my bag and lead the way out into what felt like a sauna, damp heat pushing into my body.

"Bloody hell."

In a few minutes we were driving along a straight palm-bordered dual carriageway, the darkly verdant trees matching the greenery of the central reservation. My driver's name was David Khoo, and as he talked, I matched my physiology to his, being careful with the mimicry, because when you push it all the way it's called non-verbal induction, and while I *am* an expert hypnotist, putting someone into trance while they're driving a vehicle isn't the usual practice – although if you've ever come to on the motorway, and wondered how many miles you've just driven without being conscious of it, you'll know that your unconscious can be trusted to drive a car, and you already know how to go in to trance.

By the time we were reaching the city proper, I had learned that this road was an emergency military runway – the solid-looking central divide was in boxes that could split apart and roll off-road, allowing planes to land – and that you could be arrested for drinking inside a train or dropping litter. Also that the place was spotless and safe for tourists while thousands of plainclothes officers were everywhere, making sure the citizens obeyed the stringent laws.

None of this, David said, was what he would usually tell a visitor.

The city looked the way it should, with green Chinese rooftops among the taller blocks, and the polished turquoise glass curves of the university buildings, and soon we were pulling up beneath an overhang, at the hotel which Bluejack (via a dummy company) had paid for, and at least they were putting me up in style.

Inside the air-conditioned atrium, while I waited to check in, a pretty young woman in hotel uniform came up to me with silver tray in hand, offering fruit juice and a small towel to wipe my face and hands – and I wasn't even officially a guest yet. For a working-class boy from Wandsworth, this was a long way from home.

Formalities over and with key-card in hand, I headed for one of the atrium's glass elevators, wheeling my bag behind me. Couches were set in opposing pairs, forming islands where discussion could take place, and a group of mostly men were arguing about something.

"– ray bursters were confirmed."

"But if they can't find the glitch, how can they verify the data?"

They were in shirtsleeves for the most part, but the woman from the plane was there in a two-piece skirt suit, introducing herself.

"I'm Anne-Marie, and the thing about the data reconstruction is, the different systems used different RAID-type technologies, differing checksums. Some of the data didn't rebuild, but what did, matched exactly. From totally disparate telescopes."

Beyond them, a simple flipchart bore a marker-penned message:

PSYCHO ;-) PHYSICISTS THIS WAY ==>

It pointed toward a corner exit. Some of the people in the group that this Anne-Marie Catillon had joined were beginning to drift away, presumably to this pre-conference get-together; but the thing about the dark hunger inside me is that it's hard enough to contain even without jet-lag speckling my eyeballs and making me dizzy, so I had to get away from people now.

Once in my room, the spasms hit. I'd only lasted this long because of autohypnosis, so it was all I could do to fumble at my laptop bag for the small toilet kit, and pull out the black-and-white capsules that I use *in extremis*, dry-swallowing two of the bastard things.

I sank down on the floor, muscles shaking, knowing this was going to be bad.

Shit. There's someone down there, and I'm so hungry.

The person in the room below was innocent, and I had to fight it down, the hunger, pushing the emptiness back inside me before it reached out and, and...

It's starting.

But I would *not* let this happen.

No.

Forcing myself to my knees, then my feet, I staggered toward the bed where I'd left the capsules, knowing that a third was dangerous but if the synthetic neurotransmitters didn't kick in soon I wouldn't be able to stop myself commencing the...

Shit.

The bed was rising toward my face as my legs lost all strength and I was plunging into void.

And gone.

*

There's a beginning to this tragedy. Call it my impoverished South London upbringing and the escape of books and computers, and the years at Imperial College where I matured athletically as well as cognitively, focusing on the obscure, unapplauded extremes of parkour with likeminded freerunners as we somersaulted and vaulted our way around the urban landscape, in South Bank or anywhere we could. But more particularly it was the Stanford sabbatical that was supposed to be an opportunity; yet if I'd never been to Menlo Park I'd be a normal person now.

The local freerunners – I'd found their web forum while still in England – had invited me to run the rooftops of the Stanford Research Institute with them, and so I did. Vaulting railings, bouncing from side to side down stairwells, shoulder-rolling across outdoor tables, leaping from one building to the next – all of it in the manner of Daredevil or Spider-Man, and in fact half of the guys attended ComicCon as if it were a religious obligation; but these were the fans who could move like their heroes.

At first it was fun, throwing ourselves around in the beautiful California evening, but our run ended in a hollow quadrangle with an intricate fountain at its centre, where security guards closed in, and they carried batons that they looked like they knew how to use. It's hard to vault free with a smashed kneecap, and whip-fast hardwood can generate an awful lot of torque, which we were sensible enough to realize.

They let me off with a warning, but the point was that my freerunning proclivities got flagged somewhere, and triangulated against my particular academic background, and if only I hadn't been so fucking *stupid* – but I have the neurolinguistic training to deal with unhelpful memories, so I ought to let it go, don't you think? It would be nice to forgive myself because, well, could I really have foreseen the cellphone call next morning from someone calling himself Bryant, who said he was fascinated with my hypnosis skills and the fMRI experiments, and would I like to demonstrate to his off-campus researchers, who were developing brain-controlled prosthetics for paraplegics, and get paid for doing some good in the world?

Perhaps I should have detected the manipulation in his voice – I'm supposed to be the expert – but the signal was bad and, looking back, that probably was no coincidence. And he'd called me early, before I was properly alert; perhaps that too was planned.

Late afternoon, before the sudden plunge into Californian night, I was in a seminar room with a dozen men and women, and I'd memorized their names as we'd shaken hands. After the initial talk I picked a volunteer whose body language easily synchronized with my gestures and voice inflection.

"So, Sue," I said as she sat down next to me, facing the group, "I'd like you to think about something you do every day, such as brushing your teeth. Er... I assume you *do* brush your teeth every day, right?"

My tone was joking, and the others were laughing as Sue giggled and said: "I should hope so."

It was an everyday example but that was the point, because if deep emotion were attached to the activity I'd want to pick something else, something neutral. People can link trauma to the most mundane things, or haven't you heard of phobias? I'd once cured someone of a screaming, fearful reaction to the sight of Jelly Babies, and he was a physics professor who terrified his students.

"Now imagine yourself" – I used calming tones as Sue settled – "brushing your teeth tomorrow, and really see yourself carrying out that activity, and where is the picture now?"

"It must be in my head," she said, but her facial microexpressions told me otherwise.

"You're imagining, creating a virtual image, and where is it located, precisely?"

"*Oh.*" She pointed. "There."

"Exactly there?" I positioned my hand some ten inches in front of her chin, then moved it a little further away. "Not there?" Then closer. "Or there?"

"No." Indicating the original spot. "Right where I said."

"Now imagine yourself doing the same thing in a week's time. Where's the image now?"

She pointed further away, in front and slightly to the right.

"And in six months?"

"There. No..."

I had to get out of my chair to reach where she was focused.

"That's it."

"And a year from now?"

So we'd established that her personal timeline stretched to the front and angled slightly upward.

"Imagine yourself cleaning your teeth *yesterday*. And then last week."

Sue gestured over her shoulder.

"So," I continued, "you've put the past behind you." As laughter rose in the group, I smiled. "And where did you think linguistic metaphors come from? We're looking at phenomenology more than neurology, in the sense that someone else would exhibit a different timeline – this is yours, Sue, and no one else's – but we all structure our subjective experience in some similar way, normally below the conscious level."

Blinking, Sue said, "I never knew I did that, yet I always do."

"Right, and it's the spatiotemporal grid inside your brain that activates when you're organizing memories and setting goals." Looking straight at Sue, I added: "And if you make the virtual pictures brighter and sharper, and larger in the future, you *will* achieve them."

There was an element of hypnosis involved, a reward for her willingness to be my demonstration subject.

Then, to the group, I explained how child psychologists discovered that children gain a sense of self at exactly the same time they learn subjectively to organize time-encoded memories and future plans.

"But you know about the spatiotemporal grid, just as you know about mirror neurons," I said. "So if Sue did all this again inside an fMRI, we'd be able to see it in her brain. And I hear you guys have got scanners?"

"We got the biggest scanners in the state, boy," said a bearded guy called Peterson in a mock Southern accent.

"Hoo-ah." The woman next to him was grinning.

"Playtime," I said.

*

My face was pressed against the duvet, while my feet were still on the floor. I rolled to one side, and checked the time: five a.m. I curled up, then dropped to the carpet like a monkey, bobbed up and down on all fours to test how I felt – supple and pain-free – and stood up. Not bad, considering the state I'd been in last night.

I used the bathroom, and drank two glasses of water before commencing a prasara yoga routine to get the remaining kinks out. Then I tapped acupressure points on my body, knowing I would need to be fully alert later, when the hunger came back in full, and I came to face my target, Professor Kenneth Tan.

This is awful.

But I knew for a fact that the others had deserved the fate I'd delivered – except that everything in their lives made sense to them, and whether they were triumphant or driven victims, each had been the hero of his or her personal narrative, the internal story of their life. Yet I knew nothing of Tan to indicate involvement in weapons research, which had been the theme of my earlier missions; and I wondered why Ferguson hadn't briefed me in person this time around.

Perhaps I was pretending to myself that I had a choice.

At seven I went out to run, leaving the hotel via a corridor that came out among crowded Oriental sidestreet shops, then jogging to the straight boulevard of Orchard Road. Soon I passed the gleaming glass university architecture, then angled towards Stanley Park, where I ran the trails that wound up the fortified hill, and stopped in a wooden pavilion, finally free from local observers.

I did the acrobatic stuff that had caused me so much trouble, clambering up to the pavilion roof, jumping off and shoulder-rolling as I hit the ground, and you might think it was self-indulgent but the thing was, the hunger was returning, a void of pain, and this time I couldn't take the drugs, because zero-time was a matter of hours away, so I had to fight it down however I could.

This was like working out in a sauna but I continued until my muscles rebelled, and then I slowly ran the couple of miles back to the hotel, unable to put things off any longer.

*

Sue's mind showed in the scanner as billowing sheets of colour, as intricate pulses and waves of neural excitation: cliques of neurons building up, structure upon shifting structure, the lightning magic that is mind. We explored the intricacies – her subjective timeline mapped to hippocampus activity, and the grid cells of her entorhinal cortex – and finally wrapped the session up. Afterwards, the bearded researcher, Peterson, invited me to come back for a second visit, to meet Bryant, whose initial phone call had brought me here.

Anytime, definitely, I told him, unaware of danger; and late the next night – they didn't keep normal hours any more than the Stanford academics did – a car fetched me back to the same building; and that was when disaster began.

A man called Wheelis met me in the white foyer and led me to the same fMRI room I'd used with Sue. A woman named Keele was waiting there, cappuccino in hand, sitting at the console. The screens and controls were software-driven, not hardwired, and Keele minimized an eye-catching display as I entered.

"Would you like a coffee?" asked Wheelis immediately.

"Er, yes. Please. Love one."

The other researchers might have noticed my liking for coffee, so it could have been politeness on his part; but I thought from the tightening undertone of his voice that I wasn't supposed to have seen the minimized window.

"You told Sue Carter yesterday, when she was your demo subject" – Keele sipped from her cappuccino – "that you have subjective techniques for improving biofeedback control."

"That's right."

Just like encoding timelines, when you know how your mind structures subjective experience, you can improve many abilities through the use of imagination. Controlling machines with biofeedback is easy. At Imperial, I taught a bunch of fellow postgrads to manipulate their heart rates and lie to polygraphs with ease – just as I thought the

Keele woman was lying to me now, but in what manner, I couldn't say.

As Wheelis entered with my coffee, Keele logged off one monitor, then stood.

"I'll leave you folk to it for a while. See you in a bit."

Four people followed Wheelis in, all smiling, all of them members of the group I'd seen the day before, including the likeable bearded guy, Peterson. My demo subject, Sue, wasn't with them. Wheelis gave me my coffee, and said he'd pop back in later, and have fun.

Among the newcomers, I detected no subterfuge, so we had a chat about biofeedback techniques. I got one of them to hold my wrist and detect my changing pulse, as I imagined my heart rate speeding up and then slowing right down, before we got round to looking at the fMRI setup. There was a horizontal couch that slid inside a hollow cylinder, housing the scanner, and it was lucky that my youthful claustrophobia had evaporated when I first learned the neurolinguistic techniques of change.

"So look," said one of the researchers, "at these glasses. What do you think of using these?"

They were goggles with optic fibres attached, linking them to the console.

"You're talking about feedback inside the scanner?" This was new to me. "Does it work?"

"Zero interference."

"Then I've *got* to have a go," I said.

"And we've got headphones, to provide an audio analogue, like music. The earpieces were a lot harder to insulate against resonance. Than the glasses, I mean."

"Just let me at it."

And so I saw my mind.

It is a strange and beautiful thing to stare at the oceans and chasms of thought, the many-hued fast-shifting mindscape, like geological ages on fast-forward, shaping the world, defining the spirit. And then to use the most powerful techniques of imagination, while the music of mind played in my ears, altering the patterns according to my will, whose existence was real because *I could see myself*, and if thought perceiving thought is the definition of consciousness, then for a time I was the most conscious human alive.

When they drew me out of the machine, I was blinking rapidly, coming out of a radically altered state to deal with the everyday reality of talking to people.

A shaven-headed man with a goatee had joined the group, and I knew straightaway he was Bryant; but it was the enthusiasm of the other researchers that drew me.

"You were brilliant." Peterson was smiling. "Terrific."

"It was amazing," I said. "Thank you."

"Look, we have these control patterns." Peterson held up some printed sheets with intricate patterns superimposed on shaded outlines of a cross-sectioned brain, from varying depths and perspectives. "Do you think you could try forming these patterns in your mind? They're already adjusted for you, from the scanning. And, er... This is one that Tanya Keele is working on. She'd like it if we added her pattern to the sequence."

I rubbed my face, then closed my eyes and opened them again to check that I'd memorized all the patterns correctly. I had.

"Of course I'll do it."

"When would you like to…?"

"Right now," I told him.

Because this was fun.

Once inside the machine again I embarked on the ultimate free-run, an acrobatic journey through the landscape of my mind, the geometry of me, and I played with freeform manipulation of my own neural oceanic waves; and then for fun began to form the control patterns inside my cortex, seeing them come to life around me, myself surrounding myself – knowing that I was furthering research that would allow paralysed patients to finely control devices to aid them in their lives (and as I thought that, a particularly beautiful blue-and-scarlet pattern pulsed in my mind, as I saw the wonder of my own altruistic pleasure). Finally I added the pattern which the Keele woman had devised, concentrating hard because it was a challenge, a wonderful ninefold symmetry in three dimensions, a real challenge to hold in place, but then I had it and…

NO!

…something awful plunged through me, a sickening sense of void, of hungry nothingness formed of darkness, of need, of desires that had nothing to do with humanity or our reptile brain – the lizard mind within us all – or anything of ordinary life at all. It was sick and it was worse than empty, it was pulling into itself whatever was good in the world, and all around the mindscape that was me lit up in the flaring colours of fear, while panic howled in my headphones, but that bastard pattern continued to shine inside my mind, at the core of me, a bright cage filled with darkness, more empty than the void, and if anything it was stronger now, and that was when I knew it was in me to stay.

Forever.

*

I walked through the Singapore heat, found the glass building I needed, but with half an hour to spare before the conference began. So I crossed the wide road to a European-looking coffee shop, went inside to air-conditioned coolness, and ordered a cappuccino. Paying at the till, I handed my debit card over in the normal manner, but noted the way the pretty cashier took it from me two-handed. Transaction over, she offered the card back, and I used both hands to receive it, like a perfect Zen ceremony. She smiled.

It is the minutiae that are important in communication. Our mirror neurons, matching and simulating the people we see, are a large part of what make us human, distinct from other species.

Am I still human, then?

My tutors always said I had a knack of asking the right questions, and one of them once added: "That might not always be a comfortable thing, for you or others." He was right.

With my cappuccino, I sat alone at a corner table, although a group of psychophysicists had gathered around adjacent tables on the other side of the room. One was holding up the copy of *Nature* with the famous deep-space image that people were calling The Triangle. The emissions came from the far side of a void, one of those vast volumes of space, immensely greater than galaxies, that contain nothing but dark matter, and the dark energy of the continuum itself, whose origin is incalculable to current physics.

"For God's sake, it's an equilateral triangle…"

"Only as seen from the Earth."

"…which can *not* be a coincidence."

"So you're saying it's an artefact of the telescope systems. Why not a single emission split by something like a gravitational lens?"

"But the equal-sided triangle…"

"There are such things as coincidences."

Most psychophysicists are physicists first and cognitive neuroscientists second. So it was natural that they would be fascinated by the apparent detection of three gamma-ray bursters that had appeared to explode simultaneously (as observed from Earth) as triplet hypernovae more energetic than exploding galaxies, cosmic detonations lasting only a few seconds, beyond the dark-matter void, a light-aeon away.

None of them appeared to have thought of the recent work in Beijing, where gamma-ray resonances had been shown to accompany dark matter under certain specialized circumstances, allowing the possibility not only of detection but of control.

The journals talked of dark matter manipulation as hypothesis rather than engineering, but it occurred to me – as the psychophysicists stood, coffee finished and ready for the conference – that if I got knocked down crossing the street to the university and one of these guys was present at the autopsy when they cut open my skull, they'd find something deeply different at the heart of my brain, something to make them reconsider what was possible in working with the unknown.

Perhaps I ought to kill myself.

But that was not my way, as that bastard Bryant had probably known, and for sure it was knowledge that Bluejack made use of, though it was supposed to be for my benefit as well as theirs – they assigned me only to targets who truly were the enemy of geopolitical peace. Perhaps there was a Western bias, but they were a US outfit so it was to be expected.

I followed the other guys across the road, only when it was safe to cross. In front of us, the conference building was convex and gleaming, a great glass sculpture containing some of the best minds in well-educated Singapore, one of the dynamic hearts of the new world culture.

And containing one Professor Tan, my target, soon to die.

*

They slid me out from inside the fMRI apparatus – except it was more than a scanner, I knew now – and I fell off the pad, puking on the polished floor, and I hoped it made them sick.

"What have…? Ah, shit."

I threw up some more, then pulled myself up, arms shaking, and wiped sweat from my eyes, foul-smelling stuff from my mouth.

Bryant was standing with a small dark-blue gun in his hand, with Keele on one side and Wheelis on the other – they had guns as well – and no sign of the other researchers who'd been my friends.

"You fuckers," I said.

"We've fucked you for sure," said Bryant. "That's a dark-matter particle inside your head, although vortex would be a better term than particle."

"What?"

"With your reading of microexpression clusters and all that shit, you were already a mindreader, virtually, which is why I had to be out of the room. Peterson and his friends have no idea what we're doing here. What" – with a flickering, nasty grin – "we've already done to you, my friend."

At the word *friend* I spat.

"What do you want, Bryant?"

"The question is, what are *you* going to want? And I mean, with a desperate hunger like an addict needing a fix. So we're going to supply that need."

"You're totally…"

That was when the door burst open and dark-suited men and women poured in, handguns raised and shouting: "*Freeze!* Hold still!"

It would have been dramatic or possibly funny, but my guts clenched up and I vomited again despite the shouted commands, and thought for a moment they might shoot me, while a part of me wondered if this might be for the best.

Perhaps that part of me was right.

One of the newcomers, an athletic woman with short blonde hair, pressed the fMRI's Start button. Three guns flew through the air towards the scanner, sucked by the intense magnetic field; and Bryant's weapon cut my cheek. I flinched, too late.

"Sorry," said the woman, cutting the power.

All three handguns clattered to the floor. But the dark-suited newcomers, armed, had experienced no such problem.

"Plastic weapons," the woman added. "All right, cuff the bastards and get them out of here."

Bryant, Keele and Wheelis left, wrists laced behind their backs with dark plastic, their expressions shocked. In this at least there was no trickery.

"Who are you?" I asked the woman.

"I'm Ferguson, and our employers" – she gestured at the others – "are called Bluejack, like the cheese…"

"Huh?"

There's another meaning: the more acceptable counterpart of Bluesnarfing – the hacking of devices via Bluetooth – and I'd have thought about it more but my head was whirling.

"…and I'm afraid we're going to make use of you if possible, just like these bastards were going to do. The difference is, we're the good guys."

I looked down at my vomit-spattered clothes, then up at this impeccably dressed woman. Ferguson.

"Bryant said… Something impossible."

Dark matter inside my head. And something about addiction, like heroin.

"Did he tell you that the hunger would grow? That you'd try to fight it, but fail? That you'd have to let rip, and be satisfied just for a little while, until the cycle begins again?"

"What am I, a bloody werewolf?"

"Accurate analogy," said Ferguson. "The thing is, you're a telepath."

I'm a what?

But I'm used to reading expressions if not minds; and if her words were a lie then they were also delusion, because she believed them.

"A telepath."

"Except it doesn't work the way you probably think."

*

The picking up of badges, the signing in, the calibrated smiles: just another conference, somewhere in the world. A pre-lecture breakfast buffet waited, and it could have been the States or Europe except that heated steel dishes containing dumplings and noodles were part of the offering.

"What *are* these?" asked an American voice behind me.

"Very traditional." The answer came in Anne-Marie Catillon's elegant Gallic tones. "Try that one only if you like fish."

"Nice," said another American, not meaning it.

I walked away without looking at them, not wanting to look at anyone really, because the shakes were trying to start up again and I was repeating the inner autohypnotic command of *soften* so often it was like a mantra. But this was a conference and I was here under my true name, so I decided to get a grip and go talk to some guys I knew from Adelaide the previous year.

We chatted, then a Singaporean professor in a sharp suit announced that it was time for the keynote session. Everyone drifted in to the main auditorium, which was all clean curves and comfortable seating, enough for some two hundred of us. The first talk was interesting enough, but it was the long grey hair of a fifty-something man in the front row that my gaze kept flicking to, because although he didn't turn around, he was almost certainly Professor Tan, my prey; and as a predator I wanted him centred in my visual field.

I could just walk away.

Right, and then some poor innocent bastard would suffer instead, everything good ripped from them when the hunger overwhelmed and I had to do it anyway, do the thing that made me different, forever inhuman. Bluejack gave me a purpose and an excuse, a way to live with myself; and I would not let them down.

So why didn't Ferguson do the briefing herself this time?

Forget it. The reason would be logical, an operational need for her to be elsewhere. I would not suspect her, or her colleagues. Our colleagues. It was only that Bryant, that bastard, when he'd done what he'd done to me, had manipulated me by using cut-outs, using employees who knew nothing of his objectives and therefore could give nothing away. If he'd faced me himself at the beginning I'd never have trusted him, never have stepped into that building, never…

For God's sake shut up and get on with it.

I was going to do this thing, so there was no point in flailing round inside my own guilt. After a time I was applauding along with everybody else, then leaving the auditorium, grabbing a coffee and carrying it with me,as I went to look for the breakout room where I was delivering my own small session. Professor Tan's talk was scheduled for after lunch; but five minutes before my lecture was due to start a slight man with long grey hair was among the people filing in, and I knew I would not have to wait, provided I could maintain a façade of normal humanity in front of these trained observers while I did the thing.

And of course there was a long-faced woman with dark, startling eyes who chose to sit at the back: Anne-Marie Catillon. Perhaps afterwards we could talk and arrange a meeting for some other time, like several weeks from now, because the aftermath hits me hard as a fist, always, and I'd need recovery time.

Concentrate.

There are many ways to alter your neurophysiological state, and I used several of them now, including a gesture that acted as a neurolinguistic mudra, triggering a sense of confidence, while I stepped into an imaginary column of shining gold-white light, and an enthusiastic inner voice said: "Showtime!"

I launched into my speech, standing before my props: two swivel chairs, one beneath a silver tree-like device that looked like something from a hairdresser's studio, but was in fact a next-generation fMRI, with no need to slide the subject inside a metal cocoon. Its metal branches contained atomic magnetometers, linked to a processor that broadcast via microwave to the four big plasma wall screens.

"So if you, like me, feel fascinated by the latest advances in matching neural schemata to the structure of subjective experience" – I was using hypnotic language and intonation to spellbind my audience; and Anne-Marie Catillon was one of the people smiling, recognizing what I was doing – "to understand how your unconscious can work so fast before self-awareness follows afterwards, as consciousness manifests always in retrospect, after the real cognitive processing is…"

After a time, I called for a volunteer from the audience – it was another woman, whose name turned out to be Lynn – and I settled her under the fMRI tree, with her conscious mentality displayed in beautiful shifting colours on all four wall screens. Sitting in the chair beside her, I commenced the trance induction; and her eyelids immediately began a continuous fluttering that would persist for some time.

"So my voice will go with you as you sink deeper and deeper into this relaxed neurochemical state…"

When she was deep inside, I told her that I would talk to the audience now, and she would hear the difference when it was time for me to address her once again. Then I got out of my chair, and pointed to the wall-mounted screens.

"Trance is profoundly different from the waking state, as you can see from the activity in the precuneus" – I used a radio mouse as a pointer – "and here, the anterior cingulus, which is why hypnosis is associated with suggestibility, but it would truer to say, allows the mind access to powerful resources otherwise unavailable."

It's not unusual, in a demonstration, for members of the audience to drift into trance as well – but Professor Tan's eyelids were fluttering for a particular reason, and that was when I became aware that I'd already begun the process, that Tan's world was dwindling towards finality, and nothing could prevent extinction.

At the back of the room Anne-Marie Catillon sat upright, and I knew straightaway that she was aware of what I was doing. And there was something else in her gaze – could it be hunger? – but I had to turn away, look at my spellbound subject Lynn, while Professor Tan's thoughts flooded into me, not the originals but the resonance they induced.

There's a flexible suspension footbridge in a British Columbian park – it's called the Capilano Bridge – and I once stood in the middle, staring down at the chasm, while a group of Japanese tourists crossed, their footsteps in time, setting up a resonance that made the bridge swing from side to side, oscillating with increasing amplitude, until they were all across and it slowly dampened down to stability.

Something very like that was happening right now, inside Professor Tan's mind. But the only stability achievable was death.

His chin was on his chest, and he appeared to have drifted into sleep. And in the back row there was now an empty seat.

It hurts.

It always hurts me, in so many ways.

Still, I maintained discipline, bringing Lynn out of trance and fielding questions, then bringing the session to a close, aware of Anne-Marie Catillon's absence, and I wondered if she was reporting me to the police, and how she could have known what I was doing.

Maybe she didn't know.

But I didn't need a dark-matter vortex in my brain to read a face, and I was sure of what I had seen. Very sure.

Get out of here.

It was time to move.

*

Tan's memories had slammed beneath the surface of my mind, buried as if by traumatic amnesia; but they would come back over the next few days in an agony of integration as he and I became one, knowing that I had destroyed him and brought suffering to whatever family he had. And the parts of his mind that I could get rid of, without killing my own self or eradicating memories that were useful to my employer, I would eradicate. Except that the me doing the eradication wouldn't be the same me who had landed in Singapore yesterday, because that's part of the agony, or hadn't you guessed?

I left the university building fast.

An ordinary autopsy would show cerebral haemorrhage – a tragedy that could strike anyone – and by now someone must have discovered Tan's corpse and possibly come to that conclusion already, since some of the delegates would have a medical background. If it hadn't been for Anne-Marie Catillon, I would have stayed; but Bluejack protocol was to go to ground if there was any possibility of discovery, something I'd never thought could happen.

But then I'd never thought that I could be a monster.

"What am I," I'd asked Ferguson during that first meeting. *"A bloody werewolf?"*

"Accurate analogy," she'd said.

Something like a fictional monster, but real and far less pleasant.

I walked until I found the white elegance of the Raffles hotel, went into its cool spaces, its quadrangles and balconies and overhead fans, a reproduction of British colonial times, and found a room where the maid had just finished cleaning up.

"Sleep," I told her, passing my hand in front of her eyes. It's all in the timing.

When she'd become properly amnesiac, I told her to leave the room, remembering only another normal task well done. She went out, and I was alone.

I lay on the newly made bed and tried to calm myself. It was hard work, so I defocused my eyes and used my inner voice to talk myself down into trance – we all talk to ourselves, and if you haven't noticed, ask yourself why not – with instructions to rest until dark, or come instantly awake if someone entered the room.

After sunset, I slipped out of the hotel and crossed the street. There was a mall where I could buy a change of clothes – a new image distracts surveillance – and as I turned towards the entrance, a flawlessly pretty girl on the corner looked at me and said hello, and did I like Singapore?

It wasn't a greeting but a commercial proposition; and I was so tempted for just a second, because if I needed to do anything it was to release tension – and it's not as if a person like me could ever have a real relationship – but the whole thing was a bad idea so I murmured something polite and went inside.

After choosing a shirt and cargo pants, I used my cellphone while paying, dialling the number I remembered. David Khoo said he remembered driving me from the airport, and he was on duty, and could pick me up in ten minutes.

Soon I was in his car, dressed in my new clothes, and we were heading towards the harbour district where nightclubs and bars abound. I asked him where else you could go after dark as a tourist, and he told me about a night-time zoo experience, some fifteen kilometres north of here.

It sounded perfect.

"Can you pull over a moment?"

"Sure... Here we go. What can I...?"

"Just sleep."

*

There was a southbound street that dipped below ground level in an underpass. I'd seen it this morning while out running, and I got David to drive that way now, slowing down at the deepest part. After checking the road was temporarily clear behind, I threw my cellphone onto the floor space behind David's seat, opened the door, and rolled out of the still-moving car.

Then I was on my feet and in shadow, while the car drove on, and I was sure that if the police asked David (after tracking him down via cellphone records, since the hotel and airline had my number) he'd tell them about taking me north of the city, and leaving me at the zoo, for the night-time "safari" that was so popular with the kind of tourists that didn't want bright lights and paid-for girls.

Perhaps I wasn't a fugitive from the police – but I might be, and I had to act on possibility, not knowing the facts.

At Dhoby Ghaut I went down into the station, and in a few minutes I was on the underground train heading east, towards the airport. I was wearing contact lenses that altered my eyes; and I'd inserted nose plugs, and slicked my hair back with gel: an appearance matching the passport I intended to travel on, not the one I'd used arriving here.

The carriage was spotless with few passengers. At the next station, several people got off, several others came in, and one of them was Anne-Marie Catillon.

She took the seat beside mine.

"Pretend you know me. I'm Anne-Marie." Smiling, she leaned close. "The guy on the end is a detective."

Here to watch over the citizens, ensure they did not eat or drink on board, or break any of the other successful but draconian laws that keep the city-state immaculate and safe.

"That's nice. Why should I care?"

We were in motion now.

"My employers say the authorities would like to talk to us, no more."

"Us?"

"Witnesses at the conference."

"I noticed you left early."

"Because," her voice became throaty, "there was no point in staying, when I could no longer talk to the man," she placed her fingertip against my forehead, "who's now in there."

A sick coating of sweat was suddenly covering my body.

"What are you…?"

"It's not like you're the only telepath in the world."

Oh, Christ.

There were two others at Bluejack, as far as I knew, but we'd met only at a distance and talked by webcam, because of the danger.

"You're nuts."

"No, and it's easy enough to prove." Again, she smiled. "Just read me."

"*What?* Are you" – I made my voice soften, because of the detective – "totally nuts, or merely suicidal?"

Now she was blinking rapidly.

"You think it's dangerous to read a mind like your own? Is that what they told you?"

"It's obvious that—" But I stopped, because something's being *obvious* is a linguistic marker indicating you might usefully think again, and search for evidence.

"We'd better not go to the airport yet," she said. "I know where we can go."

Espionage and warfare are increasingly the domain of private enterprise, and she'd mentioned her employers. Rivals of Bluejack? Enemies?

"What's done is done," she added, "so professionally speaking I should simply have nothing to do with you. But for people like us... Ah, God. You know."

I didn't, but I needed to find out.

"All right, so where shall we go?"

"Changi," she said. "But not the airport."

The train was already travelling above ground and soon enough we were sliding in to Changi, to an airy concrete station in the tropical night. Outside, I let Anne-Marie pay for bus tickets, and we passed brightly coloured apartment blocks and then luxurious dwellings among the palms.

We got off and began to walk in the warm, humid night. To our right was a tall modernistic wall of concrete and plastic, surmounted with shiny razor wire; to our left, across the road, beautiful family houses stood.

"That's the prison." Anne-Marie pointed. "There are two of our kind in there."

"You what?"

"Resonance tech, the way Bryant and Ferguson got the vortex inside you. The technique was discovered in Beijing. Most of the world's telepaths are from this region."

But it was her knowledge of names that disturbed me.

"Bryant's outfit did the damage." I meant to me, and to the other two guys, rescued by Bluejack after Bryant had already made them take out several targets – several *people* – each. "But that wasn't Ferguson."

"You think they were really different? For that matter, have you seen Ferguson recently?"

I was alert now, but the night was empty besides the buildings, the prison, and us.

"Has something happened to him?"

"To her, as you well know. She found out that Bluejack's owners were the same people who controlled Bryant, so I don't suppose they'll let her talk to you again, do you? Because the only way to manipulate a telepath is with intermediaries who believe the lies."

Shit.

"I believe the word you're looking for," she added, "is *merde*. Ferguson was so disturbed that she contacted my people, looking for another job, and that's how I know."

I looked at Anne-Marie's eyes, which were darkly inviting – not hungry like the void – and then I laughed.

"This is nuts. It's... I need to sit down and think somewhere."

She took my hand; an hormonal tsunami washed through me.

"I know a place."

A few minutes later, we were in a gravelled courtyard surrounded by darkened single-storey buildings, their walls the colour of bone beneath the moon.

"This is the old prison from the war," murmured Anne-Marie. "Or some of it. They moved it from inside the walls of the modern place."

"Huh."

"Come back in daylight sometime, and read the diary entries of Singaporeans who saw the Europeans shocked and helpless beneath the Japanese attacks, and realized that white men weren't the powerful, superior beings they had thought."

"Funny how perceptions can change," I said, "so quickly."

"I'm sorry to shock you. Professor Tan recently spent much time with cosmic-ray researchers, as you'll find out soon" – she meant when the memories broke the amnesiac dam and flooded into me, painful and turbulent and overwhelming – "and he believed the dark matter inside our heads came from the triple hypernovae event, the gamma-ray bursters."

That cosmic event which had coincided with systems failure among separate telescopes and satellites, making it hard to retrieve the data, shading the analyses with doubt.

"No," I said. "I don't think so."

"Carried by the same electromagnetic resonance that holds the vortices in place. Carried from the void, and you know what that word means to cosmologists, I'm sure."

"Yes."

A vast region containing only dark matter and the vacuum itself.

"But to be fair, Tan did get the hint from his Beijing friends, some of whom are military researchers. Whether Bluejack ethically targeted him, only you will be able to judge." Her fingertips touched my forearm, emanating waves of electrical reaction in my skin. "I hope you do make judgement, and ignore what they told you."

"My God, Anne-Marie." I gestured at the darkness, the relics of violence and implacable sociological forces around us. "This is so strange, so totally.... Strange."

"Read my mind, and you'll know."

Oh, my God.

She was inviting, she was asking me, and even with Tan's memories cached in the void inside me, she was enough to awaken the hunger once more.

Can I? Can I really do it?

"Two of my colleagues," she murmured, "have forged a deeper link between two people than anyone can imagine, so deeply in love that it's magical to see."

I found I was swallowing.

"I…"

Yes.

The thought triggered the process.

Oh, my God, yes. Yes!

She jerked as the connection fastened between us, the resonance began.

"*Ah, baise-moi! Baise-moi!*"

Anne-Marie fell back writhing as I twisted to once side, feeling the darkness smack into my forehead: a hammerhead migraine of abreaction, a deep sense of wrongness, of knowing this could never be.

Have you ever tried to push two magnets together, north pole to north pole?

Whatever was in her head was repellent to my own internal void, to the darkness in my core. Her colleagues might have experienced deep bonding and erotic joy, but perhaps their dark matter was from the same source, while my mine was different. Perhaps that was it.

"I'm sorry."

Sitting, she moved away from me across the gravel, silver tracks of painful tears shining under the moon.

"I'm really…"

Then she stumbled to her knees, got up, and began a jagged,

uncoordinated run, into the pervasive darkness, away from me. All I could do was watch, and feel sick, knowing the worst.

I am a monster, unpalatable, even to others of my kind.

*

Perhaps it's even worse. Because all that was hours ago; and I stand here still, on the gravel in this place of pain, looking up at the tropical night, wondering what I am. It's not just the nested layers of untruth that brought me here, the potential injustice of what I did to Tan – and soon enough I will find out for sure, as a waterfall of memory crashes through me – and I wonder if the prison guards, in the hypermodern establishment beyond the razor-wired wall, will hear me screaming and investigate.

I'm in no fit state to use the airport now. And it's worse than that.

It looked at me.

Can I trust my own internal images and feelings? Or are they lies like everything else that occurred in Stanford and afterwards? Like the rest of my life?

But before we broke contact, I saw the void in Anne-Marie's head, I swear I did – and *it looked back at me.*

Now what I'm seeing is the night, the stars of this galaxy, the darkness of voids that lie beyond, and somewhere the remnants of gamma-ray bursters that exploded an aeon ago, their emissions carrying dark packages to Earth.

And I wonder.

Just who is looking at whom?

Collateral Damage

Jaine Fenn

"I'm sorry dear, I didn't see you!"

The bitch just spilled her drink in my lap. I should cut her for that.

Or not. She's no bitch; she's topside class. And I'd been wondering about her, this stranger with her smart suit and sad eyes.

I stood up and came into the light so she could see me brush the booze off my lap (my suit's got stuff in it so dirt won't stick). Then I looked down at her to see if she'd run yet.

She hadn't, though she was trying to work me out. A downside girl alone in a topside bar, dressed for comfort, not business. What could I be?

The barman came over, abandoning the raucous end of the bar where various coves were celebrating making it big in some offworld venture. He offered me a napkin and said, "Can I get you anything else, Medame?" Then he shot the woman a look saying she might want to leg it while she still could.

I smiled at him. "No thanks. But I think my friend here'll have another…" I sniffed the soiled napkin "…jian and bitters. Light on the bitters." When I handed the napkin back her gaze settled on the bloodless wound on the inside of my wrist. I turned my smile on her and sat down.

She swallowed, her mouth silently forming the word 'Angel?'

I nodded.

She glanced at her empty seat, at the door, back at me. From the way her eyes tracked I reckoned she'd drunk just enough to wish she was sober. She smiled like a friendly corpse and said, "You're not wearing colours."

"My day off." Like I would ever get a day off from being an assassin for my City.

If my lame joke threw her, she didn't say. "It should really be me buying you a drink."

I was going to say I didn't have to pay for my drinks, but I'd already got bored with winding up people who might've spat at me in the street a few weeks ago. Instead I just said, "I'm fine." It made a change to talk to someone who didn't run or grovel, so I added, "Haven't seen you in here before."

"I don't usually drink during the day." Then she added, "Not that I'm implying anything about your lifestyle."

"Fresh citrus. No alcohol."

"Ah. Expensive. But I expect you don't pay for your drinks."

I liked this woman. "What's your name?"

"Vanna Agriet."

"I'm Malia. So, Medame Agriet, why *are* you here today?"

She took a sip of her new drink and said, "Because I've had a bad day. Are you sure you want to hear about it? It's trivial stuff to someone like you."

"Maybe, but it's the least you could do after pouring jian and bitters over my suit." She had to be fifteen years older than me, and she'd probably never spoken to a downsider in her life, let alone an Angel. I wanted to take a peek into her world, just because I could.

She took a deep breath. "Well, firstly, my business isn't going well. I import luxury foodstuffs. I've been expanding my company, but couriers' bills and import charges have been building up while customers quibbled about payments. You know how it is. Actually, you probably don't. Anyway, today I decided to distract myself by unpacking. I work from home, you see. We've only been in our apartment a few weeks so there's lots to do. While I was putting stuff away I found a woman's gold earring under our bed. It isn't mine."

"Ah. When you say 'we'?"

"My husband's name is Tolyn. We've been married eight years. Recently I've had the feeling something's wrong. Finding the earring got me worrying, and on top of the stress from work ... I decided to go out and mull things over. With a drink. Which ended up as more than one, though I think I've had enough now." She pushed her half-finished drink away. "Tolyn will be home soon."

"You going to ask him about the earring?"

"Yes, I have to, before I lose my nerve."

"Then you'd better go." Her troubles did sound trivial compared to the shit most downsiders face very day, but I didn't want to make them any worse.

"Yes. Thank you."

"For what? Not killing you for spilling your drink on me?"

"I was going to say, for listening. But yes, that too."

"I'd like to know how you get on, if you want to tell me." Since I'd become one of the City's chosen, no one talked to me like I was a normal person any more. I missed that.

"Yes, maybe. I'm not sure."

"Well I'm here every week. Same time, same dark corner."

*

I didn't expect her to come back, but she did. After saying hello she added, "Would you mind calling me Vanna? Medame Agriet sounds so formal."

"Of course."

The place was back to its usual genteel seediness after last week's party, and there were plenty of free booths. I suggested we take one, though it meant abandoning my shadowy niche.

As we sat down, Vanna gave me at odd look. "I'm sorry," she said. "But now we're in the light ... how old are you, Malia?"

"Eighteen. We grow up fast in the Undertow."

"Even so, you can't have been an Angel long. Not that it's any of my business."

She was right, and I didn't want to talk about that, not yet. Instead I asked, "How'd it go with Tolyn?"

"He said he had no idea where the earring came from. He suggested it was left by the previous tenant, and maybe we should contact the landlord in case she'd reported it lost. Which made perfect sense, when he said it."

"But you're not sure."

"I want to believe him. I want to be wrong. It's only when I'm away from him that the doubts creep in."

"You said there was other smoky stuff."

"Just odd things. Blank messages from untraceable com numbers, late nights at work. Foolish, clichéd stuff. Nothing I can confront him about."

"Why not? Why not just say 'Are you cheating on me?' Watch his face, check his reaction."

Vanna shook her head. "It's not that easy. You know how it is when you love somebody; you want to think the best of them."

My face betrayed me.

"You've never been in love, have you?"

I should have just walked off. Things had changed between us. Her natural advantages of age and experience were winning out over my unnatural one. If I came over like an ignorant downsider, I'd lose her respect. So what? In the Undertow I had to be above all that messy personal stuff but she didn't come from my world. I didn't have to make like I had all the answers with her. "I reckon love's a topside luxury."

"No, it's a human condition. Downsiders are still human."

"You sure about that? Lots of topsiders aren't."

"That's because most of the time we don't see downsiders, or if we do it's something sordid, or frightening." She continued, "And I think it's sad that you don't know love."

"Don't give me that sugar-talk. I never said I don't know love. I loved my mother; she took the fall when I was twelve. I loved my older sister; she died of a fever three years ago, left me to look after her boy, Taro. I love him too, though he's a handful. But as for being in love, the full hearts-and-flowers shit ... no, that hasn't happened yet. It might, but I doubt it."

Vanna said, "My problems must seem insignificant to you."

"You only worry about business when most downsiders worry about taking the fall, but we're all human, like you said. So, tell me about Tolyn."

"What about him?"

"Whatever you want."

She told me how they met and about their life together. Vanna wanted children in the long run but at thirty-four, she was still young. I didn't say that reaching thirty made you pretty old in the Undertow.

Vanna didn't ask me anything in return. When she left, two drinks later, she said, "See you next week."

I hoped so, but that didn't stop me looking her up on City-com. Far as I could tell, her story checked out, though there was one thing she hadn't mentioned.

*

"I can't stay long, I've got a lot of work on."

"You didn't have to come at all." Our last conversation had left me all mixed up. "Perhaps you shouldn't have, given where Tolyn works."

"What? Oh..." Her shoulders dropped. "I should have said, shouldn't I?"

"That your husband works in the Assembly? Sure as shit you should."

"He's only an aide, Malia. Not a politician, not a... potential target. But yes, I should have said. I'm sorry. I'll understand if you think it's inappropriate for us to meet up again." She shifted, as though expecting me to tell her to go there and then. When I didn't she said, "But there is something I would really like to know first, if you're willing to tell me."

Though I guessed what was coming, I still said, "All right. Ask."

"What's it like to kill someone?"

I'd been right. I could spin a lie, keep up the Angel cool. But this wasn't about looking good, this was about having a friend. "I don't know."

"You've never killed? I mean, that's what Angels do. Carry out the will of the people and, ah, remove the unwise from power."

"Like you said, I've not been an Angel long. And though I've been in a few scrapes, it's never come to killing anyone." I wondered if Vanna could only talk to me because she thought I'd taken a life, and she never would.

"Oh. I just thought... well, serves me right for making assumptions. You'll have to do it sooner or later though, won't you?"

"Probably sooner. I'll get the next removal to come up; that's usual for a new Angel."

"And until then you just wait?"

"Most of being an Angel is waiting."

"And when you do get the call, will you be able to do it?"

Shit and blood but the woman knew how to ask the right – or wrong – questions. "I'm an Angel, I kill for my City. I don't have a choice."

"Thank you for answering my question. I'll go now, if you like."

"No don't go." Not now I've found I can say anything to you. "Why don't you tell me how things are with Tolyn?"

"Well, he bought me flowers yesterday. And he hasn't been

43

working late quite so much."

As she talked I got the idea she and Tolyn were getting on better now. I wondered if, once her life was sorted, Vanna would still want to see me. I didn't ask.

And she didn't mention the fact that I'd checked up on her.

*

I missed the next week. Taro fell ill, the same fever that killed my sister. I flew him topside to get medicine. Two days later he was up and about again. Angel privilege: if I'd been an ordinary downsider he'd probably have died.

If Vanna and I had exchanged com numbers, I could have called her, but we hadn't. That wasn't how things worked. In the shadows of the bar we could say whatever we wanted to each other. Outside we'd always be strangers.

*

I half-expected her not to show the next week, but she was sitting at our usual table, drink in front of her, looking miserable.

I sat down without ordering, leaving the barman to bring my usual. "What happened?"

"Tolyn and I had a massive row. He'd been so sweet, so considerate and that got me thinking. I wondered if he was doing this to cover up. So I came out and asked him whether he was cheating on me."

"What did he say?"

"He said he was really hurt I could think that, that all the extra hours he was putting in were for us, to bail out my business. If I thought that way, then maybe we did have a problem. We ended up shouting at each other and sleeping in separate rooms."

If this was love, I'd be better off without it. "Anything I can do to help?" I sure as shit couldn't think of anything.

"You can distract me. Like you said, love's a luxury to you downsiders. Give me some harsh, downside reality. Put my silly little problems into perspective."

"What d'you want to know?"

"Tell me how you became an Angel. Assuming that's allowed."

"It is." I took a drink while I worked out if I was ready to talk about that yet. I decided I was, and she was the one to tell. "All right. I used be a ligger, bringing topside shit down into the Undertow. I'd find things topsiders had thrown out, or barter with coves – sorry, citizens – who'd deal with me. About a year ago one of my topside contacts asked me for the lowdown on some downsider deals. I refused. What happens in the Undertow stays downside, I told him. Next time I'm topside, I heard someone following me, so I waited round a corner, ready to jump them, flecks drawn."

"Flecks?"

"The blades downsiders wear on their wrists."

"Like Angels?"

"Meant to be, only flecks're on the outside of the skin. Anyway, I waited for ages, but I didn't see anyone. Then I looked round, and there's an Angel, just floating there. I dropped my flecks, but she said the cove who asked me about downside business works for the Minister, and he was testing me. You know who the Minister is?"

Vanna's eyes still glistened, but she was listening hard. "Master of the Angels, the news-nets call him."

"Right enough, though lots of other people work for him too: running errands, listening for rumours, keeping an eye on business all over the City. That's what he wanted me for, listen and report. Course I said yes. In return my topside contact gave me the prime deals."

Now the bit no-one else knew.

"There's this downsider boy about my age, name of Limnel, and he reckons girls only have one type of business with topsiders. One day, in the backstreets, he catches me. He gets his mate to hold me down and... well, he calls it teaching me a lesson."

Vanna's expression said I didn't have to say any more.

"Afterwards his mate wants a go, only Limnel says this is business, not pleasure. His mate's not so sure, he thought he'd get some too, and he lets go of me. So I reach up and punch him in the balls. He reels off and Limnel bends down to hit me back. I grab his shoulders, and head-butt him, real hard. Reckon I broke his nose; later I find blood in my hair. I run to the cove I've been working with, ask him to help me. He lets me clean up, then tells me to wait in his office. I'm scared, because I've fucked up."

I'd slipped back into downsider lingo, but the story was telling itself now. This shit had to come out.

"If I'd just let Limnel have me, that'd be it. Lesson taught, end of story. But I fought back. Things'd get nasty now, and Taro's alone in our homespace. I rush out the back door and run into someone. It's the man himself, the Minister. He just says, 'Follow me,' and walks off. Course I follow, but I'm still worried, so I say, 'I have to get downside, Limnel's gonna hurt my boy.' And he says, 'Taro will be looked after, Malia.'"

"Wait," Vanna looked confused. "He knew your child's name?"

"Of course. He's the Minister. This is his City."

"I hadn't realized he was quite so... well-informed. Please, carry on."

"He takes me all over the back-streets. When I finally get myself together enough to ask him what's going on he tells me that he's making me an Angel. I don't believe it at first. I knew the Minister chose Angels from his runners, but I never thought he had his eye on me.

"Then he leads me to this door. I remember it was red, but I got no idea how to find it again. He unlocks it, opens it... and then nothing."

"What do you mean?"

"I mean, next thing I know I'm lying in a clean bed, feeling good. Better than good. Soon as I sit up I know I've been changed. Not just the blades and the gravitics, but the whole way my body works. And in my head. I mean, I never knew what a gravitic implant was, but now I know I've got them, what they do, how to control them."

"Wow."

"No shit, wow. I'm practicing cutting air when someone chimes the door. This old woman comes in with a box. I'm floating in the middle of the room, stark naked with my blades out, but she just puts the box down on the bed and says 'You'll find a number of suits in City colours in the wardrobe. Details of your new tailor are in your com.' And she gives me stuff from the box: a com, a cred-bracelet, and then, at the bottom of the box, the case with my gun in. In some ways, I feel ready for anything. But in my head I'm still not sure, and I say, 'I never asked for this.'

"She says, 'If you had, you would not have been chosen.' Then she leaves. When I get dressed and go out, I find I'm here, in this hotel. I come downstairs to the bar, this bar, and walk up to the counter. The coves look away but the barman serves me, no question. Turns out I'd been out of it for a week. Taro was fine, he'd been looked after by our local water-trader. That was eleven weeks ago."

"And that's why you come here every week? Because it's the first place you saw when your life changed".

"Stupid, eh?"

"Not stupid. Human."

A shadow fell across our table. I looked up to see a porky cove in a rumpled suit glaring down at us. "Just what is going on?" he growled.

Vanna flinched, then said, "Tolyn? What are you doing here?"

"Looking for you. I came home early, because I wanted to apologise about last night. You weren't in and your com was off, but that nosey woman next door poked her head out and said you'd been going out drinking during the day. I tried four bars before I found you here. Where you are apparently doing all the talking you want..." his gaze painted me in contempt "... to someone I haven't had the *pleasure* to be introduced to."

Under the table, my wrists itched.

Vanna said, "If you had told me you were coming home early, I would have stayed in."

Tolyn said quietly, "And if I had any idea of the company you choose to keep when I'm not around, I wouldn't have bothered." He turned and stalked off.

Vanna looked at me, then at his back. "Damn. I'm sorry," she murmured, and ran out after him.

*

When Vanna didn't turn up next week, I wasn't surprised. Even if her husband was a shit, he was the shit she'd chosen to spend her life with. I'd only been a distraction.

After one drink, I was ready to leave. Then Vanna walked in. She looked terrible, red-eyed and shaky. She headed straight for our booth, and I waved at the barman to bring drinks over.

She sat down and said, "He's left me."

My first thought was 'good riddance', but that wasn't what she needed to hear. "It wasn't me, last week, was it?"

"No, no. Though we argued about that too. He assumed you were, um..."

"A whore waiting for trade?"

"He didn't put it quite like that, but yes. Sorry."

What a prick. "Not your fault. So, when did this happen?"

"Three, no four, hours ago. It still hasn't really sunk in." A tear ran out the corner of one eye. Looked like the last straggler from a whole lot of crying.

"You're sure he meant it?" I hoped he did. She deserved better.

"Oh yes. He turned up at the apartment just before lunch and started packing. I came out of my office and asked him what he thought he was doing. He said that I was right all along. There was someone else, and now he was leaving me for her. He said things hadn't been right for a while between us – like I hadn't noticed! – and she needed him now, because she was at a crisis point in her life. I started shouting, because if having your husband leave you with no warning isn't a crisis point then I don't know what is. I kept shouting and in the end I threw him out, without his stuff. I don't even know where he's gone."

She noticed her drink and took a long pull. Tears started to slide down her cheeks. I watched for a moment, not sure what to do, then moved round the other side of the table, put my arms round her, and held her while she sobbed.

Finally she raised her head and said, "Thank you. I'm sorry to burden you with all this, but it was so sudden. And all my other friends aren't really mine so much as 'ours'. *Were* ours. I..." I felt her stiffen and turned my head to follow her gaze.

I half expected her bastard husband to be there, but instead I saw a downside boy I didn't know standing by the bar. One of the hotel guards had the boy by the arm and they were both looking at us. In fact, everyone was.

City's sake, not now. They were waiting for me, so I nodded to the guard, who released the boy. He shuffled across the room and stopped in front of our table, bowed, then handed a sliver of plastic to me. He bowed again and walked away without a word.

Vanna looked confused. "What's going on? I don't understand."

I looked at the black-hearted dataspike in my hand, then back at Vanna. "I have to go. I'm sorry."

She caught on. "Oh," she said, and drew back.

"It was only a matter of time," I said, and slid out from behind the table.

She laid a hand on my arm. "Good luck."

I smiled back at her. "You too."

I slotted the dataspike into my com as soon as I reached the lobby and scanned the formal language of the removal request. 'By order of the voting citizens'... 'instrument of the City's will'... 'the ultimate punishment for failure to serve the people as a political Consul should and must'... down to the name, Nira Delse. It took me a moment to recall the name, though of course I kept up-to-date with all politicians on the hot-list. Delse had been involved in some sort of scam with a business interest and her husband was suing for custody of their children on the grounds of 'emotional abandonment'. Consul Delse had been bad.

And now I had to kill her.

I paused outside the hotel. Could I really kill a stranger? If I didn't I'd be declared rogue, hunted down by my sister Angels and killed, leaving my child to die.

Like I'd said to Vanna, I didn't have a choice.

I stepped forward, flexed my legs, and sprang into the air.

*

"No, not juice. What's the strongest liquor you serve?" The handful of people in the bar are all working hard to ignore both me and the newscast re-playing on the back wall. Out of the corner of my eye I see one man slip off his stool and creep towards the door.

Though the barman can't have expected to see me back, he isn't fazed. "We have burnt mash, medame."

"Downside gut-rot? Don't expect you get much call for that." The conversation feels unreal. I feel unreal. I need to hold on to the unreality for as long as possible.

On his way to fetch my drink he turns off the news.

I want to down the shot in one but my handshakes and I slop some over my fingers.

Aye, shake now. Ten minutes ago you were steady, calm. Programmed responses. Soon as I opened the case, floating high above the rooftops in my mimetic cloak, the unconscious training cut in. Assemble the gun, mark the target.

I had the skill. Now I just had to find the will.

At first I had trouble making out individual figures in the crowd milling along Constitution Street. Then, as I scanned for the mark's face I knew that I could kill any of those people right now.

Consul Delse looked scared when she stepped onto the Street, surrounded by her staff; safety in numbers. She'd have been told the hit was coming, though not when and where. Well, she'd entered politics knowing that if she screwed up, the people could demand her death. I was just the instrument of their will.

When Delse appeared the crowds got more focused. They guessed she was marked and they wanted the best view. Her people tried to clear a path, without success. I could take the shot whenever I wanted, even if that meant hitting a bystander. Collateral damage was always a risk during a removal.

The Consul turned to someone behind her. I followed her gaze. It took a second to work out where I'd seen that face before, because last time he'd been angry, and now he was shit-scared.

Vanna's words about her husband's lover came back to me: 'she was at a crisis point in her life'. No shit. Tolyn Agriet's girlfriend was facing her biggest, and last, crisis.

They changed direction to cross the Street. She was face on to me now, and I wasn't sure I had the skill to get a clean head-shot without hitting the person behind in the chest.

Without hitting Tolyn Agriet.

He hadn't worried about the damage he'd done to his wife. To my friend.

In a few seconds they'd be under cover of the buildings on this side of the Street. I should move and re-acquire.

Or take the shot now, and screw the collateral.

I paused for a heartbeat, finding that I did have a choice, after all.

Then I fired.

Before I looked away I saw the two of them fall towards each other. Raising the gun, I glimpsed chaos radiating out from them, people running, shouting.

They're still running, shouting, in my head now.

I gesture to the barman for another drink. This time it goes down in one. The mash burns and blurs, taking away the responsibility. But not the memory. That I'll never lose.

I made the removal half an hour ago. Vanna must know. How is she feeling right now? I killed Tolyn for her, because I wanted to punish him for hurting my friend. I carried out downside justice on a topsider. I'll get away with it, but up here when someone pisses you off, you sue them, not kill them. Vanna won't understand. She'll hate me, because she loved Tolyn, for all his faults.

I want her to hate me, because I'm too busy getting drunk to hate myself.

The barman fills the glass. As he turns I call after him.

"My friend... how was she...?" Words get complicated outside my head.

"She calmed down after you left, medame."

Must have cried herself out. She'll have plenty more to cry about now. "No, no. I mean, did she see?" I nod at the screen.

"Yes, medame. She was watching the news."

"How'd she take it? Did she cry? Was she angry?"

"I don't remember any particular reaction from her."

Maybe she doesn't know about Tolyn. No, they had cameras all over. She'd have seen her husband get drilled through the heart from several angles.

"She didn't react at all? Not even to the... collateral damage?"

"Not that I remember. She watched the full replay twice, then finished her drink and left."

"Just finished her drink and left?" Without screaming, without getting upset. Without any reaction at all.

Then barman says, "That's right, medame. Looking rather happier than when she came in, if I may say so."

Looking rather happier...

"Fuck." I slam my fist into the bar. My drink goes over.

The barman holds his ground, which is brave, because my blades are out and right now, I *want* to kill someone.

No, I've done my killing for the day. The blades slide back into my forearms. I raise my hand and lick the spilt spirit from my knuckles. The barman rights the glass, then refills it.

I wondered why Medame Agriet had been so eager to be my friend. Now I know.

You don't have to be the Minister to trace an Angel's movements topside. Finding out she's new is harder, but there're ways, if you've got the money and the motivation. Vanna only had to watch the hot-list to know her husband's mistress was the next likely target for removal. My first mission, as a new Angel. At worst, she'd have the satisfaction of knowing her rival's killer personally. As it was, she'd got her timing spot on. She'd played me perfectly.

She never told a lie I could prove, never did anything that would allow me legal vengeance, and if I broke the code I killed to uphold, I was as dead as her husband. Perhaps the only lie she told was to say she loved Tolyn. Or perhaps that was true too. It's not like I know anything about love.

She's been very clever. Way too clever for a poor downside girl like me.

I raise my glass. *Here's to you, Vanna Agriet. You bitch.*

Jubilee Summer

Gary Couzens

When they opened the staff training centre a couple of miles outside Greyston, I didn't want to go there. But I knew I'd have to, sooner or later.

On the way, I drive through the town itself. Although this place where I grew up is much the same as I remember, the roads in the same location, the primary school I went to still there, everything has somehow *shifted*. It's the day after the four-day Golden Jubilee holiday weekend, and the buildings seem shut in on themselves; silent, long shadows inching across the playground. I don't see any children there. Maybe it's the school holidays? I can't remember. Having no children of your own does that to you.

It's three in the afternoon. Half a dozen mid-teenage boys cluster around the entrance to the big shopping centre that's opened recently. When I and my friends were that age, we'd walk along this street, stopping when something in a shop window caught our interest, or turning our heads as a good-looking boy went past. When we were a bit older, we'd walk along here at a later hour, in our party dresses, thick make-up and too-high heels, on our way to the town's – then – one nightclub.

I've come early. The course I'm attending doesn't start until tomorrow. I knew I'd need the time.

*

The summer of 1977 was the Summer of Punk as well, but at the age of eleven I wasn't really old enough to know much of what was going on. My older sister Gemma was the real punk in our family. 1977 was the year I changed from junior school to secondary, and my life changed in so many ways.

That was the summer of Luke, too.

I often wonder what he'd be like if somehow I were to meet him again, now. Married perhaps, children maybe, possibly working up to his first divorce, while I've stayed determinedly unmarried and childless. Would we have anything in common now, as we had at eleven years old?

*

I check in at the training centre. I'm carrying my overnight bag down the corridor to my room when I hear my name being called: "Thea!"

I turn. It's Jerry, from our Docklands office; we know each other from previous courses. He's in his early forties, one of those men who combats hair loss with an aggressive number-one crop, but is too jowly and lacking the bone structure to carry off that kind of look. He's married with teenage children but regards his nights away as licence to play the field. But he's never tried it on with me, for which I'm grateful. With the unspoken understanding that there'll never be anything between us, we're much friendlier towards each other than we could have been.

He walks in step with me down the corridor. "Did you see the procession yesterday?" he says, in his broad East End accent. "Wasn't it bloody marvellous? One in the eye for those people who knock the Royal Family."

"I saw bits of it," I say. We've reached my room. As I unlock it, I add. "I was too busy listening to my CD of *Never Mind the Bollocks*."

"I never would have guessed you're a punk, Thea."

"See you at dinner, Jerry." I shut the door behind myself.

*

"The Sex Pistols? You must be joking! They can't even *play*!" That was my brother Dominic, and it was one of many arguments he had with Gemma. They were only a year apart, had gone to the same schools together, and were forever being compared. Dominic was at University, somewhere Gemma had no intention whatsoever of going herself. She'd just left school that year and was working at Sainsbury's.

These arguments never really ended, only paused. Dominic would go into his bedroom and play his Yes albums. We didn't see much of him anyway: he spent most of his first year's University vacations at his girlfriend's up north somewhere. Gemma hadn't won the argument but hadn't lost it either: she'd stand there with a little smile breaking out on her face. Dominic simply *didn't get it.*

Sometimes when we were alone in the house that summer, Gemma would hijack the record player and play her punk LPs as loud as she dared. We pogoed around the room, finally collapsing giggling onto the settee. I knew all the words to "Anarchy in the UK" and "White Riot" and "New Rose". There was the occasion when she made me up into a miniature redheaded version of Siouxsie Sioux, to my parents' horror... but maybe that was a little later. Gemma had a boyfriend, Keith alias Brian Damage, twenty years old and guitarist and lead singer of local band Cum Stains. Their first and only gig, in the back room of Keith's parents' house while they were out, was interrupted by the police. His finest hour was walking down Greyston High Street just after the council had passed a byelaw forbidding anyone with non-human-coloured hair from the town centre. He'd dyed his bright orange. He lasted five minutes before he was arrested to a chorus of jeers and catcalls. Needless to say, Mum and Dad didn't know about Keith, but Gemma spent as much time as she could with him. Once I passed them kissing in public, in Greyston High Street.

I looked up to my sister. She was seven years older than me, but somehow that age gap didn't matter. She was always protective of me – and still acts that way now – and that helped when we heard the raised voices from behind the closed door of our parents' bedroom.

Often I would ask my mother if I could go round to Luke's house, which was two blocks away. I remember Mum with bags under her eyes, or sipping at her pre-dinner sherry. I'd help her in some small way, like laying the table for dinner, and she'd let me lick the dessert spoon. With any luck she'd be in a good enough mood to allow me to do what I asked. I was the youngest, the one who was a surprise, and I played on that.

"Oh all right," she'd say.

Sometimes Luke would spend the evening here, on a Saturday night as we watched *Doctor Who* followed by *The Generation Game* and *The Duchess of Duke Street*. Occasionally it was an informal babysitting operation, and he'd spend most or all of the night on a lilo in my room while his mother went out. Or I'd be in his house until Dad collected me just before my bedtime, and sleepily half-protesting I'd go home.

*

In my room I change out of my clothes and I have a leisurely shower. Tired after a two-hour drive, I lie on the bed and distractedly watch *Countdown* on the small TV set. After it finishes, I flip through the channels, finding nothing that interests me.

Two hours until dinner. I drink a coffee which re-energises me.

I can't stay here. I know what I have to do

Ten minutes later, I'm driving out of the car park, back towards Greyston.

*

I first met Luke at the beginning of the school year, as he and his mother had moved into the area. Luke sat next to me. I don't know if that was due to our teacher sensing straight away we'd get on, or some more idiosyncratic reason such as the fact that we were both redheads. In any case, I was annoyed. The group of girls I'd hung around with the previous year had mostly gone into the other class. New alliances and friendships had been formed, and very early on it was made clear to me that I wasn't part of that emerging clique. I was too tall, growing too fast, clumsy as a result, with clothes that never fit properly.

Luke was odd from the start. He was a little smaller than average, freckles standing out against milk-white skin. He was a vegetarian, which was very unusual then. ("His mother's a bloody hippie," I heard one teacher say to a colleague.) And if you want to fit in with the rest of the class, you don't ask in the middle of a Religious Education lesson if Heaven is a different space/time continuum.

Silence fell. I could hear a boy sniggering behind me. I couldn't help but smile behind my hand.

"Er…that's a very interesting suggestion, Luke," said the teacher, after a pause. Then she changed the subject, and continued.

Luke, you see, was a science fiction fan. Not just on TV, *Doctor Who* and *Star Trek*, which most of us watched anyway. He was also reading it out of the adult section of the library, starting at Asimov and Clarke and working his way on from there. He was learning the hard way that not everyone shared his enthusiasm.

"Whatcher doing, Period Head?" As I was walking down a corridor I saw Luke, a group of boys surrounding him. One of them shoved him, while another made a grab for his satchel.

Something snapped inside my head. I knew Luke could be

annoying, but this *wasn't right*. Fired by my eleven-year-old sense of injustice, I hurried up to them. "Leave him alone! He hasn't done anything to you!"

"He your boyfriend, Thea?" said one boy, Darren, the one who had sniggered behind us in class.

"Luke fancies Thea!" someone else shouted.

I went red. "*Shut up!* Why are you so horrible to him?"

I was actually taller than most of them, having shot up three inches in height in the last half term.

"'Cos he's a spastic," said the boy.

"Oi, Luke," another boy said. "Were you the last one left at the orphanage?"

We all went silent. Everyone knew that Luke was adopted, but no one had gone so far as to say anything like this to his face. I gazed with horror at Luke, expecting him to burst into tears, lose his temper, whatever.

But he didn't. All he said was, "Your Mum and Dad *had* to have you. My Mum and Dad *chose* me." I couldn't believe how calm he sounded.

That was something else that bound us together. I wasn't adopted, although I thought sometimes I must have been, being taller than Dominic and Gemma had been at my age and the only redhead, not to mention left-hander, anyone could remember on either side of the family. But there were plenty of witnesses to the fact that I was my mother's child. I was unplanned though. Mum and Dad had had one of each sex with Dominic and Gemma, had already created their nuclear family. I was a surprise. My full name is Theodora, which means *gift of God*. A family name, after a great-aunt who was still living then, but it had seemed appropriate. It was soon shortened to Thea, and that abbreviation stuck.

That afternoon, Luke's mother was standing at the gate, and Luke introduced me to her. She shook my hand. "Hello, Thea. Luke's told me all about you." She wasn't tall, not much more so than I was then, and she had long mouse-coloured hair that almost reached her waist. She had a distinctive smell, or smells: I recognised tobacco, but there was another, heavier scent that I couldn't recognise. Years later, when I smelled it again, a shudder of recognition went through me. I could identify it then: patchouli oil.

I walked part of my way home with them, that first afternoon.

*

I drive from the training centre back into Greyston. At first I think I might be lost as I look for the road where we used to live. I may have to ask directions. But no, there's the Junior school I went to. I'm driving along the route I always walked home by. *Walking home*: that dates me. I'm willing to bet that virtually none of the schoolchildren in my old school today will be doing that. Too frightening. You don't know who might be out there.

Finally I reach the turning we lived down. There used to be a phone box on the corner, where Gemma and Keith would meet for a snatched half-hour's snog. It isn't here any more.

I park the car and walk the rest of the way up the road.

*

Luke told me stories. All his school reports emphasised his imagination, even if he was no more than indifferent in most subjects. He would tell the stories, and I would join in as best I could.

He often told me the one about the planet he came from, which wasn't in this Universe at all but in another dimension, another space/time continuum. He was the son of the King. When enemies threatened the realm, the King hid his son away so that he would come to no harm. He hid him in a different dimension, on a different planet – this one – for safe keeping. He would come back for his son when it was safe to do so. I was the Princess he was destined to marry, likewise hidden in this world when my land was conquered. There were others of us hidden away, waiting for the call. You could tell us by our red hair and our left-handedness.

"I see Luke's telling you his stories, Thea," said his mother, as she came in the room towards the end of it. "Don't let him tell you black is white, now." She wasn't critical, just smiling. She insisted I call her Beatrice. She was the first woman I ever met who called herself *Ms* instead of *Mrs* or *Miss*. I didn't even know what the title meant at first until she explained it. I liked her.

I simply smiled back, and when she had gone again, asked Luke to carry on with his story. And so the saga of Prince Luke and Princess Theodora continued. It was a serial that carried on for several episodes and many weeks, this story that Luke told just for me. As I had the neater handwriting, I wrote it down, all the details of dynasties and hierarchies, and the geography and peoples of many different planets. I started with old school exercise books and, when they were full, moved on to pads of lined A4 paper from W.H. Smith's. I still have them somewhere.

Towards the end of the evening, Dad came round to collect me. He stood in the doorway, chatting with Beatrice. They stood there for a while. As I went to the cloakroom for my coat, I glanced back and saw them, silhouetted, my much taller father framed by the doorway as he leaned over Beatrice. She had her arms folded across her chest, the sky darkening behind them. At that moment I remembered something else Luke had said: *There are always men calling round. Divorce vultures, Mum calls them.* I shook my head, flicking my hair out of my eyes. I didn't want to think that of my Dad. I didn't want to think of him and Mum arguing. That's what I came to Luke's house to avoid.

*

The road is shorter than I remembered, or maybe that's because as an eleven-year-old the world seems larger. I knew even then I wanted to explore it: childhood always seemed to me to be a restrictive experience, like a prison sentence you know will end sometime but not soon enough. You can see this in photos of me taken at the time: an oh-so-serious expression on my pale, unformed freckled face, staring unblinking out from under my fringe. I was *becoming a woman*, as Mum had said. I couldn't wait to be a grown-up. Whatever I was becoming, I wished I could hurry up and become it.

There are houses I don't recognise, a row of shops, a whole new mini-estate. Neighbourhood Watch signs. The large house that was on the corner – I remember it being demolished – is now a small close in its own right. Some of this is new, other bits are gaps in my memory which are being filled. I walk to the top and turn right. Our house was the last but one. I stand in front of it now. The front of the house has a large bay window it didn't have before and there are gnomes playing cricket in the front garden.

"Can I help you?" It's a woman standing in the front garden of the house next door.

"I used to live here," I say. "I'm just looking around. I was in the area."

The woman shrugs, lets me get on with my excursion into nostalgia. After five minutes, I've had enough, and I walk back to my car. There are tears in my eyes.

*

One morning, in the middle of May 1977, I woke up with the worst headache I could ever remember having, It pulsed inside my head and I was worried I'd be sick or faint. Spots spun and shimmered before my eyes.

I went downstairs to the kitchen, holding on to the banister in case I fell. I was just reaching for a bottle of paracetamol when I heard a voice. It didn't come from any direction, more like *inside* my head. A deep voice, an old one, reverberating inside me, as remote and vast and cold as a glacier.

No. It's not time.

"Thea? Is something the matter?" Gemma stood in the doorway, wearing only a nightdress, her hair dishevelled.

"Nothing. Just a headache." It was already beginning to recede.

"Jesus Christ, is that all?" she said. "You woke me up, you did."

"Sorry," I said.

"It's three in the bloody morning."

I said nothing as I went back to bed. I knew that something had happened, but I didn't yet know what. I didn't sleep again for some time, until exhaustion claimed me.

Luke wasn't in school that day. Perhaps he was off sick? He had been once already that year, with a cold, but his mother had rung us to let us, or rather me, know. This hadn't happened today.

"Oi, Crystal Tits," said Darren. "Where's your boyfriend?"

"Oh piss off," I mouthed back.

Our teacher saw the headmaster standing outside the door of our classroom. She went out, then a few minutes later was back in the room. "Thea? Could you come with me for a minute, please?"

Puzzled, I stood up. I wondered if I was in trouble, but something told me that it wasn't that. The headmaster, a tall man, leaned over me. His face was lined: no doubt he wasn't used to breaking bad news to eleven-year-old girls. He told me Luke had died during the night.

They sent me home for the rest of the day.

I barely remember the next few days. It was as if I had shut down, and I was locked inside myself, looking out at the world. I'm sure I cried. I remember Gemma being there. But mostly I felt numb, disbelieving.

We soon found out the cause of Luke's death. An aneurysm, one undetected and deep inside his brain, had burst. He wouldn't have felt anything and was most likely asleep at the time, which as far as anyone could tell was around three in the morning. When his mother found him, she thought he'd overslept, so peaceful was the expression on his face. Then she noticed he wasn't breathing.

The funeral was the following week, and anyone in Luke's year who wanted to go was allowed to. I went, and stood next to Gemma, who held my hand throughout the ceremony. I didn't cry: they said I was a brave girl. You can see me in the photo that appeared in the local paper.

At the funeral, Beatrice seemed to have aged ten years or more, and was supported by a woman who turned out to be her sister. Beatrice broke down during the service. Afterwards, as we filed out of the crematorium, I went up to her.

She blinked. "Thank you for coming, Thea. I really appreciate it. You were a good friend to Luke."

"He's gone back to the dimension he came from," I said.

To this day I have no idea why I said that. As I did, I knew I risked a severe telling-off from my parents. I remember everyone nearby fell silent.

Beatrice tried to smile, but her expression failed and crumbled. Tears ran from her eyes. She hugged me tight. She didn't say anything.

That was the last we saw of her. Shortly afterwards, she went to stay with her sister and soon her house was up for sale.

My parents' marriage survived a few more years, to break up around the end of the decade. Gemma had left home by then, and Mum had custody of me.

*

It's the evening, and I'm in the bar after dinner. As Jerry buys the drinks, Elaine leans over to me. "You're very quiet tonight, Thea. Is something the matter?" Elaine comes from our Paisley office. She's about my age, and we hit it off immediately when we first met, often sending emails back and forth during the working day.

"I grew up around here, Elaine," I said. "I went and had a look around."

"Och, that's always a mistake," she says. "It'll never be like you remembered. Was it?"

"No, it wasn't." I don't say any more, deciding to leave the full story for another time, preferably when Jerry isn't around.

"Nostalgic are we?" says Jerry, resting all three drinks on the table. "Oh sorry, I forget I'm talking to an old punk rocker."

"You weren't a punk, were you Thea?" Elaine asks. "Aren't you a bit young for that?"

"I'm thirty-six now, so work it out," I say. "My sister was more into all that, really."

"Bunch of antisocial arseholes," says Jerry. "No talent or anything. Couldn't even play their instruments."

I smile thinly, having had this argument with many people in my time. And I'm not inclined to have it again now.

But Jerry has only started. "You know what annoys me, what really pisses me off? All this *I Love the 70s* on TV. Well, I hope you don't mind me saying, girls, but I'm a bit older than you are and I *remember* the 70s and they were *shit*. Three-day weeks, power cuts, the Winter of Discontent, the miners going on strike all the time. Well, Maggie sorted *them* out. Someone had to…"

Elaine and I glance at each other during this diatribe. Our eyes meet and suddenly we're both laughing.

Jerry stops in mid-sentence, his face reddening. "Why? What's so funny?"

*

Nine o'clock at night, I've left the bar early claiming a long day, tiredness, things to do. I'm now in my room, calling Gemma on my mobile. "Oh hi, Thea. Did you get there okay?"

"Yes thanks. Just a boring course tomorrow, that's all."

"Lucky you." I can hear her children in the background, the sound of a television. "Auntie Thea," Gemma whispers to someone.

"I went back to have a look at the house."

"Bet it's changed a lot."

"It has."

"Quite a lot of memories."

"Yes, I thought of Luke again."

"Luke..." She paused. "Yes, of course I remember him, the poor kid."

"He died right at the end of the summer term. Just before the Silver Jubilee celebrations. He was looking forward to a street party, even if his Mum wasn't. He liked all that royal stuff."

"Is that so?"

"He never got to see it."

"That's so sad."

I still think of those words I heard that night. *Not my time.* When it is my time, will I be taken the same way as Luke was?

When will my time be?

From time to time, I see others like us. The overweight man at the bar, ginger hair sprouting around his shirt buttons, gazing across at me and my friends. Was he left in this dimension for safekeeping? The red-haired woman in a pinstripe suit, flicking her lighter with her left hand, enjoying a last cigarette in the minutes before her train arrives, grinding it out half-smoked under the sole of her court shoe. Is she waiting for her call?

As Gemma and I chat, I think back to that summer. *No future*, we sang, but at least we thought, hoped, there would be one. Now we look back to the past, picking it over as if to find something we missed, to put something right that we got wrong first time round. But we can't go back.

I can't go back there again.

I think of Luke in his other dimension, summoned back to fight alongside his father the King. I hope they have been successful in defeating their enemies. Maybe when they have they will call me back for that destined marriage.

Sometimes, I hope that will be soon.

Noble Deceit

Juliet E. McKenna

I'd always known the call could come. I'd never worried about it. Knowing they were there was nothing I need fear. I shared their secret. If I couldn't tell anyone else, that simply made the secret more precious, something to hug to myself when other children called me names.

Not that I suffered any more passing spite than other artisan quarter boys. No one knew I was special apart from Madam Sima. I wondered about that as I grew older. Had one of my brothers said something? We were all learning our letters at her school around the time we realised I was the only one who could spin substance out of shadows. To make a ball to play with when the long summer evenings sneaked through the bedroom shutters our father had bolted.

To make a lumpy frog spring out of the chamberpot, when Seppin went to pee, first as always. He yelled and fell backwards and pissed his nightshirt. But he didn't tell on me, not even when our mother slapped him, calling him a dirty barge boy. We stuck together, four of us with barely three years between our birthdays first and last. Besides, we didn't think much of it. Seppin could add up numbers in his head. Rachik could whistle like a willow finch. I could make frogs out of shadows and Marlil could roll his tongue into a tube. He was only five, so that was worth praising.

Then Madam Sima tapped my shoulder one day as we sprang up from our benches when the noon bells called us home for lunch.

"Thian, I have something for your mother."

I thought nothing of it. She'd hardly trust whatever it was to Marlil, and Seppin had been first out of the door, followed by Rachik.

All of us lads were eager for the afternoon's work around our fathers' looms and lathes. Most were already counting the new moons until their tenth birthday when they'd leave the school Madam Sima had made of her dead husband's weaving shed. I enjoyed my lessons more than most but, like my brothers, assumed I'd take up the joinery trade.

So I dutifully followed Madam Sima across the yard and into her kitchen. She surprised me by leading me into the parlour.

"Sit down, dear. I want to show you something."

I was expecting a book. She had a whole shelf full and she trusted a few of us to read quietly when she drilled the rest in their letters. I can picture her still, standing by the alphabet wall-hanging, straight-backed despite her years, her dress and lace-trimmed cap always mourning grey.

Sitting opposite, she spread her wrinkled fingers on the table's embroidered cloth. I sat uncertain as she stared at the empty linen. Then I caught my breath.

Something was taking shape. Like the bridge tower's turrets coming into view as the sun burned through spring mists. Madam Sima was drawing something out of nothing into a patch of sunlight.

A cat. Not a real cat, one barely as long as her forefinger. Ginger and white with different coloured eyes? I gasped with delight. It was Basu!

"Make Lagan," I begged, "and the black heron."

That was my favourite tale about the wily cat and the yard-hound and the curious things the river brought them.

Madam Sima stroked tiny Basu's head. It stropped itself around her finger just like a real cat. "Why?"

That flummoxed me. "Why not?"

"What would I do with a pocket-sized dog and a bird the size of a clothes pin?"

Her voice was kind. She never asked questions like Havas, our father's journeyman, heavy with sarcasm to show you were a fool.

"I could have them?" I suggested hopefully.

"How would you explain that to your mother?" Her blue eyes twinkled. "Or your brothers? What about Kettle-cat?"

Our mother's cat, named for his habit of sleeping among the pans, had a reputation as a rat-killer the length of our street.

"I could keep them in a box," I said uncertainly.

The tiny cat rolled on its back and Madam Sima gently tickled its belly. "Wouldn't that be cruel?"

"It's just a toy." I was itching to stroke the marvellous creature myself.

She sat back. "Is it?"

The tiny Basu sprang up, just like Kettle-cat. I stretched out one finger. It pushed at my fingernail with its little nose. I stroked its silky fur, warm from the sun.

It flopped down and rolled over. Tentative, I touched its belly. Wrapping its forepaws around my finger, it bit, hind legs raking. Father played this game with Kettle-cat. None of us did, convinced we'd lose a hand.

"Ow!" I laughed but little Basu's teeth and claws were sharp as pinpricks.

"It's quite real," Madam Sima said. "Now I've made it, I must care for it until it fades. It's my responsibility."

I had no notion where the frog had gone, I realised guiltily.

"There aren't many of us who can make things like this." She gently unhooked the tiny cat, scooping it up in her palm. "We must take care."

I looked at her, wretched. "There was a frog…"

"I know," she nodded, untroubled. "It'll have faded by now and, being a frog, I don't suppose it thought much about anything. But this one." She smiled as the little Basu jumped down from her hand to explore the table top. "I'll need eyes in the back of my head for a few days."

"What will happen?" I wondered.

"It'll go to sleep and then it won't be here any more." Madam Sima curbed the tiny cat's attempt to climb down the table cloth. "It would fade sooner if I didn't feed it but that would be cruel."

"Why did you make it?" I blurted out.

"To show what you can do." She looked at me. "So you realise what you mustn't."

"I won't," I promised fervently. If the notion of making tiny animals thrilled me, the thought of them dying mere days later was horrid.

"You might, by accident." Her eyes were ice-bright. "You could wake in the night and find the marsh bear you've been dreaming about. Or a mud serpent under the bed might strike at your foot one morning."

I was only seven years old. Suddenly this was terrifying.

"I'll teach you how to make sure that doesn't happen," Madam

Sima reassured me. "But this must be our secret."

"Why?" I demanded.

"Why do you think?" she chided.

I bit my lip. "Seppin wouldn't leave me be if he knew."

"True." She laughed. "That's not the most important reason."

"No?" Seeing her unconcern sparked faint hope in me.

She gathered up the tiny cat. "When needs must, Thian, if danger threatens, you and I and others like us will defend the city."

I gasped. "How?"

"By shaping things to terrify the enemy, to drive them away, to block their path."

"But…"

She understood my incoherent protest.

"I know the paramount kings have ruled in peace since before your grandsire's day but that could change. Then, if some enemy knew our city's defences relied on the likes of me and you, they'd kill us first, wouldn't they?"

I was struck dumb with fear.

"Provided no one knows who we are or what we can do, we're safe." She stroked the tiny cat curled up asleep in her palm. "So tell no one and all will be well."

I nodded. If Madam Sima said, this was how it must be.

She smiled. "Now, run home with some pickled cherries."

I can't recall how I found my way home, or if my mother was pleased with the cherries. But I can still picture that tiny cat and recall the hollow in my stomach when I found its basket empty three days later.

*

Summer turned to autumn and the dank days of winter. I stayed in school for half a chime each day after the others left. Madam Sima told my parents I was clever enough to apply to the Horned God's school. She would prepare me for the priestly tutors' examination.

She told me not one in a thousand can draw imagination into reality. First she challenged me to make everyday things like bricks and chairs. I was a biddable child and did as she asked. So she challenged me to create a blooming rose. I never thought I would master that but eventually I did. Gradually I became proficient at making creatures, mostly birds which no one would remark on if they escaped.

Thankfully I never woke up to find some nightmare become reality by my bed. Madam Sima taught me meditations to clear my mind before sleeping.

I proved particularly good at unmaking things. Perhaps because the more skilfully I shaped birds, the less I liked doing so. I would unmake them as soon as the sheen on their feathers stilled, before they could look at me.

Once I mastered the challenges of this strange power, its thrill receded. Madam Sima was adamant I tell no one and I dared not disobey her. Besides, I knew children made outsiders of people they thought too different, too strange. I didn't want to find myself friendless. As I grew older, I saw adults had their own fears and prejudices and I didn't want to end up chained in the madhouse.

Madam Sima told me time and again I must do my duty if I was ever called upon. I never questioned that but daydreams of saving the city from some peril I took care not to imagine too precisely faded after a while.

I had scant time for such fancies because Madam Sima was serious about presenting me to the priests. She taught me history and mathematics and natural philosophy and I was enthralled. The tutors at the Horned God's school recognised my enthusiasm when my father took me to face their questions. So when Seppin and Rachik took up their chisels, I was learning geometry and metallurgy. By the time Marlil joined the workshop, I was apprenticed to a master builder whose magnificent many-windowed house overlooked the Golden Goddess's own temple.

I saw Madam Sima occasionally on visits home. Once, I brought a girl to meet my mother. Falling into conversation with us, Madam Sima drew me aside to warn against plucking trinkets out of the air to impress my sweetheart. She need not have worried. It had honestly never occurred to me.

The next time I went home Mother told me Madam Sima had died in her sleep. I grieved for her and life went on.

*

The call came on a summer's day. Having long since left masonry and mortar for the lofty heights of the drawing house, I was calculating the width of beams for the new ropemakers' hall. Hearing boots on the stairs, I looked up. Instead of some guild messenger, I saw a youth barely old enough to shave but wearing fur-trimmed velvets.

"Thian Hindrie?"

"Good day." I rose from my stool and bowed. He could only have come from one of my master's richest clients.

"Madam Sima told you your duty." The young man stretched out his hand and an azure butterfly coalesced out of nothing. "We need you."

I watched the butterfly soar up to the attic's skylights. "The city's threatened?"

My master was alert to every whisper carried up and down the great rivers. I'd heard nothing.

"In a manner of speaking." The youth's face gave nothing away. "Come with me."

He was ordering, not inviting me.

My throat tightened. "My master…"

"Will be thrilled that you're summoned to the palace." His smile wasn't reassuring. "Appalled if you demur."

He was noble, he spoke with Madam Sima's authority and he was right. My master would insist I go. So I followed the youth down the stairs and we crossed the cobbled square in front of the Golden Goddess's temple.

"Who are you?"

"Eion." He slid me a sideways glance. "The Margrave of Jedfal's third son but that's not important."

I wondered about that, as we walked along the broad avenue to the pleasure gardens beyond the palace. He headed for a distant summer house, shuttered up and draped with tarpaulins.

"Thian, good day." As my companion unlocked a side door and ushered me in, a man turned from examining a mouldering fresco. Grizzled and weather-beaten, his shirt was creased and he smelled of stables.

"Good day." I glanced at my companion

Eion was locking the door. "This is Alace, the queen's groom."

I swallowed. "How may I serve?"

Alace thrust his hands into the pockets of his stained leather breeches. "By shaping a facsimile of the paramount king."

"Treason!" I spat.

"I'm glad that's your first thought." He smiled without humour. "But no, we are all loyal."

Eion spoke up. "The king has been stabbed."

"Silence." Alace scowled at him.

"Forgive me." The youth ducked his head, meek as milk. When his rank entitled him to have the groom horsewhipped for such impertinence.

"Madam Sima told you we defend the city." Alace challenged me with a penetrating stare. "These days our enemies don't send armies. They send spies and assassins and one has left the king for dead."

"Prince Perisen is so young." I was aghast. "Who will stand as regent?"

Eion's father? The other margraves wouldn't like that.

"There will be no regency because the king will recover, goddess be praised," Alace said firmly.

"Barely ten people know of the attack," Eion added.

Alace nodded. "The queen and the royal children have been sent away…"

"Princess Kemeti has toad-pox." I remembered one of my fellow draughtsmen mentioning it a few days since, prompting us all to reminiscences of the tiresome childhood ailment.

"Quite so," agreed Alace. "As far as the world and his wife are concerned, the king has also succumbed. Unfortunate but no cause for alarm."

I was confused. "Then why…"

"Whoever wants the king dead will spread the word he's been stabbed." Alace looked murderous. "To kill that rumour, he must be seen. Thankfully, being seen at a distance will suffice." His eyes strayed towards the main palace. "His doctor will permit him to appear on the eastern balcony to greet the midsummer sun. Alone, naturally, to avoid an epidemic laying the whole court low. Then he'll join his family to convalesce in peace."

That made sense. Toad-pox is virulently contagious and while not life-threatening, adult sufferers were left exhausted. Whenever the king returned, no one would wonder if he looked thin and weary. Provided he survived his wound.

"Who did this?" My mouth was dry.

"That's not your concern," Eion snapped.

Alace looked at me, unblinking. "Shape us a kingly puppet to walk from his majesty's apartments to the balcony, to smile and wave at his subjects and depart in a closed carriage."

"At the queen's command?" I was still struggling to believe all this.

"Succeed, and you will be hired to rebuild this pavilion." Eion waved a hand at the crumbling plaster. "The first of many such commissions. This time next year, you'll have the coin to set up your own business and to wed in fine style."

So he knew about Meriah. We had hopes of marriage within five years if I prospered.

"What if I can't?" I asked hoarsely.

"You can." Alace was unyielding.

"In three days?" I shook my head.

"You're saying you won't?" Eion raised his brows. "Then your promising career will founder on such a scandal…"

"Enough." Alace's hand cut him short. "We only ask that you try. I'm confident you'll succeed, given what Sima told me. If you cannot…" he shrugged. "You cannot."

"If you cannot, every margrave in the sixteen cities will fasten on rumours that the king is dying. Half will start calculating their chances of ascending to paramount rule," Eion said savagely. "We needn't fear upland horsemen or raiders from the marshes if we start fighting amongst ourselves."

Civil war had ravaged the peace of the realm during the last regency and I had to keep faith with Madam Sima.

"I can try," I said hesitantly.

"Good." Alace momentarily betrayed his relief. "Eion will see you have all that you need."

"What?" I didn't understand.

"You'll stay here till it's over." The groom walked to the door.

As I stood like a sun-addled fool, he left, locking the door behind him.

I looked at Eion. He had a key.

"Don't be a fool." He twitched back his scarlet cloak to show his sword. "Do this and you'll be well rewarded. Turn stubborn and we'll ruin you."

I rubbed my face. "I can't stay here. I'll be missed."

"I've left word that you and I are surveying a project on my father's estates."

Abruptly I realised Alace hadn't answered my question. "Are we doing the queen's bidding?"

Eion shook his head. "No one knows about this but you, me, Alace, the king's physician and his majesty's valet."

*

Was it treason? I could only hope not. Would they reward me? Perhaps. Eion was certainly sincere in his threats to ruin me. So I tried. What else could I do?

That first day I made and unmade four hopeless puppets that sagged and collapsed.

Eion wasn't impressed. "I thought you were an architect."

"If it's so easy, do it yourself," I snapped.

But his words prompted a thought as I unmade the fifth shapeless manikin sprawled on the dusty tiles. "Get me paper and charcoal."

He left me locked in. I examined the shuttered windows while he was gone. I could have smashed my way free. But Alace had known Madam Sima and she'd said this call would come. Besides, the challenge was beginning to intrigue me.

Eion returned with parchment, pen and ink. I searched my memory for everything the Horned God's priests had taught me of anatomy. Medicine was merely one of the mysteries they safeguarded in his name.

A maidservant brought us food and a lamp. There were tables and chairs upstairs. Later she returned with blankets and pillows. I don't know what Alace told her and I didn't ask. I was too busy thinking.

Only a fool builds a house without foundations, without load-bearing walls, rafters and trusses to support the roof. By the time the light faded, I knew what to try next.

When Eion opened his eyes in the morning, he yelled and scrambled to his feet, shirt flapping around his bare backside. I laughed, remembering Seppin and the frog.

"What's that?" He dragged on his breeches.

"Scaffolding."

More precisely, it was an approximation of a skeleton. I hunkered down to contemplate the manikin's feet. Remaking those to my satisfaction, I shaped its knees and hips and worked my way upwards.

The next puzzle was making the thing move. Levers and pulleys. Mechanical advantage. I used such things without thinking on a building project.

"Eion, take off your shirt and your breeches."

Thankfully he was well-enough muscled for me to see what I needed. Though I don't know what the maid thought when she brought us our lunch.

Drawing pale substance out of the air, shaping it with my fingers like clay, I spent the rest of the day carefully crafting a bloodless semblance of flesh.

"It looks like a flayed carcass." Eion shivered as the manikin finally lurched across the room. "And moves like a drunken whore."

"Madam Sima said function follows form."

Maybe Eion didn't know that, if he could only make butterflies. Whenever I'd made a bird well enough, it had always known how to fly. I could only hope this simulacrum would walk like a man when I'd finished it.

I yawned. A day hauling stone on a building site couldn't have tired me more. "I don't suppose it'll try to leave in the night but you had better keep watch."

My bed was all the cosier, knowing he was sitting vigil in the dark with my uncanny creation.

Alace came to see our progress. The manikin was smooth as a waxen image once I had laid a skin over the underlying workings.

"Well done," he approved.

"I don't know what the king looks like close to," I warned.

"What about clothes?" Eion asked.

Alace nodded. "I'll see to it."

He came back the following morning with brocade doublet and breeches, silk stockings and shoes.

"Do we dress it?" Eion was becoming ever more nervous around the manikin.

"Let's try." His unease perversely calmed my own misgivings.

It proved disturbingly easy. As I lifted its hand, the creation held itself ready. I slid on a sleeve and it lowered its arm without needing my touch. When I knelt and raised its foot, it kept its balance as I rolled on the stockings.

"What about the face?" Eion demanded harshly.

"Here." Alace produced a miniature portrait, oils on an ivory oval.

I hesitated. I'd never tried shaping something to a specific resemblance. "How is the king?"

"Holding his own." Alace looked grim. "Rumour's running rife. He must be seen by the populace tomorrow."

"I'll do my best." It was all I could say.

As I summoned up hair to clothe the smooth head, I concentrated on the rich chestnut of the portrait, just as I had imagined the purple-shot black of a gable crow's wing. Smoothing colour into the face, I shaped the king's angular nose with my mind as much as my hands. Deft strokes of my fingers drew his brows and his beard.

It took me the rest of the day, with any number of false starts. Eion and Alace examined my efforts from all angles, interrupting to object or correct me. Initially I couldn't amend any mistake, forced to return to that pallid blankness. Gradually I learned how to make changes, crudely at first, then with growing subtlety. The last of the summer twilight was fading when Alace finally pronounced himself satisfied.

"No," Eion said suddenly. "It's not right."

Trembling with fatigue, I rounded on him. "If you think…"

He stepped back, hands raised. "He's supposed to have toad-pox."

It took me a moment to understand. I struggled to recall the pustules my brothers and I had scratched, twenty and more years ago. Slowly, I raised them on the manikin's face.

"Good." Alace approved

"Goddess!" Eion knocked over a chair

As I touched the creature's cheek it opened its eyes. Brown, just like the king's.

The breath froze in my throat. I hadn't done that. Blood pounded in my head and I stumbled backwards, dizzy.

Alace guided me to the chair as Eion retrieved it. The creature's vacant gaze followed me.

"Close your eyes!" My voice broke on the command as my knees buckled. "Face the wall!"

To my relief, it turned around.

"Goddess," Eion breathed.

"I'll be glad when tomorrow's over." Even Alace's composure was shaken. "Right, get some sleep. We must get it to his majesty's apartments before the dawn chimes."

He left me and Eion looking numbly at each other.

"Stay awake till midnight and then rouse me," he said abruptly.

I nodded. There was no way I'd sleep without someone keeping watch over the creature either.

*

Alace appeared at first light with the yawning maidservant bringing hot water. She fetched bread and meat and warm spiced ale while Eion and I washed and shaved. Alace produced clean clothes for us; maroon liveries like the one he wore.

"Has it moved?" He studied the creature as we dressed.

"Not yet."

As I spoke, it stirred.

Alace threw me a hooded cloak. "Hide its face."

Steeling myself, I draped the heavy cloth around its shoulders. As it looked at me, I saw its eyes were no longer so vacant. Was there was comprehension behind that gaze now?

I hid my unease with a curt order. "Follow me."

I followed Alace and it followed me. Eion brought up the rear.

Alace led us quickly to the palace and in through a servants' entrance. Back stairs and uncarpeted passageways took us to a plain door where a stern-faced man in doctor's robes waited. Silent, he unlocked the door and ushered us into an antechamber hung with ornate portraits. We must be in the king's apartments.

"Remove the cloak," Alace ordered.

I stepped forward but the creature was already throwing back the hood. As it untied the cloak, it looked faintly puzzled.

Function follows form. It looked like a man. Could it begin to think like one? How quickly?

Alace took the cloak and looked the creature in the eye. "Go with this man." He pointed to the doctor.

The creature looked at me, like a hound unsure of its master's wishes when another voice gives it commands.

I cleared my throat. "Go on."

The doctor led the manikin out into a richly carpeted hallway. Alace disappeared though a side door.

"Come on." Eion ducked his head, hands folded, every measure the humble lackey.

I followed his example and when the doctor and the creature halted, we both hurried to throw open the double doors ahead. I saw a wide window open from floor to ceiling on the far side of the room.

The doctor didn't seem to find the manikin disconcerting. He led it out onto the balcony. "Stand and wave and smile."

It nodded, walking through the lace curtains fluttering in the breeze. A great cheer went up from the crowds gathered on the parade ground below. I had often stood there, at midsummer and midwinter, when the nobles left their upstream estates to mingle with artisans and merchants and all the countless lesser folk thronging the alleys and crowded tenements of the dockside quarters. The whole city celebrated the peace secured by the benevolent rule of the paramount kings.

Sooner than I had imagined but not so quickly as to prompt discontent below, the doctor urged the creature back inside.

"Where will the carriage…"

As I turned to Eion, a man rushed into the room. He wore the same maroon livery as us. Then I saw the flash of steel. I lunged for him but Eion tripped me. I scrambled up, torn between punching Eion or seizing this newcomer. Too late. The assassin plunged his knife into the manikin's chest.

It staggered and recovered its balance. Puzzled, it tilted its head, frowning. Dumbfounded, the attacker stabbed again. The blow was equally ineffective. Ripping his blade free he looked incredulously at the shining steel, unstained by blood.

Eion moved, twisting the assassin's hand so viciously he dropped the dagger. Wrenching the man's arm behind his back, he forced him face down to the floor.

"Get him on his back." The doctor dug in a pocket.

"Help me!" Eion glared at me as the assassin struggled.

I kicked the knife out of reach and we rolled the writhing man over. Eion pinned his arms and I leaned on his legs.

"Do you recognise him?" The king stood in the doorway.

At his side Alace gripped a sword. "No, Majesty."

The king didn't look like a man who'd been stabbed. Though the toad-pox story was true, judging by the scars on his drawn face.

Looking from the king to the manikin, the assassin gaped, astonished.

The doctor seized his chance to thrust something into his mouth.

The assassin would have spat it out but the doctor's strong hands held his jaw shut, long fingers pinching his nostrils closed for good measure.

The man struggled in vain. A few moments later, he lay limp. Eion stood up.

I did the same. "Is he dead?"

"He'll wake," the doctor assured me. "Ready to tell all he knows."

The king entered the room and walked slowly around his counterfeit. The creature regarded him with amiable interest.

"Astonishing," he marvelled. "You made this?"

"Only to serve," I mumbled, bowing low.

The king nodded before turning to Alace. "See this vermin is carried below and questioned. I shall join the queen and tell her all is well." He favoured us all with a charming smile and departed.

The doctor followed, pausing on the threshold. "Clear up. No one must know."

As the door closed, I looked at the unconscious assassin. "He knows about the creature."

Eion laughed callously. "You think he'll tell anyone?"

Alace retrieved the fallen dagger from beneath a chair. "A gallows in the cellars will silence him once he's given up his paymasters."

I didn't want to think about that. "You said the king had been stabbed."

"That was their plan." Alace tossed the dagger into the air and caught it. "We needed to know if you knew anything of it before we brought you into this masquerade."

"You suspected me?" I was horrified.

"No." Eion shrugged. "We don't take any chances though."

"We've let the rumour spread through a few selected courtiers." Alace closed the windows to the balcony. "We're watching to see who's insufficiently surprised."

Eion nodded. "And for anyone expecting some calamity today."

"Of those few who knew the king would be making this unannounced appearance." Alace smiled coldly.

I saw the manikin was looking from one to the other as they spoke.

"You had to lure the assassin," I realised, "but you couldn't put the king at risk."

"Thank you for your service." Alace smiled. "You'll be well rewarded. Now, unmake it, quickly."

"What?" Incredibly, I hadn't thought beyond making the creature. The intensity of the task had consumed me.

"You must unmake it," Eion insisted.

How could I have been so foolish? "Of course."

"No."

In that single utterance I heard the creature's confusion, its fear and defiance. Growing intelligence shone in its eyes.

"Unmake it!" Alace snapped.

The creature shot him an angry look. Its glance took in his sword and the door beyond.

I closed my eyes and tried to imagine the creature pale and featureless. But when I looked once again, it was still there, unchanged.

"No," it said defiantly. Lifting a hand to its cheek, it wiped away the pox marks I had raised there.

"Kill it." Alace threw me the assassin's dagger.

I caught it instinctively before protesting. "No."

"You're the only one who can." Eion was barring its way to the window, a dagger I hadn't known he carried in his hand. "It can't attack its maker."

"Not yet," warned Alace. "It'll soon break free of you."

A bird loose amid the flocks that roosted in the city's towers and bridges was one thing. A man wearing the king's face, something that wasn't even a real man wandering the streets? That couldn't be permitted.

Besides, the creature was frightening me now. I wanted rid of it, all evidence of what I had done obliterated.

"Stand still."

I walked slowly forward. The creature struggled to raise its hands. I saw it couldn't ward me off.

"A single blow suffices, provided you truly intend to kill it." Eion moved to stand behind me.

"Go on!" Alace's shout spurred me to action.

I thrust the assassin's knife into its belly. It gasped just like a man of true flesh and blood. Tears brimmed in its brown eyes.

"I beg you…"

Before it could plead further, it vanished, gone as though it had never existed.

I collapsed to the floor, dizzy and nauseous and darkness claimed me.

*

I came to my senses tucked in a bed. Evening sun slipped through the narrow window. From the slope of the ceiling I guessed this was some servant's garret. Trying to move, I found I was as weak as a man after ten days of fever.

"Thank the goddess."

I rolled my head on the pillow to see Eion sitting on a stool by the door.

"How…?" My mouth tasted stale.

"Three days." Eion shrugged. "As long as you took to make it."

"You knew," I accused him weakly. "That's why you didn't do it."

"Would you have tried, if you'd known?" I hadn't seen Alace, slumped in a chair beyond the foot of the bed. He rose and came over. "Well done, Thian. You even passed the final test, the hardest one of all."

"What…?" What else had Madam Sima not told me?

"You killed it, thankfully." Eion rose to his feet. "If you couldn't bring yourself to do it, I'd have had to kill you."

The door closed behind him.

"Well done," Alace repeated, looking down at me. "Now you're truly one of us."

*

They cosseted me for six days as I gradually recovered my strength. I took the king's commission to rebuild the summer house back to my master, along with assurances of work for the Margrave of Jedfal that were promptly honoured. I was certified as a master by the masons' guild by midwinter and married Meriah on the first day of spring.

That was seventeen years ago. Every morning, my first thought is still terror: that this will be the day the call comes again.

Tales From the Big Dark: Lie of the Land

Pat Cadigan

"Bicycles," said Shiva, staring across the boulevard. Just opposite where we were sitting on a bench in the small rest area, a traffic warden had pulled over half a dozen cyclists for riding two by two. "A billion lightyears from home, there are bicycles." The snow-white hair that started at the crown of his dark brown head and ended at the base of his neck in a narrow, horse's-mane shape fell to one side as he turned to look at me.

"Yeah, well. There you go." I winced inwardly. For all the years I've done this job – hell, for all the years I've been here – you'd think I could come up with something sage, or at least not so lame and empty. I thought he'd been staring at the traffic warden, who had particularly vivid plumage. Feathered bipeds are quite the novelty for the rest of us. Most of my patients are still goggling at them long after the first few layers of strange have worn off everything else.

Of course, there's plenty more strange after that. Out here in the Big Dark, there's no shortage of reminders that it's not your universe, you just live in it. Sometimes it's a race of mammals with feathers rather than fur or hair and other times it's finding out just how common the commonplace really is.

"Have they always had bicycles here?" Shiva asked, his radiant dark brown features even more aglow with curiosity.

"I don't know about *always* – I'm not quite *that* old." I grinned at him. "They weren't new when I got here so I guess as far as we're concerned, that's *always*. Close enough for government work."

Shiva burst out laughing. "Oh, I *love* that. Everyone in the universe has bicycles and government work."

The translator behind my right ear didn't hum even slightly, which meant we were talking about exactly the same thing. Apparently government work was a bigger joke among Shiva's people than it was among mine.

"When you think about it, it's perfectly natural," I said. Shiva erupted with laughter again. "I mean bicycles," I clarified, laughing a little myself. "You know, once humanoids have the wheel, it's really only logical. We have bicycles where I come from, as well as unicycles, tricycles, and four-wheeled vehicles with and without motors, all of which are here. Scooters and skateboards, too." I'd half-expected to get at least a hum from my translator on that last but there was nothing, of course. Have no idea why I'd thought there would be since I'd just been running my mouth about the universality of the wheel. Just my own shock of the commonplace, I supposed. The *frisson* of the familiar, as Jean-Christophe always put it.

Damn. I sneaked a look at my watch and saw that I'd managed to go almost two hours without thinking of Jean-Christophe. I shifted uncomfortably on the bench.

"I suppose you're right," Shiva was saying. "Still, seeing bicycles surprises me more than anything else. Even feathered humanoids." Pause. "Or people with only one sex." He looked at me sidelong. "Is my talking about that a *faux-pas* or a sign of full-blown mental defect?"

Faux-pas. As if there really was no English equivalent and my translator had had to borrow from French. I spoke no French at all so I never heard anything but English when Jean-Christophe talked to me.

"Excuse me, did that translate right?" Shiva touched the bare skin above his left ear where his own translator was located, as if he could actually feel it. A lot of new arrivals think they can but that's strictly psychosomatic. The translator's a nano device; the buzz is nerve stimulation and it happens only when there's a shortfall in translation. I hadn't felt so much as a hum on anything Shiva had said and I told him so.

"I just wanted to make sure," he said, looking concerned. "In case it wasn't working right…"

"That never happens."

The white mane of hair fell to one side again as Shiva tilted his head. "You're really that certain."

"I am." I pulled his hand gently away from his head and placed it atop his burgeoning belly.

"Tell me the truth," Shiva said, smiling. "If you were in my place…"

"I was once," I reminded him.

"I know. Indulge me anyway. If you had just woken up in an artificial habitat millions of light years from everything you knew with no memory of how you got here and no way to get home and *I* was the medic looking after you, what would shock you most – feathered people, a dually-sexed human referred to as male when pregnant, or bicycles?"

I was almost tempted to tell him that what was really bothering me was the nagging suspicion that my translator had deliberately used French to make sure I kept thinking about Jean-Christophe. But even if I'd been so unprofessional, I wasn't sure either of us would have been able to hear anything over the buzzing.

"Good question," I said after a bit. "Too bad you weren't around to ask it when I first woke up here. But now I think it's time to get you back to your room."

Shiva let me help him to his feet, his attention back on the cyclists. The traffic warden had them riding off one by one at carefully timed intervals so they wouldn't bunch up. Even if they didn't, they'd be stopped again farther on by another traffic warden who would insist they ride two-by-two. Unless they hit an orientational anomaly – then they'd all be riding on the ceiling, out of reach. I smiled at the thought and Shiva, thinking it was directed at him, smiled back.

*

A cluster of circles in various sizes and colours floated in mid-air above the console-desk in Dr. Neep's office. S/he was using a light-pen on them, moving them around till s/he found one s/he wanted. Then s/he changed the setting on the pen so the circle swelled to several times its original size and strange unreadable (to me) symbols appeared on it. Neep scrolled through them in various ways – up and down, sideways, diagonally – added more symbols and erased others before making the circle smaller again and pushing it off to one side. Paperwork is a lot more psychedelic out here in the Big Dark. Well, some people's paperwork. Neep's system was far too abstract for me. Even after all these (subjective) years, I still wasn't completely comfortable using only the cartoon-style graphics on a flatscreen without any actual files that I could physically hold in my hands.

After a while, Neep paused to look over her/his shoulder at me. "Are you warming that chair because you really think you have something important to tell me about Shiva or are you trying to delay going to see Jean-Christophe for as long as possible?"

I sighed. "For the record: have you re-checked his due date? Because when I took him out for exercise and orientation, I thought I saw signs of pre-labour."

Neep echoed my sigh perfectly. For some reason, all dually-sexed species have the ability to mimic other voices with astounding accuracy. "For the record: I re-checked his due date the first time you asked me and I re-check it every day in anticipation of your asking me again, which you always do. Today's reading shows that he's not due for another eight days. Yesterday's reading showed he was not due for another nine days. Tomorrow's reading will show that he's not due for another seven days. And if you ask Shiva himself, he will give you a more precise answer in hours rather than days because he is much more sharply attuned to the biological process. Did you ask Shiva today?"

"I asked him yesterday."

"Next time, make a note of the answer so you won't forget."

"I didn't forget."

"Oh? I thought that was why you were asking me."

"No, I'm asking you because Shiva needs his rest. It wouldn't be fair for me to tire him out so I can put off going to see Jean-Christophe." I sighed again.

"Oh, of course. Better to hang around my office and interrupt me while I'm updating patient files."

"I didn't mean to interrupt. You can go on working. Ignore me. I can't read your written language so it's not like I'm seeing anyone's confidential information."

Neep's dark red-gold face looked put-upon. "I know, but it feels funny anyway. How would you feel if I were looking over your shoulder while you did *your* paperwork?"

I couldn't help grinning at the last word. I've lost count of the number of species I've met in the Big Box, humanoid and otherwise, and *paperwork* translates perfectly for every single one. Even those who don't ride bicycles. "I see your point. Suppose I sit with my back to you?" I swiveled around in the chair.

"Suppose you sit in Jean-Christophe's room? He's been in and out of consciousness for the past two hours. Charlie's been with him but Maintenance wants *you* on the case and no one else. Unquote."

I swiveled back to face her/him, a bit startled. "They told you that? Personally?"

Neep looked even more put-upon. "No, I'm lying because the truth is so boring."

"Did Maintenance also decide to explain why they didn't send him to some other humanoid sector where no one knows him? Since he's supposed to be a new arrival and not someone who's lived in the Big Box even longer than I have."

"This may surprise you but no. Still."

"It *would* make more sense."

"No, it would be easier on you. Maintenance have their own ideas of what makes more sense. You know what they're like. Now, please, Hannah. Let me finish my paperwork before it eats my brain and I die of tedium." S/he made a shooing motion with both hands.

*

Charlie all but jumped up from his chair as soon as I walked into Jean-Christophe's room, relief large on his bony face. "*Really* glad you're here. He's going to wake all the way any minute."

I shrugged, irritated. "So? This isn't your first day on the job. Or did Maintenance wipe your memory, too?"

"Keep your voice down!" Charlie grabbed my arm and pulled me into the far corner. "What if he heard you?"

"What if he did?" I looked past him at Jean-Christophe, stirring slightly. "Maybe he ought to. This is bullshit. We've all got better things to do, Jean-Christophe included."

Charlie's grip on me tightened. "Yeah, but it's Maintenance's bullshit. You want to get in trouble with them, go ahead but leave me out of it."

"Sorry," I said, prying my arm loose. "Honest. I'm just upset about this."

"I know," Charlie said, sympathetic now. "I'm upset for you. I don't understand why he couldn't have been sent to some other part of the Big Box, either. I don't understand why he couldn't have just gone back to rehab if he was having a breakdown. Whenever any of us has a breakdown, we go back to rehab. I don't know what was so special about Jean-Christophe that they had to re-set him."

"Don't ask me," I said. "I only saw him for a few minutes in the Terrarium. He told me he was leaving. Then you called me back to the shelter for a pick-up. As a matter of fact, I was just with Shiva."

"Oh? How is he?" Charlie asked conversationally.

"More pregnant that I'd have thought possible for any life-form, mammalian or otherwise. In good spirits. Still amazed by bicycles."

Charlie nodded. "Everybody's got their own special kick in the head."

"Don't I know it." I looked over at Jean-Christophe who was stirring a little more. "I think he's about to surface. You'd better go."

Instead of running for the door, Charlie surprised me by hesitating. "Maybe I *should* stay."

"This is my problem," I said, giving him a little push. "You're my assistant, not my slave." There was a slight buzz on the last word and I remembered that slavery was unknown on Charlie's planet. Why our translators didn't simply choose an equivalent to subordinate or some other state having to do with expected obedience without buzzing was yet another of the translator's many mysterious quirks. Or features. Not that I found it any more mysterious than how Charlie's branch of the human race didn't comprehend slavery.

"But I know how it is with you two," he was saying. "Jean-Christophe is bad for you. He always has been. Who's to say that'll change just because Maintenance wiped his memory?"

"Who's to say it won't?" I gave him a more forceful push toward the door. "I might not interest him at all this time around."

"But what about you? Will *he* interest *you?*"

"Not if he's my patient," I said firmly, hoping I wasn't lying. I never have gotten involved with a patient in that way.

Jean-Christophe stirred some more and mumbled something. I managed to get Charlie out of the room and locked the door behind him.

Just pretend it's any other case, I told myself as I went over to the bed. *Maintenance cut off his hair and shaved his beard as well as wiping his memory. This makes him no different from anyone else who's ever been abducted by aliens and then left off at the shelter. As far as he'll know, he is no different. He'll feel the same way they all feel when they first come here. He'll go through the same stages of adjustment as you guide him through rehab.*

I felt myself start to relax. There was no reason why I couldn't be his medic. In fact, there was no reason why I *shouldn't*. Knowing him as well as I did, I was the best choice to take him through rehab and see that he adjusted – again – to spending the rest of his life in the Big Box. Perhaps he would adjust so well under my care that he would have fewer breakdowns. Maybe even none. While I would benefit because my professional standards would prevent me from falling madly in bed with him. No more ill-advised love affairs. Well, at least not with Jean-Christophe, who had always been bad for me.

Had that been Maintenance's reason for re-setting him – to give him a fresh start? Possibly, although it was just as likely that they were merely experimenting for the hell of it, or for some reason that wouldn't have made any sense to mere mortals like me and Jean-Christophe.

I pulled a flatscreen out of the frame of his bed and had a look at his vitals. He was definitely waking up now. Leaning over him slightly, I took his hand. His fingers moved over my skin until they found mine and entwined themselves in a familiar way. Old habits die hard, I thought, trying to ignore the pang in my heart.

"Hello?" I said, keeping my voice soft so I wouldn't startle him.

His eyes opened and he looked up at me. Those green eyes still seemed to look right through me. Maybe this was going to be too hard after all, I thought, hoping I appeared a lot more professional than I felt.

"You've been asleep for a long time so you might feel groggy for quite a while…"

"Hannah," he said.

I froze. *You misheard that,* said a small, desperate voice in my mind. *He actually said* Hand, *because you're holding his. Or he was trying to say* Where am I? *Because that's what they all say…*

"I'm back, aren't I?" He squeezed my hand. "I guess it's true – once you've been abducted by aliens, you're far more likely to have it happen again." He let out a resigned breath. "Or did Maintenance send a crew after me to bring me back?"

I didn't even think about it; I just reached over and slammed the panic button in the wall beside me as hard as I could.

*

"I wish you'd stop doing that," I said as Neep topped up the sedative in my system.

"The panic button is for *patients* who become hysterically violent."

"He scared me." I wasn't slurring my words but my muscles felt like half-filled water balloons. "It's OK to hit the panic button if a patient scares you. I *thought*. It *should* be."

"You ended up scaring Jean-Christophe."

"Sorry." It came out *shorry*. Neep frowned and made a small adjustment to the collar resting on my neck; immediately I felt more alert, although not enough to get up off the table in the treatment room. "It's Maintenance's fault. They said they wiped his memory. I thought he was supposed to be like a new arrival."

Neep dipped his/her head non-committally. "Obviously we misunderstood."

"You mean they *lied*."

"We don't know that."

"We know that nobody ever leaves the Big Box. Once you're out in the Big Dark, there's nowhere to go and no way back home. For most abductees, that's the hardest thing, the worst. When this gets out, what do you think is going to happen? We'll be lucky if there aren't riots. How could Maintenance *do* this?"

Neep's red-gold features were disgusted. "I don't know. All I can think is that they deliberately allowed him to escape."

I stared at her/him with my mouth open for some unmeasured period of time. "They – what?"

"Probably as part of some experiment," s/he went on. "You know what they're like. Which is to say, nobody knows what they're like, or what they're thinking."

"How could Jean-Christophe have escaped?" I demanded.

"My theory? He crawled through conduits in the infrastructure to the travellers' area and talked one of the more irresponsible crews into taking him with them. Probably the Dacz.va. You know what *they're* like."

"That's impossible."

"I used to think so."

"*Neep*. Think for a minute." I tried to will my arm to reach for her/him but I was far too limp.

S/he frowned at me. "About what?"

"Jean-Christophe didn't go anywhere. Maintenance screwed around with his memory so that he *thinks* he did."

"Oh?" Now there was no expression at all on Neep's face. "Did they *screw around* with my memory, too?"

I hesitated. "I don't know. How long do you think Jean-Christophe was gone?"

"By our reckoning? A few hours."

"Well, there you go." I couldn't help laughing a little. "That isn't enough time to…"

Neep was shaking her/his head. "You know time gets very slippery out here in the Big Dark."

"Not *that* slippery. A few hours isn't long enough to travel from one end of the Big Box to the other, let alone all the way back to Earth and then back here again."

"You're an expert?"

"No, but…"

"Neither am I. Very few are. Among those few, however, are Maintenance."

"And Maintenance has somehow convinced you that this is possible. Even though you're not an expert, you would know if they were lying."

"Why *would* they lie to me? Or you, or Jean-Christophe, or any of us? It wouldn't give them any advantage they don't already have. They run everything. If they were going to lie, I'd think it would be to tell us Jean-Christophe *didn't* leave. That would save them a lot of trouble. Now, however, they'll have people clamouring for more information and saying they want to leave, too."

Neep was still going on as I let myself drift away.

*

The uproar about leaving the Big Box that I had predicted never materialized. A few people got vocal about wanting to leave. Maintenance responded with a detailed demonstration of how security measures had been beefed-up to prevent any more contact with travellers. I had expected them to trot out Jean-Christophe and have him speak about how he regretted his escapade – how his second abduction had been even more cruel than the first one or somesuch – but that never happened.

At least Maintenance no longer insisted that I handle his case. They gave him over to another medic working on a different clock and I never had to see him, even in passing. It should have been a relief and mostly it was. But he stayed in the back of my mind like a little barbed hook that had caught there and somehow never really let go.

*

Eventually he came to me and I didn't run the other way as fast as I could. I told myself that I was surprised at this but it wasn't true.

He said he knew that I didn't believe he had really gone back to Earth and then, in an effort to convince me, launched into a long, detailed account of what things were like there. I let him talk on the grounds that it was probably better for him to spill out all the lies and false memories that Maintenance had given him instead of walking around with it all bottled up inside.

All right, I'll admit it – I was curious. And maybe, deep down, I hoped to hear something that might mean it could have been true after all. But it turned to be an enormous disappointment. Most was stuff the latest abductee from Earth had told us; the rest was too absurd.

I mean, our particular branch of the human race has never been what anyone would call enlightened, but not even the Dacz.va would be stupid enough to damage their own planet so badly that they could see it dying around them and do nothing about it. And we're nowhere near as dumb as the Dacz.va.

Are we?

It crossed my mind that perhaps Maintenance was just trying to make us feel better about being out here in the Big Dark – like, not only less homesick but actually glad we're not there any more. That's almost funny, in a tragic sort of way.

But there are two things I know for certain are true:

a) I don't know why they decided to play this silly charade with Jean-Christophe.

b) He's just as bad for me as he ever was.

Anything else, I'm not buying.

The Moth

Neil Williamson

Markady Veitch stumbled through the empty city, searching for somewhere to hide. His feet bled through the holes in his ruined court shoes, his silk trousers were soot-blacked from the road through the scorched fields, and his neck ached from the impulsive twisting at every skitter and skite that echoed from the countless dingy alleymouths. Convinced that he was being followed, he imagined flittering movements in the corner of his vision but, when he looked, Nothing was ever there but bare cobbles, blank walls. Knowing that the city was abandoned was no comfort. It only increased his anxiety, and his fingers gripped tighter to the note.

GO TO KARPENTINE. I WILL FIND YOU.

He clutched the paper to his perspiring heart and blundered on. When he arrived at the main street, he encountered a litter of shell-like husks. In his haste there was no way to avoid them, and they were crushed under his worn-through soles. If he had not recently learned what he had, he would have been in fear of his life.

Safety, though, was a relative issue. The fluttering returned, no mistaking it now. And this time he felt a feathering at his cheek, caught a blur of white wings each with a dark spot like inked eyes. The creature was the size of his fist. It hovered in the air for a second longer before arcing off once more. Markady's skin crawled with revulsion, clammy with shock. *Oh, mother, oh father.* The last thing he needed was *moths.*

After that, he redoubled his efforts to find a bolt hole. Occasionally he paused to catch his ragged breath, push at a door, test the latch of a window, but for all the brick and shadow, shadow and black brick, he found nowhere that would conceal him.

Then he saw the last splashes of molten sun outlining a crooked tower ahead, and he took it as a sign. He tripped up the uneven steps to the weathered shop door. The creaking shingle proclaimed it as a seller of books. Ink and paper were what had brought him here. That had to be a sign too. The iron handle would not budge, but to the side the lingering light limned a star-shaped hole in the glass of the shop's display window. Whether it had been made by soldier's rifle or looter's rock back in the last days of the evacuation, or by some unknown agent in more recent times, he didn't know, but to Markady it was the third sign of his salvation. Careful, so careful, he slipped his white hand through the jagged aperture, worked the latch and entered stealthy as a thief. Once the comparison would have shamed him, but he recognised that he had resigned all claims to being an honest man some weeks ago. He was still congratulating himself on his nimbleness when he slipped from the sill and fell inwards in a landslide of dusty tomes.

Markady lay listening as sunset-blazed dust settled around him. He waited until he was certain the clodhopping of his heartbeat was not masking the clatter of soldiers' boots before daring to rise from the floor. The street outside was silent, but that was unsurprising. No Family would send an army to catch a spy. If they were intent on tracking him at all it would be nothing as obvious as men with guns. A soft-shoed assassin would be more their style, and if that were the case there'd be little he could do about it, but for now at least there was no sign. He snicked shut the latch and arranged the displaced books in what he hoped resembled an old fashioned window display.

A volume on top of the pile caught his eye. A slim, stylish book among the pulpy romances and mysteries that had been faded by age, bloated with damp. This one had slipped from his own pocket. Of the three items the charabanc driver had handed him when he abandoned Markady on the dark road some miles out of Abergaard, this was the most mysterious. The note was for his soul, the candle to preserve his sanity through the night in a city without power. Good gifts in such a hurried situation, but the book? Markady stroked the title.

Lost Tales: Stories for Children

He slipped the volume back into his pocket and then busied himself with finding a place to hole up. Higher, he reasoned, would be preferable to lower. All the better to see his enemies – or rescuers – coming.

I WILL FIND YOU, the note said, and once again he took heart from that.

Opening doors at random, Markady gathered an armful of useful supplies before finally locating the foot of the tower stairs. The climb was a steep and claustrophobic one, and he was breathless by the time he reached the top. In the emberish light, he looked around the odd, octagonal room and saw that it appeared to have been used both as a store room and a small office. Quickly, he stacked packing crates to blockade the door, and then built himself a nest under the desk. Only once he was squeezed into that small space did he dare to light the candle.

The flame took with a sputter before settling down to a gentle glow. A reminder of the hearth of his home where by rights he should have been sitting had events turned out differently.

"Well, then, what have you achieved today?" he asked himself aloud and, on hearing the flat amplification the enclosure gave to his words, wished he hadn't. An echo of the authoritarian tones of the schoolroom, which were stencilled in his heart, as they were in that of every Abergaardian child. The daily challenge to justify their contribution to society.

What *had* he achieved today?

Well, after thirty-seven years of asking himself that question, with mostly satisfactory results that had heaved him turgidly through school and up into the lower-middle rungs of the civil service, today – *today* – he had for once excelled. In one moment of indiscretion, he had been revealed as a spy and, with that slip of the tongue, discarded all those years of slow but steady progress. It was such a stunning anti-achievement that, had the circumstances been different, he would have been wallowing in self-loathing. But on top of all that, his head was now full of other people's secrets, *and those people knew about it,* and fear had swamped all other emotions.

Now, though, he needed to master himself and consider his position. Employing his plodding, but trustworthy, talent for methodology, he set out the consequences of the day's events in order of importance. What had he *really* achieved? Never mind the loss of his job, his position and status; and with all that his modest but comfortable home. Never mind that his hard-earned contract of engagement to Minne would by now have been torn up by her Family, and that the Weathermakers' matchmakers would already be spinning a new web of links and alliances for that pleasant young lady. And never mind that his life was probably forfeit – it was worth precisely nothing now anyway. No, worst of all was that he had failed his – only in his heart did he dare to think of her this way, but what else could she be? – *patron.*

It had begun with a note. An innocuous letter, *sans* envelope, folded once and requesting, of all the banal things, weather reports covering the whole of the northern peninsula from some years before. Someone had slipped it beneath the door of his office. The paper had been a thin, utilitarian bond; the handwriting neat, unhurried; the tone formal. Naturally, it was unsigned. But none of those factors were unheard of. The civil service was not prescriptive in its practices. In fact the only really unusual thing about the note was that it had been addressed to him. Private arrangements with the Council's civil servants were usually entrusted to senior officers, the ones with contacts and influence. That a Family had chosen to engage Markady naturally had both piqued his interest and plumped his self-image. This was an honour he had hardly dared to dream of but, on rereading the request, he saw no reason why he should not be rewarded for his years of patient application. Further consideration suggested that his impending connection to the Family Weathermaker had also brought more than a little influence to bear on his selection.

He had done what was asked of him discreetly and quickly. It had taken little more than a day to collate the records, and the following morning a boy (presumably the same one who had delivered the note) had arrived to bear them away. Markady had asked the lad if he might be permitted to know who had contracted his services. Expecting the answer to be one of the ancillary Families, such as the Telegraphers or the Accountants, he had been stunned to learn that his employer was the Lady Moraine Otterbree of the Inksmiths, and had known then for certain that his star was on the rise.

More requests followed. The investigation, as he had pieced it together – for it was clear that was what it was, even if the reason behind it was not – appeared to centre around some sort of research programme that the Weathermakers, in league with the Artificers Animeaux, had been carrying out in secret for some years. The paper trails mentioned both Families frequently and when the information had become difficult to obtain in documented form and the nature of his enquiries had changed to face-to-face contact, the strangers he had found himself befriending in pubs were invariably of one family or the other. Markady found this daunting. He had never been the most sociable of people, but after a few jars the conversation flowed more easily than he would have believed. He gained introductions from his fiancée, ingratiated himself with uncles of wives of cousins. Each exchange required a little more leverage, a careful application of libation here, a coded offer of favours there, and each had pushed closer to the limits of what he was legally allowed to do within the remit of his position. He had been nervous when the tasks had first moved away from his beloved paperwork, but his apparent aptitude emboldened him. Nevertheless, the transition from the grey to the wholly illegal had not been without qualm. He hesitated, prevaricated, delayed, and it had taken one further note to seal his loyalty. This entreaty appeared on luxuriant creamy weave, in a strong, feminine script that would become as familiar to him as his own hand, and had been initialled at the bottom *M.O. Ink.*

Anyone who worked in the Abergaardian civil service knew that there was under the surface as grand a tradition of bribery and alliance, horse trading and coercion as there had been in any great democracy. Great putsches were achievements of legend. Factions formed, splintered and reformed in a constant flux of powermongering and the newspapers were bloated with commentary on the state of power in the city.

The Inksmiths did not make the newspapers, although they made the news in quite a different way. The Inksmiths supplied the ink for the pens and the presses, the ribbons for the typewriters, but their influence ran deeper than that. Their product was the oil that lubricated the political machine. They were always there or thereabouts, lending support in one place, opposition in another, donating cash and influence to steer events to their advantage. Achievement Stocks soared and crashed at the slightest of nods from the Inksmiths.

Markady could never have imagined that he might one day be associated with such a powerful Family. The only disappointment was that he had to keep it a secret. He wished he could have told someone; boasted to his friends in the service, finally pleased his always coaxing, always encouraging parents, shoved it in the face of his patronising teachers. *Markady shows a talent for following instructions with meticulous attention to detail* – his final school report had read – *but little imagination or initiative. Not recommended for a managerial career.*

Well, he could tell no one from his current position. He peered bravely out from under the desk. Through a window on the opposite side of the room there was the deepening sky, and elsewhere under that same sky was Abergaard. For a moment he wondered whether it had really been necessary for him to flee, whether he shouldn't contemplate attempting to return in the morning. Then something pale and quick passed the glass that sent his heart careening his chest.

Bloody moths.

No, he'd stay here as instructed. He was safe here. He had the note, and that meant he had a protector.

The flow of clandestine instructions had been supplanted by a more personal correspondence. As each assignment had inched him deeper into the realms of espionage, gaining and betraying the confidences of higher and higher ranking officials, the more Markady had expressed his doubts, and the more his Lady's notes had assuaged them.

YOU HAVE A NATURAL TALENT FOR THIS WORK, she wrote. And when he read it, he could not deny it. AND IT IS UNCIVIC, IS IT NOT, TO FAIL TO MATCH OUR ACHIEVEMENTS TO OUR TALENTS?

In a later exchange he had confessed his fear of discovery in an engagement with an officer of the Artificers Animeaux of whose trust he was uncertain. The reply had come with gladdening urgency. There were two notes. One sealed – which later unlocked the reluctant informant's tongue like a golden key – the other for him, and before he had even so much as read the words, he had laughed at himself because he could sense her gentle, chiding humour in the darkling loops that caressed the paper.

YOU ARE NOT AFRAID, the note said. BY YOUR HAND I KNOW WHAT SCARES YOU, AND IT IS NOT DISCOVERY. HAVE NO FEAR, MY MARK, ESSELENE MORAN HAS NO CONNECTION WITH THEIR INSECT MAKERS. YOU WILL MEET NO NASTY OLD MOTHS IN THE DARK TONIGHT.

And indeed she had been correct. Moths terrified him. It had not occurred to him before, perhaps because few of the creatures frequented the windy Bridges district where he had grown up and still lived, but the moment he had seen those words written down he realised exactly how loathsome the creatures were. Even the word *moth* on its own had made him twitchy just to look at it. How she had known simply from his handwriting about a phobia so private that even he had not been aware of it, he could not think, yet that, he supposed, was the skill of a master in pen and ink. The knowledge that she knew him so intimately had redoubled his confidence in his patron.

But now he had finally failed her. He didn't mind the exposure – she had been right about that too, in a way it was a relief – but she would be so disappointed. If he had any hope now, it was that she appreciated at least how hard he had tried.

In the light of the candle, Markady retrieved her final note. He smoothed it out on the floor. The lovely paper was crushed now, soiled with his desperation, but the ink still glittered like precious jet. He read the words again. They inspired hope, but only went so far. If anything, it was the surety of the penmanship – a work of art in itself, as you would expect of an Inksmith taught from birth to develop a hand that did justice to the ink that flowed from it – executing perfect lines, wasting not one drop, that saved him from despair. It was almost as if the ink itself gave him strength. He traced the loops and curves, the drops and serifs with his finger.

GO TO KARPENTINE. I WILL FIND YOU.

Seven words, and not a letter more. But they were enough to reassure him of safety in a place that most recently had been famous for one thing.

Plague.

It had been twelve years since the abandonment of Karpentine. Twelve years since the black night when the citizens of Abergaard's smaller port neighbour had been roused from their beds with shouts of "infestation" and "disease", and marched up the road to where the Families of its larger sister waited to console the refugees. Twelve years during which the city had been abandoned to the foreign white beetle. And twelve years during which numerous attempts had been made to cleanse the place – it would certainly be a prize, a jewel of achievement, for any Family that could claim it – but the city had never yet shaken off the spectre of contagion.

What Markady had discovered was that someone *had* managed it. He still did not have the full picture – he didn't know what role the Artificers played, although possibly there was a need for guinea-pigs, so to speak, to test the environment before any public claim could be announced – but the evidence had fleshed the rumours of the Weathermakers' scourging clouds with fact, and if his Lady thought it safe for him to be here, then he trusted that.

But *Karpentine*. It was a name to frighten children.

Markady hunkered deeper under his desk. The blanket he had scavenged was coarse and smelled of mildew, but he did not want for warmth. Indeed, he began to find the room stuffy. He fixated on the candle's flame, watched it lick as it consumed oxygen. The air was as soft as deadening ash, and he could hear nothing beyond the beat of his own blood and the candle's hiss. He felt his eyelids droop, once, twice, then snapped himself awake in such a panic that he bumped his head on the desk. However tired he may be – and his throbbing feet and aching limbs told him he was exhausted – he could not risk falling asleep. Any second not spent listening for a signal from the agents of his Lady or anyone else abroad in the desolate town, was a second closer to his demise.

Markady found himself contemplating opening the window. Just a crack to let the thinnest breath of night air into the room and take the edge off his drowsiness. The candle was shaded by the screen of crates. Just a crack of air would not give him away.

Markady crawled out of his hole and crept to the window. Through the grubby quarterpanes he saw a glitter of early stars. The city below was completely in darkness. He strained gently at the sash, felt it budge, but not enough. He applied an ounce more pressure and the window shot upwards with a bang that was forceful enough to dislodge one of the panes. Markady watched it tumble into the shadows. The distant tinkle of breaking glass was not nearly distant enough. Too late, he yanked the window shut again and fled back to his den.

The draft from the missing pane threatened the candle, chilled the air. Markady pulled up the hood of his coat and scrabbled under his blanket again but he could still feel the breeze nipping his skin. He wondered if the Weathermakers could have fashioned a poisoned frost and sent it to seek him out, but the idea seemed fanciful. His subtle probing of Minne's great uncle, their Engineer General, a ruddy-faced sot with too much money and a penchant for poker, had revealed that developing the technological capacity to create their sterilising rain had been an extensive and expensive undertaking. He told himself that they would not waste such resources just to dispose of one lousy spy. No, he was simply overanxious. He was well hidden here. What he needed was a distraction. And at last he realised the reason for his third gift.

He fished the storybook out from his pocket, riffled through the pages.

Lost Tales

It looked old. The cover sported a colour-washed pen and ink drawing of a schoolboy dressed in old-fashioned clothes – short trousers and a jacket, black lace-up boots. The boy stood at the edge of a dense forest, and was looking over his shoulder with an expression of anxiety. The faded sky was the palest of blues, the grass a green that had vanished almost to grey, the lad's skin sucked of life save for a single spot of pink on his cheek, but the trees – a dense clustering of line and shadow – had lost none of their inky lustre. The density of their rendition increased towards the centre, it drew the eye inward, and in doing that offered a clue as to what it was about this forest that was persuading the boy, against all his mother's warnings and his own sense of self-preservation, to enter. There's mystery here, the trees said; there's danger, yes, but also excitement and treasure and the unknown.

And you knew that the boy was lost.

The image was compelling. Holding this book in your hands, Markady imagined, in this very shop you'd need a will of steel not to have bought it, and then read it from cover to cover the moment you got home to discover the mystery in the trees. And it would have cost you a pretty penny to be so persuaded, a book like that.

Markady opened it.

The boy's name was Malcolm, the story said. Those were the only words on the first page, but Markady knew that such an expensive book was more than the words it contained. The author could sit down beside you and tell you the same story, use the same words, and enthral you with his tale, but your experience of the story would be different than if you held the book itself in your hands. This kind of book was a pact of effort on behalf of the papermaker and the bookbinder, of the typesetter and the illustrator. And, of course, the inksmith. Because it was ink that engaged you with the words, that bound you to the story.

This kind of book was an *achievement.*

The boy's name was Malcolm, the words said. But the paper added that he was a pale, sickly child. The meagre gutter margin, providing little safety between the words and the binding's fissure, hinted that he was never far from unsuspected danger. The thorny serifs contributed that he was prone to sudden and destructive jags of mood, that perhaps danger was what he sought, although he might not yet know his heart well enough to be aware of this. The page's illustration, sketched with such simplicity and, Markady now realised, not washed out by time's ravage, but drawn intentionally insubstantial, underlined the lad's barely tangible sense of self. However, it was the thundery blue-black ink that shadowed the treeline with terror and hinted in every measured drop of murder. It was the ink that told you this story would end tragically, but compelled you to read on nevertheless.

Markady turned the page and followed Malcolm into the woods.

Some time passed before a sound made him lift his head from the book. A ruffling of air, at first indistinguishable from the other forest sounds that had been playing out in his mind's ear as he stumbled along with Malcolm deeper and deeper into the darkening forest. The sound of wings in the boughs.

Markady looked up, and of course the wood above him was not boughs, but the underside of the bookshop's old desk. Markady rubbed his stinging eyes. His cheeks were cold, wet with tears.

The noise came again, a dreadful thrum. Markady's ears pinpointed the source of the sound near the broken window, but then it moved. Louder, closer. He felt a stir of air above the desk, and then a flitter of shadow, a drift of diamondine dust that sizzled green sparks from the candle's flame as the moth alighted on the wall. At the sight of the fat, furry delta Markady shrank back. It made his skin crawl, and he wondered if it was the same one that had scared him in the street earlier. Maybe. The wings were dappled like the face of the moon, and the scintillating powder that sloughed off when it flick-stretched was almost beautiful. There were probably thousands of moths with similar markings circulating lazily in the city tonight, but those two sooty circles watching him like patient eyes made him feel hunted all over again. A thought occurred. Was it possible that the Weathermakers had subcontracted not only guinea-pigs from the Artificers Animeaux, but also animal spies to monitor the efficacy of their secret rain?

That made no sense. Had his patron not told him herself that insects were not involved? Once again, he chafed at how little he knew.

He made himself look at the moth again, choked down the rising bile at the twitch of its feathery antennae. It looked real enough but they were artists, those Artificers. Now, though, he thought he saw inconsistencies. The wing pattern was too regular, the movement too mechanical, the watching wing-eyes too attentive. And so *much* dust could not be a natural thing, could it?

In fact, on closer inspection, that soft powder looked lethal.

So that was it.

There was to be an attempt after all to silence him, to keep the news of a cleansed Karpentine secret. He had half-expected it, but his imagination had failed him in regard to the shape that it would take. He didn't even merit an assassin after all. Markady pulled the blanket protectively over his nose and mouth, and then fumbled out the note once more. He held it close to the candle so that the strong words glowed.

I WILL FIND YOU.

Too close to the candle. As the lower half of the paper began to brown, he snatched it away fearful of its burning clean through. But instead of catching alight, he noticed something remarkable. There was more writing on the paper than he had supposed. Where the paper had reacted to the candle flame, letters in *white ink* had appeared.

Of course. This was his patron's plan all along.

Having sent him on his way in her charabanc, she had known that if he made it as far as Karpentine, he would at some point put the candle and the note together. Only then could she tell him the rest of her plan for his escape. A nomad train, perhaps, to take him across the desert, or a boat to transport him to a comfortable foreign exile.

Oh, those clever Inksmiths.

Carefully, Markady brought the paper close to the candle again, and watched the message reveal itself in full.

THANK YOU, MY MALCOLM, MY FINDER-OF-SECRETS, the words said. YOUR ACHIEVEMENT IN FACILITATING THE RECLAMATION OF KARPENTINE FOR THE PRESTIGE OF THE INKSMITHS WILL BE RECOGNISED. HOWEVER, THAT CAN'T, I'M AFRAID, BE FOR SOME TIME TO COME, SO FOR NOW THE SECRET MUST REMAIN SO.

YOU WILL UNDERSTAND BY NOW, MY MARK, HOW EASY IT IS FOR LOCKED LIPS TO BE LOOSENED, BY A COIN, A WORD, A DROP OF INK. THE INKSMITHS BECAME THE FAMILY THEY ARE TODAY BY EXPLOITING THAT WEAKNESS IN OTHERS, AND ELIMINATING IT WITHIN THEIR OWN. SO, YOU WILL UNDERSTAND, MY FOOL, IF I THANK YOU ONCE AGAIN, IN THE CERTAINTY THAT YOU WILL NOT BETRAY US.

Markady goggled. Read the words again, expecting this time that they would make a different sense.

The ink glowed white.

His nose itched, his throat felt thick.

White as a kindness.

The moth watched, twitched its moonsmilk wings.

White as a command.

The letters disintegrated, an accelerated leprous demise. Became choking smoke.

White as a betrayal.

But that was all right. The ink told him so.

Underbrain

Tony Ballantyne

Andeel doe Resthispil bumped into her sister at the pheromone counter of the *Gallerie Artemis*.

"Capel," she said, kissing her on the cheek, and then "Oh dear!" as she took the little diamond phial from her sister's hand. "Surely not *Dark Nights*? Isn't that a little, well, passé?"

"Don't be so bloody stupid," replied Capel, taking back the scent. "It's not for me. It's a gift."

"For someone you don't like, I assume?"

Capel raised a dark eyebrow. Her sister had no sense of humour: Capel allowed herself a little smile at Andeel's unintentional rudeness. It was good to see a familiar face after three weeks spent looking over her shoulder, and despite their differences, Capel was fond of her sister. The two of them were alike in so many ways: their assured manner, their immaculate dress; and yet both Andeel and Capel would agree on, and both be smugly satisfied by, the fact that Andeel had been born with the looks, and Capel the brains. And that would be an understatement. If anyone were ever so ill-bred as to speak the truth, they would report that Andeel was incredibly shallow, Capel incredibly ugly.

"Good to see you out in public," said Andeel approvingly. "Not hiding away in your rooms. I heard about the hatchet job the *Times* did on that lecture you gave at the Academy. Uncalled for, I thought."

Capel handed the phial to the waiting sales assistant to be gift wrapped.

"Really?" she said, unable to keep the surprise from her voice. "You mean you agreed with my theory?"

White diamonds flashed in the light as Andeel gave a dismissive wave of her hand. "Capel, I don't care about your theory one way or the other. As far as I'm concerned, there was a time when it simply wasn't *done* to attack a person of substance in the press. This is just another example of Alharian morals encroaching upon our society! There are those who say that we should do all we can to avoid war with that country. *I* say we are at war already! Alharian culture is displacing ours and we appear powerless to stop it!"

As if on cue, a low rumble shook the perfumed Gallery. All present looked up through the wrought iron and glass dome that crowned the store to see three triangular jet planes fly by, very slow, very low. Three lines of black smoke hung in sullen silence over the city, bars against the scarred face of the minor moon.

"Caletptrian markings," observed Capel as she turned back to the assistant. The gift was returned to her; she dropped the silver and red striped foil parcel into her elegant little handbag and neatly changed the subject.

"Andeel, your husband has written to invite me to Resthispil. It seems he wishes to speak to me in person."

"Gelda?" Andeel raised her eyebrows in surprise. "What on Capth could he want with you?"

"I've no idea. He's your husband. I rather thought you would know."

"Me? I haven't spoken to him in weeks. When the children are off at school I let him handle the affairs of the estate. I have more important things to attend to. I'm flying to Parador on Thursday. Didn't you know?"

Capel tutted in annoyance. "I should have done. It's almost Appassionata, isn't it?" She frowned. "This is a nuisance. I hoped you could shed some light on the invitation. What do you suppose Gelda knows of my work?"

"Dear sister, whyever do you think that I would know that?" Andeel snorted. "You don't have eight legs, do you? Because if you don't, I can't imagine why my husband would want to speak to you. You want my advice? You stay here in Fourways and show that you don't give a damn about these rumours. You know as much about the Standard History as anyone else in this State, you spoke the truth as you saw it in that lecture, and *damn* right too. I say *that* to the underpolice." She snapped her fingers.

Capel looked thoughtful. "I don't know, Andeel. I feel as if I may have acted rather hastily. There is a war coming, and perhaps now is not the time for people to be controversial. I rather think I might go and visit Gelda."

"Oh, but Capel, he's such a dreadful bore. If it isn't Herder Spiders it's business problems. As if *I* care about what goes on in his slaughterhouses."

"You married him, Andeel."

"He provides money and manages the estate and leaves me free to travel. I always think…"

But Capel didn't hear the rest; she was distracted by the grey-suited man at the next counter, ostensibly staring at a range of pheromones. *Is he watching my reflection in the glass*, she wondered? *Surely it doesn't take that long to choose? Didn't I see him following me when I came in the store?*

"Capel! Capel, are you listening?" Andeel took hold of her hand. "What's the matter with you?" she demanded. "Didn't you hear me? You can't really be serious about visiting Gelda!"

"I think so," said Capel, heart pounding. "I think I shall." The grey-suited man at the next counter had been joined by his wife. The two of them walked off, arm in arm, chatting happily. "Yes," said Capel weakly. "I will go. I need to get away from the city for a while."

*

That Thursday Andeel flew to Parador on the StratoLiner, soaring through the sullen and suspicious skies that brooded over the seas that separated the two continents.

The same day, Capel picked out a beautifully made set of dove-grey travel luggage from the Galerie Artemis, packed it with something suitable for a week's visit, and drove herself to the Resthispil estate and her appointment with her sister's husband.

Her copy of the Standard History lay on the passenger seat beside her, dogged and worn, the pages covered in tiny, precise notes, and Capel found herself glancing at it as she drove, her mind constantly straying back to her lecture.

She was an expert driver. The Dundal 450 was a notoriously temperamental car: it was not unknown for a beginner to frighten its biological part through overhandling; in extreme cases it was even possible to short the vehicle's nervous system, but Capel managed the car with firm patience. The route to Resthispil led through what should have been a rural idyll. The roads through this part of Caleptria were straight and well-tended, lined with poplars and marked with white stones, but still she couldn't relax. She found herself constantly checking her rear view mirror to see if she was being followed.

Her mind drifted back to her lecture. *This world is not our own*, she thought. *We don't control our own State, though we believe we do. Look at this countryside, so sweet and tame, with fields that have been ploughed and harvested for hundreds of years, and hedgerows and elms and ditches that have bestrode this land for generations. So safe and homely and familiar. But we did not make it this way. We live in a house that we believe was constructed by our fathers for our convenience, but the builders hide unseen in the walls; they stand in the background of the friezes and murals and laugh at us because we don't see them for who they are. And I was foolish enough to speak this truth and now those builders will have me silenced lest the truth be heard...*

A little grey van had been following her for at least twenty minutes. The car picked up on her panic and began to misfire. Her eyes kept being drawn to the following vehicle. It was just like those used by the underpolice, *it was following her, they were coming to seize her and...*

The little van turned off at a pretty crossroads by a thatched tavern and Capel felt a bubbling relief rising within her.

*

Capel reached the Resthispil estate in mid-afternoon, her nose pink from the bright sun: she was looking forward to changing out of her travelling outfit.

The estate was bounded by neat white fences and yellow stone walls. The main gates were of black iron, and they were firmly closed. Capel tooted the horn a couple of times but no one came to open them. In the end she got out of the car and pushed them open herself. She imagined Andeel's reaction at returning home and having to open her own gates, the tantrum she would throw. Why she had ever married Gelda was a mystery to everyone.

Except it wasn't really. It was funny how people looked at things in different ways, Capel reflected. Gelda doe Resthispil had married for status and the connections to help his business grow. An unexpected bonus was finding a wife who would not get in the way of his interest in herder spider husbandry. Andeel had married for money and a husband who left her alone to move in fashionable society. Both thought they had the best of the deal: in some ways, theirs was the perfect marriage.

As for Capel, she had never married, and she had cared neither for fashion nor herder spiders.

There was a particularly large specimen standing in the shade of the trees that marked the edge of the doe Resthispil estate. It watched her as she drove slowly through the gate, the brass bonnet of her car covered in condensation. There was a fluttering in her mind as the spider felt its way around her brain, trying to gain a foothold there, but she shook it off and the spider turned its attention back to the flock of sheep it tended; set them back to grazing at the grass right up to the verges of the gravel road.

Still she could feel the creature was watching her. Glancing in her rearview mirror she made out a suggestion of eight bony legs that rose almost to the drooping canopy of willow, and there, looking out coolly, as if from under the brim of a hat, a pair of green eyes staring straight at her. Six red eyes glared madly above them.

Those cool green eyes in particular made Capel feel uneasy. There was an air of intelligence there, an air of ownership. She gunned the car's engine and sped down the crunching gravel of the long drive, eager to be away from the animal. In the mirror, she saw it step out onto the road behind to watch her go.

The doe Resthispil estate was large, but not enormous. Capel liked its style: simple but elegant. The place had been designed to complement the landscape; sloping gently from the green forested hills to the north through a patchwork of hedge-lined fields down to the rolling grassy downs to the south. The house itself was built of yellow stone in the Dorphan style; it faced down a wide valley with a pleasant prospect. Three farmsteads had been moved in order to improve the view. Of course, that had been two hundred years ago. They didn't do things like that now in Caletptria. Capel smiled at the thought: Andeel would say that was the Alharian influence.

Power and control. The doe Resthispil estate had once been nothing more than some pretty landscapes where one was assured of good hunting and fishing. Under Gelda's management, the estate had assumed a different, more agricultural feel. Herder spiders roamed free across its rolling acres, marshalling the cattle and sheep. Sheep moved over distant fields, grey white coats thick and ready for shearing. Nearby, a herd of Emmental cows came to drink from the ruffled surface of the lake that lay to the right of the road. The sinister black water, unfathomed by the sunlight: Capel wondered what secrets could lurk in its depths.

She pulled up at the front of the house and climbed stiffly from the car. Her tan driving suit may have been the height of couture, but it was utterly impractical for its purpose. The skirt was too short; her legs had stuck to the leather seat. Feeling vaguely annoyed, she pulled her cigarette case from her handbag and selected a yellow Peach City Strand. She was just lighting up, taking a deep lungful of marijuana when a bearded man in a long pair of green boots came trotting towards her down the steps of the house. He was carrying a long electroprod, brass rod tipped in silver, the handle wrapped in black tape. He looked angry.

"This can knock out an adult female spider," he growled, his voice low and menacing. "Just imagine what it could do to you…"

Capel drew on her cigarette. Unlike her sister, she found the man's rough, working class accent rather pleasant. There was something honest about it.

"Gelda," she said reproachfully. "Is that any way to greet your sister-in law?"

The man squinted down at her.

"Capel doe Mistletroe. Is it you?"

"Of course it's me, Gelda doe Resthispil. Who else would it be?"

Gelda realised he was pointing the electroprod at Capel. He let go of the trigger handle; there was a sizzle as the prod discharged its load.

"I'm sorry," he said. "The livestock have been acting up here over the past few days. One of the spiders was found dead on the road you've just driven down." His eyes narrowed as he scanned the fields. "Somebody is playing games with me," he murmured, but then he suddenly remembered his manners. "But what am I saying, leaving you here like this!" he called. "Come inside! You'll want a drink after your journey."

Capel took a last deep drag on the cigarette and dropped it on the yellow gravel, where she ground it beneath her shoe. She followed Gelda up the steps into a wooden panelled hallway and watched as he sat down and pulled off his long green boots.

"We'll go through to the library," he said. "Halma!" he called. "Carrenth tea and ether for my guest. Or would you rather have beer? No, I'm teasing! And, Halma, prepare the yellow room. I'm sure Capel will be staying here for at least tonight!" He looked questioningly at Capel as he spoke.

An old man in a blue-striped jacket nodded confirmation from the doorway and withdrew.

"Only me and Halma left here," apologised Gelda. "He came out of retirement when all the staff were swept up by the draft." His face clouded for a moment. "They're all off in Resthpitham learning how to polish boots and cook rations the army way." Then he grinned. "My cook trained in Peach City. Now they have him in a tent peeling potatoes. I wonder how his airs and graces will go down now with his colleagues whilst he serves food to squaddies?"

Gelda laughed loudly at the thought as he led Capel down a passageway lined with antique prints of hunting parties. Silver-jacketed men and women rode on spider mounts chasing foxes, deer and wolf hare.

"But that's his problem," said Gelda, throwing open a set of double doors and striding into the octagonal space of the library. "Really, it is a pleasure to meet you again after so long, doe Mistletroe."

"And you too, doe Resthispil. Andeel sends her regards."

Something softened in Gelda's eyes for the briefest of moments, but he brushed that aside with and impatient gesture. "Yes, yes. I read in the *Times* about your lecture, you know."

Capel had been looking at the grey and tan bound books that lined the library walls. Now she turned and fixed Gelda with a long stare. "And what did you think?"

Gelda looked solemn. "I think it treachery to suggest the Caletptria is going to lose the war with Alharia."

Capel felt a stab of anger.

"It's not treachery to speak the truth!" she snapped. "Caletptria is a fiction! The Caletptrian state is not of our making. This house, this landscape, the towns and the cities… All of the political and artistic and technical advances of the past five hundred years are the product of unseen forces. Someone or *something* has led our society to its zenith, and now the baton of progress is to be handed to the Alharians. The forthcoming war is just another step in the play that has been written out for us."

She glared at Gelda.

"So you said, Capel," he said.

"Yes! And so I say! We are all actors in our own history. Read the *Standard History of Caletptria*. Read between the lines and you will see that what I say is the truth!"

The door opened and Halma entered carrying a set of hot towels on a tray. He seemed not to notice that Capel had lost her temper. He picked up a towel in a set of silver tongs.

"To freshen up after your journey, doe Mistletroe."

Capel took the towel and meticulously wiped her face and hands. Gelda watched her, expression hidden by his thick dark beard. He waited for Halma to leave the room and then spoke in a low voice.

"Capel, I did not say that *I* thought you were a traitor. I may not be the expert on the Standard History that you are, but even a working class lad like me is capable of reading between the lines, and I can see that the State is very worried about what you said. I may have spent most of my life selling meat but I've learnt something about people on the way. There's only one thing that upsets folk that much, and that's the truth."

"Of course," said Capel. She was calm now. A skeleton of a herder spider caught her eye. She walked across to the corner of the room where it stood, mounted on a wooden plinth.

"Is this a model?" said Capel. "I didn't think Herder Spiders grew so small."

Gelda waved a dismissive hand.

"Dwarf species. Long extinct. I found that specimen frozen in the tundra north of the Epherenian steppes. Broke a shovel getting it out of the ground. Hah! That was nothing compared to the trouble I had bringing it back home. As we headed south, the air grew warmer and the flesh defrosted and began peeling away. The stink! I tell you, I had to shove the thing in the ice bucket Andeel had been using to chill the Carrain wine."

"Hmm." Capel ran a finger along a greenish leg bone, feeling the strange double curve typical of a herder spider's skeleton.

Gelda stroked his thick black beard. Suddenly he was all businesslike. "Capel, I'll be honest. I heard your lecture, and I agree with you. And I'm not the only one. A lot of people think the same as you: our society is not our own. Something else is controlling us."

Capel almost retained her composure, but Gelda saw how her eyes widened.

"Oh come on, Capel. You're a clever woman, it's true, but you don't suppose you were the first to notice the clues?"

"N…no…" lied Capel

"You did, didn't you?" said Gelda. "And you didn't think anything about speaking out so publicly. I don't know whether that was bravery or recklessness."

Capel was an ugly woman, and she knew it. Maybe if she had Andeel's looks she would have evolved different strategies for dealing with people. Maybe. As it was, she found bluntness to the point of rudeness the most effective way of getting what she wanted.

"What do you know of bravery, Gelda? Sheltering here in your estate whilst my sister travels the world on your money. If you knew the truth, you should have spoken it years ago!"

Gelda smiled.

"What? And risk torture and death? Capel, don't you realise that the only thing that has kept you alive so long is your title? You made plain in your lecture some secrets that have been known but hidden for years. Centuries even. Secrets that no one dared share before. Maybe the time was right for someone to make them known, but how could you know that?"

"How could I know otherwise? I thought that only I knew the truth!"

Gelda held her gaze for a moment.

"You're so like your sister. Utterly self-centred."

"Don't you speak about my sister like that!"

"Why not? She's my wife." He shook his head. "Listen Capel, you have only touched on the truth. There is more, so much more…"

"Other secrets? Like what?"

"We're not the first, Capel. Whole nations have been destroyed and wiped from the histories before us. Whole races of people. Whole species!"

Capel gazed at him, anger burning slowly inside her.

"What are you talking about, Gelda? Are you playing games with me? What can you know of this subterfuge? How could you know secrets I have spent my career unearthing? You're nothing but a glorified slaughterman! A meatpacker who has made enough money to breed herder spiders."

Gelda laughed. A brittle laugh, entirely without humour and with more than a little despair.

"Capel, all that research, and you never realised? It's the herder spiders that are controlling us! We think that we farm them, but throughout history it has been the other way around."

Capel held his gaze for a moment, and then something seemed to snap inside her. She began to laugh.

"Don't waste my time, Gelda. Herder spiders don't have the power to control humans. You know that. And if they did they wouldn't have the intelligence to build a society like Caletptria. There's no evidence of anything like that in the Standard History."

Gelda flew his hands wide with despair.

"And you're the woman who says that the Standard History is a fake? Did it not occur to you that the powers controlling our society would have ensured they were written out of the history?"

Of course it had occurred to Capel. The fact that Gelda said this to her in his flat, working class accent only made her more annoyed.

Capel wiped her hands on a towel. She resorted to the icy language of academia.

"Anyway, Gelda, one can claim as many omissions from the text as one wishes, but you cannot write a history from omissions. Do you have any evidence to support your assertions?"

"What," asked Gelda, "more evidence than this skeleton?" He patted the bones of the dwarf herder spider. "Extinct for five thousand years. This species is not mentioned in the Standard History." And he fixed her with a hard stare. "It was mentioned in the Apocrypha, though."

That silenced Capel. The fear that had been with her the past few weeks suddenly receded to leave her standing on the brink. This was the moment, this was the time when she would either step forward and be swallowed up, or she could pull back.

Gelda stood in silence for a moment, as if pondering, and then he appeared to come to a decision. Wordlessly, he crossed to one wall of the library and its shelves of identically bound books. He ran a finger along the leather spines of one row, paused, and then slowly pulled clear a slim grey and tan volume, just like any of the others. Capel's heart was suddenly pounding in her chest. It couldn't be true. Gelda *couldn't* have a copy. Surely the Apocrypha had all been destroyed? And yet here was Gelda, giving a wry smile as he open the book and began to thumb his way through it, holding it deliberately away from her so she couldn't see the contents as he searched for a page. This *had* to be a bluff, thought Capel. And yet Gelda was now handing her the book, and, hands trembling, she took it.

"Read this," he was saying, but she was running her fingers down the paper of a page, so old and yellow that the ink thereon faded to a pale brown.

And she knew. This was the real thing.

Heart pounding, she began to read.

*

Domina dragged the fork through the earth, pulling out yet more of the round grey rocks that filled the thin soil. Saxicale bent down before him, dark patches of sweat staining her smock beneath her arm pits and her heavy breasts. She patiently lifted the rocks into the basket, ready to carry them clear of the tilled area. Three children and seventeen years of back-breaking work had taken their toll on her. What is it that keeps a man with a woman at this time when his seed has been spent and his children nearly grown? Surely he would live a better life if he cut himself free from such impediments and set out on his own?

It was not a feeling born of logic that bound Domina tightly to Saxicale.

*

"Domina...Domina... where have I heard that name before?" whispered Capel to herself. She ran her fingers over the yellowing pages of the book, feeling their age, a complete contrast to the smooth newness of their binding: their camouflage, their disguise. "I can't believe you have a copy of the Apocrypha," she whispered. "Does Andeel know about this?"

"Of course not," said Gelda. "I wouldn't put her in such danger. If the underpolice suspected she was complicit in my crime..."

Capel wasn't listening. She was too engrossed in the book. "The style... It is that of the Standard History. It has an eye for detail and character unknown in any of the other works written at the time."

Gelda gave a laugh.

"Of course it does. It was written to be part of the Standard History. But then someone decided to have it excised."

Capel wasn't used to being on the back foot — not where the Standard History was concerned. Nonetheless, she read on.

*

No other animal on Capth moves like a spider. Its passage registers in a unique way on the human consciousness.

Saxicale dumped the basket of rocks on the spreading pile at the edge of the forest and turned to see the green and white striped body of a spider picking its way through the rows of cabbages and potatoes that stretched over half of their clearing.

"Domina," she said, her voice flat with exhaustion. In those days, there was little energy left over after work was completed for a person to breathe life into the finer sensibilities.

Domina made his way across the rock-strewn ground, the mud sticking to his leather boots in clumps as he went, making his walk high and unsteady. The wolf spider paused and bent its head down, blue eyes staring at him, almost as if in challenge. The cabbages were half unfolded, the green stalks of the potato leaves still half grown.

"Take your fork and kill it," said Saxicale, coming to his side. "Drive it through its rotten heart."

The spider looked back at her with its four green eyes, its two blue eyes. It bent its legs…

*

Capel's heart was pounding with excitement. They were going to kill a spider? There was nothing like this in the Standard History. "There is a break here," she said, fighting to appear calm. "The text resumes in a different hand."

Gelda gave a nod. "I suspect the passage you have just read is a dramatisation. Read on."

Capel did so.

*

Cal's people came to the homestead, tired from their travels. They saw a rude hut, set in a clearing of the forest. The green trees that bordered the rock-littered ground bore white bleeding bands of pale wood where they had recently been ringed.

"There are three dead over there," said Fel. "A woman and two children. They bear many wounds."

Cal walked across the clearing, taking in the damage done to the land where some simple crop had been planted. The soil was churned up by many feet, green stalks trampled into the earth. Something rose inside her as she saw the bodies of the two children, clasped in the arms of their mother; their blood dried black on the ground.

"This is a tale that is told too often," said Cal. Her hand touched the pommel of the sword she wore at her belt. "Iron is no match against the wolf spider."

"Over here," called one of her tribe. "I have found the father and his daughter. What's left of them, anyway…"

*

Capel placed a finger on her place in the book, and paused, thinking. She was imagining another world, one that had been hidden from her. One where spiders preyed upon humans. Through the wide windows of the library she had a view across Gelda's estate. A brown and white herder spider guided a flock of sheep across a field, its long curved legs seemingly wading through the white foam of their bodies. Was it all an act, she wondered, was that familiar shape engaged in some subterfuge?

"It can't be right," she said. "Nothing like that is mentioned in the Standard History…"

Gelda gave a laugh.

"For you, of all people to say that, Capel doe Mistletroe…"

Capel gave a slow nod. She looked back down at the book.

"There seems to be a jump here. The story of Domina ends." She read the start of the next passage.

*

Cal decreed the City of Fourways should stand at the heart of the Empire…

*

"What happened to Domina? Blast! Why *does* that name sound familiar?"

"There is a passage in the Standard History, of course." Gelda went across to one of the yellow wood shelves of the library and pulled out a bound copy of the History. He turned to a page near the beginning and showed it to Capel.

She began to read the words from the passage she had just seen in the Apocrypha. Now she remembered where she had head the name before. Domina and the parable of the Tithe Spider. It was a small passage, tucked away in *Values and Virtues*.

She scanned down the page, seeking the part where the text diverged from that of the Apocrypha.

*

"Take your fork and kill it," said Saxicale, appearing at his side. "Drive it through its rotten heart."

"Peace, wife," said Domina. "Each of us to our place. The herder spider guards our land from other intruders. It keeps us safe. Let it take its allotted portion."

They looked to their cabin. Saxifrage, their youngest daughter, stood in the doorway, eyes filled with quiet acceptance as she watched the tithe spider step over to the far side of their cleared ground and pause for a moment. It looked to where Domina and Saxicale worked so hard to increase their livelihood, raking white rocks from the earth to leave usable soil.

Saxicale gave a heavy sigh. "Our fathers stripped the bark from these trees that surround us in order that they might die and this clearing form. They laboured long to dig the dead roots from this rock-stirred land so that we may plant food and live. This spider has not toiled as we have! Instead, once a year it comes out from the forest and takes its tithe. It is not right…"

Domina placed a hand on her shoulder. "Peace, wife," he said again. "It protects our land from wild animals and those who might rob us. It has earned its tithe."

*

"The spider taxes and tithes," said Gelda. "An excellent parable for the model of the feudal society from which Caletptria grew. One can see an example to all the peasants and workers written down in the Standard History on how to behave. Is there any wonder that the description of the wolf spider was dispatched to the Apocrypha?"

His tone changed as he spoke about the book, Capel noticed, his accent became less harsh.

"They changed the History," she said. "They changed the History to suit themselves. But how come I have never heard of a wolf spider?"

"Because someone doesn't want us to know about them. Because a long time ago there was a fight between humans and spiders on Capth, and the humans looked to be the winning side. Just suppose that amongst all those forgotten creatures there was a breed of herder spider that could control human minds. One that was more intelligent than the rest. A breed intelligent enough to see that they couldn't win by brute force and so they hid themselves away from us and they learned to stay hidden throughout the centuries. They learned to change the books to wipe out the knowledge of themselves…"

Both Gelda and Capel gazed at the Standard History. Gelda began to flick through the pages, searching for something. He gave a Capel a familiar passage to read.

*

Cal walked out to meet them, bearing green branches as a sign of peace. The leader of the Eastpeople reined in his spider-mount and looked down from the saddle. The beast watched Cal too with its eight yellow eyes and two disturbingly intelligent red ones.

*

"Eight yellow eyes and two red ones," repeated Gelda. "An East Rondel red. I used to have one of them on my estate. It died of poisoning three years ago. Andeel forgot to close the door to the meat locker. Mutton does not agree with a herder spider's metabolism."

He sighed at the memory, and then flicked further through the book, showed Capel another passage.

"That describes a Norren brown. The old Norren Empire used them to help control slaves. Did you know that? No? They fitted bronze spears to their front legs. The spiders couldn't really kill a man – they didn't have the strength – but they could make a nasty wound. The threat was enough to keep the slaves in order."

He looked at Capel, eyes disturbingly bright above his thick black beard.

"The Standard History lists the seventeen modern species of herder spider. A further five distinct species can be identified, thought to be now extinct. But it doesn't mention the wolf spider…"

Capel had heard enough. Something inside her rebelled.

"No," she said. "I can't believe it. This can't be true. There is no such thing as a wolf spider."

At the Gelda's expression became very odd.

"I think there is something you should see," he said.

*

There was a stone flagged room at the rear of Gelda's house, a place for people to change out of muddy boots and rain-soaked coats. Oiled jackets and tweed caps hung in neat rows along the walls; a set of shelves held well waxed and polished boots of all sizes. Capel sat on a low bench and changed out of her slim tan shoes into a clumpy pair of walking boots. Gelda helped her fasten a pair of green gaiters over them, smiling at the incongruity of her outfit: neat little figure-hugging tan suit and great heavy boots. He swung open the outside door and led Capel across the white gravel, through an afternoon where the pale spring sun had not yet warmed the chill of winter from the countryside. Taking a deep breath of smoke-tinged air, Capel looked out across the neat green fields that surrounded Gelda's estate. Three hundred years of careful cultivation had produced a picturesque scene that ran in a brown and green patchwork to the distant low hills. She could make out the odd curving motion of a herder spider, picking its way across a distant field.

"This is a beautiful place," said Capel.

"Hmm," grunted Gelda, leading them towards a low block of whitewashed stables that stood off to the side of the house. "Remember it. Once Alharia invades it will be altered forever. A society that thinks of nothing but profit will not understand the sense of obligation that keeps this place running."

"I don't know," said Capel. "I have seen estates in Alharia. They have a savage beauty of their own."

Gelda opened a door and led them into the dim warmth of a stable. Capel smelled horses and hay; she saw straw and stalls and well kept tack. And in the middle of the floor...

"A herder spider. It's dead!"

"Look closer," said Gelda. "Describe it."

"It is green and white. It has four green eyes and two other eyes, both closed."

"They were blue," said Gelda. "Does that sound familiar to you?"

Capel looked at Gelda, and the last dregs of doubt drained away.

"The spider that Domina described in the Apocrypha. A wolf spider." Her voice was thin and colourless. The world had lurched and lurched again, and now she found herself standing in a completely alien place. The smell of the stables, the thickness of the walls, the reassuring normalness of it all no longer seemed to touch her.

"I'm sorry Capel," said Gelda gently. "I know it's a shock. They were hunted nearly to extinction, I think. Someone was trying to remove all trace of their existence. But there are a few left alive, in the remote corners of the world. I found this one up in the mountains of Parador. Poor Andeel never suspected what it was, she thought I was mad having it shipped back here. I had it hidden here for years on my estate, until last week. Someone killed it."

Capel shook her head, struggling to take this all in.

"But who? And why?"

Gelda didn't meet her eyes.

"I don't know, Capel," he said. He was almost mumbling now.

"But why?"

Now he looked at her again. "To hide the evidence?" he suggested. "Someone built up our society and has secretly controlled it these last few hundred years. And now that their secret is beginning to emerge, that someone is destroying all of the remaining evidence, starting with poor old Nora here."

He placed a tender hand on the white fur-like mat that covered the spider's head.

"But some secrets will not be so easy to hide…"

And at that he took an axe from the wall and brought it down hard in the centre of the spider's skull, splitting through the chitin covered bone with a harsh cracking sound. Clear jelly ran from the spider's head, thin and sticky and shot through with green threads. Gelda raised the axe into the air once more, and, breathing heavily, struck the skull again, and again. Capel covered her nose with a handkerchief. The jelly gave off a foul smell.

"What is that?" she asked, as a strand of clear jelly flew from the axe and stuck to her skirt.

"The overbrain," said Gelda, hacking open a hole in the spider's football-sized skull. "We need to clear it away so that you can see what lies beneath." He gave one last blow with the axe, and then bent and picked up a triangular piece of bone. There was a hole in the middle of it. He fiddled with the bone shard, foul-smelling jelly dripping down his fingers.

"Look," he said, pushing a clear green disc across the middle of the hole. "One of the overeyes." He held out the bone to Capel. "Come on, Capel. There're girls of fourteen earn a wage in my gutting rooms who every day have their arms up to the elbows in worse than this. Take it."

Stomach churning, she did so. Gelda resumed his hacking at the inside of the spider's skull.

"The eye structure is typical of type B life," he said, hacking away. The thunking of the axe resonated deep in Capel's stomach, nauseating her. Gelda didn't seem to notice.

"Basically it is nothing more than a set of light sensitive cells plumbed straight into the overbrain," he continued.

Capel had overcome her nausea. Truth be told, she wasn't normally so squeamish. It was just the unreality of the situation that unnerved her. She gazed through the green disc, holding it up to one of the ceiling windows. It seemed to glitter with yellow light.

"Ah, got it!" Gelda was straddling the green and white body of the spider and reaching deep into the skull. He was trying to pry away the bone at the bottom.

"You have to be careful here," he muttered. "Don't want to damage the Type A structures."

"I don't understand," said Capel, thoroughly confused. "What is Type B life? What is an overbrain?"

Gelda paused. He looked up at Capel, his grey trousers stained with foul jelly, cotton sleeves slicked to his arms. His expression was a mixture of disbelief and amusement.

"Type B life?" he said. "Capel, you're one of our foremost historians. Don't you know anything about *Natural* History?"

"Very little," said Capel, primly. "I studied the classics."

"Of course you did," he said bitterly. "That's why Alharia is going to defeat us. Their best scholars study mathematics and Natural History, whilst ours reread the Standard History and translate it into Dorphan. All our best minds are either working in the factories and gutting rooms, or they have married into the aristocracy to act as breeding stock for the next generation."

Capel scowled. "You made your choice, Gelda. Don't expect sympathy from me. Now, stop wasting your time lecturing me. Tell me about Type B life."

Gelda resumed picking away pieces of skull, trying to reach something deep in the spider's head. He spoke as he worked.

"At some time in pre-history, two separate types of life evolved on Capth. It is not fair to say two branches of life, for this would imply that they connected at some point in the past. No, it is true to say that two completely distinct types of life have thrived upon Capth, and have diversified until they fit into every niche of the planet's ecosystems. We belong to type A life, along with grass and trees and potatoes, pigs and sheep and mosquitoes and roses."

He rubbed a hand across his sweating forehead, smearing it with green-tinged jelly.

"Then there is type B life," he continued, "which includes things like the sea spiders and the mountain plankton, air ribbons and land clams."

"Then you don't see much type B life in Caletptria," observed Capel. "Not like Parador. I remember visiting that country as a girl. The plankton glows pink on the peaks of the Charamin mountains."

"That's because Parador is still undeveloped," said Gelda. "Andeel thinks it's a wonderful place to mix with the right sort of people – especially during Appassionata." His voice was bitter. "I think it's a backward society, an example of all that is wrong with Caletptria in microcosm." He seemed to remember himself. "Ah, but as for the landscape! Most of the second continent is a fascinating place for the study of flora and fauna, but the mountains of Parador... I think there are stranger things waiting to be discovered there than old Nora here."

Capel nodded slowly. "I once saw the snail paddies in the southern Alaharian states. I don't think I've ever seen anything so odd..."

"Yes!" said Gelda, delighted. "Yet they used to be common here in Caletptria, thousands of years ago! No longer." He pulled away some more bone. "The thing about the two forms of life, is that they are, as I said, completely separate. Type A life feeds only on type A life. As we have planted grain and forests here in Caleptria, so we have restricted the habitats and food sources of Type B life. The encroachment of Type A life is not yet so advanced on the second continent."

"Good," said Capel. Gelda smiled.

"We'll make a Natural Historian of you yet, Capel. Now, look at this."

Capel leant and peered inside the hollowed-out skull of the herder spider. Gelda had peeled back the floor of cavity to reveal a second bony chamber beneath. Nestling in the middle of it, grey and wrinkled, was a brain the size of Capel's fist.

"That looks like a human brain," she said.

"A mammal brain," said Gelda. "It is. A Type A brain. Almost exclusively of all life on Capth, the Herder Spider bridges both types. And virtually no one seems to know this, and those who do don't seem to care why." His voice sounded almost wistful for a moment. "Almost as if we were being made not to notice..."

"If you look here…" he said suddenly. He pointed to where two thin strands emerged from the base of the grey brain and ran upwards, branching and branching into ever finer strands.

"What are they?"

"Interface to the overbrain. This is how Type A life controls a Type B brain."

Gelda gazed at her intently.

"This makes you feel sick, doesn't it?" he said.

"Yes. I need to go outside. I need a cigarette."

She half ran for the door, fumbling in her bag for her cigarette case. Gelda followed her out, eager to make his point.

"It *is* sickening, isn't it?" he said. "The way one brain controls the other. Why is that, do you suppose?"

"I don't want to think about it," said Capel. She snapped open her lighter, yellow flame bursting into the cold afternoon light. She drew smoke into her lungs, trying to escape the foul smell of the stables. Gradually, the marijuana relaxed her. She looked out across the patchwork of fields. White hawthorn blossom lit up the hedges, the branches of the ash trees still bare against the pale sky. Brown fields, ploughed and ready to be planted with Type A life. Gelda was at her shoulder.

"There is something unsettling about the spider's brain, isn't there? Something that resonates in your gut."

"Leave it," said Capel. Gelda pressed on.

"But that sort of thing is written through our world. Look at your car, the way it has a mind of its own plumbed into the machinery. Why is that?"

"I said leave it!"

"It makes me think of what you've seen hidden in the Standard History. Something concealed underneath our society. It makes me think of branching green strands reaching up, controlling us. And that's not all…"

"What?" asked Capel. "What's not all?"

But Gelda wasn't listening. He was looking over her shoulder, puzzled.

"Something is up."

Capel followed his gaze. A tall herder spider stood at the edge of the field that bordered the gravel path upon which they stood. Absolutely motionless, its green eyes stared at her with cool intelligence.

That's the underbrain looking at me, she thought.

Gelda was looking around.

"It shouldn't be here. There is no reason for it to be here." Suspicion gripped him. "Unless… of course! Damn! It's you! Why didn't I guess?"

Capel began to back away from Gelda. His ragged beard, his tanned skin did not seem the chirpy working class man any more. Suddenly, he was dangerous.

"Capel," he asked, a dizzy edge to his voice, "what are you doing here?"

Capel was genuinely puzzled.

"What do you mean, what am I doing here? You invited me. I got your letter."

"What letter?" Gelda frowned. "I never sent you a letter."

The thumping fear that had followed Capel all the way here from the city welled up all around her again. It churned in her stomach, it filled her limbs making them weak and heavy, it pounded in her chest.

"But why bring me here…" she began. "Who…?"

Nearby, ever so slowly, the herder spider lifted one leg over the fence and placed it upon the path with a crunch of gravel.

"What's it doing?" asked Capel, voice hoarse. The spider began to raise another leg.

Gelda's voice sounded strained. "It's protecting me… Look…"

How long had they been here, Capel wondered? Men and women

in grey suits and coats. Walking up by the side of the fence, leaning against the walls of the stables. Filing into view so quietly, so inconspicuously, you'd barely notice them. It was a valuable skill. One learned in basic training by the underpolice. Had someone been waiting on the estate, spying on them? Had they gone and summoned reinforcements whilst they were in the barn? Capel felt sick.

Now a man walked forward. Tall and thin and hollow-cheeked. His eyes were as green and as mad as a wolf spider's.

"My name is Polossa Gunnil," he said in a voice that was just a little too high-pitched. "I am here to arrest you both for crimes against the State."

"Get off my land," said Gelda with cold authority. "You have no place here."

Capel felt something tickling at the back of her mind, something creeping into her brain, but the feeling was drowned by her fear. She had encountered the underpolice before, had been on the point of entering one of their grey vans to be driven off to their neat little headquarters. That time she had managed to maintain her external composure; this time it was as if all the fear she had suppressed before had caught up with her. From nowhere, a vision arose in her mind of a white-tiled room and a sharp little knife. Just her and a knife and so much time.

"N…No…" she stammered.

The herder spider continued the process of stepping over the fence, one complicated leg motion after another.

Polossa Gunnil tilted his head, gazing at Gelda as if puzzled.

"I have no place here?" he said in a piping voice. "But this is just the place to be, Gelda doe Resthispil. Away from prying eyes and inconvenient questions."

"You mean away from a fair hearing," spat Gelda.

Polossa Gunnil was unperturbed.

"Different rules apply during wartime."

"I wasn't aware war had yet been declared."

Polossa Gunnil sucked in his hollow cheeks. His green eyes shone madly. "You talk very well now, don't you, *doe* Resthispil. Not just a slaughterman now, are we? Learnt a lot from our fine wife, haven't we? Got your money's worth? She certainly has. Using your cash to travel to Parador to be serviced by other men…"

Gelda's temples bulged.

"Leave it, Gelda," said Capel, her voice shaking. "He's not telling you anything about Andeel you didn't already know. Let's keep calm. Think of what to do next."

Polossa giggled.

"Think what to do next? Leave the thinking to me, *doe* Mistletroe. And let me tell you, Gelda *doe* Reshispil, that we've been at war to all intents and purposes for some months now. The actual declaration is a mere formality." He smiled. "Now, to business. We know what you have been breeding on this estate. Abominations. Lies to discredit the Standard History of the Caletptrian State. False creatures! Do you deny it?"

"I do not deny that I have been breeding spiders on this estate…"

"I am *so* pleased," said Polossa, sarcastically. "Then, if you would be so good as to follow me…"

Something was walking through Capel's mind, casting webs as it went. She tried to concentrate, but she was distracted by a crunching sound. Tyres on gravel. A grey van was rolling slowly towards them. A prison van. Come to take them away to a little room and a sharp little knife. Involuntarily, she gave a low moan.

Gelda seemed confused. "I don't think I can follow you," he said. He nodded towards the herder spider that had crossed the fence and was now picking its way slowly down the gravel road towards them.

Polossa was suddenly holding something in his fist. Something small and compact. A gun. He was no longer smiling.

"I will say this once only. Move."

"I'm sorry, I don't think I can," said Gelda. And then, to Capel's horror, Polossa raised the gun and pulled the trigger. Tried to pull the trigger. Nothing happened. His finger jerked again, and again. Capel flinched each time.

"No! Stop it!" Capel's voice was thin and wobbly. Years of good breeding drained away just like that, all at the sight of the gun and the cold-blooded way in which Polossa frowned and said: "I don't seem to be able to move my finger enough." He shook his head in puzzlement. "What's the matter with me?"

"You're trying to kill him," whispered Capel, almost crying with the meanness of it all. "All he has done is stand up for himself and you are going to *kill* him."

"We are at war," explained Polossa, earnestly, his finger still jerking ineffectively at the trigger. "Examples must be made. People like you are talking us into defeat."

"We are at war," said Gelda, "but not with Alharia."

He reached out and took the gun from Polossa's unresisting fingers.

"Hold still," he said. Polossa did so.

Gelda levelled the gun. He licked his lips. He fired once, taking off the top of Polossa's head. The underpoliceman registered no surprise, no shock or pain. His body simply went limp and slumped to the ground. Capel stared at the space in his skull in disbelief. She took a step backwards, and another.

"No," she whispered.

"I didn't do that," said Gelda miserably.

"No," repeated Capel.

"I didn't do it," said Gelda. "It was the spider."

Capel couldn't move her legs: there was something in her mind, it wandered through her head, touching silken strands to her neurons, gathering them up like puppet strings.

"Gelda…" she said. He didn't seem to notice. He was too busy checking the gun's action. "Gelda," she called again. "Something is in my head…"

And then, without willing it, she took a step forward. All around, grey-coated men and woman were doing the same. The whole crowd began moving and Capel joined them as they formed themselves into ranks under the patient eyes of the Herder Spider.

"Gelda! What's happening?"

Gelda took hold of Capel's arm, pulled her away from the crowd. He shouted at the spider.

"No!" he called. "Leave her alone. She's with me!"

Capel found herself struggling against Gelda. She couldn't help herself. She bumped into a grey-coated man. He grunted, looked at her with wide eyes, and then returned to his place in the forming ranks.

"Stop it!" called Capel. "Make it stop!"

"I'm trying to!" said Gelda. He was trying to appear calm. His grey face betrayed him. "It's only protecting its estate." He explained. Then he turned and waved his hand again. "Leave her alone!" he called.

"*Its* estate?" Her voice was shrill. Now nearly all the underpolice had fallen into ranks. Gelda let go of her arm and she took her place amongst them. Gelda stood alongside her, uncertain as to what to do.

"We all have different perceptions," he muttered. "I think that I own this place. Your sister believes that I am trapped here, tending the estate to provide the money that allows her to travel as she likes. I think that spider is something that I bred, the result of matching suitable mates for years, hoping to strengthen their telepathic powers, seeking to prove my theories. That spider sees me as just another one of its herd, one useful animal that arranges for the fences to be mended and the winter feed provided."

"And it sees me as a threat!" yelled Capel. "Get it to let me go!"

"I can't!" said Gelda. "It's too strong..."

And then, in perfect time with the others, Capel stepped forward on her left foot. The grey-coated ranks of the underpolice began to march along the gravel road, the herder spider walking alongside them, looking for all the world as if it was beating time.

"Where is it taking us?"

"The lake," said Gelda, and his voice was hollow. "Always the lake."

"You mean it's done this before?"

"More than once."

"And you let it?"

Gelda gave a laugh that was entirely without humour.

"Capel, there is a war coming. If that spider were to have let me, I would have been long gone, sitting safe in Parador waiting for Caletptria to fall. Waiting for when it was safe to return and take my place in the new Alharian State that is going to be established in this land. As it is, I am forced to stay here and tend to my stock. What can I do but maintain my catalogues and library and await the Alharian troops?"

Up ahead, Capel could see the dark lake. She heard someone moan nearby.

"Gelda," she said, half frantic now. "You don't have to let it do this."

They were at the lake now; a cold wind was blowing across the water. The people in grey were to be put down because they endangered the estate, and Capel was to be put down with them. The first row were already kneeling, pushing their heads under the water, kicking forward, slipping below the surface. A woman in the second row turned to look at Capel, a desperate plea for help in her eyes. Then she too knelt and ducked under the lake's surface.

"Gelda," said Capel. "Please."

Gelda looked miserable.

"Trust me, Capel," he said. "It has to be this way."

"Why? Stop it! Do something!"

But she was stepping forward again. She felt cold water at her feet. She knelt down and slipped forward into the dark embrace of the lake.

*

She awoke coughing, Gelda's concerned face above her. He was speaking to her. Gabbling. Gradually the words made sense.

"Are you okay?" he was asking. "Speak to me!"

She coughed again, coughed up water.

"I had to let you pass out!" said Gelda. "I had to wait until you were unconscious. It had no control over you then!"

She couldn't stop coughing; she curled up, hacking up water. She was lying on gravel. Her back, her side, her knees stung with the sharp stones.

"I'm sorry," said Gelda. "I'm sorry, I couldn't tell you. I couldn't let it know!"

The coughing eased. She rolled upright.

Nearby she saw the body of Polossa Gunnil, greenish jelly leaking from the skull. Capel finally succumbed to the urge that had been building in her. She rolled forward and was violently sick. She continued to retch for some time after her stomach was empty.

"Are you all right?" asked Gelda.

"No," said Capel. Her eyes were drawn back to Polossa Gunnil's skull. "Green jelly," she said. "Like the spider's brain! He wasn't human. He wasn't human at all."

"He was human," he said, looking down at the empty shell on the ground that had once been a living thing. "As human as you or I. Open up your skull and you will find exactly the same arrangement inside. Underbrain and overbrain."

"No," said Capel. "That's not right. I *know* that's not right."

"How do you know? Before today, how many skulls have you looked inside?"

"I don't know. Many. That's not what a brain looks like."

"Have you really looked inside skulls? Or have you just seen pictures in books?"

"Oh."

"Peel back the skin of our world, Capel. There is something very wrong beneath it. We are not who we think we are!"

She shook her head. "I feel so weak. Take me to the house."

"I can't, Capel. Get in your car. You need to get away from here before the spider realises you're still alive."

The spider! She shook her head, tried to feel its silken webs in her mind. There was nothing.

"Where shall I go?" she asked.

"As far away as possible. Go to Merliosta."

"But that's at the other side of the country!"

"Exactly. You can't go back to Fourways, and you can't stay here. You need to start running, Capel. You need to start running and shouting the truth as loudly as you can. It's your only chance. They can't arrest everyone!"

"But they'll shoot me!"

"After what happened here they're going to shoot you anyway. Let the secret out, what have you got to lose? Take this with you."

He handed her a book, bound in tan leather.

"The Apocrypha!" she said. "I don't want it. It's not safe."

"You're not safe whether you have it or not! You're the foremost scholar of the Standard History, Capel. Well, take that book, and maybe you can learn the full truth. For all our sakes!"

He took the book back from her and flicked through the pages.

"Look there," he said, pointing to a picture. People, men women and children. Just like her and Gelda but with one difference.

"They're all black. I don't understand."

"There used to be black people on Capth, Capel. There were black people and yellow people and all sorts, and they were all wiped from this world. And now it's our turn. Alharia will launch its attack and Caletptria will be removed from the Standard History and something else will be written in its place."

"But why?"

"Because, because..." He seemed to be struggling to express himself. "Because I think that once there was a time for strong leadership from a chosen few. Now I think that time is passing. The day of the individual is dawning. I think it is Alharia's time. Or at least I think that is what the creatures who control this world believe."

"You mean the herder spiders?"

"I don't know, Capel." He looked at the book for one last time, then closed it and pushed it into her hands. "And, Capel, if you see Andeel, tell her…"

"Tell her what?"

He looked at the ground.

"Tell her to take care."

He looked back at her.

"Now get in your car, and go!"

She stared at him for a moment. She was filthy, her clothes cut by gravel. She stood near a pool of her own vomit and the green jelly of another human being's brain. The world seemed to teeter around her. And then she regained her composure.

"Thank you, doe Resthispil," she said.

"You're welcome, doe Mistletroe." He gave a grim smile. "Please come again."

"I'd be delighted," she replied.

She climbed into her car, and pushed the starter button. Somewhere amongst the machinery there was a nervous system and brain. Why? She could think of that later. Now was the time to get away. She gunned the engine, skidded on the gravel, driving too fast, eager to get away from the place, roaring down the drive towards the gates.

In the rear view mirror she saw Gelda, raising a hand in goodbye as she left. Master and prisoner of his own estate, she reflected.

She drove her car out of the open gates and back into the outside world.

Out into another prison.

Underfog
(The Wreckers)

Tanith Lee

Oh burning God,
Each of our crimes is numbered upon
The nacre of your eternal carapace,
Like scars upon the endless sky.

'Prayer of the Damned'
(Found scratched behind the altar
in the ruined church at Hampp.)

We lured them in. It was how we lived, at Hampp. After all, the means
had been put into our grip, and we had never been given much else.

It is a rocky ugly place, the village, though worse now. Just above
the sea behind the cliff-line, and the cliffs are dark as sharks, but eaten
away beneath to a whitish-green that sometimes, in the sunlight, luridly
shines. The drop is what? Three hundred feet or more. There was the
old church standing there once, but as the cliff crumbled through the
years, bits and then all the church fell down on the stones below,
mingling with them. You can still, I should think, now and then find
part of the pitted face of a rough-carved gargoyle or angel staring up at
you from deep in the shale, or a bit of its broken wing. The graveyard
had gone, of course, too. The graves came open as the cliff gave, and
there had been bodies strewn along the shore, or what was left of them,
all bones, until the sea swam in and out and washed them away. Always
a place, this, for the fallen then, and the discarded dead.

By the days of my boyhood, the new church was right back behind
the village, uphill for safety. The new church had been there for two
hundred years. But we, the folk of Hampp, we had been there since
before the Domesday Book. And sometimes I used to wonder if they

did it then too, our forebears, seeing how the tide ran and the rocks and the cliff-line. Maybe they did. It seemed to be in our blood. Until now. Until that night of the fog.

*

My first time, I was about nine years. It had gone on before, that goes without saying, and I had known it did, but not properly what it was or meant. My nine-year-old self had memories of sitting by our winter fire, and the storm raging outside, and then a shout from the watch, or some other man banging on our door: "Stir up, Jom. One's there." And father would rise with a grunt, somewhere between annoyance and strange eagerness. And when he was gone out into the wind and rain, 1 must have asked why and Ma would say, "Don't you fret, Haro. It's just the Night Work they're to."

But later, maybe even next day, useful things would have come into our house, and to all the impoverished houses up and down the cranky village street. Casks of wine or even rum, a bolt of cloth, perhaps, or a box of good china; once a sewing machine, and more than once a whole side of beef. And other stuff came that we threw on the fire, papers and books, and a broken doll one time, and another a ripped little dress that might have been for a doll, but was not.

On the evening I was nine and a storm was brewing, I knew I might be in on the Work, but after I thought not and slept. The Work was what we all called it, you see. The Work, or the Night Work, although every so often it had happened by day, when the weather was very bad. Still, Night Work, even so.

My father said, "Get up Haro." It was the middle of the night and I in bed. And behind the curtain in my parents' bed, my mother was already moving and awake. My father was dressed. "What is it, Da?" I whispered. "Only the usual," said my father, "but you're of an age now. It's time you saw and played your part."

So I scrambled out and pulled on my outdoor clothes over the underthings I slept in. I was, like my father, between two emotions, but mine were different. With me that first time, they were excitement, and fear. Truly fear, like as when we boys played see-a-ghost in the churchyard at dusk. But in this case still not even really knowing why, or of what.

Out on the cliff the gale was blowing fit to crack the world. There were lanterns, but muffled blind, as they had to be, which I had heard of but not yet properly seen.

Leant against the wind, we stared out into the lash of the rain. "Do you spot it, Jom?" "Oh ah. I sees it." But I craned and could *not* see, only the ocean itself roughing and spurging, gushing up in great belches and tirades, like boiling milk that was mostly black. But there was something there, was there? Oh yes, could I just make it out? Something like three thin trees massed with cloud and all torn and rolling yet caught together. "You stay put, Haro," said my father. "Here's a light. You shine that. You remember when and what to do? As I told you?" "Yes, Da," I said, afraid with a new affright I should do it wrong and fail him. But he patted my shoulder as if I were full-grown, and went away down the cliff path with the others. Soon enough 1 heard them, those three hundred feet below me, voices thin with distance and the unravelling of the wind, there under the curve of the crumbled white-green cheese of the cliff-face. Though I was quite near the edge, I knew not to go too far along to see, but there was a place there, a sort of notch in the crag, whereby I could see the glimmer of the lamps as they uncovered them. And I knew to do the same then, and I uncovered my lantern too.

So we brought it in. The thing with the clouded trees that was adrift on the earthquake of great waters. The thing:that was a ship.

She smashed to pieces on the rocks below, where the tallest stones were, just under the surface at high tide, against rock and shale, and the faces of angels and devils, and against their broken wings.

This was our Night Work then. In tempest or fog we shone our lights to mislead, and so to guide them home, the ships, and wreck them on the fangs of our cliffs. And when they broke and sank, we took what they had had that washed in to shore. Not human cargo, naturally. That counted for nothing. It must be left, and pushed back, and in worse case pushed under. But the stores, the barrels and casks, the ironware and food and, if uncommon lucky, the gold, those were rescued. While they, the human flotsam, might fare as wind and darkness, and their gods – and we – willed for them, which was never well.

I saw a woman that night, just as the great torn creature of the vessel heaved in and struck her breast, with a scream like mortal death, to flinders on our coast. The woman wore a big fur cloak, and also clutched a child, and in the last minute, in intervals of the storm-roil, I saw her ashen face and agate eyes, and he the same, her son, younger than I, and neither moved nor called, as if they were statues. And then the ship split and the water drank them down. But there was a little dog, too. It swam. It fought the waves, and they let it go by. And when it came to land – by then I craned at the cliff's notch, over the dangerous edge – my father, Jom Abinthorpe, he scooped up the little dog. And my reward for that first night of my Night Work was this little innocent pup, not yet full-grown as neither I was. Because, you will see, a dog can tell no tales, and so may be let live.

But the ship and her crew, and all her people, they went down to the cellars of the sea.

*

I was always out to the Work with the men after that. By the time I was eleven, I would be down along the shore, wading even in the high savage surf among the rocks, with breakers crashing sometimes high over my head, as I helped haul in the casks, and even the broken bits of spars that we might use, when dried and chopped, for our fires.

Hampp is a lorn and lonely place; even now that is so. And when I was a boy, let alone in my father's boyhood, remote as some legendary isle in the waste of the sea. But unlike the isles of Legend, not beautiful, but bony bare. There were but a dozen trees that grew within a ten mile walk of the village, and these bent and crippled by the winter winds. In summer too there were gales and storms, and drought also. What fields were kept behind their low stone walls gave a poor return for great labour. And there was not much bounty given by the ocean, for the fish were often shy. The sea, they said, would as soon eat your boat as give you up a single herring. No, the only true bounty the sea would offer came on those nights of fog or tempest, when it drew a ship toward our coast and seemed to tell us: *Take it then, if you can.* For to do the Work, of course, was not without its perils. And to guide them in too required some skill, hiding the light, then letting out the light, and that just at the proper angle and spot. But finally the sea was our accomplice, was it not, for once drawn into that channel where the teeth of the rocks waited in the tide, and the green skull faces of the outer cliffs trod on into the water and turned their unforgiving cheeks to receive another blow, the ocean itself forced and flung each vessel through. It was the water and the rocks smashed them. We did not do it. We had not such power, nor any power ever. And sometimes one of our own was harmed, or perished. Two men died in those years of my boyhood, swept off by the surge. And one young boy also, younger than I was by then, he broken in a second when half a ship's mast came down on him with all its weight of riven sail.

But ten ships gave up their goods in those years between my ninth and fourteenth birthdays, and I was myself by then a man. And the dog had grown too, my rescued puppy.

I called him Iron, for his strength. He had blossomed from a little, black soft glove of a thing to a tall and long-legged setter, dark as a shadow. He was well-liked in our house, being quiet and mannerly. Also I trained him to catch rabbits, which he killed cleanly and brought me for my mother's cooking. But he hated the sea. Would not go even along the cliff path, let alone to the edge with the notch, or down where the beaches ran when the tide was out. Whenever he saw me set off that way to fish, he would shift once, and stare at me with his great dark eyes that were less full of fear than of disbelief. Next he would turn his back. And here was the thing too; on those nights when the weather was bad, and the watch we posted by roster spied a ship lost and struggling, Iron would vanish entirely, as if he had gone into the very air to hide himself.

I thought after all he did not know what we were at. Certainly, he would eat a bowl of the offal of any beef or bacon or whatever that came to my family's portion out of a wreck. By then, I suppose, it had no savour of the sea.

He had not known either that we let his ship, his own first master likely on that ship, be drowned. Iron only knew, I thought, that my father, and next I, had plucked him from the water after all else was gone.

For a while I had recalled the cloaked woman and her son. I said nothing of it, and put it from me. And soon I had seen other sights like that, and many since that time. The worst was when they tried to save each other, or worse yet, comfort each other. Those poor souls. Yet, like my dog, I would stare then turn my eyes away. I could not help them. Nor would I have, if I could. We lived by what we took from them, lived by their dying. All men want and will to live. Even a dog does, swimming for the shore.

*

Iron is here now. He leans on my leg and the leg of the chair. Strange, for there is iron metal there also, but he does not know this. They are kind, compassionate to have let him in. Well then. Let me tell the rest.

*

I had seen fogs often, and of all sorts. Sea-frets come up like a grey curtain but they melt away at Hampp and are soon gone. The other sort of fog comes in a bank, so thick you think you might carve it off in chunks with your rope-knife. And it will stay days at a time, and the nights with them.

In such a fog sometimes a ship goes by, too far out and never seen, yet such is the weird property of the fog that you will *hear* the ship, hear it creak and the waves slopping on the hull of it, and the stifled breathing of the sails if they are not taken in and furled. It is often worthwhile to go down with extra lanterns then, and range many lamps too along the cliff by the notch, for the ship's people will be looking for landfall and may see the lights, even in the depths of the cloud. But generally they do not. They pass away like ghosts. After they were gone men cursed and shrugged, wasting the lamp-oil as they had and nothing caught. But now and then a ship comes in too far, misled already by the fog and by the deep water that lies in so near around our fanned rocks. For surely some demon made the coast in this place to send seafarers ill, and Hampp its only luck. These ships we would see, or rather the shine of their own lanterns, and they were heard more clearly, and soon they noticed our lamps too, and sometimes we called to them, through the carrying silence, called lovingly in anxious welcome, as if wanting them safe. And so they turned and came to us and ran against the stones.

That night of the last fog I was seventeen years, and Iron my dog about eight, with a flute of grey on his muzzle.

I had been courting a girl of the village, I will not name her. But really I only wanted to lie with her and sometimes she let me, therefore I knew we would needs be wed. So I was preoccupied, sitting by the fire, and then came the knock on the door. "Stir up, Jom Abinthorpe. Haro – waked already? That's good. There is a grey drisk on the sea like blindness, come on in the hour. And one's out there in it, seen her lamps. Well lit she is, some occasion she must have for it. But sailing near, the watch say."

So out we went, and all the village street was full of the men, shouldering their hooks and pikes and hammers, and the lanterns in their muffle giving off only a pale slatey blue. By now I did not even look for my dog Iron, though a few of the men had their dogs with them, the low-slung local breed of Hampp, with snub noses and big shoulders, that might help too pulling the flotsam to shore.

We went along the cliff, near the edge now all of us, but for the youngest boys, three of them, that we posted up by the notch. Then the rest of us went down to the. beach.

It was a curious thing. The fog that night was positioned like a fret, one that stayed only on the sea, and just the faintest tendrils and wisps of it drifted along the beach, like thin ribbons of smoke from off a fire.

The water was well in, creaming clear on the shale, the tide high enough, and not the tips of the fangs below showing. even if the vessel could have made them out. But the ship was anyway held out there, inside the box of the fog, under the fog's lid, like a fly in thick grey amber.

It was a large one, too, and as our neighbour had said, very well lit. In fact crazily much-lit, as if for some festival being held on the decks. We all spoke of it, talking low in case our words might carry, as eerily they did through these fogs. The watchman came and said he reckoned at first the ship had caught fire, to be so lighted up. For she did seem to burn, a ripe, rich, flickering gold. How many lamps? A hundred? More? Or torches maybe, flaming on the rails –

A dog began barking then behind us, a loud strong bell of a bark. Some of the men swore, but my father said, "It's good. Let them know out there land is here. Let them hear and come on. Let's show the lanterns, boys. I'll bet this slut is loaded down with cash and kickshaws – we'll live by it a year and more."

And just then the vessel slewed, and the line of it, all shown in light, altered shape. We knew it had entered the channel and was ready to run to us.

Something came rushing from the other way though, and slammed hard against my legs, so I staggered and almost fell. And turning, I saw my dog there. He was standing four-square on the shale, panting and staring full at me with eyes like green coals. Brighter than our uncovered lamps they seemed.

I said Iron would never come to the sea, nor anywhere near it.

"Wonders don't cease," said my father. "The dog wants to help us with it too. Good lad. Stay close now…"

But Iron turned his eyes of green fire on my father, and barked and belled, iron notes indeed that split the skin off the darkness. And then he howled as if in agony.

"*Quiet*! Quiet, you devil, for the sake of Christ! Do he want to sour our luck?" And next my father shouted at me. I had never seen him afraid, but then I did. And I did not know why. Yet my whole body had fathomed it out, and my heart.

And I grabbed Iron and tried to push him back. "Not now, boy. Go back if you don't care for it. Go home and wait. Ask Ma for a bit of crackling. She knows when you ask. She'll give it you. Go on home, Iron."

And Iron fell silent, but now he sank his teeth in my trouser and began to tug and pull at me. He was a muscular dog, though no longer young, and tall, as I said.

The other men were surly and restless. They did not like this uncanny scene, the flaming ship that drove now full toward us and cast its flame-light on the shore, so the cliffs were shining up like gilt, and the opened lanterns paled to nothing – and the dog, possessed by some horrible fiend, gnawing and pulling, his spit pouring on the wet ground in a silver rain, as if he had the madness.

And then there came the strangest interval. I cannot properly describe how it was. It was as if time stuck fast for a moment, and the moment grew another way, swelling on and on. Even Iron, not letting go of me, stopped his tugging and slavering. And in the hell of his eyes I saw the wild reflection of the gold fire of the ship growing and moving as nothing else, for that moment, might.

"By the Lord," said my father softly, "it's a big one, this crate." It was such a foolish, stupid thing to say. And the last words I ever did hear from my father.

They call them she; that is, the seafarers call each ship *she*. As if she were a woman. But we did not. We could not, maybe, seeing as how we killed them in the Night Work. Just as we ignored the women who died with the ships, and the children who died.

But now I must call it she. The ship, the golden ship.

Believe this or not. as you will.

I do not believe it, and I saw it happen. I never will believe it, not till my last breath is wrung from me. And then, I think, I shall have to.

The moment which had stuck came free and fled. We felt time move, felt it one and all. It was as if the two hands of a clock had stuck, and then unstuck, and the ticking of it and the moving of it began again.

But as time moved, and we with it, it was the *ship* instead that froze. Out there at the edge of the grey slab of the fog, under it, yet visible now as if only through the flimsiest veil. She was well in on the last stretch. She could not stay her course. No vessel, mighty or slight, could have stayed itself now. So far she had driven in, she must hurl on towards her finish against the rocks, and on the faces of the cliffs around, those that crowded out into the sea to meet her. Yet – she did not move. Our clock ran, hers had halted. But oh, something about her there was that moved.

I behold her still in my mind's eye. So tall, six or seven decks she seemed, and so many masts, and all full-laden with her sheets. There was not a man on her that I could see. None. Nor any lamps or torches to light her up so bright that now, almost free of the fog, half she blinded me. No, she blazed from something else, as if she had been coated, every inch of her, in foil of gold, her timbers, her ropes, her sails – coated in gold and then lit up from within by some vast and different fire that never could burn upon this world, but maybe under it – or high above. Like the sun. A sun on fire at her core, and flaming outward. Lampless. *She* was the lantern. How she burned.

Not a sound. No voice, no motion. Even the ocean, quiet as if it too had congealed – but it moved, and the waves came in and lapped our boots, and they made, the waves, no sound at all.

And then the dog, my Iron, he began to worry at me, hard, hard, and 1 felt his teeth go through the trouser and he fastened them in my very leg. I shouted out in pain and turned, not knowing what I did, as if to cuff him or thrust him away. And by that the spell on me was rent.

I found I was running. I ran and sobbed and called out to God, and Iron ran by me and then just ahead of me. It seemed to me he had me fast by an invisible cord. I had no choice but to fly after him. And yet, oddly, a part of me did not want to. I wanted only to go back and stand at the sea's brink and look at the ship – but Iron dragged me and I could not release myself from the phantom chain.

I was up on the cliff path when I heard them screaming behind me and some one hundred and fifty feet below. This checked me. I fell and my ankle turned and a bone snapped, but I never heard the noise it made, for there was no sound in that place but for the shrieking of the men, and one of them my father.

Of course, I could no longer stir either forward or back. I lay and twisted, feeling no pain in my foot or leg, and stared behind me.

And this is what I saw. Every man upon that shore, every lad, even the youngest of them, ten years old, and the dogs, those too, and those screaming too as if caught in a trap, all these living creatures – they were racing forward, not as I had inland, but out toward the sea, toward the fog, toward the golden glare of the ship – but they howled in terror as they did so, men and beasts, nor did they run on the earth. They ran on *water*. They ran through the *air*. The three children from the cliff-top – they too – off into the air they had been slung, wailing and weeping, and whirling outward like the rest. And up and up they all pelted, as if racing up a cliff, but no land was there under their feet. Only the ship was there ahead of them, and she waited. The thin veil of the outer fog hid nothing. The light of her was too fierce for anything to be hidden. The men and the boys and the dogs ran straight up and forward, unable to stay their course until, one by one, they smashed and splintered on the cliff-face of the golden ship, on the golden fangs and cheek and rock of the ship. I saw so clear their bones break on her, and the scarlet gunshot of their blood that burst and scattered away, not staining her. As they did not either, but fell down like empty sacks into the jet black water. Till all was done.

After which, she turned aside, gently drifting, herself as if weightless and empty, and having moved all round she returned into the fog, under fog, and under night and under silence. She slid away into the darkness. Her glow went soft and melted out. The fog closed over. The night closed fast its door, and only then I heard the waves that sucked the shale, and the pain rose in my leg like molten fire.

*

They will be hanging me tomorrow. That is fair; it is what I came to the mainland for, and made my confession. At first I never said why I had had to. How I had crawled up the path, with my dog helping me. And in the village of Hampp, all the faces, and seeing that each one knew yet would not speak of it. My mother, she like the others. How I stayed two months there, alone, until I could walk with a stick, and by then almost everyone had left the place, the empty houses like damp caves. And then I left there also. But I came here, and my dog quite willing to cross water, and I found a judge, and was judged.

Men have gone to search the waters off the coast, below Hampp. They find nothing of the dead ships. We took all there was to take. As for corpses, bones, theirs and ours are all mingled, like the gargoyles and angels in the stones of the beach.

When I did tell the priest of the ship, he refused to believe me. So I have told you now and let it be written down, since I was never learned to make my letters.

You see there is an iron manacle on my ankle, but it is quite a comfort. It supports the aching bone that snapped. The rope perhaps will support my neck and then that will be crushed, or it will also break, and then I will leave this world to go into the other place, from which golden things issue out.

It is kind they let me say farewell to Iron, my dog. Yes, even though he is no longer mine. They have told me a widow woman, quite wealthy, is eager to have him, since her young son is so taken with Iron, and Iron with him likewise. I have witnessed it myself, only this morning from this window, how the dog walked with the child along the street, Iron wagging his strong old tail that is only a touch grey to one side. The child is a fair boy too, with dark sad eyes that clear when he looks at Iron. And certainly his mother is wealthy, for her cloak is of heavy fur.

That is all then. That is all I need to say.

No. I am not sorry for my village. No. I am not afraid to go to the scaffold. Or to die. No, I am not afraid of these things. It is the other place I fear. The place that comes after. The place they are in, the men of Hampp, and my father too. The place where she came from. The Ship. I cannot even tell you how afraid I am, of that.

They Left the City at Night

Sarah Singleton

They left the city at night. Anna was sitting in her bedroom when the men arrived. She was dressed in furs, staring in the mirror. Her candlelit reflection was faded and insubstantial. She had become a ghost already.

The men didn't knock. They ran up the stairway, boots clopping on the marble steps, carrying with them the bitter cold of the night, the perfume of vodka and churned snow.

"Anna, it's time," the elder man said. He too wore a fur coat and hat. The younger man, in long boots and a military jacket, picked up the leather case by the door. On a bed draped in crimson, between creased sheets, a baby began to cry. Anna stood up and lifted her son into her arms, pressing her lips against his smooth forehead. She ran her fingers over the lick of fine, honey-coloured hair.

"We'll take good care of him," the elder man said. His voice was gruff and impatient but not unkind. An old woman, the nanny, stepped into the doorway and held out her arms. Anna was shaking. Now, at the very moment, could she do as she had undertaken? They watched her, all four, the father and son, the old woman, the infant Evgeni, just six weeks old, so new-hatched he was still a piece of her, as though the severance of the umbilicus had not, in fact, split them one from the other. Her flesh cried out at the prospect of separation.

"Come, Anna. We must hurry," the elder man said. He moved towards her, prepared to take the baby forcibly if needs be. But Anna stepped aside, avoiding him, and placed her baby instead in the arms of the nanny. The baby clasped a strand of Anna's hair in his fist, tugging painfully as she drew away, leaving several golden strands in his fingers. The old woman bent over the child and took him from the room.

"It's time," the elder man repeated. Without a word, Anna drew on her fur hat and gloves, fastened the buttons on her coat and followed the two men out of the house.

Snow lay over St Petersburg like an enchantment, covering the

city's habitual coat of soot and filth. Lights burned in the windows of
the grand houses, even so late. Gutters and railings carried baroque
ornamentations of ice. High above the roofs, stars poured in a cold
white river, brother to the Neva, flowing through the city, now sealed
beneath a crown of dense, grey ice.

The carriage rumbled through the streets. Inside, Anna attended to
the instructions of her father-in-law. He held lantern, and in its pale
light gave her papers and complicated instructions. His agents and
friends would help, he said. She would not be alone. As they drew away
from the centre of St Petersburg the lights grew fewer. The father-in-
law finally fell silent. His younger son stared at Anna, his eyes fever-
bright, clutching her bag upon his lap. Anna gazed through the window
at a darkness that grew more palpable with every passing mile. She felt
nothing, as though her body were a shell from which all light and
warmth was slowly bleeding away, leaving only an exterior; a brittle,
empty form.

The carriage drew to a halt at a crossroads on the edge of the city.
The driver called out, words Anna couldn't hear. Her father-in-law
jumped down from the carriage and strode across the snowy road to a
second vehicle, which she could make out only dimly despite a brace of
carriage lamps. Words were exchanged – then he returned, gestured for
her to climb out and, grasping her again by the elbow, hurried her to
the other carriage.

"There," he said, settling her into a seat, placing rugs over her lap.
The son placed her leather bag on the floor beside her feet. The father
looked at her once, picked up her gloved hand, and pressed it to his
lips.

"Goodbye Anna Arkadyevna. Send Anatolyi my love," he said.
"Tell him – tell him –" His voice faltered: "Tell him to be safe, that we
are proud of him, that we will never forget him."

He shut the carriage door, exchanged another word with the driver
and backed away. A whip cracked. The driver called out to the horses
and the carriage jerked forward. The wooden wheels lurched over ruts
in the road, splintering long bones of ice. Anna gripped the seat.
Beyond the window she saw her father-in-law, still carrying the lantern,
standing in the middle of the dark, snowy road, and beside him the
silent younger son. She would never see them again, nor her friends,
nor the city, nor the infant son she had conceived and carried and

nursed. It was all over: all.

They travelled through the night and into the late, January dawn. Anna could see little of her surroundings. She slept for a while, a period of mental vacancy without any dreams, and woke to see pine forests covered with snow beneath a leaden sky. She hadn't spoken with the driver, nor clearly seen him the night before. Where was he taking her? She couldn't remember the instructions her father-in-law had given. Hunger came, and went. She slept again, and woke shivering with cold. Later in the morning the forest gave way to agricultural land, snowy fields laced with frozen streams. The carriage drew to a halt outside a country house and the unseen driver jumped down from his box, opened the door and helped Anna descend. His scarf was wrapped around his face, his fur hat low over his brows, so Anna could see only his blue eyes, reddened by hours of cold and darkness. The horses, heads hanging, plastered with mud and filth, were wretched with exhaustion.

"Shall I take my bag?" She was helpless, not knowing what to do, a package to be passed between strangers. The driver nodded. He gestured to the door of the farmhouse.

"They're expecting you," he said.

The farmer and his wife were relatives of her father-in-law, prosperous people with a son studying in the city and a daughter just married to a neighbouring landowner. The farmer's wife welcomed Anna with open arms, and evinced sincere and cheerful delight to be taking part in an intrigue. Anna was guided to a comfortable chair by the fire in the kitchen, given hot milk to drink, bread and a bowl of mutton soup. After an hour or so, she was ushered to her feet again and out into the yard where a black horse stood, saddled and ready, a groom standing by its head.

"I understand you're a strong rider, Anna Arkadyevna," the farmer's wife said. "You will need to be. The next town is four hours away. Just follow the road – it's easy enough, and no one has reported any wolves this winter. Keep up a good pace to arrive before dark. I hope the weather is kind to you." The woman, square and stout with thick, iron-grey hair, put her hand to her forehead and stared anxiously at the sky. She passed Anna a piece of paper.

"Here is the name and address of your next contact. They will be expecting you. Travel safely."

The groom helped Anna mount and tied her bag to the back of the saddle. The horse stamped its hooves and tugged at the bridle, cold and impatient to be moving.

"Thank you," Anna said, gathering the reins. "Thank you for your help." Her breasts were sore and tight with milk her son would never drink. Her body ached as though she'd been beaten. The horse danced in the snow, snatching its bit. Riding astride, she closed her legs against its sides and it sprang into a canter, throwing crusts of snow from its hooves. Slowly the farm disappeared; when she glanced back the white huddle of buildings was swallowed by the greater white of the receding landscape.

*

The road was silent. The horse slowed to a rhythmic trot, the sound muffled by the hard-packed snow. They passed vast fields, the occasional stew of peasant homes, where mud churned the snow in yards littered with straw and manure, and coils of smoke rose from the huddled buildings. She encountered an old woman, bent under a burden of sticks, two boys herding geese, a stout country gentleman (a doctor perhaps?) on horseback as she was. He tipped his hat as he passed. Otherwise, only the limitless winter landscape spreading away, the white horizon melting into the pale sky.

Snow began to fall. The horse slowed to a plod. Soft flakes settled on the animal's mane. Anna's hands and feet grew numb. She lapsed into a dream, allowing the horse to find its own way through a swirl of white that swallowed up the rest of the world. She closed her eyes.

The horse stopped. Anna fell over its shoulder onto the ground. She'd fallen asleep. But for how long? She tried to stand but her feet were stones of ice. She clutched at the reins, hauled herself up. The snow had cleared a little. The road – where was the road? They were standing among naked birch trees, in a clearing. The horse's hoof prints had already been obliterated by the falling snow. A trail of sorts, only just discernible – would this take them back to the road, or lead them deeper into the wood? Hopelessness welled, a bubble of it, bringing tears and a desolate ache of longing for the life she had left behind. What did it matter, if she died here, alone in the cold? But Tolya was waiting for her, mustn't forget. Tolya was the reason for her exile. Except that she hadn't seen him for six long months, hadn't seen him since the birth of their son, since his arrest.

She led the horse forwards, along the track. Snow crunched beneath her boots. High in a birch tree three crows, blots of ink, ruffled their feathers and cawed as she passed. How far to the road? But there was no road. Instead the trees opened up and Anna saw a summer house standing before her, and beyond it, the iced grey of a lake. The horse stopped abruptly, threw its head up and stared at the house. How inviting it was, at first glance, with tall windows, kirtled with snow.

"Come along," she said to the horse, tugging at the reins. The animal snorted, reluctant to move any closer. A shadow appeared at a window, perhaps the light reflecting on the glass. Anna narrowed her eyes and the shadow moved, momentarily resolving itself, becoming an old woman with pale hair. Anna waved, but the shadow broke into pieces. She shivered. It would be dark soon. The place would have a stable, surely? So it proved, with damp straw underfoot and musty, aged hay. It was the best she could do.

The door at the back of the house was locked. Anna peered through the window into the darkness. How to get inside? She walked around the house, but the door at the front was also locked. The prospect of breakage wasn't pleasing, but what choice did she have? The sun was sinking behind the birch trees, the frost crystallising on the surface of the snow. She picked up a stone from the ground and smashed it against a window. The glass cracked, splintered and fell into the house. Anna slid her hand inside, turned the latch, and slowly raised the window. She lifted her skirts and climbed inside.

How long had the house stood empty, Anna wondered. Her footsteps echoed against the walls. Dried leaves lay upon the dusty wooden floors in vacant rooms. A double staircase from the hall led to three large bedrooms with huge wooden beds. In one, a vast mirror hung from the wall, gold-framed, fly-blown and dirty.

She had nothing to eat, no light, nor the means to make a fire. As night fell, darkness flowed into the house, settling on the ground floor and slowly inking in the stairway and the upper rooms. Anna curled up on one of the giant beds, already shivering. She closed her eyes, trying to ignore the cold. She thought about her baby, wrapped up warm in his grandfather's house, and her body ached with the yearning to hold him. And Tolya, where was he? Far away, perhaps alone and cold in the winter night, as she was. Anna wrapped her arms around herself. The wind whined through the window. Downstairs the draught picked at the leaves lying on the floor. Her mind drifted.

"Anna. Anna." Tolya lent over her, placed his hand against her cheek. She was dreaming, let herself be carried by the dream. "Wake up, Anna," he said. Warmth, utterly delicious, spread over her body. She was lying in the garden behind Tolya's house in St Petersburg, beneath trees covered in blossom. Tolya sat down beside her and grasped her hands, smiling. He looked very young and beautiful, as she remembered him from their first meeting, with pale, perfect skin and thick chestnut hair brushed back from his forehead. He bent down and kissed her cheek, smiling still.

"Will you marry me?" he said.

"When you are free, of course I shall," she answered, as she'd done many times before. Tolya was already married. His wife lived on her country estate. Anna was his mistress in the city.

Anna soaked up the sun's heat, enjoying the warmth on her face, revelling in the knowledge of her lover's proximity, the contact between them. Blossom danced above her head, scattering beads of sunlight. A disturbing recollection needled her mind.

"You were arrested," she said. "How are you here?" Anatolyi was a lieutenant in the Russian cavalry. On December 14 he and other high-ranking officers had marched armed troops into the city. They wanted freedom and reform – the end of serfdom, the beginnings of democracy. But the uprising was beaten down, its leaders arrested, executed or exiled. Anatolyi was stripped of his rank and titles, taken from the city and sent to live out the rest of his days in Siberia.

"Are you coming with me, Anna?" he asked. "The church has decreed the wives of the Decembrists should consider themselves widows. My legal marriage is over. Will you follow me to Siberia?"

And so she had agreed. In truth she had been persuaded by Anatolyi's family, and she had none of her own to support her, though she hadn't known she was pregnant and would have to leave her baby behind. For a moment the dream frayed, revealing behind its unsubstance the reality of the empty house. Anna shifted on the bed and briefly opened her eyes. What could she see? A shape like smoke, leaning over her as Anatolyi had done in the dream. She remembered how the light on the window had taken on the form of an old woman. This time the old woman had knitted herself from the darkness in the room. Anna closed her eyes again. The presence, while uncanny, was also comforting. She wanted to return to Anatolyi and the sunshine.

"Anna," he called again. "Wake-up, sleepy." Yes, she was back in the garden. She sat up and put her arms around Tolya. He kissed her gently on the mouth, kissed again, sliding his tongue between her lips. Desire blossomed, a bud opening in the pit of her belly. Tolya squeezed his hand into the top of her dress, pressing his fingers against her breast. Then he took his mouth from hers, though his head was still close to hers, and said:

"Come inside."

"No, stay here. No-one will see us." She wanted to stay in the sun.

"Come inside," he said again, stepping away, tugging her after him. And Anna succumbed. They hurried into the house, to Anatolyi's room where the tall French windows were open and the summer air toyed with the gauze curtains.

Had she ever been so happy? The moment was all perfection, an unreal distillation of the long months of their affair. Such languorous hours of love-making, of talking, laughing and sharing. She breathed the clean, masculine perfume of his skin, relished the sensation of his hands on her body. They chatted idly, reweaving the story of their affair, recalled the time of their meeting at a coffee house in the city, famous for its radical clientele, and the argument that broke out, the flowers he sent in amends... Anna sighed. Here, in this dream place, the sense of bliss and sunshine, of homecoming, this rapture, rose to a crescendo; for a moment she hovered, seemingly suspended, until the bubble of heat and light and love expired, as though the memories, the passions had been drawn out of her and sucked away. Anatolyi, the garden and the sunlight faded and disappeared. She woke up, stiff with cold, aching with loss for the emotion conjured up inside a dream. She hugged her arms around herself, shivering. Perhaps she should get up, walk about, try and warm herself. The window revealed itself, a faint pallor painted on the otherwise featureless darkness; the moon had risen over the trees and shone upon the snow. She closed her eyes again, willing sleep to obliterate the long hours before sunrise.

A little boy ran down the stairs and through the hallway to the front door, which stood open. Anna stood at the bedroom door, looking down at him. Sunlight, dust, pollen made the house golden.

"Evgeni!" She followed him. The boy stopped, looked back over his shoulder, then ran on out of the door and into the summer heat.

Anna hurried after him. Evgeni (how old was he now – about seven?) laughed and skipped away, around the house to the lake. Sunlight glittered on the water. On a wooden pier over the water, Anatolyi lay on his back with his arms outspread. The lightest of winds touched the reeds at the lake's margin.

Evgeni jumped over his father, and clambered down from the pier into a rowing boat. Six white geese flapped away as he splashed with the oars. Anna laughed.

"So, if you won't study, will you at least let me share your boat?" she said.

Anatolyi sat up abruptly and cursed, his son having showered him with water.

"Wait," he said. "Wait for your mother." Anna trotted along the pier and stepped down into the boat.

"I'll row," the boy said. "You sit at the front of the boat."

"Are you sure? Can you manage?"

"Yes. Father taught me."

Anna glanced back. The boat was already drifting from the pier, where Anatolyi was now sitting with his legs hanging over the side, shirt damp with lake water. He nodded:

"He'll be fine."

Evgeni fooled with the oars, struggling to control them. The boat turned on some unseen current. Anna stared over the side into the grey water, seeing the dark weeds and the darker grey of a carp. At last they began to make some purposeful progress over the water. The pier, the house, grew smaller. The birch trees repeated themselves on the surface of the lake. Except for the slight splash of the oars, all was silent.

"I told you I could do it," Evgeni said. He was proud and smiling, his young face damp with perspiration from the heat and his effort.

"So you did. And you were right." She lay back, shading her face with her arm. The slight movement of the boat was soothing. The sun made her drowsy, and in this moment before sleep a cold, dark corner of her mind reminded her that she was in fact already asleep and this idyll of lake and sun (and son) was a fantasy soon to be snatched away.

"What's that?" Evgeni had stopped rowing and pointed across the lake, away from the house. Anna sat up. As she opened her eyes the sunlight dazzled.

"What is it?"

"There, on the water. Ahead of us."

They were a long way from the lakeside now. Anna glanced back at the house, still staring at them over the distance.

"There! You see?"

Anna peered over her son's shoulder.

"Oh yes. I see." A large, black shadow lay on the water, seemingly without a source. Like an ink blot, it extinguished the glint and glitter of light on the lake. Although Evgeni had let go of the oars, the boat continued forwards, and the shadow grew nearer. Anna felt the clutch of panic. She grabbed the oars.

"Perhaps there's something under the water. What if we run into it?" The boat gained speed, the current ripped the oars from her hands and they slipped through the rowlocks and dropped onto the surface of the lake. Evgeni dipped his hand over the side of the boat, reaching for the water as the prow cut into the patch of black.

"No, leave!" Anna shouted, but too late, Evgeni lost his balance. He slid, headfirst, into the water and sank like a stone.

As soon as the boy had gone, the boat stopped moving, as though pulled by a rope which now had gone slack. Anna leaned over the side, frantic, calling out her son's name. Where was he?

"Evgeni! Evgeni!" Far away on the pier, Anatolyi was lying down, oblivious to the accident. Anna stood up in the boat and waved her arms, desperate to get his attention. The boat rocked beneath her and, in their wake, the oars slowly floated away.

"Evgeni!" There he was – staring up through the black water, eyes open, hands reaching up towards her. His hair floated in the water, his lips parted and slow, white bubbles drifted between them, up and up to the surface of the lake. Anna dropped to her knees and plunged her arms into the water to grab him. Too deep – he was too deep. She lent over the side of the boat, further and further, till the boat reached a precarious tilt. Why didn't he swim towards her? What was holding him down? She strained towards him, her son, drowning. The boat tipped and she dropped into the water. The shocking cold embraced her. Sun, light, the summer scene, were obliterated in an instant. Evgeni was beneath her still, hands still outstretched, slowly sinking into the depths.

Anna made her own slow descent into the darkness, reaching out for her son, but he sank faster, falling away, until he entirely disappeared into the bowels of the lake. She felt such loss, like a rending physical breakage, as though her passion for her son was sucked from her flesh and blood just as the water drew the life-heat from her body.

"Evgeni!" she shouted one more time, and the water flooded into her throat and down to her lungs, ice-cold. She clutched her throat, fighting to breathe, choking on the water.

Upright, on the bed in the old house, her hands on her neck as if she were throttling herself. Anna sucked the biting air into her lungs, as though, in accordance with the dream, she had been holding her breath. Evgeni had been taken from her – the meaning of the dream wasn't difficult to fathom. She had lost him. He was dead to her, wasn't he? Perhaps, more accurately, she was dead to him. He would never know, nor have any memory of her.

She climbed from the bed and went to the window. The night was drawing away now. Pale light bloomed over the bare birch trees. Moonlight glimmered on the frozen lake. Anna put her hand to her cheek, feeling how cold she was, though strangely she had stopped shivering. For the moment at least, the dreams had purged her emotions. She thought of Tolya and Evgeni, tentatively raised them in her mind, and felt a new detachment, as though they were characters in a story no longer her own. Her heart had been numbed, as her body was now indifferent to the cold.

The old woman had returned, though Anna understood she had been her constant companion since her first arrival in the house. As Anna stood at the window, the old woman stood at her shoulder, her shrunken hand rested gently on Anna's arm. Without turning to look, Anna said:

"How long have you been here?"

The other didn't reply but her hand pressed more firmly on Anna's arm.

"I'm not afraid of you," Anna said. "Why's that?" Far away, on the hems of the lake where dead reeds poked from the ice, a fox emerged like a shadow and tip-toed through the snow. Anna watched the fox and then turned to the companion who had walked beside her in the house and had so closely studied her as she slept.

The old woman had a long, heavy dress that dragged on the floor, a cloak with a hood, a coil of grey hair, an aged face – these were not so much evident as suggested, the form engendered from the shadows in the house, and not entirely substantial despite the pressure of a hand on Anna's arm. The woman hinted, with a nod of her head, that Anna should sleep again. She guided her, like a child, and indicated she lie down on the bed. The old woman sat down beside her and took Anna's hand in her own. The ghost's hand was warm.

Anna closed her eyes.

When she opened them again, a warm, golden light flooded the room and the old woman had gone. Anna rose from the bed and looking through the window, observed that autumn had come. The leaves on the birch trees were sulphur yellow, the mass of the forest beyond, scarlet and bronze. Dead leaves lay on the bare floor of the bedroom, tumbling around her feet. When she walked from the bedroom the leaves followed behind her, in a train. The front door stood wide open and a young woman dressed in a smart navy-blue riding outfit strode into the hall, dropped her hat and whip on a table, and without speaking to Anna, marched into the living room. Anna followed. The dried leaves whispered around her feet.

The room was tastefully furnished and very comfortable, with a fire burning in the hearth, plump sofas and cushions, bookshelves, and paintings of landscapes on the walls. The young woman sat down beside a table where tea and cake waited on a tray. Anna took the seat opposite, placed a cake on a plate and stared at her host. Observing the room, the young woman and the leaves now clambering onto her lap Anna understood she was dreaming again.

"Mother," Anna said. The young woman glanced at her then. Their eyes met with a kind of defiant shock.

"Anna," the woman said. "What are you doing here? I left you at home." Anna had been a nuisance, always.

"I was travelling to Siberia, to be in exile with my lover. After his arrest, well, his family wanted me off their hands."

"But they wanted your son," the young woman said, sipping her tea. "You made a mess of things."

"Falling for Anatolyi? Yes I can see that was a mistake. I had no idea where it would lead."

"Having a child," the young woman said, raising her hand. "That is always a mistake."

Anna felt again the acute, unique pain of her mother's dismissal. She thought she had left it behind, this child's sense of loss.

"Yes, a nuisance," Anna said. "I expect it bored you, having a child. Diminished your value."

"As it has for you," the woman jumped in. "Look at you now, on your own, with nothing."

Tears sprang to Anna's eyes.

"Anatoyli's waiting for me."

"Yes, in a prison. Is that what you wanted?"

The future rose up, the long years of cold and dirt and drudgery. The past receded, a glass globe glittering with light and comfort and grandeur, already seeming to belong to someone else. It was snatched away.

She pressed the heels of her hands to her face. A sudden sense of panic rose up, a clutching onto life. She jumped to her feet and sprang at her mother, hands in claws, wanting to tear her in pieces.

But the scene dissolved. Woman, sofa, fire all disappeared. Anna was bent over on her hands and knees on the floor in an empty room. With some difficulty, she climbed to her feet and made her way up the long, arduous stairway to her bedroom. A dark shape lay on the bed. Was she asleep now, and dreaming, or wide awake? It was no longer possible to tell for sure.

She looked in the huge old mirror on the wall, striated with cracks on the left side. Black freckles covered the silver beneath the glass. It was light now. The sun had risen over the snowbound forest and the iced lake. Her reflection was broken and multiplied but still she could see an aged face, a coil of dun hair and a body obscured by the dragging dress.

The young woman on the bed got up, brisk and purposeful. She swept by Anna and the eddies of her passing broke up the reflection Anna saw in the mirror, sent it swirling like a cloud of ash which only slowly reassembled itself into the drab figure she had seen before.

She moved, very slowly, to the window, brought her face to the glass and looked out over the white yard where the new Anna led out the horse and climbed lightly into the saddle. Alone in the house, Anna turned over her memories. Of course, there was nothing left. Everything had been taken.

The new Anna urged the horse into a trot and set off through the gates, down the lane and back towards the road. She would not go to Siberia, of course. This woman was stronger than Anna. She would return to St Petersburg, create another, more brilliant life.

Once she glanced back, no doubt seeing, as Anna had on her arrival, the hint of a face at the window, in the darkness of the house.

The God Particle

Steve Longworth

"Never be absolutely certain of anything." (Bertrand Russell)

The Director, to say the least, was non-plussed. He stared at his unexpected guest for an uncomfortably long time before hesitatingly extending his right hand.

"Er…welcome to CERN," he said at last.

"Thank you," said God. "I'm very pleased to be here."

With the inauguration of its brand new Large Hadron Collider – the world's biggest ever atom smasher – the Director and his team at the European Organisation for Nuclear Research had set out to prove the existence of the Higgs boson, the so-called 'God Particle' that was theorised to be the source of mass for all other sub-atomic particles.

CERN's scientists were also looking for evidence of physics beyond the theoretical framework of the current 'standard model' but the first experiment with their brand new multi-billion-Euro toy had succeeded in a way that even their most 'out-there' theoretical thinkers had failed to imagine.

An awkward silence descended. Well, the Director felt awkward. God simply radiated serenity.

"Can I get you anything?" offered the Director. "Tea? Coffee? Water?" If you don't fancy water you can always turn it into wine, he thought, then immediately regretted this. Oh God! he thought. If He really is omnipotent He probably heard that thought. Or knew I was going to think it even before I thought it. And I wonder if He was offended by me thinking 'Oh God!'

"No thank you," said God, "Though I might trouble you later to use your phone. I ought to call my Representative On Earth."

"And that would be…"

"Why the Pope of course," said God with kindly smile.

"Certainly, certainly," replied the Director, nervously fingering his collar and flicking at a non-existent fleck of dust on his sleeve.

"And don't worry about the mind-reading," said God, "I've turned it off for this particular manifestation. I will experience all interactions in real-time. Well, in your version of real-time at any rate."

Silence.

"I imagine you have many questions," said God.

You're not kidding! thought the Director. He turned the flat screen of one of his computer monitors towards his guest.

"Your, uh, arrival inside the Large Hadron Collider coincided with the appearance in our detectors of these previously unknown subatomic particles," and he pointed to a pair of tracks on the monitor.

"Ah yes," said God. "Ambiguons."

"Ambiguons?" echoed the Director.

"Yes," replied God. "When you isolate a Higgs boson it immediately releases a quantum of ambiguous energy and decays into two ambiguons, a reality particle and an anti-reality particle. These are what you have here."

"But how did…"

"The pulse of ambiguous energy created in your experiment caused the spontaneous symmetry breaking of reality which induced the phase transition that brought me here."

The Director's head buzzed.

"The breaking of reality? Anti-reality?"

"Does this come as a surprise?"

"Well…" and he searched for a reply. "I'm sorry but we always believed that if the Higgs boson existed that it would decay into top anti-top quark pairs. But…anti-reality?"

God smiled indulgently.

"This sort of thing always comes as something of a shock. Do you know Piet Hut?"

"Of course," said the Director, "he's an Astrophysicist at the Institute For Advanced Study at Princeton."

"Indeed. As he has pointed out, Copernicus upset the moral order by dissolving the strict distinction between heaven and earth. Darwin did the same by dissolving the strict distinction between humans and other animals. The next step is the dissolution of the strict distinction between fiction and reality."

The Director snorted contemptuously. Then, remembering whom he was talking to, he started to stutter an apology.

God waved his hand dismissively, "Don't worry about it. But consider the impact of Copernicus on the prevailing psychology of the 16th century; and of Darwin on the 19th century. The paradigm change they precipitated was nothing short of a cataclysm; and now it's your turn."

The Director breathed deeply. Quantum physics was a field that required the ability to think outside the box, but what was happening now required one to think that perhaps the box didn't actually exist in the first place. But if you could embrace the idea that a positron was actually an electron travelling backwards in time, was it such a big leap to accept that reality had an anti-state?

"Cataclysm?" repeated the Director.

"A sudden violent upheaval. That's what you have here, isn't it?"

*

"Perhaps," said Dr. Chetty, "the main determinant of the manifestation of God is the psychosocial milieu into which the influence of ambiguous energy is released."

Father Mendes raised an eyebrow.

Dr Chetty circled his hands at the sides of his head in an expansive gesture. "Where are we? In the heart of Christian Europe. God has appeared in the form of the prevailing cultural archetype. One might almost say prevailing caricature. What would have happened if we had built a particle accelerator in India and tried to run the same experiment there? Perhaps Lord Shiva would have appeared rather than a bearded elderly male Caucasian in flowing white robes."

Manuel Mendes, Director of the Vatican observatory, doodled a spiral galaxy in the margin of his briefing notes.

"We are certain that this is not simply an elaborate hoax?"

The Director sighed. He would have loved nothing more.

"Sadly, yes."

The astronomer-priest placed his pen on the conference room table. As the most senior Catholic physicist in the Vatican at the time the Holy Father had taken God's call, he had been dispatched to CERN post-haste.

"Does anyone else have a theory?"

An eclectic mix of eminent scientists, holy men, politicians and PR gurus had been hastily convened at CERN headquarters astride the Franco-Swiss border near Geneva. The Director glanced out of the window at the chaos outside. It was impossible to keep a lid on this. A rapidly drafted security force was struggling to control the swelling multitude. The irony was not lost on him. The site of the world's biggest-ever scientific experiment would soon be the world's most famous religious shrine.

The President of the European Commission grunted.

"How many theories do you want?" He gestured at his laptop. They all knew what he meant. The Net was on fire with theories – cosmological, religious, conspiratorial, to name but three categories. A wave of tension-relieving laughter rippled through the room. Even Father Mendes chuckled.

"I think what the good Father means," said Professor Bonnaire, "is 'does anyone have a theory we can test?'" She flicked rhythmically at her lower lip with an earpiece of her spectacles, a behaviour loop indicating deep mental engagement. "I agree. After all, what does 'anti-reality' actually mean?"

"We did ask God to elaborate," replied the Director, "but He said it was important that we work it out for ourselves."

"Where is He now?" asked The President.

"He requested a room to Himself so that He could meditate. We've given Him one of the offices out of sight of the public."

"Why does God need to meditate?" asked one of the PR experts.

"Is He God?" asked another.

"Well, if He's not God what's going on?" demanded the Chief Rabbi of Geneva and at that the room descended into an argumentative ruck.

The Director held up his hands. "Ladies and Gentleman, please, please." Order returned. The Director sighed and rubbed his eyes. It had been a long day and he had had little sleep since God had appeared. "I think we need to take a break. Let's reconvene in an hour."

*

The Director knocked quietly on the office door.

"Come in," said God. He stood from the lotus position and

gestured the Director towards a chair. "You look tired. Have you made any progress?"

"Not really. How are you?"

"I'm God," said God, "how would you expect Me to feel?"

"I'm an atheist," said the Director. "I have no expectations."

"An atheist? Still?" said God, eyebrows raised archly.

"Yes," replied the Director, "still an atheist."

"So who do you think I am?" asked God in amusement.

"I don't know yet. Your arrival here is certainly a challenge to our model of the Universe, but not a fatal one. This is not the death of science. It is a threat, certainly, but also an opportunity; an opportunity for deeper understanding. You know what Sir John Vane used to say?"

"Of course," said God. "'Never ignore the unusual.' I should think from the crowds gathering outside your institution that you are having great difficulty ignoring Me. But don't worry. I have to go soon."

"Go where?"

"Go back," said God. "There's work to be done."

*

They had reconvened in the conference room. Dr. Chetty was holding forth again.

"Perhaps magic and religious experiences occur when the environment contains a surplus of anti-reality particles. Perhaps occult rituals and holy ceremonies are ways of creating an imbalance in the ratio of ambiguons that keeps our own reality stable. Perhaps there are natural or random fluctuations in the ratio that correspond with the emergence of myths and legends and the visionary experiences of great religious leaders."

"Double Dutch," ventured one of the PR gurus.

"Double Dutch?" repeated Dr Chetty. "You think that's what I've been speaking?"

"No doc," replied the guru, "I think that's what you've been smoking."

Dr Chetty laughed. "Not allowed by my religion, I'm afraid."

"You're religious?" asked Father Mendes. The Chilean clergyman was curious. "How does that square with being a theoretical physicist?"

"As a Hindu I see no contradiction," replied the Indian mathematician. "In contemporary usage Hinduism is also sometimes referred to as Sanātana Dharma, a Sanskrit phrase meaning 'eternal law'. That is what we seek here at CERN, to uncover the eternal law behind the universe."

"A theoretical physicist and a practicing Hindu," mused the EC President. He smiled. "Isn't that somewhat…ambiguous?"

"Dr Chetty laughed again. "My dear Mr President, everything is ambiguous if you contemplate it for long enough. Hinduism itself is not one single simple religion but a complex and diverse system of thought with beliefs spanning all the way from monotheism through polytheism to atheism. How ambiguous is that? Did you know that the swastika is a Hindu symbol? It indicates auspiciousness. What could have been less auspicious for mid-twentieth century Europe than the rise of the Nazis?"

"Electrons and photons, are they particles or waves?" said Father Mendes. "This is the ultimate ambiguity at the heart of quantum physics."

Professor Bonnaire turned to the priest. "Vatican astronomer?" She looked at him over the top of her spectacles. "With the Roman Catholic Church's track record on the suppression of scientific truth, and of the nature of the solar system in particular, surely your role is particularly ambiguous?"

Father Mendes shrugged and spread his hands.

The Director rapped the conference table impatiently.

"Yes, yes, all very fascinating, but can we please get back to the point? We are here to discuss the apparently spontaneous manifestation of God inside the Large Hadron Collider during an experiment in which we fired protons at anti-protons. How do we explain what occurred? What is real and what is apparent?"

"I'm not a scientist," said the EC President, "so you will have to bear with me. Surely what has happened here is scientifically impossible. It *must* be proof positive for the existence of God."

"No," said Professor Bonnaire, "all that it proves is that we don't fully understand the laws of physics and the structure of the universe. But this event is not inconsistent with current theories of the origin of the cosmos."

"Exactly!" exclaimed Dr Chetty. "The multiverse!"

"The multiverse?" said one of the PR gurus. "Sounds like the Chilean national anthem."

Father Meneds laughed. "You are right. It does go on a bit longer than necessary. But Professor Bonnaire is correct. The multiverse theory says that our universe is only one of many 'pocket universes' created by the Big Bang. In all directions beyond the event horizon at the edge of our observable universe may lie a whole patchwork quilt of 'pocket universes' each one with slightly different versions of the laws of physics. There is nothing intrinsically 'fundamental' about what we refer to as the fundamental laws of the universe. They may simply be local 'by-laws' that came about randomly."

"But how could your multiverse explain what has happened?" asked the senior PR guru.

"The multiverse allows for an infinite number of realities governed by an infinite series of possible rules," said the Priest. "Which means that somewhere there is a universe where what has just happened is possible. Here, it would seem."

"That's pretty mind-blowing," said the junior PR consultant.

Father Mendes shook his head and smiled ruefully.

"Not as mind-blowing as what I am about to suggest. Perhaps what we have here is the answer to the greatest question in cosmology, which is of course 'where did the Universe come from?' There are two major competing types of theory. The oldest sort of theory is supernatural: the idea that an omnipotent God created the universe. Modern science postulates a number of possibilities such as the idea of 'infinite expansion'. There is another theory that says that the cosmos spontaneously erupted into being from a singularity into which spacetime was so compressed that time was another dimension of space. There are various other scientific theories. But the point is that we have two broad theoretical categories that are mutually exclusive: supernatural and scientific. The problem with both schools of thought is that they fail to answer the most fundamental question of all. Where did God, or the expanding universe or the singularity actually come from? So with the appearance of God at CERN, perhaps we have the answer to this conundrum in the shape of the most unexpected but greatest imaginable unifying event in religious and scientific history. Science has called God into existence so that He can create the scientific universe."

"Wait a minute," said the President, "how can God create what already exists?"

"Simple," replied Father Mendes evenly. "By going back in time."

There was a stunned silence.

"Time travel?" The President sounded shocked.

"This is completely consistent with the Max Tegmark model of the extreme multiverse," continued the priest, patiently. "Tegmark proposed that all possible worlds of any description really exist, not just those flowing from a specific mathematical model such as string theory or infinite inflation. The extreme multiverse explains everything because it contains everything. Anything that might happen, given an infinite number of possibilities, clearly must happen. One of those possibilities is a universe that creates its own creator. And now it would appear that it is this specific creator-creating universe that we inhabit."

There were gasps and snorts of incredulity from half of the people in the room and slow nods of unfolding enlightenment from the rest.

"What a minute, Father," interrupted the senior PR guru. "I'm no scientist either," and he glanced at the President of the EC, "but this sounds fishy to me. God and science reconciled via an improbably convenient experiment followed by time travel?"

Professor Bonnaire gave a bemused smile. "Not fishy at all. It follows inevitably from the existence of an extreme multiverse populated by observer-participants. Us."

"This is what God meant when He said that He had work to do and He has to go back," said Father Mendes. "He has to go back to the beginning of the universe in order to create it."

"The quantum universe is indifferent to the direction in which time travels," added Dr Chetty. "The equations work equally well if you run them forwards or backwards. The idea that our universe engineered its own self-awareness through a self-consistent causal loop mediated via quantum backward causation is a respectable scientific theory."

"'Respectable' is a bit strong," muttered the Director, but Dr Chetty was not listening. The Hindu mathematician gestured rhythmically back and forth with his hands.

"Now we have a self-consistent causal loop in which the Universe creates God and God creates the Universe. There is no longer any need to ask what came before."

"So what happened during the Higgs experiment?" interjected the President.

"And how does this account for the appearance of God?"

demanded the Chief Rabbi.

Father Mendes was getting into his stride. "The current 'standard model' of physics postulates something called the Higgs field. This invisible energy field interacts with matter to give it mass. What if ambiguous energy is actually another invisible all-permeating field that interacts with matter to give it *reality* and hold it together? God said that the pulse of ambiguous energy created in the experiment caused the spontaneous symmetry breaking of reality. This induced a phase transition; a phase transition that created the physical manifestation of God out of the all-pervasive ambiguous energy. A phase transition from fiction to fact, from fantasy to reality." He paused. "A transition from faith to certainty."

"Are you sure you are being objective here?" asked the senior PR guru. He was a well-respected popular science writer and had the knack of getting to the hub of a complex argument. "After all, as a priest and an astronomer you have a vested interest in seeing religion and science reconciled."

"Of course you're right," said Father Mendes, "and I am trying to put aside any presumptions in formulating these ideas; but remarkable events require remarkable concepts. Consider this remarkable fact: up to now, 96% of the mass of the universe was unaccounted for. Some of this is in the form of dark matter, but most of it is in the form of 'dark energy'. We have no idea what form this energy takes or where it resides. But what if 'dark energy' is the same as 'ambiguous energy'. What if the role of this ambiguous dark energy is to hold the structure of spacetime together, consistently, from moment to moment, allowing a coherent and self-consistent reality to arise. And what if ambiguous energy straddles the boundary between what we can observe and know, and what we can't, between what we know *does* exist and what *might* exist, between fact and fiction, between fantasy and reality. In certain extreme circumstances – such as might exist for an infinitesimal amount of time during the Higgs experiment – might reality collapse in on itself and allow…a miracle? In a multiverse the concepts of possible and impossible may well be meaningless."

"Is this what you physicists mean by 'quantum weirdness'?" asked the junior PR consultant.

"There is no end to the potential weirdness." Dr Chetty was now in full flow. "When we sleep we dream. We think of sleep as a necessary restorative to allow us to continue with our 'real' lives. But what if our dream life is the true reality, and our waking life is the necessary restorative that allows us to dream? What if we exist as nothing more than nominal, marginally integrated entities with arbitrary labels such as 'Dr Chetty?' Perhaps the self is an ever-shifting conceptual chimera."

"Not a new idea," said the Chief Rabbi. "It was proposed by the philosopher David Hume in the 18th century."

"And before that by the Buddha!" exclaimed Dr Chetty.

"Please, please, we are all getting a little carried away here," pleaded the Director.

"But if we could understand and harness ambiguous energy," said Professor Bonnaire, "to what mind-boggling uses could we put it? Might the only limitation be the depth and breadth of our own imagination? Could we use ambiguous energy to live forever, to visit other galaxies or to travel back in time? Did you know that in quantum physics there is, as yet, no agreed-upon interpretation of time?"

"Precisely!" declared Dr. Chetty. "We must ask ourselves: do past, present and future actually exist? Are our individual personal histories simply fantasies? What does the extraordinary result of our experiment tell us about the ambiguous nature of what is real?"

There was a silence.

"Got any of that Double Dutch left, Doc?" asked the senior PR guru.

*

The Director's temples throbbed. Yesterday, without explanation, God had disappeared. The Director had spent a gruelling morning in front of a frenzied international media. Now he was now preparing to supervise a repeat of their initial experiment.

"Ready to go," said the Deputy Director.

The Director sighed. Their ad-hoc expert committee had discussed this deep into the night. In the end, the decision to re-run the experiment had been easy. They were under intense scrutiny. They were in charge of the biggest particle accelerator on the planet. They had to do something – and after God's mysterious disappearance what the hell-else were they going to do?

"Go," he said, struggling to prevent himself from crossing his fingers.

*

The Director sat alone in his office watching the twin monitors on his desk. One showed dozens of different views of the Collider ring. Everything looked normal. The other monitor contained real-time live feeds from the ring detectors. There was the usual cacophony of subatomic particle traces. He was looking for two particular patterns. He waited. The tension mounted. Nothing…and then suddenly, there they were! But one was reversed, a mirror image of when he had seen it the first time. He was staring at the screen, trying to make sense of it when the Deputy Director burst into his office.

"Director, come quickly! It's happened again!"

*

The Director, to say the least, was very non-plussed. He stared at his second unexpected guest for an uncomfortably long time before hesitatingly extending his right hand.

"Er…welcome to CERN," he said at last.

"Thank you. I'm very pleased to be here."

"Can I get you anything?" offered the Director. "Tea? Coffee? Water?"

"Perhaps some rum mixed with hot chilli sauce. Half and half."

"Certainly, certainly," replied the Director, nervously fingering his collar and flicking at a non-existent fleck of dust on his sleeve. A faint sulphurous whiff brushed his nostrils and caused him to rub his nose.

Silence.

"I imagine you have many questions," said the new arrival.

You're not kidding! thought the Director. He turned the flat screen of one of his computer monitors towards his guest.

"Your, uh, arrival inside the Large Hadron Collider coincided with the appearance in our detectors of this previously unknown subatomic particle," and he pointed to the mirror-image track on the monitor.

"Ah, yes. One thing my predecessor failed to mention was that, like quarks, anti-reality particles have paired properties. As you know, quarks have six properties or 'flavours'; up and down, charm and strange and top and bottom."

The Director loosened his tie. He was feeling decidedly warmer.

"In the same way anti-reality ambiguons have plausibility and implausibility, possibility and probability…oh, and of course, good and evil. Have a guess which of those properties was in the ascendant during my phase transition?" asked their visitor, flashing a perfect set of pearly white fangs.

The phone rang. He picked up the receiver with a shaking hand.

"Director!" squawked his Deputy. "The Collider!"

The Director's head whipped around to the computer screen monitoring the Collider ring. He jumped and dropped the phone back into its cradle. "I don't believe it," he whispered; "it's gone!"

"But of course. We shan't be needing that again."

"Oh my God!"

"God?" replied their new guest. "God is the God of the Past, confined to a self-consistent loop between the beginning of time and yesterday. The future belongs to me."

"What happens now?" croaked the Director. He felt as if a loop werer tightening around his neck.

There was an awkward silence. Well, the Director felt awkward. He nervously mopped his brow as his guest calmly stroked one of the sharp bumps on his own forehead before leaning forward and pointing a clawed finger.

"May I trouble you for the use of your phone?" His smile grew wider. "I ought to call my Representative On Earth."

"And that would be…?"

"Why the Pope of course," said the new deity with a wicked grin.

The Great Gig in the Sky

Una McCormack

The twelvemonth and the day being up,
The dead began to speak:
"Oh who sits weeping on my grave,
And will not let me sleep?"

Trad.

I'm summoned by the phone in the dead of night. I leap out of bed and sprint downstairs, heart racing. It could be anything. I'm standing barefoot in the hall, bitter cold, chest thumping as if Bonzo's bashing out *Moby Dick* on my ribcage.

And it's Dave. "Guess what I've just seen."

"Jesus Christ, mate, I thought someone had died!"

"Nick! God! You're a real old woman these days."

"Can't it wait till morning?"

"No, it can't."

It might be a line about us in the *Evening News*, or a call from Annie Leibovitz about the cover of the *Rolling Stone*, but there's only one reason it can't wait. Dave doesn't want Simon getting in first. "Go on," I sigh. "What have you just seen?"

"A poster! A bloody *tribute* band! And guess what they're called – go on, guess!"

He's livid when I get it in one. Well, what else could it be?

*

Of course, I'm the poor sod that has to tell Simon. I brood about how to do it all weekend and get nowhere. Monday, I studiously ignore my phone, and it still isn't done. I end up sticking a flyer in my pocket and taking it round on Tuesday. Tuesday night: fish and chips at Simon's. Thus it has ever been, or at least since the divorce. Simon's not really listening; there's a programme on about one-hit wonders and I think he's hoping there'll be a clip. While he's still distracted, but before he's disappointed, I shove the leaflet under his nose. He smoothes it out over his knee, reads, and goes red. I worry again about heart attacks. This isn't fussing. We're all at a vulnerable age.

"'The Missing Link'? At the Corn Exchange?" His voice rises a tone at the end. We've never played anywhere that big. I keep quiet and watch him fold the flyer in half. "We won't see a penny from this, will we?"

I know better than to say anything once that track is playing and, besides, I don't mind listening, not that much. It's not Simon's fault he's the way he is, not really. I bet Gandhi would struggle too, supply teaching. I give the ketchup bottle a patient thump and, when Simon's finished, glance at him surreptitiously. He isn't quite as red as he was, but I pretend to watch the television for a bit longer, before saying, casually, "I might go and find out what they sound like."

I venture a look. Simon's glaring at me over his haddock. "By yourself?"

"I doubt it, Simon."

He skewers a chip and turns his wrath back towards *Monster Mash*. Infinitely more deserving target. "Somebody should be looking after us. I'd better go too."

There's that sigh of mine again. Yes, I'm the one who will have to tell Dave.

*

That Thursday we have a long-standing engagement at the Salisbury Arms folk club. It's friendly and eclectic and two quid at the door. It was a quid until 1991 (when Simon joined the committee) and from the outcry you would have thought we were being privatised. Dave fumed for months, although Sandy and I got a good laugh out of the whole business.

We've played the Salisbury on and off for nearly fifteen years, so you'd think this would be home ground, but this particular Thursday a spectre is haunting Cambridge and it goes by the name of The Missing Link. Dave's all over the place from the start, which is exactly what winds Simon up most. It's cut-throat out there for a while and then, halfway through, it's as if Simon gives up. He starts dashing for the end, so then Dave is chasing to get there first. I just about hold it together, but when it's finished and I'm consoling myself with beer, I wonder again whether we should have just packed it in. Because this is nothing like playing with Sandy.

The last time The Link was just me, Dave and Simon was thirty years ago. March 1968. We're straight out of school, stuck in a provincial town, fed up with college and go-nowhere jobs. We've got a band that's going to take us somewhere, but we're a man down, so we put the word out round town that we're looking for someone to complete the line-up. We've already got a guitarist (Dave's been saving out of his wages) and a drummer (my old man astonished me on my eighteenth birthday) and a lead singer (that was always going to be Simon). What we're missing is a bassist. What we get is Sandy.

Sandy, who swears he's seventeen, and while we don't believe it for a second we're still young enough not to give him any hassle. Sandy, who can barely look you in the eye or speak above a murmur. Sandy, who – after we've been playing for twenty minutes or so – whispers, "I brought some songs along with me..."

"Cool," I say, reaching for the sheets he's clutching.

"If we're being scrupulously fair, we've still got people to see—"

"Jesus, Simon, you're such a wanker!" Obviously this comes from Dave, so it was Dave who settled it, which is odd when you think about what happened later. Anyway, Sandy's in, of course, and we keep going for hours after on the strength of his songs. They're magic, and so is he.

"'Night, Nick," Sandy says, as he's leaving. "See you soon?"

That question mark. He still can't believe we rate him, never mind how much. "See you soon, Sandy," I say.

Thirty years later, after closing time, the wind's blowing and I can feel a few drops of rain. We huddle on the corner outside the Salisbury Arms. Simon begins to speak, but Dave clears his throat, cutting him off. I honestly don't know if it was intentional, but the upshot is that we end up standing in silence, the gap between us bigger than it's ever been. I struggle to come up with some words to make it all right again, but the more I try, the less there is to say. Hopeless.

In the end, Simon makes the move. He takes a step back from us, and gives me a smile tempered by a lifetime's familiarity. "Well... I guess I'll see you around."

*

Bank Holiday Monday. I've not slept much, mostly for fretting about Simon. I don't feel like facing the Corn Exchange, but I've agreed to meet Dave and Jan there, and I suppose I might regret missing it.

The place isn't packed, but it's certainly not empty, and as things turn out I needn't have worried about Simon. When we get to the bar, he's already there, looking happier than he's been in ages. Seeing him like that I know for certain that we won't be playing together again. People keep going over to shake his hand and congratulate him. I hadn't thought of tonight as a celebration before. Certainly beats going to a wake. When Simon sees us, there's a moment's pause, and then he comes over to say hello. He gives Jan a kiss, and then holds up four tickets like a royal flush. "For upstairs. Compliments of the management."

Dave badly wants to refuse, but Jan takes charge before he can get a word out. "I've waited years to watch you lot from a decent seat," she says. "I bet this is the closest I get. Thanks, Simon." Simon's genuinely pleased and, to his credit, it's not only because he's one up on Dave. Dave looks as if he's been trumped, but he cheers up measurably as we go upstairs. Someone coming down grabs Simon's hand and starts pumping at it. "Good Lord!" he says. "I'd assumed you were dead too."

At the seats, there's an awkward shuffle while we put the maximum distance between Dave and Simon without anyone admitting what's going on. I end up sandwiched in the middle with Simon on my far side. There's an uneasy silence which I fill by tapping the armrests. "Thanks for the ticket."

"You're welcome."

"I tried calling you on Friday."

"Yeah?"

"Not just Friday, I mean, I tried on Saturday too." Sunday I was hungover but Simon will know that already.

He's wearing the same small strained smile he got outside the pub on Thursday. "It's all right, Nick. Really. Forget it. It doesn't matter anymore."

I'm saved by the lights going down. We get the opening bars of *This Time There Won't Be No Reply*, and then The Missing Link appear.

"*Fuck,*" says Simon, who I haven't heard swear since his daughter was born, and I know what he means. We were solid enough, competent, but The Missing Link are *good*. The guitarist has all Dave's enthusiasm but more self-control. The singer has Simon's care and precision, but the tone is richer and a touch more self-possessed. As for the bassist…

Whoever he is, he's gone to a lot of trouble to get it right, and it's not like the world's full of magazines with our faces on the cover. (No, Annie never called.) He's wearing one of those black t-shirts Sandy always put on so he didn't have to worry what he looked like. He's got the fringe, oh yes, that's bang on. He even stands like Sandy did, eyes only for the guitar, and when he looks back at me – at the drummer, I mean – it's exactly how Sandy did, like the magic was a secret only us two shared.

"Christ," I tell Simon. "I mean, *Christ*." Because every so often, this Sandy does something our Sandy would have died before doing. He faces the audience, takes their measure, and then he turns back to the others and when he does *that*… the four of them pull together, tight as wire. And that's when they really sound nothing like us. They sound out of this world.

Sometimes I can't always quite say everything I'm feeling, not the way I'd like to, but if it isn't clear yet – I love live music, I mean, *really* love it, the way other people love cars or films or football. If this were any other band, I'd be out of this world with them right now, as happy as you can get and still be alive. But… all his songs, sounding how they must have done in his head, how they could have been if only we'd been better or had more time. Long before the end, long before they reach the single, I'm in tears. But I was always sentimental, and my dead friend Sandy Fraser knew all there was to say about regret.

*

After, Simon comes over with us to the Eagle and Dave shoves a whisky mac under my nose. "So…" Jan asks, "what do we think?"

Simon begins to laugh. "I think they're a lot better than us."

Sure as death or taxes, Dave's hackles rise. "*We* could have been that good!" Jan takes hold of his hand. "All right, love, shush… Nick, what about you?"

The three of them are staring at me as if I'm about to say something monumental. Honestly, how long have these people known me? Anyone would think we were strangers. What I want to say is: *I wish Sandy were here*, but instead I get the same hopeless feeling I had outside the Salisbury and her question goes unanswered. Our table falls silent. Jan starts stroking Dave's hand with her thumb, the fond kind of habit that can make you believe some things remain the same, and then a devilish smile crosses her face. "You know, there's someone we haven't asked yet. We haven't asked Sandy."

Myself, I can't decide if that's funny or in extremely bad taste, but Simon's perfectly clear. "I believe," he says frostily, "that's not actually within the realms of possibility."

Jan's smile acquires a brittle edge. "They were doing it on the telly the other night..."

"Not for real, love," Dave says into his glass. Jan's face falls, and that's when I get what she's trying to do. It's the kind of thing we used to do in the pub all the time, years ago, before the little things started intervening, little things like life and death and taxes. Jan draws back from the table, looking really sad now, as if she's given it her best shot and it's still not worked. I suppose this sounds stupid, but looking at her it strikes me for the first time that I'm probably not the only one missing Sandy like hell.

I clear my throat and shift forward in my seat. "I'll give it a go, Jan."

It earns me a lovely smile, which quickly turns wicked. "That's the spirit!" Groans. Eye-rolls. Jan hops out of her chair and goes to gather up beer mats. Back at the table, she takes a couple of pens from her handbag and we both get to work scribbling letters onto the beer mats. I'm actually feeling an awful lot better. "Pass us that ashtray, Dave," Jan says as we finish writing. "Then put your hands on the table – just *do* it, *and* you, Simon, don't start – make sure your fingertips are touching, that's right..."

At the next table, they've been watching all this unfold, and one of them calls out, "Is there anybody there...?" Dave mutters, "Fucking students," but before that can go any further, the pub doors burst open, and there's a blast of cold air. Enter the band, The Missing Link, their Sandy leading from the front. He points at us and turns to his friends in glee. "See! I *told* you it was them!"

*

We all move round so that there's space for them. We're pulling up chairs when the bassist says his name, so I don't catch it, and before I can ask again, he's already introducing the others. There's a seedy American on drums called Jim who I'm sure I've seen before. The singer's called Greg, thin as a pilgrim and quieter than the grave; he nods hello and then makes himself popular by going to the bar. There's another Nick, although this one plays guitar. "Nick Mark Two," their Sandy says. He grins across the table at me, like he's my best friend. That's Sandy's black leather jacket he's wearing.

Dave's all over Nick Mark Two. "You were amazing. As me! *I* was amazing!"

"We think he's sold his soul to the devil," Jim drawls, and Nick Mark Two lights a cigarette and smirks like he reckons he got the good end of the deal. "Don't mention it when Greg gets back, for God's sake," their Sandy laughs from behind the smoke. "He doesn't think it's funny."

Once the beer arrives, people start talking about the early days. After Sandy joined us, we started meeting at my place – my parents' place, as it was then – most nights and all weekend. Dave gets onto one of his favourite subjects. "I wish you could have met Nick's old man... Terrifying. Used to scare the life out of me."

"He wasn't that bad..."

"He absolutely was," Dave tells Nick Mark Two, his new best mate. "He'd waylay you in the hall and you'd have to make conversation. He used to call me 'David'..."

"So what? He used to call *me* 'Nicholas'."

"And I'd call him 'sir'. I've never done that with anyone else, my whole life."

Poor Dad. Sometimes I'd see him out of the corner of my eye, looking in on us from the door, elderly and bookish and bewildered, wondering when this was all going to pass but relieved I was doing something at last.

Their Sandy moves forwards eagerly in his chair. "Spring sixty-eight, yes? The house on Glisson Road." I'm trying to get a proper look at him, but Dave has started squaring up to him and blocks my view. "So you think you know your stuff?"

"Let's see how good he really is," Simon suggests. He and Dave weigh each other up for a moment, and then Dave says, "All right," and starts firing off dates, to see whether he knows where we were and what we were doing.

"June sixty-eight."

"Much too easy. First paying gig. King's May Ball."

We got that gig because Simon was seeing a girl on the Ball committee. We weren't bad but, forming a habit that would last us a lifetime, we weren't brilliant either. We mostly did covers, one or two of Sandy's songs, or at least that's what Dave claims and I'll have to take his word on it. What I remember most vividly is sitting with Sandy as he threw up from nerves and later from champagne.

Simon turns out to have a picture from the following morning in his wallet and he passes it around. Jan puts on her specs and then snorts with laughter. "My God, boys, look at those shirts! What were you all thinking?"

Myself, I cannot believe the blonde on Simon's arm. He had a string of beauties round about this time, college girls who thought it would be smart to go out with a townie, all stunning, all of whom he'd ditch when the new set of freshers turned up. If I recall correctly, though, this particular lovely ditched him for a lawyer at Magdalene. When the photo gets back round to Simon again, I watch him smile down at it for a while before he tucks it back in his wallet. All these years, and I never knew he carried that around with him.

"April sixty-nine," says Dave.

"Pick a day. I'll tell you which student union you were at."

Dave's just about to try when Jan declares, "In April sixty-nine, one of us *gave birth.*" That earns her cheers all round, hugs from Dave. More drinks arrive. While they're going down their Sandy passes the rest of the union test. "I can't remember half of these," Dave admits. "He could be telling us anything."

"I remember," Simon replies. "He's doing fine."

Then, of course, they're all talking about doing the record. You know, I never thought my name should be on it, not really, but Sandy wouldn't go ahead if it wasn't, like he needed company or protection or something. It still turns up in front of me on the stall every so often: *The Unquiet Grave, Trad., arr. A. Fraser and N. Marks.* My father was pleased, I think. Perplexed, but pleased.

After that came our fifteen minutes. November 1970, *Top of the Pops.* "Was that the same week T-Rex debuted?" Jim asks.

"The week after," all four of us say, at exactly the same time, and then all of us around the table are laughing – because that's it, isn't it, our story summed up, right there – a day late and a lot more than a dollar short. Except Sandy never stopped writing and since Sandy never stopped, neither did we.

Until now. I sit for a while drumming on the table, listening to the others being happy. After a moment or two, someone reaches over from behind me to stop the beat I'm making. "You look like a man in need of beer," their Sandy says.

He points in the direction of the bar, and then summons me to follow with a long guitarist's finger. As I get up from my chair, the bell rings for last orders, and everyone else gets up too. I lose sight of him in the crush. I inch my way forwards, and then I feel someone touch my shoulder. And when I turn round it's *him* – exactly as he was when I saw him last that autumn night on Tenison Road, just past forty, salt-and-pepper hair, still as thin as a teenager. He puts his long pale hand round my wrist, and his eyes hold more regret than one of his own songs.

"October ninety-six," he says, voice as quiet as when we were still strangers. "You three meet up for the first time after. Dave says that Simon was jealous of Sandy from the start and that's why it all went nowhere. Simon says that Dave can go to hell." The bell rings again. "And what did you say, Nick?" Someone pushes past, breaking us up, and before I can answer, I've lost sight of him again.

I get myself to the gents as quickly as I can and throw cold water on my face. What did I say? What I always say. I said nothing. I listened to Dave and Simon lay into each other, and I wished that somehow Sandy would walk through the door and save us from all this.

That's what killed it: the worst kind of lie, mixed with the truth and told in grief. Of course Simon would have sold his soul to write like Sandy. Who wouldn't? There's a good reason all those people turned up tonight, months after Sandy went and died on us. But that isn't why we went nowhere. What happened was Sandy didn't want to go anywhere if it meant going without his mates. We were company, we were protection. That's what I always thought. Was I wrong? Did I miss something? What was Sandy trying to say through all those songs?

*

Was it him? You'd have to be old or drunk to think so and I was both. I hurry back to the table and, when Jan says I've just missed him, I rush straight out into the street.

"Sandy!" I call after him, like the old fool I am, and when he turns round, the moon and the street light get all mixed up together, and I see him anew – Sandy at sixteen, thin as bones, with the fringe his mother hated falling over his eyes, with the boy's smile he always kept, hopeful and shy.

"You know, don't you," he tells me, "that I wouldn't change a single thing? Not one second of it. Not for the world." He heads off, but at the crossroads he stops to look back. "'Night, Nick. Maybe we'll play together sometime. Sometime soon."

I lift my hand to wave goodbye but he's already gone. Back inside, though, Simon and Dave are still at the table, and it looks almost as if they're talking to each other. Maybe we will.

Time, Like an Ever-Rolling Stream...

Nik Ravenscroft

According to the man's antique analogue watch, the boy hadn't moved for thirty-five minutes. Sitting on the slope leading down to the river, so close that his shoes were partly over the edge of the bank, his bony knees drawn up, long arms folded on them, chin resting on his forearms; from the bank he was almost hidden. His straight, dark hair was stirred by the warm breeze, as were the sunlit willow branches, but he was motionless. A casual observer would not even have noticed him.

The man walked over the short grass and sat down about a metre away, throwing his own jacket down to sit on as the boy had done with his blazer. He didn't expect a response from the child, wrapped as he was in black, adolescent despair to the exclusion of all else. It almost made him smile: adults, as he knew, tended to have their concentration broken by the demands of colleagues, or lovers or offspring – even utility companies. It was wonderful how often arguments with funding bodies occurred just as he was settling into deep despair over his latest failure.

The peace of the Backs wrapped itself about him, as he waited to be noticed, to be challenged. He allowed it to soothe him, luxuriating in the freshness of the day, the light on the leaves and the water: the perfection of Cambridge in late spring. The sun reflected off glass and warmed mellow stone, and even the hurrying students and tourists were distant, a pleasant backdrop to his own idleness. He stretched out long legs on the grass and understood that he had never taken time to enjoy all of this when he could have done. There had always been too much going on and he'd spent so much time in seminar rooms and lecture theatres and hot little pubs. Before he knew it, his three years had been over and then London, with its grimy pavements and the crush of the tube, had claimed him.

A glance showed that the boy's stance was unchanged. His school shirt strained across sharp shoulders already gaining their full adult width without, as yet, the complement of muscle, the bones of his spine lifting like partly excavated remains. The dark hair was rather long, overlapping the collar by a good three inches. The man smiled, a hand reflexively at his own nape. He still wore his hair student-long, but tied it back nowadays out of deference to Health and Safety rules and to avoid being confused with his own post-grads. He remembered some spectacular collisions with school authorities and judged the boy's current length to be just at the collision stage.

He found a small stone under his fingers and flipped it at the river. It hit a partly submerged willow root and skipped sideways.

The boy's head moved, his attention snagged by the white pebble, the small splash.

*

The pitiless beauty of the day was bad enough, without having to share it. Toby wanted to yell at the stranger to make him go away but didn't have the courage. Or the energy. Everything seemed to be too much effort. Even getting away from school with no difficulty – his forged note accepted, the Cambridge train due in – had seemed less like Fortune smiling on him, and more like part of a pre-ordained doomed path. He had been unable to think, even after promising himself that when away from the morass of school, he would analyse everything properly. His thoughts refusing to clear, the countryside had flickered past the window unnoticed.

A loop in his head was replaying the most hateful moments of the week. Sometimes, he watched his mother screaming at his father as if he, Toby, weren't there. He'd known something was wrong, but until then, they'd kept up the pretence whenever he was around. The naked aggression had been scalding. "…and as for 'Not in front of Toby', I couldn't care less about bloody Toby! Sod the selfish pair of you!" The door slamming had reverberated through his chest and he'd felt physical pain, as if someone had punched him hard below the sternum. The pain continued, even after she'd explained, or tried to.

Sometimes, he saw Tally's laughing mouth. So pretty, so soft and shiny, touched with something that tasted vaguely of fruit sweets whenever he managed to snatch a kiss. She insisted the flavour was strawberry but he preferred it when her lips no longer tasted of anything but Tally. Now he remembered only her laughter. Laughing with Gavin. Gavin's apparently concerned enquiry: "I mean, are you all right, mate? Going all religious, are you?" The hoots of derision; Gav's hand hard on his sleeve. "Or can't you do it with girls? You gay or something?"

Why couldn't someone tell you who to watch out for?

He could hear the laughter, the suggestions for his failure, and all through it, Tally had laughed, too.

The sun was warm along his shoulders and his eyes filled with splinters of light from the river.

If only you could somehow be warned – who to love; who to trust; what to avoid, in case it came back and hit you.

Just thinking about that afternoon made him sweat. If he could go back, he would have said something. Or just turned and walked away a little faster, so he wouldn't hear the comments, the Viagra jokes, the sniggering. She had seemed so understanding at the time... He hadn't been ready, hadn't wanted to go so far so fast.

Why couldn't someone tell you what was going to hurt? Why couldn't you tell when people were lying?

He tried to convince himself that he didn't care.

In front of him, the river flowed calmly on, clear and brown and gilded with sunlight. Its waters were quiet, carrying leaves and bearing ducks towards him in a stately procession. He had nothing for them.

Another voice echoed in his head. "Toby, you have to buck up – this mark is terrible. What's got into you?" A tart, desiccated voice that had pierced his protective shell of silence and roused him to unwise response. To swearing at her and storming out, in fact.

They'd all wanted to know what was wrong – Ms Grant, the Head, his housemaster – and he couldn't say. There was too much that was wrong. He seemed to have lost his ability to think, and that was truly terrifying. Without that, he had nothing left.

*

The splash made him see the river properly and the ducks investigated the disturbance in its smooth surface for a moment before resigning themselves yet again to mild disillusion and sculling off downstream.

The water reminded him of the hymn they always sang at the end of term. His lip curled as he thought of the melody -- and then heard it. The man who had come to sit by the river was humming the tune and the soft air was bringing it to him. The words came without bidding. *Time like an ever-rolling stream/ Bears all its sons away...* The sentiment always made the girls cry.

"It's not a stream," he muttered, fingers ripping. He threw some grass blades at the water. A few got there.

"What isn't?"

Toby ducked his head defensively. He hadn't meant to be heard. Damn. He cleared his throat.

'Time. It's not a stream," he said. Getting the words out seemed to free the rest. "That's *such* rubbish. I *hate* having to sing that damned thing every end-of-term – sentimental, religious crap for the hard-of-thinking. Time is so much more than that, it's fascinating and they reduce it to... some anodyne pap for soothing the barely conscious." The anger was in the wrong form, directed at the wrong audience. Still, he hadn't asked the bloke to interfere, had he? "If you try to talk to anyone about it, all they go on about is Doctor Who and the sodding Tardis. That's the level of scientific discussion you get. And this is the country that produced Newton. I give up." He drew breath and realised that he was ranting. The shame that had been washing over him all day did so again. He was so off-balance: he seemed to have no idea how to behave anymore. He shoved his fingers into his hair. "Sorry." It sounded ungracious even to himself; a sullen mutter. "I mean, if it's your favourite hymn or something."

'Not really. I quite like the tune, that's all.'

Toby glanced around and away. He got an impression of a long body, dark hair, casually worn clothes. 'Wish they'd write some better words for it.'

There was a low laugh and then another burst of song. "*In the beauty of the lilies, Christ was born across the sea?*"

Despite himself, Toby snorted with derisive laughter. "Oh, *quite*! Exactly! I spend the entire time wondering about that. I mean, it can't be hygienic, can it? And how the hell 'the soul of time' is to be 'His slave' is anyone's guess. Why do they write such stupid rubbish?" Oh, God... He felt himself scarlet again. What was the matter with his mouth? It seemed to be on automatic. He hunched into himself, wanting to vanish.

"Agreed." The answering voice was mild, amused. "You're a scientist, then?"

Was he? Ms Grant didn't seem to think so. And if he didn't get his university place – well, he might just as well forget it. His entire future was a terrifying blank that he just couldn't face.

"And you're thinking about time?"

Toby wondered what the stranger's interest was. Could he be some kind of social worker? It was obvious that he, Toby, was bunking off: he was still in school uniform. Another glance to the side showed the expensive kind of boots that Toby yearned for; pale linen trousers…No. He didn't look like a social worker. He had to be at least as tall as Toby himself, but broader with it. Toby felt confident about one thing: he wasn't a sexual predator. He had learned that to be over six foot three, bony and awkward, was to be deeply unattractive. Which was why Tally had seemed such a miracle.

He told himself not to think about her; she didn't matter any more.

"It's an interesting subject," the man was saying. "Did you catch that interview on the radio this morning? About time distortion?"

In the seething heat of his humiliation, something cool touched his sore mind. He could remember that, at least.

"Yeah."

"I missed the last half – sounded interesting, but I didn't catch it."

"You got the bit about black holes distorting time?" Toby looked round to see a nod. He hoped his eyes didn't still look red. He cleared his throat and tried to be in control of his voice. "The Einsteinian bit? So what they've done is to try to duplicate a twisting of time by distorting space. Using light – light beams that circulate, using mirrors to create a sort of swirl in space." He thought. "The next part wasn't explained very clearly but the gist seemed to be, if you twist space, you twist time as well. You cause a loop – so that the past, present and future are all connected. And I suppose the theory then is that there can be travel from one part to the other."

As he said it, he wished, urgently and painfully, that he could have travelled into the future to know what Gav would do. Or tell himself from his more informed future, who not to trust. How not to act… Not to be there when Mum snapped. He turned away. Misery swamped him and the sunlight darkened again.

"Impressive. How will they know whether or not it works?"

The enquiry drew him out of the darkness again. Toby shook his hair away from his eyes and had to clear his throat once more in order to speak. He felt as if his emotions were choking him. He wanted them to be gone, exhausted, and he didn't think he could stand it much longer. He tried to concentrate. "It's going to be at the neutron level…Sub-atomic only and God knows how much energy *that* will take."

"No human travel then?"

"I shouldn't think so. One thing they were saying was that it could be used to send information – warnings. About earthquakes and that sort of thing? You could save lives or stop environmental disasters. Imagine…"

Even as he said it, telling a total stranger, he felt that welcome coolness again. Reducing the heat of shame, it took him away from himself, as if dropping his body into a well of deep, still water. The powers he was describing loomed about him, vast and impersonal, shrinking his troubles to nothing. The Earth felt uneasy, shifting, and he spread his fingers on the cool grass, sensing the warmth of the surface, the huge benign mass of the moist soil underneath it all. Space and time, aching depths and heights, filled his mind and he was suddenly dizzy, as if he might fall into his own vision and be lost forever. Wonder and terror blended and overwhelmed all else.

Even as he took a shuddering breath to try to steady himself, he got another strong sensation. Thousands of people – somewhere, on the other side of this moment, there were thousands of people and they were looking to him, as if he were able to do something for them, as if he were somehow in their thoughts. They tugged hard at him and he didn't know what they wanted. His heart pounded – excitement? Fear? He almost felt as if he might pass out, but it wasn't quite that sort of feeling – more light: more clear, somehow.

Then the vision dropped him, dumping him unceremoniously back into his body, his place on this small riverside. It took him a moment to feel his own thoughts. *How odd not to feel at home in your own head…* What a strange place it was…

Feeling the old pain, it seemed too small to trouble with. And as for anyone from his own future coming and sparing him any of this – *Get real, idiot…*

It just wasn't important enough.

"It would be stupid," he said carefully, "to use it for some kind of idiotic time tourism, when you could do so much more."

The man nodded. "So no Doctor Who?"

"No." The answer seemed to come from somewhere else, somewhere certain. "At least," and Toby remembered to be cautious – this wasn't his research, after all. How could he know? "I shouldn't think so. Imagine the energy you'd need to send a person back – I can't think it'd be worth it. Whereas, an image – or information..." The idea was taking hold of him, despite his efforts to keep his distance. "But how to prime the past – how would they know they were getting a message? And how would you choose what to warn against?" He thought. "Maybe – what about Cassandra? Was that a failed attempt? Moses? Abraham..?" He stopped and drew a startled breath. "What if all the major religions were just some scientist trying to influence humans into not being so shitty to each other? I mean... That would be a responsibility and a half!"

"So much for the ivory tower," the man said wryly. "Not to mention stopping the military using it to alter the outcome of wars."

Toby grinned. "Yes, but what a thing to be doing! It's amazing – and sort of pre-ordained, isn't it? I mean, if they've done it, it's done already, so..."

The man was following him. "...so they have to do it."

"And no-one would ever know. Because," Toby was feeling that secure rush of enthusiasm he got whenever an idea took him in the right direction, "if a disaster has been successfully averted or the right thing happens, then no-one knows about the alternative... Which must mean that it alters the present. Or that there's a parallel reality being formed..."

"So is it worth doing? If it doesn't affect the reality you're in?"

"Of course it is! Oh, of course! Everyone matters – everything matters..." He heard himself about to launch into what Gav always referred to as his 'righteous rants' and skidded to a halt. Not that the man had seemed to mind.

"You're right," the man said. "And if that's so – well, you have it in you to do some fine work. Hold on to that."

That reminded Toby of Ms Grant and the dreadful test marks. It also reminded him that he didn't know who this man was.

"Look, I'm sorry. But are you something to do with school?"

*

The boy flushed as if he realised how rude he sounded but the man smiled and leaned back on his elbows, closing his eyes against the sun.

"No. And before you ask, your name is on the label in your blazer."

He watched the boy glance down: the tape was in capitals: toby maitland but he could be seen thinking that it was upside-down and very small, surely, from that distance. So it was time to close. The hands on his watch were indicating as much.

"And, I think, when it comes to it, you should choose Imperial," he continued. "You'll get offers from other places, but you need to be careful."

"What?" The boy was looking straight at him now, his face pale and eyelids still swollen with old weeping, but the spark was there. Curiosity.

"When you decide on your research place. Don't be seduced by dreaming spires. When things start getting weird – and they will. Very weird indeed – you need someone backing you who won't get scared and try to bury your research and you with it." He sat up, taking another look around the idyll before he left it. There would be no return visit.

The boy looked confused, trying to follow. He gave up and pursued what mattered. "What do you mean, weird? How weird will it get?"

*

Toby was not upset by the man's laughter. It was relief, in a way. He had always supposed that adults lost their capacity to laugh freely – but here was proof that this needn't be so. Unless the guy was mad. And maybe sitting on a riverbank, talking scientific theories with complete strangers, reviling hymns… Well, it was possible. Except that he, Toby, had just done the same and *he* didn't feel mad. He watched the man get to one knee.

"Oh, it'll get weirder than you can imagine, Master Maitland," the man said, still grinning and then leaned over. Half-kneeling, he slid the box of tablets from the blazer pocket. "You won't be needing these," he said confidently.

Toby felt himself flush but found the wit to shake his head, looking at the blue and white packet. He avoided the man's eyes and spoke to the tablets instead.

"How did you know they were there?"

'Inspired guess? But you won't, will you?'

Toby shook his head. Without another word, the man stood, shook out his expensive, crumpled jacket and paused. He spoke over Toby's head, as if it was an after-thought.

"You know, I've always thought that the advice you give yourself is the only kind that matters." He seemed to be waiting for an answer. Toby thought about his own adjustment in perception, the sudden sense of proportion – the correct end of the telescope for once. He nodded tentatively. Without another word, the man turned and strode off, an imposing, impressively tall figure, soon lost behind the swaying willow branches.

*

Toby sat and watched the water for a long time. Inside, he began to feel again, not the sickening heat of shame but the warming fire of anger. Somehow, anger freed logic.

Looking down the correct end of the telescope, he could dismiss half of his troubles. Six months from now, he'd be in London at university. There'd be new friends, new girls – and his family could sort itself out. In the meantime, he could get on with his studies while they bickered and fought amongst themselves. How dare they threaten to mess up his life with their stupid problems? And it would take more than Tally to break his heart. He needed to get his grades – so nothing would stop him. Gavin could sod off, too, even if he pretended it was all a big joke. With friends like him...

Anger did help. In its comforting heat, he got to his feet, collected his blazer and climbed back to the path, shrugging himself into the navy wool. He could catch a reasonable train back: no-one would know he'd gone and on-one would ask stupid questions. And the tablets were gone from his pocket, now.

His fingers automatically checked and came into contact with a piece of card, instead. It was the right size – nearly – for a rail ticket but it wasn't that. His was zipped into his inside pocket. He'd only bought a single, of course, which now looked puerile and melodramatic. He grinned and decided to forgive himself that piece of idiocy. He paused for a moment, enjoying the classical postcard beauty of the view and the elegance of the stone spanning the river, engineered to perfection.

His mind felt clear. Maybe all this could be his, after all.

As he walked along the dirty yellow gravel, he drew out the business card and glanced down at it. Plain cream-coloured card, it must have been slipped in at the same time as the tablets were removed. Idly, he turned it over, about to flip it into the bin by the bridge. Instead, he stopped, staring.

In neat black copperplate, he read *'Dr Tobias Maitland.'*

Followed by a string of qualifications and *'Director: Institute of Temporal Studies.'*

*

Ignoring the Japanese tourists and the hurrying students, he stood in the middle of the path, questions swarming in his mind, too many to answer – too many even to think about. The world seemed to turn about him, dizzying…

Then he tucked the card carefully into his breast pocket. Excitement swelled beneath his breastbone and, for a moment, he felt breathless. He forced himself to move.

As he walked along the old paths, under the shadows of ancient learning, he felt his mind fizzing with ideas, possibilities, impossibilities…

Weirder than this? Oh, I doubt it. I can imagine some very weird things indeed, Dr Maitland.

*

On the lee side of the trees further up the bank, Simon Amies stopped and leaned against rough bark. His legs shook, hollow and boneless with the sudden rush of reaction, and his heart pounded as terror surfaced. He took deep breaths to try to steady himself. God, but that had been worse than he'd expected.

Had the boy found the card yet?

Like most, he'd seen Maitland in the media. At first on scientific news sites and then propaganda 'documentaries' then later, of course, Maitland's face had been familiar from news footage of the War Crimes Tribunal at The Hague. But Simon had seen the old monster in the flesh once, outside the crowded entrance to a conference. Maitland's expression had always been cold and analytical, but his physical presence conveyed chilling messianic certainty. Simon had accidentally caught his eye. The memory made him shiver even now. Ironic then that Simon of all people had been closest to him in height and build, so that, from being the purely theoretical lead psychologist working on the Maitland data, he had become the active field agent.

At least he had been prepared for his own reaction. Killing dreams, even those that ended in horror, was never going to be easy and the hesitant, rather charming boy was a world away from the Maitland he'd known. He was not surprised to feel pity for the bright, vulnerable child.

That boy would go to Imperial and waste his efforts, never meeting the right people, never making the right connections. Someone else might get there but not – crucially, thank God – *not* Maitland.

He glanced at his watch but the ancient object was too inaccurate to tell him anything. He wasn't sure what he was waiting for. The kinder of the physicists had tried to explain – "Look, Simon, imagine the transition object is a rubber duck in your bath. Stop laughing! I'm serious! The force we exert pushes it below the surface – that's the present – into the past, underwater. Without the power, it bobs back up. We let go – you bob back up into the present."

But…

Simon had carefully not explained the extent of his findings. The team had trusted him. The stolen access to the transition equipment meant that time was tight and no-one questioned his conclusions. No-one else, apparently, had worked out that Maitland diverted meant the likely end of the very technology they were using and he had kept his secret to himself for fear that the others would baulk at the cost.

Now, as he waited, he had time to wonder about that careful lack of speculation.

He had been prepared to sacrifice the temporal technology as a price worth paying but standing on this peaceful riverbank, it struck him with the force of utter certainty. They had known, too.

They had known but had kept it from him, the naïve non-physicist.

He thought of the team on the other side of time, perhaps feeling guilty and wretched, and wished for a moment that he could have told them he was prepared. There had been no need to keep it from him. He smiled, sudden tears in his eyes.

Cool clear sunlight filtered down through leaves and on to his face as he looked up into a sky that was blank and innocent. Another line from Maitland's despised hymn came into his mind: *They fly forgotten, as a dream / Dies at the opening day.*

The boy would have found the card by now.

The future was already gone.

Multitude

Dave Hutchinson

1.

The elves came in around eight o'clock, just as the place was starting to get busy. There was no fuss. The door opened and three of them just walked into the lounge bar and stood looking around and every conversation stopped dead in its tracks.

The elves stood watching us for a few more moments, then two of them went and sat down at the table under the window. The third came up to the bar.

"Guinness," it said.

"We don't have any Guinness," I said without thinking, and the moment the words left my mouth I felt my heart do the Lambada.

The elf's expression didn't change. The lantern-light painted flickering shadows across its thin face. "Real ale," it said without missing a beat.

"I don't want any trouble," I told it.

"Then give us real ale."

I turned my head and looked at Wendy, who was standing frozen with a pint glass overflowing under one of the lager taps.

"Wendy," I said. "Wendy."

She blinked hard and suddenly realised there was beer all over her hand and dripping on her trainers. "Shit!" She looked at the elf, which was watching her with some interest. "Oops. Sorry."

The elf smiled and tipped its head to one side.

"Three pints of Old Aitken's," I told her.

"And whisky," said the elf.

"And three whisky chasers," I said to Wendy. "On the house."

"You're not fucking serving them, are you?" Colin Woodhouse called from the other side of the room.

There's always one. I sighed. "Unless you can suggest a good alternative, Col, then I think I will serve them, yes."

"Well I'm not fucking staying here with them things." And he got up, grabbed his duffel coat, finished his pint in one go, and stormed out into the cold and the wind.

This broke the spell for most of the other customers, who finished their drinks with faintly obscene haste, wrapped up warm, and followed Colin out into the night. Which left the place occupied by the elves, me, Wendy, Roger, and a couple of the old lads from up the coast who were so drunk that God Himself could have walked into the pub without them noticing.

"Wonderful," I said. I looked at the elf. It was still standing at the bar, its head tipped over to one side, looking at Wendy and smiling dreamily. Like the others, it was wearing jeans and a Barbour jacket and a thick black sweater and walking boots. "Hey," I said. "Hey, you."

The elf looked at me. It had long grey hair and yellow eyes. It had stopped smiling. We stared at each other for a little while and then I looked away.

"Go and sit down," I said. "I'll bring your drinks over."

It did a little half-bow, turned, and went over to its friends, who were sitting silently at their table and watching us. They weren't smiling, either.

Outside, the wind picked up a notch, making howling noises in the chimneys and hurling rain at the windows like handfulls of gravel.

"Sort their drinks out," I told Wendy. "Then go home." I nodded at Roger, who was standing down at the end of the bar with his mouth open. "And take Idiot Boy with you." At this, Roger closed his mouth and scowled at me.

"Will you be all right?" Wendy asked.

"I shouldn't think I'll be rushed off my feet tonight," I said.

"You know what I mean."

Wendy was short and dumpy and not all that good-looking, but she had a heart of gold and half the village, me included, was a little in love with her. I sometimes thought she was the only reason some of them came into the Duke of York. I wondered if she would be enough to get them to come back after tonight.

"I know what you mean," I said. I turned to look at the elves. Now all three of them were sitting at their table watching us. It wasn't the spookiest thing I'd ever seen, but it wasn't far off. I took a deep breath.

"Well, if they want to do something they'll just go ahead and do it and there's nothing we can do to stop them. It's probably best if you and Rog go home."

"What about Toby and Albie?"

Once upon a time, Toby and Albie had worked in a big brokerage house in London. The Crash had taken care of that, and they'd drifted up here over a period of years and a few dozen temporary jobs. Now they painted and fished and then they came into the Duke of York to drink what they'd earned painting and fishing. Tonight – I leaned to one side slightly so I could see into the corner of the bar – tonight they were at their usual table, muttering to each other over their pints, oblivious to what was happening around them.

"I'll look after them," I said.

"I'll get Simon to come over," Wendy said.

Simon was Wendy's fiancé, and although it was unlikely he'd be too much help if the elves did decide to do something violent, I knew I would find his presence comforting, which right now counted for a lot.

"You can tell him what's happening," I told her. "Say I don't want him to get involved, but if he feels like coming in for a pint I'd love to buy him one on the house. Tell him not to wear his uniform."

Wendy nodded and got on with pulling the pints. I told Roger to do some clearing up, and he went out into the bar and started collecting glasses and emptying ashtrays, but he stayed well away from the side of the room where the elves were sitting. When Wendy had the drinks ready, I told them both to go home and then I loaded up a tray and took the elves their order.

"It's a windy night," said the elf who had spoken to me earlier.

"Happens a lot," I told it, putting the drinks on the table. "Not too much between the Norfolk coast and Russia, really. Wind just howls down off the steppes and across the North Sea." I closed my mouth, aware I was starting to babble.

"You're not from this area," it said.

"No."

"You're Polish. From the mountains. Zakopane."

I put the last glass of Scotch down and straightened up, wondering if I looked as scared as I was. "Enjoy your drinks."

I turned to go, but the elf reached out and took my wrist. "Have you perhaps seen or heard of other elves in this area?"

The elf's hand was cool and dry and ever so slightly rough, the tips of its fingers calloused. I said, "No."

"You're sure, now?"

"I would have heard about it, I promise you."

"And if you had heard about it, you'd tell us, wouldn't you?" The elf looked me in the eye and smiled, but it wasn't the nice dreamy smile it had used when it was looking at Wendy. "Of course you would." It released my wrist.

"Enjoy your drinks," I said again, and retreated back behind the bar. When I got there, I discovered that I had sweated entirely through my sweatshirt. I mopped my face with a clean bar towel and poured myself a treble vodka. I didn't normally drink the vodka we served in the bar, because it wasn't Polish and it was warm, but this evening those distinctions didn't seem to matter too much.

I had never seen an elf. To my knowledge, no one in the village had ever seen one, either. They were enormously violent and enormously quick to anger, and in the decade or so since they had emerged from hiding to take over Britain they had slaughtered thousands of people and destroyed whole towns, and if some of them wanted to come into my pub and have a drink I wasn't about to stop them.

The door opened and a gust of wind blew leaves and rain into the bar as Simon came in, blocking out a reassuring amount of that end of the room. I saw to my relief that he was dressed in jeans and a parka rather than his police uniform.

He let go of the door and it closed slowly, the springs fighting the wind. The elves glanced disinterestedly at him and then went back to their drinks while he walked over to the bar and stood looking at me, rain on his face and bits of twigs in his hair.

"Well," he said finally. "Isn't this an interesting evening."

"Have a pint," I suggested, reaching a clean glass from under the bar. "On the house."

"Is that supposed to make me feel better?"

"It will if it happens often enough."

He grunted and took off his parka. He was wearing a chunky red sweater underneath. He draped the sodden parka over a nearby table, pulled a stool up to the bar and sat and watched me pulling his pint. "It's a dirty night out there," he said.

"Raining?" I put his drink down in front of him.

"Thanks. Bucketing down." He sipped his beer and looked at me. We were both thinking about the house on Princess Close, and if elves really could read minds, as some people believed, we were in big trouble.

I said, "How's Wendy?"

"Agitated." He drank some more beer and put the glass down, scanned the lounge slowly, saw Toby and Albie. "Jesus, are those old blokes still here?"

"They just won the lifetime award for Most Faithful Customers."

Simon shook his head. "Is it my imagination, or are we being really calm about this?"

"I don't know," I told him, turning to replenish my glass of vodka from the bottle behind the bar. "You're calm because it's your job. Toby and Albie are calm because they're colossal alcoholics. Speaking for myself, I'm scared shitless."

Simon laughed and the front door opened again. A young woman stepped through. She was wearing a black duster coat, jeans and a black cowboy hat. Well, why not? I thought. The evening's obviously not surreal enough already.

She took off her hat and ran a hand over her short chestnut hair while she looked around the bar. She saw Toby and Albie. She saw the elves. She saw Simon. She saw me. She unbuttoned her coat and flapped some of the rain off it.

"Are you still serving?" she called to me.

No, the evening obviously wasn't surreal enough already. "Yes," I said.

"Good. I'll just use your loo. Back in a minute." And she made her way towards the toilets.

Simon and I watched her go, then we looked at each other. Simon raised an eyebrow. "Tourist?"

"Come to sample the delights of the Norfolk coast on a stormy night in October," I said. "Of course." I nodded at his glass. "Another?"

"If it's still on the house." He drained his glass and handed it to me.

I was still pulling Simon's second pint when the young woman came out of the Ladies'. She had taken off her coat and was carrying it over one arm. Underneath, she was wearing a grey sweatshirt and a short denim jacket. She pulled up one of the tall barstools, sat down beside Simon, and propped her elbows on the bar top.

"So," I said, "what can I get you?"

She blew out her cheeks. "Wow," she said, looking at the rows of bottles on the shelves behind me. "What have you got?"

"Beer. Spirits. Crisps. The usual pub stuff."

"Is the beer here any good?"

I shrugged. "As good as anywhere else, I suppose."

"Okay." She was patting the pockets of her denim jacket, a manoeuvre which, given the length of the jacket, was faintly erotic. "How good is that?"

"I have no idea how people around here drink it." Simon laughed again. He was right: we were being awfully calm. There were whole moments when I was forgetting that the elves were there.

"Fine." She finally located a tin of small cigars in one pocket and a lighter in another. "I'll have a whisky and water. No ice."

While I got her drink, she turned on the stool and looked around the room again. "Slow night?"

"We were busy earlier," I said with what I thought was admirable understatement.

"Hm. I'll bet." She lit a cigar and leaned on the bar again. Before the elves, there had been a smoking ban in workplaces and restaurants and pubs. Oddly enough, that had been one of the first things to disappear. "Do you have rooms to rent?"

This was such an unusual question that it took me a few moments to process it. "You want to stay here?"

"Not necessarily. Are there any bed-and-breakfasts in the village?"

"There are a couple," said Simon, whose mother ran a B&B.

She turned to him. "Yeah? What are they like?"

"Most of them are pretty shitty," he said. "There's one that's not too bad."

"Maybe you could give me the address?"

"I can do better than that," he said smoothly. "I'll take you there in a little while." He put out his hand. "Simon Smith."

She shook his hand. "Did you bring the dancing bear?"

Simon said, "I beg your pardon?"

"It's an old song," she told him. She looked at me, but I probably looked even more at a loss than he did. "Simon Smith And His Amazing Dancing Bear. Or something like that." And to my amazement she sang a couple of bars about Mister Smith and the eponymous Bear. I looked across to see what the elves were making of all this, but they were just sitting drinking.

"I've never heard that one," said Simon.

"It's a really old song," she said. She shrugged. "I'm Edie Hamilton."

"Pleased to meet you," Simon said. "Have you been introduced to Kaz?"

Edie looked at me. "He got me a drink," she said with a grin. "Where I come from, that counts as an introduction."

Simon chuckled. It was amazing how we were behaving as if nothing was wrong, while three sylvan psychopaths were sitting around a table in my lounge bar. Simon nodded at me and said, "Edie Hamilton, meet Kaz Mackowiak." Even after all these years, he still pronounced it `Mac-koviak,' as if I was Scottish. I waved hello while I pulled him another pint of bitter.

"So," said Edie. "Does this sort of thing happen often?"

"You mean…?" Simon inclined his head towards the elves, and Edie nodded. "First time. Ever."

Edie turned and looked over at the elves. "Which sort of makes you wonder what the fuckers want, doesn't it?" And at that point the elves got up, walked over to the door, and left.

"That's great," I said, watching the door close behind them. "They come in here, destroy my business, alienate my customers, get me a completely undeserved reputation, and then they just fuck off without even saying good night."

"Don't shout, Kaz," said Simon, unable to disguise the relief in his voice.

"It's my pub," I told him, "and if I want to shout, I will shout."

"I bet they didn't pay, either," Edie said.

"There is that also," I said. "Simon, this is a disaster. All my customers have gone, and as we speak my reputation as an elf-lover is being circulated to every village, hamlet, house and outbuilding within a fifty mile radius."

"I'll sort it out, Kaz," he said, which I thought was a rash sort of statement to make. He picked up his glass, gulped half of his beer, and put it down again.

"Simon's our local police Sergeant," I told Edie.

"Really?" She turned back and looked at him. "I love a man in uniform."

Simon blushed all the way up to the roots of his hair.

I was usually the first person to appreciate the comic possibilities of a situation, but this was ridiculous.

"You know, this doesn't happen in London," said Edie. "You see them all over the place down there. Shops, clubs, walking in the street, in pubs." She drew on her cigar, blew out smoke. "Never seen them drink anything before, though," she said thoughtfully.

"London," said Simon, and shook his head. He said to her, "You know, you have to register with me if you intend to stay in the area for more than two days."

"Which begs the question of whether I plan to stay here for more than two days." Edie looked thoughtful. "Okay, you'd better register me."

"I'll need to see some ID," he told her.

"Oh, Christ," and she was suddenly in motion again, patting her pockets while Simon and I watched with great interest. "That's no problem."

She came up with a little credit card wallet, which she flapped open so that we could both see the plastic card inside. The card had a photograph of her embossed on it. Her hair had been longer when the photo was taken. The card also had the eagle-and-sickle of the Rykov-Forsyth Commission embossed on it.

"Lovely," said Simon, nonplussed.

"Long hair suits you," I told her. I was going to have nightmares about this evening for the rest of my life. However much longer that might be.

2

Pubs don't run themselves. They need help. Which is why we have pub landlords and landladies. People go into pubs and all they see is clean ashtrays and hoovered carpets and a nice range of spirits behind the bar and professionally-pulled pints, and they think all that stuff just happens, but it doesn't. It takes a lot of work and planning. I spent ten hours a day serving behind the bar, and another fourteen hours worrying about it. It was no wonder my hair was going white; it was amazing I wasn't bald. After last night, it was a miracle I wasn't a raving lunatic.

I was up at six the next morning. I made myself a mug of coffee and wandered downstairs and stood behind the bar in the lounge smoking a cigarette and wondering what else the world could possibly throw at me.

There is something really sad and abandoned about a pub in the morning, before the cleaners have been in. Something else the punters never see and probably never think about. Dirty glasses stacked on the bar. Piles of ashtrays collected on one table. Mud and cigarette ash trodden into the carpet. Stale smell of tobacco smoke on the furnishings.

I went and opened the doors to let some fresh air into the place, stood in the doorway and smoked my cigarette and drank my coffee. The storm had blown itself out sometime during the night and the air smelled fresh and cool. There was a hint of sunrise on the edges of the clouds. It was very very quiet.

The Duke of York stood on the edge of the village, a little half-timbered building with a leaky roof, six chimneys and two stars in some long-forgotten tourist guidebook. Over a century of Norfolk coastal weather had picked and pried at the rendering, forcing cracks in which moss had established itself. When I took over the pub from Big Keith I had wanted to get rid of the moss, but Mister Ross, the owner of the local microbrewery, had been of the opinion that these days the moss was the only thing holding the Duke Of York together, and removing it would have left us with a pile of bricks and old timber. The moss stayed.

The view from the front door of the pub wasn't the most inspiring in England. I could see the car park, and beyond it the road that twined through the village and off towards Norwich, and beyond that was a long high sloping bank covered with long grass, and beyond that was the sea, which had managed on two memorably stormy occasions in the six years since I'd become landlord to make its way over the bank, inundating the car park and flooding the cellar. Last night's storm, by comparison, had been little more than a fairly muscular wind accompanied by some rain.

My cleaner didn't turn up, which was no great surprise. I tidied up the bars, did some inexpert and rather desultory hoovering. Wendy came in at half past ten, gave me a brave little smile, and went through to the kitchen to start getting the bar lunches ready.

She needn't have bothered. I opened up at eleven, and three hours later when Wendy and I sat down to eat a couple of her bar lunches we were still the only people in the pub. Roger hadn't bothered to turn up.

I said, "If Simon's putting the good word around about me, he isn't making a very good job of it."

She looked sad. "Kaz…"

I got up from the table. "Lock up and go home, Wendy," I said. "I'm going for a walk."

Even by the standards of this part of the world, Aitken's Wold wasn't a large village. A few dozen houses, a little supermarket, a newsagents, a garage and the pub, and that was it. In the winter and during stormy periods it felt as if we were living on the edge of the world.

I walked through the village, fists jammed into the pockets of my parka, and though no one actually crossed the road to avoid me no one looked me in the eye, either. Which rather suited me. The mood I was in, I was more than likely to snarl at anyone who tried to speak to me.

On the other side of the village there was a newer estate. Newer in the sense that it only dated from just after the death of the Princess of Wales, which explained the names of its streets. I turned off the high street and onto Althorp Avenue. Left into Spencer Road. Right into Princess Close. I walked down to the end of the Close, up to the front door of Number Seven, and rang the bell.

The door was opened, after quite a long interval, by a beefy blond young man in jeans and a sweatshirt. He was holding one hand behind his back and he glowered at me and said, "What."

"It's okay, Jeff," came a voice behind him. "It's only Kaz. Let him in."

Jeff stepped to one side to let me in. As he closed the door behind me, I saw that the hand that had been hidden behind his back was holding a new-looking Heckler & Koch flechette pistol. I stood in the hallway, looking up the stairs. Christina was standing about halfway up, holding a pistol and looking annoyed.

"I heard you had an interesting evening," she said.

"You heard right," I said.

She waved with the gun. "Come on up."

The Princess Estate had been built in those long-ago days when it seemed that this part of the coast might attract young, upwardly-mobile couples and their young, upwardly-mobile families, and apart from two enormous houses on Diana Drive all the buildings were identical, a little clump of detached red-brick homes with a kitchen, reception hall and a big lounge/dining room downstairs and three bedrooms and a separate bathroom and toilet upstairs.

Number Seven Princess Close was on the edge of the estate, and its garden backed onto a little bit of woodland, which was useful for Christina because most of her friends preferred to sneak in under the cover of darkness rather than using the front door. I presumed that Jeff had arrived this way because I had never seen him before. It was all right for me to be seen entering the house, because Christina was widely assumed to be my girlfriend. This was not true, but again it was useful for her.

"Thanks for the warning, by the way," she said as I followed her upstairs.

"I had a crisis of my own last night, Chris," I told her. "Give me a break."

"I should give you a slap, Kaz. I thought we had an understanding."

"Absolutely," I agreed. "I do as you say and you don't shoot me. That's always seemed clear enough."

She glanced back over her shoulder. "Don't push your luck, Kaz."

"After last night, I think I'm all out of luck."

On the landing at the top of the stairs was a ladder, rising up through a trapdoor and into the attic. Chris went up first, and as I climbed behind her I heard her say to someone up above, "This is Kaz. He's supposed to be a friend of ours."

The attic was full of cardboard boxes and wiring and water tanks and pipes. Half a dozen battery-powered worklamps, of the kind used by mechanics, were clipped to the joists with huge crocodile clips.

In the middle of all this, three rough pine folding picnic tables had been set up, and on these sat a very old-looking Sony laptop. Plugged into the computer were several beige plastic boxes of indeterminate purpose. A young Asian man was sitting on an upturned wooden box in front of all this, holding an automatic pistol and looking nervous.

"It's okay, Mike," Chris told him. "I told you about Kaz."

"You told me you couldn't trust him as far as you could kick him," said Mike.

"Yes, well." She looked at me. "Kaz is on probation, sort of."

"You'll get us all killed."

"Excuse me?" I said in the polite tone of voice I reserved for speaking to armed guerillas. "Would you mind not talking about me as if I wasn't here?"

Chris sighed. Mike shook his head and put his gun down beside the computer and started typing on the laptop.

"Simon came round last night," said Chris. "He told me what happened. We got as many people as we could out of here, but Mike didn't want to go."

"It's taken me two days to get this fucking thing set up," Mike said, still typing. "I wasn't going to unplug it all and lug it across the fields in the middle of a storm."

"Yes, I know, Michael, dear heart," Chris said in her long-suffering voice. "I do seem to remember having this conversation already."

Mike grunted.

"Turns out it was a false alarm, anyway," Chris went on. "Those three elves moved on up the coast after they left your place. They killed fifteen people and burned two farms to the ground."

I closed my eyes.

"Oh, don't worry," she said. "They'll get what's coming to them."

"And then their friends will come up here and burn down another couple of farms," I commented. "Maybe leave a few smoking holes in the ground where some villages used to be."

She looked at me again. "We're fighting a war, Kaz."

"Yes." I rubbed my eyes. "I know."

A couple of years ago a gang of armed lunatics had been roaming East Anglia in a fantastical lashed-together gasogene lorry, robbing shops and pubs late at night and burning them down in what I could only rationalise as some strange neurotic reaction to the elves' occupation of the country.

Which was why, when I heard someone banging on the back door late one night in the middle of December, I pulled up a couple of the floorboards in my bedroom and took my AK from the space underneath before going downstairs to see what the noise was all about.

I shouldn't have worried. Well, with hindsight of course I should have worried, but at the time the two starving, rag-clad, more or less completely frozen figures crouching in a howling blizzard outside my back door didn't seem remotely dangerous, and I took them in, warmed them up, made them coffee laced with brandy, and hot soup, and gave them hot baths and dry clothes.

One of them was named Chris, a pretty girl in her early thirties who did all the talking. Harry, her companion, was too busy hoovering down warm foodstuffs to speak.

At some point, Chris looked over at the Kalashnikov, which I had laid on the floor near the door, and said, "If the elves find out you've got that, they'll kill you and reduce this place to a pile of smoking rubble."

It was against the elves' law for human beings to have firearms, but I'd brought the AK with me from France and I was rather attached to it. They were such marvellous, simple, reliable guns that you still found them all over the world, some of them well over a hundred years old and still in perfect working order.

I said, "The elves have to find out first."

Chris smiled dreamily at me. "Yes," she said. "Have you ever thought about joining the Resistance?"

I never saw Harry again, but Chris decided the village would be an ideal base of operations, bought the house on Princess Close, and set about turning it into Resistance Central.

Christina liked to describe it as a country-wide movement with thousands of members, all waiting for the right moment to rise up and overthrow the elves, but the truth was that I had no idea how large or widespread the Resistance was; for all I knew, it comprised Christina and her dozen or so weapons-mad friends, skulking about the countryside and killing the occasional elf here and there.

Weapons were the one thing the Resistance never seemed to be short of, which wasn't terribly surprising. The elves' law notwithstanding, I suspected a large amount of military kit, from both the Union and the Alliance, had made its way across the Channel after the War; in the weeks and months following the Crash the chaos had been so bad that I could have brought in half a dozen battlefield nukes and no one would have noticed.

"All right," said Mike.

"Go on, then," Chris told him. "Stop keeping us in suspense."

Mike hit the laptop's return key and one of the little beige boxes emitted the unmistakeable dialling notes and screech of a modem trying to find a connection. There was a moment of silence, and then the screen went black and the computer switched itself off.

"Fuck," Mike muttered.

*

Even this long after the event wild rumours and legends abounded about the Crash. There were still parts of the country where you could find someone who would swear blind to you that it had been the work of aliens, or that it had been the result of the intervention of older, wiser beings from Atlantis, or that Arthur himself had risen from Avalon and, gathering his Round Table knights about him, had ridden out into the countryside cutting telephone wires.

The mundane and rather embarrassing truth was that just as the War was getting entirely out of hand, someone had released a computer virus. It might have been part of some strategy of cyberwar, but it might equally have been the work of some clever adolescent in Dushanbe or Warsaw or Birmingham, Alabama. There would never be any way of knowing.

What was fairly evident was that it was unlike any of the other viruses that had once troubled the Information Superhighway. It breezed past firewalls, was invisible to virus scans, and crashed every online computer system on Earth, and many systems that had only ever been tangentially online. Stock exchanges were erased. Banks ceased to exist. Telecommunications disappeared. Economies dried up and blew away.

Less than an hour later, the War was over.

*

Chris made coffee. We sat at the kitchen table, smoking cigarettes. Mike was still up in the loft, dismantling the computer gear and preparing to leave.

I said, "Did I just watch you and your chocolate soldiers attempting to do something unimaginably stupid?"

Chris shrugged and half-turned on her chair so she could look out of the kitchen window. "You know the Crash didn't get everything?" she said finally without looking at me. "We only found that out a couple of months ago. There's stuff out there that's still running, still uninfected. Some military nets, a few corporate intranets, stuff that never was part of the Internet, or was offline for some reason when the Crash came through."

"And you just tried to hack into one of them."

She turned back to face me and rubbed her eyes. "Weeks of work," she muttered, picking up her coffee mug. "The virus is still fucking well out there, somewhere." She shook her head. "How does it do that? The Internet's gone."

"I don't know," I said. "I'm only a pub landlord."

She looked at me and snorted. "Sure you are."

I stubbed out my cigarette. "There's no need to quote me that thing about omelettes and broken eggs, but can we presume that you've just helped to crash one of those uninfected networks?"

"Do you know what wins wars, Kaz?" she asked. "Guns don't win wars. Communication wins wars. The ability to talk to each other, to organise, to plan. That's what wins wars."

In my experience, and notwithstanding all the stuff that they teach in officer school, what actually won wars was a colossal superiority in numbers and weaponry, but Chris didn't want an argument, so I just nodded.

"We've got to get back in contact with people," she said. "We tried ham radio, and we talked to guys in Sierra Leone and Auckland and a few other places, but we always lose our radio operators. Always. We don't know how the elves do it, but they always find our radio people."

I didn't know what to say. I poured myself some more coffee from the pot on the table, lit another cigarette.

"They won't let us get the telephone system up and running," Chris went on. "And have you noticed how long it's been since you got a letter? We don't know for sure what's happening anywhere else. We get a whole bunch of wild rumours about what's going on in Europe, and we don't know anything at all about America or China or Australia. How are we supposed to organise ourselves and fight back if we can't talk to each other?"

"This is all very interesting," I said, "but you all seem very relaxed about the chances of the elves tracing your little experiment. Much more relaxed than I am, for example."

She shook her head. "They don't do computers. They do do radio, so wi-fi's out of the question, but if we can plug into a phone line we're fine. Or we would be if the Crash wasn't still out there."

I heard footsteps on the stairs and Mike came to the kitchen doorway carrying a heavy-looking rucksack. "All done," he said.

Chris turned to look at him. "No evidence?"

"No evidence. The laptop's toast. I'll ditch it somewhere."

"All right. Get some sleep, Mike. We'll move you out of here after dark."

I watched Mike go back up the stairs, leaving his rucksack in the kitchen doorway. It was a miracle there was a Resistance at all, if they were all like this bunch of amateurs. Unfortunately, I was stuck with them, and when they got themselves killed they were going to take me down with them.

*

I spent the first six months after the Crash working on a farm near Caen. Apart from a few pockets where Union and Alliance forces still fought each other because they couldn't think of anything else to do, the War was over. Half the great cities of Europe were uninhabitable, for one reason or another, and the countryside from the Algarve to Ukraine was full of refugees and troops who just wanted to go home. The French coast was a nightmare, but the farm was deep in the countryside and the War and the Crash seemed to have passed it by. I approached it down a long wooded track, my hands on my head, until I reached a farmhouse that looked as though it had been built shortly before Napoleon's venture in Russia and the owner came out carrying a shotgun that may well have taken German lives during the First World War.

The farmer, whose name was Claude, spoke no English or Polish, and my French was limited to a number of phrases which were frankly unsuitable for this situation. Claude looked at my clothes and the AK which I had laid on the ground and stepped away from. He watched me miming hunger. He watched me miming mucking-out a stable and then miming eating. He watched me miming using a sickle to harvest corn and then miming eating. He watched me doing this for a lot longer than I thought strictly necessary in order to get the message. Finally, he nodded and beckoned with the gun and we went into his farmhouse, where he gave me my first decent meal in three days, followed by a glass of Calvados that almost dissolved my liver.

The whole time I was there, we hardly spoke to each other, communicating in mime and grunts. He set me to work repairing storm-damaged outbuildings. I managed to get Claude's rusty old petrol-driven tractor working again, and every week or so I hooked it up to a trailer and used it to drive Claude to the nearest village to barter for supplies.

There was still no phone system, landline or mobile. There was no internet. But there was gossip. Brittany had become the home of a fairly large British ex-pat population long before the War, and sitting in bars or waiting in shops I started to piece together bits of overheard conversation about what was happening in the wider world. Most of it was wild rumour and supposition, but one day I heard something that made me drive Claude back to the farm, wait until dark, and then simply walk away while the old man slept.

I walked for a long time, doing odd jobs for people as I went, in return for some food or a night's lodging. I kept moving. I walked to Calais, where I found a local fisherman who was willing to take me to England simply because he liked the idea.

And one evening, a year after the end of the War, I beached a little inflatable dinghy onto the shingle at Deal, and walked off into the Kent countryside.

About six months later the elves started to appear. And two months after that many of Britain's cities were in ruins, millions of people were dead, and the elves ruled the country.

*

It was starting to get dark when I got back to the Duke of York. There was light in the windows, and I blessed Wendy for lighting the lanterns. I pushed open the door and took a quick look around the bar.

Toby and Albie were in their usual corner, already drunk. Wendy was putting clean ashtrays on the tables. The only other person in the pub was Edie Hamilton.

I went down and sat beside her at her table. "That's two nights in a row you've come in here," I said. "You'll get yourself a reputation."

Edie glanced at Wendy, who was looking daggers at us across the bar. "I know it's Simon's mum's place," she said in a quiet voice, "but I can't spend another night in that B&B, Kaz. The place stinks."

I nodded. Everyone in the village knew that Mrs Smith's bed-and-breakfast did, indeed, stink, although nobody was quite sure what it stank of.

"Can I stay here?" Edie said. "I'll pay whatever you want, within reason."

"Sure," I told her. It had been that kind of day.

3

At first there were only a handful of them. Then a few hundred. Then a few thousand. Then tens of thousands. Nobody knew where they were coming from. Britain had been brought to its knees by the Crash, and the elves were determined never to let it get back to its feet again. They forbade us internal combustion and electricity – although solar-cell batteries were apparently okay. They would not allow us the use of telephones, mobile or otherwise, although the landlines remained and something somewhere was keeping them running. They would not allow us a postal service or weapons or music or films or cameras. They killed without notice, in enormous numbers, for the slightest infraction. The British tried to fight them, and failed. If the British hadn't given up, the country would have been a cratered smoking ruin, devoid of human life. Chris said there were fewer people in England now than during the reign of Queen Elizabeth I, but I thought that was bullshit; there was no way she could have known.

After a while, order emerged, of a sort. It was a testament to that order that Aitken's Wold could have as near an ordinary existence as it did. We got news – rumours, really – of what was going on elsewhere in the country, from people passing through, traders, refugees, the crazy and the hopeful. Elvish rule had not stopped a town near Sheffield turning itself into a fortified state; the elves, apparently, found that amusing. The elves had only taken over Britain – although once again I had to wonder how anyone could know that, considering no reliable news reached us from anywhere else in the world. They only wanted Britain, because once, long ago, they had ruled here before our technology drove them away, and they wanted their land back. They wanted revenge. They were all insane.

"Morning."

I looked over my shoulder. Edie was standing behind the bar, bleary-eyed, her hair standing up on one side where she'd slept on it. She was wearing a teeshirt with the face of some dead American pop star on it.

"Did you sleep all right?" I asked.

"Like a top. This place smells a lot better than Simon's mum's." She yawned and rubbed her eyes. "You?"

"Oh," I said, turning from the door, "as well as could be expected. Breakfast?"

She nodded. "Breakfast would be nice."

*

Bacon, eggs, sausage and another mug of coffee made the coming day seem more approachable. Edie had seconds of everything but the eggs.

"You know," she said, "you are allowed to talk to me."

I nodded.

She sat back and picked up her mug. "If this makes you feel awkward, I can go somewhere else."

I looked at her. Then I shook my head. "It's just a little strange. First the elves, then you."

She laughed. "All these undesirables suddenly coming into your pub."

"No, it's not that." I lit a cigarette. "I don't know. I'd sort of half-convinced myself the War never happened, half-convinced myself the elves never happened." I watched her reach for my cigarettes and take one. "Maybe a lot of people around here have done that. We're a long way off the beaten track."

Edie lit the cigarette with my Zippo. "And I thought what I saw the other night with the elves was just normal hostility."

"We've never seen an elf around here," I said. "We've never had the chance to feel normal hostility towards them. It's a miracle there weren't a couple of lynchings."

She tapped ash into the ashtray in the middle of the table. "And if there had been we would have been having this conversation in the middle of a smoking hole in the ground."

Britain was dotted with smoking holes in the ground where the elves had happened upon things that didn't please them. I said, "Do you know what they were doing here?"

Edie shook her head. "Nothing to do with me. Did you speak to them?"

I shrugged. "They ordered their drinks. I took them over. One of them asked me if I'd seen any other elves around here. You came in. That was it."

"Have you? Seen any other elves around here, I mean."

"I told you, we've never seen an elf around here."

"That's right; you did." Edie yawned and rubbed her face. "Sorry. Still not up and running on all cylinders."

I said, "I suppose this makes whatever you're doing more complicated. Elves being here."

She looked levelly at me through a haze of cigarette smoke. "Now you know I can't talk to you about that, Kaz."

"I just wondered," I said.

She shook her head. "They've never interfered with the Commission."

"I heard somewhere that the Commission was being wound up."

She put her elbow on the table and rested her chin on her hand. "Kaz," she said, wide-eyed. "Where did you hear that rumour?"

Shit. I scowled. Low blood-sugar. Too many late nights. Mouth working before brain is fully engaged. That sort of thing gets people killed.

"Because we all know the phones don't work," she said, still wide-eyed but smiling now. "We all know the Internet doesn't work. We all know that national news doesn't get to places like this, let alone international news." She laughed and shook her head. "You should see your face."

I rubbed my eyes. Well, whatever. "So the Commission's not being wound up?"

Edie shook her head and stubbed out her cigarette. "We still have a lot of work to do."

I heard the sound of hooves on the tarmac outside, and then someone leaning on a battery-powered horn. Edie raised her eyebrows. "Delivery day," I told her, getting up from the table. "Although I'm not sure why I'm bothering. None of my customers will ever come back."

*

"Heard you had a bit of fun the other night," said Brian when I went outside.

"You know," I said, "you wouldn't think news would travel that quickly here any more, would you?"

"Bad news has been travelling quickly since we were all living in caves, Kaz," he said, jumping down from the drivers' seat of his wagon. "It's a law of Nature."

"Oh," I said. "Is that what it is?"

"It is." Brian looked at the pub. "Everything seems all right."

"Seems that way."

"I heard they killed some people up the coast."

"I heard that, too."

"Mister Ross says he'd appreciate a visit sometime soon," he told me. "Put your side of the story."

Mister Ross's microbrewery supplied a dozen or so pubs over an area of about a hundred square miles. He was a big Captain Of Industry type and he was a complete pain in the arse. He mostly left me in peace to run the Duke, but he seemed to think that running the only brewery in the area meant he owned the pub and me with it, which irritated me. Local rumour had it that he'd made a lot of money racketeering in London during the War, only to see his fortune blow away like faery gold when the elves took over.

"Tell him I'll be over when I can," I said.

Brian looked doubtful. "Now, Kaz, that sounds awfully uncertain, doesn't it? Mister Ross, he doesn't like uncertainty."

"Monday," I said. "Tell him I'll come and see him on Monday. It's always a quiet day."

"Monday it is, then," said Brian. "So. Usual, is it?" He was a chirpy little sparrow of a man, a one-time English lecturer from Manchester.

"I think trade is going to be a bit lighter than usual for a while," I said. "Two bitter, two lager and two mild ought to do it."

"No stout?"

"I keep telling you, Brian, nobody around here drinks it." Except, apparently, the elves, and I didn't want to give them any excuses to come back.

He smiled. "All righty. Neville!"

From his nest among the barrels on the back of Brian's horse-drawn dray, his son Neville stirred, forty-two-years old, with the mind of a fourteen-year-old, the smooth untroubled face of a baby and the strength of two men. He and his father had drifted down here sometime between the Crash and the beginning of the Elvish Occupation. The elves had come here and turned gangsters into feudal lords and English lecturers and their educationally-subnormal sons into enforcers. Or had we done that for ourselves?

"Two bitter, two lager, two mild!" Brian called, and Neville got on with unloading the dray's ramp and rolling the relevant barrels down it and over to the cellar hatch at the side of the pub. I dug a wad of notes out of my pocket and counted most of them into Brian's palm. He looked at me. "We've got a case of Scotch," he said.

My heart sank. "These people are beer drinkers, Brian," I told him. "We go through a litre of Scotch in maybe two weeks. Vodka even longer. They're not spirit drinkers."

He raised his eyebrows so far they almost disappeared under the brim of his bowler hat. "All the way from Scotland, Kaz," he said.

I wondered how many of the other publicans on his round he'd tried this on. The Scotch would be some dreadful thing distilled by a lunatic in a barn somewhere. It would be about six weeks old and it would have travelled no more than fifteen miles and I wouldn't dare let anyone drink it. And I found I didn't care any longer.

"How much?" I said.

Brian tipped back his hat and looked at the money remaining in my hand. "That'll about do it, Kaz," he said, and he reached out and took it from me, looked over his shoulder and called, "And the whisky, Neville!" He grinned at me. "We've all got to make our way, haven't we, Kaz?" he said.

"Some of us more than others, Brian," I said.

This offended him. He took a step back while folding up the money – making sure to keep the whisky money separate – and pushing it into a back pocket of his jeans. "We're all honest men trying to make a living, Kaz," he said.

I was too tired for this bollocks any more. I leaned forward and said quietly, "In any civilised society, you and your master would be in prison right now, Brian."

Perversely, this seemed to cheer him up. "Well, thank Christ this isn't a civilised society any more, eh?" he said. He thought about it. "Or a society at all, really."

"Personally, I would be ashamed of myself if I was doing what you do."

He tipped the brim of his hat down over his eyes again. "I'm looking after my boy, Kaz," he said. "And I remember you being keen enough to get involved when you had no job and no money."

Of course, there was no way to deny this because it was only the plain honest truth. I said, "Get out of here, Brian."

He turned to get back on the dray. "I'll tell Mister Ross you'll see him on Monday, then," he said.

"Monday," I said. "While I'm there I might mention to him your sideline in whisky that blinds people and then kills them."

His expression hardened. "You might have made better decisions, Kaz."

But I have friends in the Resistance, I almost said, and a representative of the Rykov-Forsythe Commission is staying at the pub. But I didn't. All I said was, "You might be right, Brian."

He nodded at me, from the driving seat. "All right, then." He shouted, "Neville!" over his shoulder without taking his eyes off me, and his son vaulted back onto the wagon, and Brian grabbed the reins and snapped them and the horses took up the strain and pulled the dray back onto the road.

I watched them go for a long time, and when I turned away and went over to the cellar hatch I found that they had only left me one barrel of mild and no whisky at all.

Edie was still in the kitchen when I got back. She said, "Kaz?"

I looked at her and for a moment I actually saw my life flash before my eyes. It just went on and on, a landscape of bad decisions and weakness and endless killing.

"Enough," I said, and for a moment she kept up the pretence that she didn't know what I was talking about.

Then she nodded and got up from the kitchen table and went upstairs to get dressed, and I sat down and lit a cigarette and a few minutes later I heard her let herself out by the back door.

*

By the time Wendy arrived I'd stacked all the furniture in the car park and I was pushing the pub's antique manual carpet-cleaner around the lounge bar. She stood in the doorway watching me for a few seconds before she said, "What are you doing?"

I stopped pushing the carpet cleaner. I was on my third circuit of the lounge and the carpet looked just the same as it had when I started. I said, "Nobody's going to be coming in here for a while. I thought I'd take the opportunity and do some spring cleaning."

She frowned. "Kaz, it's October."

"Autumn cleaning, then."

She looked at me for a few more moments, obviously wondering just how much of my mind I'd lost. Then she said, "Well, it'll take you all day on your own. Where do you want me to start?"

*

Nobody bothered to turn up for lunchtime opening, which was fine by me. Wendy and I washed and wiped and polished and brushed and by the time the light was failing and Wendy was going around lighting the lamps we had the furniture back in place and both the bars looked cleaner than they had when I took the pub over. We took turns to have a wash upstairs, and when I came back down Wendy was sitting in the lounge bar with Simon and Chris, which was not what I wanted at all.

I went over and sat down at their table. Toby and Albie were in their usual corner, sharing a spliff, but apart from them we were alone. Wendy had lit the fire and the bar was warm and cosy in the lamplight. For a moment I just sat looking around me, thinking how proud I was to have been here with all these people.

I turned to Chris and said, "You should leave –" and the door opened and Edie came into the bar. She looked at me and there was no spark of humour in her eyes. She let the door go and it started to close, but the elf behind her pushed it open again and stood there looking at us. Wendy gave a little scream.

"Shit," said Simon.

Chris put her hand in her jacket pocket and started to stand up, but I grabbed her wrist and held her down. Very quietly, I said, "Please tell me you haven't been so stupid as to come here armed…"

"Let me go, Kaz," she muttered.

"It's all right," I told her. "They haven't come for you." I looked at Edie and said, a little louder, "Have you?"

"You know who we're here for, Major," she said. She waved a hand to indicate the elf. "This is Elrond. Well, obviously, it isn't. But that's what it calls itself. Thinks it's funny, don't you, Elrond?"

The elf hadn't taken its eyes off us for a moment. It let the door go. "Not enough humour in the world," it said.

Well, there certainly wasn't enough right here. I said, "Unusual."

"I'm on official business," said Edie. "When I'm on official business, I get a minder. To make sure I don't become compassionate."

"Too much compassion in the world," said the elf, and it smiled.

"What's all this about?" Simon said, and I was proud of him for how calm and matter-of-fact he sounded.

Edie stepped a little further into the bar. The elf stayed where it was. "I've been investigating a war criminal who's been living here in Aitken's Wold," she said.

"I beg your pardon?" asked Simon.

Edie unbuttoned her coat and pulled a stool over from the bar and perched herself on it. "After the War, the Union and the Alliance recognised that war crimes had taken place on both sides. Crimes against Humanity. The Crash made things more difficult than they might have been, but eventually they set up the Rykov-Forsythe Commission to investigate atrocities and bring the perpetrators to justice. And that's who I work for."

I was still holding Chris's wrist. I could feel her trembling, whether with fear or rage I couldn't tell. My bet would have been rage.

"So," Edie continued. "Europe has been devastated by a war, civilisation has been knocked off its feet by the Crash. Why on Earth are we still investigating? Well," she took out a packet of cigarettes and lit one, "because the elves think we're great, don't you, Elrond?"

Elrond didn't reply.

"They like the idea of us going around killing each other so much that they insisted that we carry on our work."

"Not enough humour in the world," Elrond said again.

"You could have said no," Chris said in a monotone.

Edie shook her head. "There's no `no' in the elvish language, is there, Elrond?"

"No," said Elrond.

"All right," said Edie. "That was obviously a lie. But you don't say no to the elves. Not twice, anyway. You do as they tell you. And to be honest, it's only what we were doing before they arrived."

"I don't understand," said Wendy, bless her. "What are you doing here?"

Edie tipped her head to one side and smiled at her. "The Union had something they called `Police Battalions,'" she said. "They were supposed to come in behind the conventional forces and make sure there was civil order behind the front lines. No looting, no criminal activity, no disgruntled locals taking it upon themselves to set up a Resistance." She got up and walked over to the fireplace and looked at the old photographs of Aitken's Wold that hung on the chimney breast. "And some of them did just that," she said without looking at us. "But for most of them it was just an excuse to rape and pillage and murder." She looked over her shoulder and smiled. "The Major, here, for instance. Of the 378th Police Battalion, commanded by Colonel Rodrigo Suarez. The 378th were such a bunch of bastards, weren't they, Major?"

Everyone in the room looked at me. Even Toby and Albie.

"Kaz?" said Simon.

"That's not his real name," said Edie. "He'd have had to be insane to live here under his real name, knowing we might be looking for him." She looked at me. "Will you introduce yourself, Major?"

"I think not," I told her, although I wasn't sure why it mattered.

"I have some photographs," Edie told everyone. "They took photographs of themselves, standing beside the things they did. Would anyone like to see the photographs?"

"No," said Chris.

"Yes," said Simon.

"Absolutely right, Sergeant," Edie said, reaching into her inside coat pocket and pulling out a little wad of printed photographs. "You'll need to see the evidence, won't you?" She handed them over.

Simon went through the photographs slowly. Then went through them again. I watched all kinds of emotions pass across his face, but mostly betrayal. He looked at me and held the photographs towards me. I recognised the faces in the top one. One of them was mine. I recognised the pile of burned bodies behind them, too. I couldn't remember where it had been, though.

I shrugged. "Faked," I tried, and then I was on the floor and Simon was standing over me shouting and there was a great painful roaring in my head and Edie was shooing Simon back with the gun. I got to my knees, righted the chair, and climbed back onto it. I put a hand to the side of my head and it came away bloody. The photographs were scattered all over the floor. I looked at them. We all looked so young.

Edie was speaking again. "Did someone tip you off in France?"

I pressed my hand to the side of my head and grimaced. "I was in town shopping," I said. "I was buying some tools for the tractor." I looked at her. She had no idea what I was talking about. "I overheard someone talking to someone else about a Commission officer in the area asking questions about Poles." I shrugged. "The fisherman?"

"About six weeks after he brought you across the Channel he decided to try it again," said Edie. "This time he tried to do it with forty kilos of pretty manky heroin and the remnants of a Russian special-ops team who wanted to make a new life for themselves in England and were happy to pay him for the opportunity. Was Europe that bad back then?"

"It was fairly lively. I'm disappointed a bunch of Russian spec-ops boys couldn't hack it, though."

"Anyway, he ran into a Coastguard patrol while he was dropping his cargo. They got the heroin, they got the Russians, they got the fisherman. He was already singing like a diva while they were still pulling in to Dover harbour. He gave you up a couple of days later."

"He looked the type," I said.

"We got in touch with Commission headquarters in Tallin, where there was a big fat file on you. They couriered it over to us. And then..." She gestured at Elrond.

"Inconvenient," I said. "Still, Justice never sleeps, eh? The Great Work goes on." Actually, I was rather impressed that they'd found me at all, however long it had taken them.

Her expression hardened. She took a deep breath. "Under the powers vested in me by the Rykov-Forsythe Commission, I find you guilty of crimes against humanity," she said to me. I looked at her. "I sentence you to summary execution." She pointed the gun at the middle of my face. "Get up, Każimierż," she said.

"What are you going to do?" Christine said loudly, standing up. Simon stood up as well. I stood up too, just so I wouldn't feel left out.

"We're going for a walk," said Edie without looking away from me. "Sergeant?"

Simon moved in behind me, grabbing my upper arms and propelling me towards the door. I heard some scuffling behind us and Christine shouted, "You fucking bitch!"

"Każimierż is going to take part in a little experiment," Edie said, her voice a little muffled. As she moved past us to open the door, I saw blood on her mouth and a couple of scratches on her face and I smiled at her. She didn't smile back. "Każimierż is going to have the experience." She looked up, pointed the gun past me. "And no one is going to stop us, are they."

"Chris," I said. "Calm down."

"Kaz!" she shouted. "She's insane! She's going to kill you!"

Then maybe it's about time, I thought. I said, "Get out of here, Chris. Get your people together and get out of the area as fast as you can. Simon."

No reply, but I felt his fists tighten around my biceps.

"Make sure she's all right, Simon," I said.

"I don't have to do anything you tell me, you twat," he muttered, mouth close behind my ear. "But I'll make sure nothing happens to her. Now walk." And he marched me out into the dark.

*

As if the evening hadn't already been interesting enough, there was a car in the car park. An electric car, to be true, but a car nevertheless, as banned by the elves on pain of death and mass destruction.

"Perk of the job?" I asked Edie, and Simon cuffed me across the back of the head.

The elf that called itself Elrond was already in the car. In the driving seat, I saw with some interest. We got in, Edie in the passenger's seat, Simon and me in the back. Edie turned and pointed the pistol at me around the headrest of her seat.

"Are you going to make any trouble for me, Major?"

I shook my head.

"All right." She glanced at Elrond. "Let's go."

The elf started the car, put it in gear, and drove off without bothering to switch on the headlights. I briefly entertained a scenario à la The Fugitive, but after a couple of minutes or so it was obvious that Elrond could drive as well without lights as I could with them, and I shelved that particular plan of escape. And then I shelved all of them. Simon was too strong, Edie had the gun, they had an elf with them. I was going to die, whatever happened.

And maybe it really was about time.

The Colonel was insane. That had never really been in question. He used to talk of setting up his own country, when the War was over. He didn't seem to think it mattered who won. He even had a place ready, he said, up in the deep forests that straddle the border between Poland and Lithuania. Just a little country, he said. Four hundred square kilometres, no more, he wasn't greedy. He was going to have his own currency printed up, and passports and stamps everything, and he was going to rule it along similar lines to the Divine Right of Kings. When the War was over.

There was a point when I believed the War would never be over, when I believed the Colonel would march us back and forth across Europe, killing and killing and killing.

And then, somewhere in Belgium, it didn't matter any more. We were friends, comrades. We were strong. The killing made us strong, and the ones who found excuses not to kill, the ones who sneaked away into the woods or pretended to be sick, they weren't capable of doing a man's job. We tolerated them, but they were somehow less trustworthy.

By the time we reached St Ursula, it was just routine, mechanical. We could have been doing it for the Alliance, we could have been doing it for the Union, it didn't matter any more. We did it because it made us strong, because it held us together, because if we stopped we might never be able to live with what we had done. None of us were bad men – except the Colonel, who was insane -- but we learned to kill. We learned to kill innocent people in great numbers. And some of us learned to enjoy it. Because we could.

St Ursula saved us. We'd left other villages unmolested in our journey – the Colonel had long since stopped listening to orders and seemed to be choosing our victims according to some unfathomable internal compass -- and if we hadn't stopped there we would have been in Paris the next day.

But the Colonel's compass settled on St Ursula. We went through the village in the cool Summer pre-dawn light and we rounded up every living person and we took them to a nearby football pitch and we shot them all. Then we carried all the bodies into the little village school and stacked them up inside. Because we could. Dusk was falling by the time we finished.

The following morning, while we were preparing to leave, the Crash happened and civilisation slumped.

The War was by then not being run by people in their right minds, but the Crash drove away whatever reason remained. The Alliance lobbed battlefield nukes onto Paris. The Union Fifth Army put the

Vatican to the torch. Someone -- nobody ever found out who -- turned Barcelona into a charnel house with biological weapons.

The Colonel stopped functioning, a man whose internal compass had suddenly stopped working. He sat at a child's desk in the school, looking at the pile of dead bodies, waiting for word from whatever voices drove him, but no word came. We waited for orders but no orders came. The men became restless. Days went by, while the Alliance rendered Paris uninhabitable for the next ten thousand years. There were fights in the Battalion.

Finally the senior officers, Krause and Sanchez and I, had a meeting. Then we formed the men up in front of St Ursula's church and we told them their War was over. We told them we were victorious. We told them anything. We told them to flee. Dump their uniforms, find civilian clothes, and run. And run they did, like men waking from a dream of godhood to find that they were, after all, only men.

And when the men were all gone, one of us went into the school and put a bullet into the Colonel's head.

"Shall we have a story?" Edie asked from the front seat. "Make the journey go more quickly?"

"Sure," I said. "Why not?" If it helped take my mind off being driven at seventy miles an hour down winding lanes at night without headlights by an elf, that was fine by me.

"All right," said Edie. "Well, a long, long time ago the elves ruled the world, didn't you, Elrond? How long ago was that?"

"A long, long time ago," said the elf. "The North Sea was still a great wooded valley."

"A long, long time ago," Edie agreed. "And then something happened. The elves know what happened, but they're not saying, are you, Elrond?"

"I don't know what happened," said Elrond.

Edie patted him chummily on the shoulder. "Of course you don't. Anyway, whatever happened, when it was over there were only a handful of elves left and they were suddenly outnumbered by us. And there weren't all that many of us back then. Hairy men and women in animal skins, carrying spears." She looked at Elrond and beamed. "But we remembered you, didn't we? All that time ago, we never forgot you." She glanced at me, then looked back out through the windscreen.

"Anyway, the elves who were left went away for a while. But before they went away, they did something to the trees."

"I beg your pardon?" said Simon, who I thought had already demonstrated remarkable forbearance by not saying 'I beg your pardon?' at the end of every sentence.

"Did you know that trees can think?" Edie asked. Then without waiting for an answer, she went on, "Oh, not very much. But an individual brain cell can't think very much, either. Put a whole lot of them together and link them up in the right way, though, and that's a different thing."

Simon shook his head, baffled.

"The elves call it the experience," Edie said. "It's an artificial intelligence made up of every tree on Earth."

"Doesn't sound very artificial to me," I said. "If it's made up of trees."

Edie snorted. "It didn't exist until the elves created it. Is that artificial enough for you?" She shook her head. "Every tree, every plant, every blade of grass. The elves went away and left it behind and it's been watching us for almost the whole of human history, studying us, waiting for us to make a mistake, waiting for us to be vulnerable."

"The Crash," said Simon.

"Absolutely. The Crash. The Crash came, the experience alerted the elves, and, well, here we all are now." She looked at Elrond again. "Only the elves can talk to – interface with, I suppose you'd say – the experience." She paused. "Well, that's not quite true. Anybody can do it. But it doesn't kill the elves."

"And that's what you're going to do with…"

"It's all right, Simon," I said. "You can say my name. I won't tell anybody." He nudged me, none too gently, to be quiet.

"One hundred percent fatal to humans," Edie said. "The elves like it. It hurts a lot."

"You know," I said, "I do have to wonder how this fits in with the Commission's Charter. I'm supposed to have a trial, and I believe the prescribed method of execution is firing squad."

Edie sighed. She was probably starting to find me tiresome. Screw her. "That was the way things were in the eighteen months or two years after the Crash," she said. "After the elves arrived all of that went out of the window."

"Well, if you're not working to the Charter any longer, you could just drop me off…oh, somewhere around here, and we won't mention this again." Simon nudged me again, but a little more gently this time.

"There's no statute of limitations on war crimes, Kaz," Edie said. "I'm going to keep working until I've done my job."

I tipped my head to one side and looked at the back of her head. I thought of the house on Princess Close, with its handy little bit of woodland to hide people who didn't want their arrival or departure noticed. If this experience was everything Edie said, the woodland was watching people creeping in and out of Chris's house at funny times of the night. If it was everything Edie said, the Resistance was doomed. On the other hand, either the elves had decided not to act on its information and arrest Chris just yet, or it hadn't told them. Either way, something odd was going on.

"The elves love the Commission," she went on. "They give us all the help we need. They think we're funny. Don't you, Elrond?"

"Yes," said Elrond, although it didn't sound all that amused.

"Isn't it?" I said. "Isn't that funny, Elrond?"

"Everyone's talking too much," said the elf.

"People on their way to their execution do tend to babble, don't they?" I said.

The elf didn't reply for a moment. I wondered if it was consulting this great vegetable artificial intelligence, which knew everything about us, looking for guidance. Finally all it did was say, "Everyone's talking too much," again.

"Out of curiosity, and because I'm going to die soon anyway," I asked, "who's in charge here? The elves or the experience?"

Edie looked around the headrest at me again. "You won't survive this, Kaz," she said. "It isn't funny."

"It isn't? It's hard to keep track of what's funny and what isn't, all of a sudden."

"Everyone's talking too much," Elrond said again.

"And you decided I was guilty pretty damn fast," I muttered to Simon. But I wasn't surprised, really. The elves allowed us to have police but it was hardly a career choice these days and the command structure of the County Constabulary was in ruins. Edie represented Higher Authority, someone to give orders and to take responsibility. In his way, Simon wasn't all that different from the men in the 378th, who killed and did worse things just because we told them to. Someone from the Commission had told him I was guilty; that was all he needed to know.

The car started to slow, then we turned off the road onto a bumpy track. Outside, I could see trees in a solid wall beyond the window. One of the old Forestry Commission plantations, maybe. Of course. Deep in the heart of the experience.

We drove for another few minutes, then Elrond brought the car to a stop and Edie leaned around the front seat and pointed her gun at me. "Out."

We all got out, Simon hanging on to me in case I made one last bid for freedom.

"This way," said Elrond, and in the moonlight through the trees I saw it set off deeper into the plantation.

"Stalin's men did it this way," I said. "In forests. Thousands of Polish officers and intellectuals murdered in the Katyn forest. Do you think the experience was watching back then?"

"Shut up, Kaz," said Edie. "Here."

We had not walked far from the car, after all. Elrond was standing beside a young tree. The elf said, "Put your arms around this tree."

"You're joking," I said. Edie poked me in the ribs with her pistol, and I walked over to the tree and hugged it. I could just get my arms far enough around to clasp my hands on the other side. Edie went around and held my wrists so I couldn't step away, and then she said, "All right. Do it."

Elrond moved faster than I would have thought possible. Its hand came up against my face and all of a sudden there was a small rubbery mass in my mouth. My whole head filled with the smell of forest and decay. I tried to cough it out but the elf was clamping my jaws shut with one hand and massaging my throat with the other. Its hands were smooth and hard, like polished wood. My head filled with roaring darkness. Then the elf's hands were gone and I was swallowing. I felt the mushroom go down. I turned my head and looked into Elrond's eyes. It was smirking at me, and all I wanted to do was kill it.

I heard my pupils contract. They made a sound like an oncoming locomotive.

And then the whole of Creation was inside my head.

*

I was lying on my back with my eyes open, staring up at the stars. From the way my eyes were smarting, I might have been doing this for quite some time, without blinking. I wondered whether all those little unwinking points of light had burned themselves on to my retinas.

"Are you awake?" asked Edie.

I turned my head and looked at her and blinked. She was standing a few metres away, Simon and Elrond beside her.

"Kaz?" she said. "What did you see?"

I took a deep breath. My first, it seemed, for a very long time. "Everything," I said.

Edie half-turned, put the muzzle of her pistol to the side of Elrond's head, and pulled the trigger, all in one easy movement. The elf slumped to the ground like a dropped sack of potatoes. Simon took a few steps back.

I sighed. "You're with the Resistance."

Elrond stirred on the ground and then started to get back to its feet. Edie shot it in the head again and it slumped bonelessly once more.

"Nobody ever survived the experience before," she said.

"Your recruiting methods suck," I told her. "How many people have you killed looking for someone who can interface with this thing?"

"It's a two-way thing," she said. Elrond started to move again. It rolled over on its stomach and started to lever itself into a kneeling position. Edie emptied her pistol into the back of its head and it sprawled flat. She popped out the clip, loaded a fresh one, cocked the gun. "You look at the experience and it kills you, but the experience absorbs your personality at the same time. It all adds to the sum of knowledge. The elves think it's rather neat. That's how we talked them into letting us use it for executions. God damn you, stay dead." This last addressed to Elrond, which had started to move again, even though its head was more or less bloody mush by now. Edie fired a couple of shots into its back and planted a foot on its neck. She looked at me. "How do you feel?"

"Oh, super."

"What did it say to you?"

"It didn't say anything. But it wanted to know who I was. It wanted to know why I wasn't an elf."

"Do you know why it didn't kill you?"

I shook my head. "Maybe it just liked my face."

She looked at Simon. "Help him up." When he didn't move, she said, "For God's sake, Simon, I'm not going to hurt you. Enough people have already been hurt."

"I thought he was a war criminal," said Simon.

"I am," I said. "But now I'm a useful war criminal."

"Help him up," said Edie.

Simon walked hesitantly over to me, grabbed me by the upper arm, and hauled me to my feet, which was harder than it sounds because my legs wouldn't support me. I had put my arm around his neck and sort of hung off him. He said quietly, "Your face was…" and his voice tailed away.

I said to Edie, "They're quite difficult to kill, aren't they?"

She looked down. Elrond had started to move its arms and legs again, trying to find enough purchase to turn itself over. "Oh, fucking hell," she muttered. She looked at Simon and started rummaging in one of her coat pockets. "We'll have to do it the hard way." She took her hand out of her pocket and tossed a bunch of keys at Simon. He caught them awkwardly but almost dropped me. "There are some things in the boot we can use. Put him down and go and get them."

Simon looked at me and I nodded tiredly and he deposited me on the ground in a more or less sitting position while he went over to the car. He opened the boot and looked inside and I heard him say, "You're fucking kidding."

"If this great vegetable brain of yours really is watching everything we do and reporting back to the elves, they probably have some idea of what you've done by now," I said.

"We have some lead time," she said. "Not much, but enough."

"How about the villagers?" I asked. "Do they have enough lead time?"

She looked at me. Simon was coming back from the car. Edie said, "Do you know what wins wars?"

"A massive superiority in men and weapons," I said.

"Communication. That's what wins wars." Simon had reached her. He was carrying a petrol can and a long-handled axe. He held them out and she put the gun in her pocket so she could take them from him. This was the moment to get to my feet and make a run for it; the moonlight kept disappearing as clouds scudded across the sky. I might have made it. But my legs weren't interested in making a run for it. So I sat there and watched Edie use the axe to dismember the elf. At some point, Simon moved away from her and came to stand over me. We watched her pour petrol over the hacked-up but still moving bits of Elrond and throw a lighted match at them. There was an acrid yellow flash of fire, then the elf began to burn with a green flame.

"Communication," Edie said again. She was breathing heavily. "The experience knows all about us, but it knows all about the elves too. Strengths, weaknesses, where they are, what they're doing, what they want."

"And that's worth the lives of my friends," I said. Simon looked down at me.

"Of course it is." She took her gun from her pocket and walked over to us. "I know someone on the coast who can get us to Holland."

"What about the lives of his friends?" Simon asked.

"Once we're in Holland you can contact the experience again." Edie patted her pocket. "I've got lots of mushrooms and I can get more. The experience works for the elves, but the elves are the only ones who've ever talked to it. If we can talk to it, somehow make it see our point of view…"

"You're out of your mind," I said.

"I'd say you were out of options."

"What about the lives of his friends?" Simon asked again.

"The elves know what we've done here," I told him. "They'll come looking for us but they'll make an example of the village."

"Kaz," Edie warned.

"There'll be nothing left," I said. "We'll be lucky if anything ever grows there again."

Edie pointed the gun at Simon. "Kaz," she said.

"We'll be lucky if anyone can tell there was ever a village there," I said. "They'll kill everyone. Then they'll go to the next village and kill everyone there too. Maybe in the whole county."

Simon nodded slowly and said, "Okay," and he reached out and calmly closed one huge hand over both the gun and Edie's fist. Then he raised his arm until the gun was pointing at the sky and Edie was pulled up on tiptoes. She swore, imaginitively and at some length.

Simon looked at me. "What are we going to do?"

"We're going to Holland," I said. "You, me, Edie, your mother, Wendy. The rest of the village will have to take their chances, but we are going to warn them."

"There's no time," Edie said furiously.

"Give me the gun," I said. Simon took the pistol from Edie's hand and gave it to me. I pointed it at her.

"You can't make me," she said.

"I can just give myself up to the elves," I told her. "What difference does it make to me? You, on the other hand, even if you managed to get out of the country, you'd have to find someone else like me. And now the elves know what you're doing they'll never let another human near the experience." I shrugged. "And all the time, the experience is watching us argue. Doesn't it make you proud to be human?"

Edie glared at Simon. "Put me down."

He didn't move. I said, "Let her down, Simon." He lowered his arm and released her. I said to her, "Well?"

She nodded.

"All right." I said to Simon, "We're going back to the village and we're going to warn as many people as we can, tell them to run for it. We're going to stay no longer than ten minutes, we're going to get your Mum and Wendy, and then we're going to see if Edie's friend really can get us to Holland." We didn't stand a chance, of course, but it might be interesting to find out how the elves had managed to keep the country isolated for so long.

"We'll never all get in that car," Simon said uncertainly. "You know Mum's claustrophobic."

I burst out laughing, and it was only a fraction away from being hysteria. "We'll open all the windows, Simon."

"We're all going to be killed," Edie said bitterly.

"Quite possibly," I said. I looked up at Simon. "But first you're going to have to carry me to the car. My legs don't work any more." I looked at Edie. "The experience didn't kill me, but it appears to have crippled me instead. Isn't that funny?"

Edie sighed. "Yes," she said without any detectable trace of amusement. "That's war for you."

The Rhine's World Incident

Neal Asher

The remote control rested dead in Reynold's hand, but any moment now Kirin might make the connection, and the little lozenge of black metal would become a source of godlike power. Reynold closed his hand over it, sudden doubts assailing him, and as always felt a tight stab of fear. That power depended on Kirin's success, which wasn't guaranteed, and on the hope that the device the remote connected to had not been discovered and neutralized.

He turned towards her. "Any luck?"

She sat on the damp ground with her laptop open on a mouldering log before her, with optics running from it to the framework supporting the sat dish, spherical laser com unit and microwave transmitter rods. She was also auged into the laptop; an optic lead running from the bean-shaped augmentation behind her ear to plug into it. Beside the laptop rested a big flat memstore packed with state-of-the-art worms and viruses.

"It is not a matter of luck," she stated succinctly.

Reynold returned his attention to the city down on the plain. Athelford was the centre of commerce and Polity power here on Rhine's World, most of both concentrated at its heart where skyscrapers reared about the domes and containment spheres of the runcible port. However, the unit first sent here had not been able to position the device right next to the port itself and its damned controlling AI – Reynold felt an involuntary shudder at the thought of the kind of icy artificial intelligences they were up against. The unit had been forced to act fast when the plutonium processing plant, no doubt meticulously tracked down by some forensic AI, got hit by Earth Central Security. They'd also not been able to detonate. Something had taken them out before they could even send the signal.

"The yokels are calling in," said Plate. He was boosted and otherwise physically enhanced, and wore com gear about his head plugged into the weird scaley Dracocorp aug affixed behind his ear. "Our contact wants our coordinates."

"Tell him to head to the rendezvous as planned." Reynold glanced back at where their gravcar lay underneath its chameleoncloth tarpaulin. "First chance we get we'll need to be ask him why he's not sticking to that plan."

Plate grinned.

"Are we still secure?" Reynold asked.

"Still secure," Plate replied, his grin disappearing. "But encoded Polity com activity is ramping up, as is city and sat-scan output."

"They know we're here," said Kirin, still concentrating on her laptop.

"Get me the device, Kirin," said Reynold. "Get it me now."

One of her eyes had gone metallic and her fingers were blurring over her keyboard. "If it was easy to find the signal and lock in the transmission key, we wouldn't have to be this damned close and, anyway, ECS would have found it by now."

"But we know the main frequencies and have the key," Reynold observed.

Kirin snorted dismissively.

Reynold tapped the com button on the collar of his fatigues. "Spiro," he addressed the commander of the four-unit of Separatist ground troops positioned in the surrounding area. "ECS are on to us but don't have our location. If they get it they'll be down on us like a falling tree. Be prepared to hold out for as long as possible – for the Cause I expect no less of you."

"They get our location and it'll be a sat-strike," Plate observed. "We'll be incinerated before we get a chance to blink."

"Shut up, Plate."

"I think I may–" began Kirin, and Reynold spun towards her. "Yes, I've got it." She looked up victoriously and dramatically stabbed a finger down on one key. "Your remote is now armed."

Reynold raised his hand and opened it, studying with tight cold fear in his guts the blinking red light in the corner of the touch console. Stepping a little way from his comrades to the edge of the trees, he once again gazed down upon the city. His mouth was dry. He knew precisely what this would set in motion: terrifying unhuman intelligences would focus here the moment he sent the signal.

"Just a grain at a time, my old Separatist recruiter told me," he said. "We'll win this like the sea wins as it laps against a sandstone cliff."

"Very poetic," said Kirin, now standing at his shoulder.

"This is gonna hurt them," said Plate.

Reynold tapped his com button. "Goggles everyone." He pulled his own flash goggles down over his eyes. "Kirin, get back to your worms." He glanced round and watched her return to her station and plug the memstore cable into her laptop. The worms and viruses the thing contained were certainly the best available, but they wouldn't have stood a chance of infiltrating Polity firewalls *before* he initiated the device. After that they would penetrate local systems to knock out satellite scanning for, according to Kirin, ten minutes – enough time for them to fly the gravcar far from here, undetected.

"Five, four, three, two... one." Reynold thumbed the touch console on the remote.

Somewhere in the heart of the city a giant flashbulb came on for a second, then went out. Reynold pushed up his goggles to watch a skyscraper going over and a disk of devastation spreading from a growing and rising fireball. Now, shortly after the EM flash of the blast, Kirin would be sending her software toys. The fireball continued to rise, a sprouting mushroom, but despite the surface devastation many buildings remained disappointingly intact. Still, they would be irradiated and tens of thousands of Polity citizens reduced to ash. The sound reached them now, and it seemed the world was tearing apart.

"Okay, the car!" Reynold instructed. "Kirin?"

She nodded, already closing her laptop and grabbing up as much of her gear as she could carry. The broadcast framework would have to stay though, as would some of the larger armaments Spiro had positioned in the surrounding area. Reynold stooped by a grey cylinder at the base of a tree, punched twenty minutes into the timer and set it running. The thermite bomb would incinerate this entire area and leave little evidence for the forensic AIs of ECS to gather. "Let's go!"

Spiro and his men, now armed with nothing but a few hand weapons, had already pulled the tarpaulin from the car and were piling into the back row of seats. Plate sat at the controls and Kirin and Reynold climbed in behind him. Plate took it up hard through the foliage, shrivelled seed husks and sword-like leaves falling onto them, turned it and hit the boosters. Glancing back Reynold could only see the top of the nuclear cloud, and he nodded to himself with grim satisfaction.

"This will be remembered for years to come," he stated.

"Yup, certainly will," replied Spiro, scratching at a spot on his cheek.

No one else seemed to have anything to say, but Reynold knew why they were so subdued. This was the come-down, only later would they realise just what a victory this had been for the Separatist cause. He tried to convince himself of that…

In five minutes they were beyond the forest and over rectangular fields of mega-wheat, hill slopes stitched with neat vineyards of protein gourds, irrigation canals and plascrete roads for the agricultural machinery used here. The ground transport – a balloon-tyred tractor towing a train of grain wagons – awaited where arranged.

"Irrigation canal," Reynold instructed.

Plate decelerated fast and settled the car towards a canal running parallel to the road on which the transport awaited, bringing it to a hover just above the water then slewing sideways until the vehicle nudged the bank. Spiro and the soldiers were out first, then Kirin.

"You can plus-grav it?" Reynold asked.

Plate nodded, pulled out a chip revealed behind a torn-out panel, then inserted a chipcard into the reader slot. "Ten seconds." He and Reynold disembarked, then, bracing themselves against the bank, pushed the car so it drifted out over the water. After a moment, smoke drifted up from the vehicle's console. Abruptly it was as if the car had been transformed into a block of lead. It dropped hard, creating a huge splash, then was gone in an instant. Plate and Reynold clambered up the bank after the others and onto the road. Ahead, waiting about the tractor, stood four of the locals, or 'yokels' as Plate called them – four Rhine's World Separatists.

"Stay alert," Reynold warned.

As he approached the four he studied them intently. They all wore the kind of disposable overalls farmers clad themselves in on primitive worlds like this and all seemed ill-at-ease. For a moment Reynold focused on one of their number: a very fat man with a baby face and shaven head. With all the cosmetic and medical options available it was not often you saw people so obese unless they chose to look that way. Perhaps this Separatist distrusted what Polity technology had to offer, which wasn't that unusual. The one who stepped forwards, however, clearly did trust that technology, being big, handsome, and obviously having provided himself with emerald green eyes.

"Jepson?" Reynold asked.

"I am," said the man, holding out his hand.

Reynold gripped it briefly. "We need to get under cover quickly – sat eyes will be functioning again soon."

"The first trailer is empty." Jepson stabbed a finger back behind the tractor.

Reynold nodded towards Spiro and he and his men headed towards the trailer. "You too," he said to Kirin and, as she departed, glanced at Plate. "You're with me in the tractor cab."

"There's only room for four up there," Jepson protested.

"Then two of your men best ride in the trailer." Reynold nodded towards the fat man. "Make him one of them – that should give us plenty of room."

The fat man dipped his head as if ashamed and trailed after Kirin, then at a nod from Jepson one of the others went too.

"Come on fat boy!" Spiro called as the fat man hauled himself up inside the trailer.

"I sometimes wonder what the recruiters are thinking," said Jepson as he mounted the ladder up the side of the big tractor.

"Meaning?" Reynold enquired as he followed.

"Me and Dowel," Jepson flipped a thumb towards the other local climbing up after Reynold, "have been working together for a year now, and we're good." He entered the cab. "Mark seems pretty able too, but I'm damned If I know what use we can find for Brockle."

"Brockle would be fat boy," said Plate, following Dowel into the cab.

"You guessed it." Jepson took the driver's seat.

Along one wall were three fold-down seats, the rest of the cab being crammed with tractor controls and a pile of disconnected hydraulic cylinders, universal joints and PTO shafts. Reynold studied these for a second, noted blood on one short heavy cylinder and a sticky pool of the same nearby. That was from the original driver of this machine… maybe. He reached down and drew his pulse-gun, turned and stuck it up under Dowel's chin. Plate meanwhile stepped up behind Jepson and looped a garrotte about his neck.

"What the…" Jepson began, then desisted as Plate tightened the wire. Dowel simply kept very still, his expression fearful as he held his hands out from his body.

"We've got a problem," said Reynold.

"I don't understand," said Jepson.

"I don't either, but perhaps you can help." Reynold nodded to one of the seats and walked Dowel back towards it. The man cautiously pushed it down and sat. Gun still held at his neck, Reynold searched him, removing a nasty-looking snubnose, then stepped back knowing he could blow the top off the man's head before he got a chance to rise. "What I don't understand is why you contacted us and asked us for our coordinates."

Plate hit some foot lever on Jepson's seat and spun it round so the man faced Reynold, who studied his expression intently.

"You weren't supposed to get in contact, because the signal might have been traced," Reynold continued, "and there were to be no alterations to the plan unless I initiated them."

"I don't know what you mean," Jepson whispered. "We stuck to the plan – no one contacted you."

"Right frequency, right code – just before we blew the device."

"No, honestly – you can check our com record."

Either Jepson was telling the truth or he was a very good liar. Reynold nodded to Plate, who cinched the garrotte into a loop around the man's neck and now, with one hand free, began to search him, quickly removing first a gas-system pulse-gun from inside his overalls then a comunit from the top pocket. Plate keyed it on, input a code, then tilted his head as if listening to something as the comunit's record loaded to his aug.

"Four comunits," said Plate. "One of them sent the message but the record has been tampered with so we don't know which one."

Jepson looked horrified. Reynold tapped his com button. "Spiro, disarm and secure those two in there with you." Then to Jepson, "Take us to the hideout."

Plate unlooped the garrotte and spun Jepson's seat forwards again.

"It has to be one of the other two," said Jepson, looking back at Reynold. "Me and Dowel been working for the Cause for years."

"Drive the tractor," Reynold instructed.

*

The farm, floodlit now as twilight fell, was a great sprawl of barns, machinery garages and silos, whilst the farmhouse was a composite dome with rooms enough for twenty or more people. However, only three had lived there. One of them, according to Jepson, lay at the bottom of an irrigation canal with a big hydraulic pump in his overalls to hold him down. He had been the son. The parents were still here on the floor of the kitchen adjoining this living room, since Jepson and Dowel had not found time to clear up the mess before going to pick up their two comrades. Reynold eyed the two corpses for a moment, then returned his attention to Jepson and his men.

"Strip," he instructed.

"Look, I don't know–" Jepson began, then shut up as Reynold shot a hole in the carpet moss just in front of the man's work boots.

The four began removing their clothes, all with quick economy but for Brockle, who seemed to be struggling with the fastenings. Soon they all stood naked.

"Jesu," said Spiro, "you could do with a makeover, fat boy."

"Em alright," said Brockle, staring down at the floor, his hands, with oddly long and delicate fingers, trying to cover the great white rolls of fat.

"Em alright is em?" said Spiro.

"Scan them," Reynold instructed.

Plate stepped forwards with a hand scanner and began running it from head to foot over each man, first up and down their fronts, then over them from behind. When Plate reached Brockle, Spiro called out, "Got a big enough scanner there, Plate?" which was greeted with hilarity from his four troops. When Plate came to the one who had been in the grain carriage with Brockle, he reacted fast, driving a fist into the base of the man's skull then following him down to the floor. Plate pulled his solid-state laser from his belt, rested it beside the scanner then ran it down the man's leg, found something and fired. A horrible sputtering and sizzling ensued, black oily smoke and licks of flame rising from where the beam cut into the man's leg. After a moment, Plate inspected the readout from his scanner, nodded and stepped back.

"What have we got?" Reynold asked.

"Locater."

Reynold felt cold claws skittering down his backbone. "Transmitting?"

"No, but it could have been," Plate replied.

Reynold saw it with utter simplicity. If a signal had been sent, then ECS would be down on them very shortly, and shortly after that they would all be either dead or in an interrogation cell. He preferred dead. He did not want ECS taking his mind apart to find out what he knew.

"Spiro, put a watchman on the roof," he instructed.

Spiro selected one of his soldiers and sent him on their way.

Having already ascertained the layout of this place, Reynold pointed to a nearby door. "Now Spiro, I want you to take him in there," he instructed. "Tie him to a chair, revive him and start asking him questions. You know how to do that." He paused for a moment. They were all tired after forty-eight hours without sleep. "Work him for two hours then let one of your men take over. Rotate the watch on the roof too and make sure you all get some rest."

Spiro grinned, waved over one of his men and the two dragged their victim off into the room, leaving a trail of plasma and charred skin. Like all Separatist soldiers they were well versed in interrogation techniques.

"Oh, and gag him when he's not answering questions," Reynold added. "We all need to get some sleep."

Reynold turned back to the remaining three. "Get in there." He pointed towards another door. It was an internal store room without windows so would have to do.

"I didn't know," said Jepson. "You have to believe that."

"Move," Reynold instructed.

Jepson stooped to gather up his clothing, but Plate stepped over and planted his boot on the pile. Jepson hesitated for a moment then traipsed into the indicated room. One of the troops pulled up an armchair beside the door and plumped himself down in it, pulse-gun held ready in his right hand. Reynold nodded approval then sank down on a sofa beside where Kirin had tiredly seated herself, her laptop open before and connected to her aug. Plate moved over and dropped into an armchair opposite.

"That's everything?" Kirin asked Plate.

"Everything I've got," he replied.

"Could do with my sat-dish, but I'm into the farm system now – gives me a bit more range," said Kirin.

"You're running our security now?" Reynold asked.

"Well, Plate is better with the physical stuff so I might as well take it on now."

"Anything?"

"Lot of activity around the city, of course," she replied, "but nothing out this way. I don't think our friend sent his locator signal and I don't think ECS knows where we are. However, from what I've picked up it seems they do know they're looking for a seven-person specialist unit. Something is leaking out there."

"I didn't expect any less," said Reynold. "All we have to do now is keep our heads down for three days, separate to take up new identities then transship out of here."

"Simple hey," said Kirin, her expression grim.

"We need to get some rest," said Reynold. "I'm going to use one of the beds here and I suggest you do the same."

He heaved himself to his feet and went to find a bedroom. As his head hit the pillow he slid into a fugue state somewhere between sleep and waking. It seemed only moments had passed, when he heard the agonized scream, but checking his watch as he rolled from the bed he discovered two hours had passed. He crashed open the door to his room and strode out, angry. Kirin lay fast asleep on the sofa and a trooper in the armchair was gazing round with that bewildered air of someone only half awake.

Reynold headed over to the room in which the interrogation was being conducted and banged open the door. "I thought I told you to keep him quiet?"

Their traitor had been strapped in a chair, a gag in his mouth. He was writhing in agony, skin stripped off his arm from elbow to wrist and one eye burnt out. The trooper in there with him had been rigging up something from the room's powerpoint, but now held his weapon and had been heading for the door.

"That wasn't him, sir," he said.

Reynold whirled, drawing his pulse-gun, then tapping his com button. "Report in." One reply from Spiro on the roof, one from the other trooper as he stumbled sleepily into the living room, nothing from Kirin, but then she was asleep, and nothing from Plate. "Plate?"

Still nothing.

"Where did Plate go?" Reynold asked the seated guard.

The man pointed to a nearby hall containing bunk rooms. Signalling the two troopers to follow, Reynold headed over, opening the first door. The interior light came on immediately to show Plate, sprawled on a bed, his back arched and hands twisted in claws above him, fingers bloody. Reynold surveilled the room, but there was little to see. It possessed no window so the only access was the door, held just the one bed, some wall cupboards and a sanitary cubicle. Then he spotted the vent cover lying on the floor with a couple of screws beside it, and looked up. Something metallic and segmented slid out of sight into the air-conditioning vent.

"What the fuck was that?" asked one of the troops behind him.

"Any dangerous life forms on this world?" Reynold asked carefully, trying to keep his voice level.

"Dunno," came the illuminating reply. "We came in with you."

Reynold walked over to Plate and studied him. Blood covered his head and the pillow was deep red, soaked with it. Leaning closer Reynold saw holes in Plate's face and skull, each a few millimetres wide. Some were even cut through his aug.

"Get Jepson – bring him here."

Jepson seemed just as bewildered as Reynold. "I don't know. I just don't know."

"Are you a local or what?" asked Spiro, who had now joined them.

"Been in the city most of my life," said Jepson, then shifted back as Spiro stepped towards him. "Brockle … he might know. Brockle's a farm boy."

"Let's get fat boy," said Spiro, snagging the shoulder of one of his men and departing.

Brockle came stumbling into the room wiping tiredly at his eyes. He almost looked thinner to Reynold, maybe worn down by fear. His gaze wandered about the room for a moment in bewilderment, finally focusing on the corpse on the bed.

"Why you kill em?" he asked.

"We did not kill him," said Reynold, "but something did." He pointed to the open air-conditioning duct.

Brockle stared at that in bewilderment too, then returned his gaze to Reynold almost hopefully.

"What is there here on Rhine's World that could do this?"

"Rats?" Brockle suggested.

Spiro hit him hard, in the guts, and Brockle staggered back making an odd whining sound. Spiro, obviously surprised he hadn't gone down stepped in to hit him again but Reynold caught his shoulder. "Just lock them back up." But even as Spiro turned to obey, doubled shrieks of agony reverberated, followed by the sound something heavy crashing against a wall.

Spiro led the way out and soon they were back in the living room. He kicked open the door to the room in which Jepson's comrades were incarcerated and entered, gun in hand, then on automatic he opened fire at something. By the time Reynold entered Spiro was backing up, staring at the smoking line of his shots traversing up the wall to the open air duct.

"What did you see?" Reynold asked, gazing at the two corpses on the floor. Both men were frozen in agonized rictus, their heads bloody pepper-pots. One of them had been opened up below the sternum and his guts bulged out across the floor.

"Some sort of snake," Spiro managed.

Calm, got to stay calm. "Kirin," said Reynold. "I'll need you to do a search for me." No reply. "Kirin?"

Whatever it was had got her in her sleep, but the sofa being a dark terracotta colour had not shown the blood. Reynold spun her laptop round and flipped it open, turned it on. The screen just showed blank fuzz. After a moment he noticed the holes cut through the keyboard, and that seemed to make no sense at all. He turned to the others and eyed Jepson and Brockle.

"Put them back in there." He gestured to that bloody room.

"You can't do that," said Jepson.

"I can do what I fucking please." Reynold drew his weapon and pointed it, but Brockle moved in front of Jepson waving those long-fingered hands.

"We done nuthin! We done nuthin!"

Spiro and his men grabbed the two and shoved them back into the room, slamming the door shut behind them.

"What the fuck is this?" said Spiro, finally turning to face Reynold.

The laptop, with its holes...

Reynold stepped over to the room in which Spiro and his men had been torturing their other prisoner, and kicked the door open. The chair lay down on its side, the torture victim's head resting in a pool of blood. A sticking trail had been wormed across the floor, and up the wall to an open air vent. It seemed he only had a moment to process the sight before someone else shrieked in agony. The sound just seemed to go on and on, then something crashed against the inside of the door Jepson and Brockle had just been forced through, and the shrieking stopped. Brockle or Jepson, it didn't matter now.

"We get out of here," said Reynold. "They fucking found us."

"What the fuck do you mean?" asked Spiro.

Reynold pointed at the laptop then at Kirin, at the holes in her head. "Something is here..."

The lights went out and a door exploded into splinters.

Pulse-fire cut the pitch darkness and a silvery object whickered through the air. Reynold backed up and felt something slide over his foot. He fired down at the floor and caught a briefly glimpse of long flat segmented thing, metallic, with a nightmare head decked with pincers, manipulators and tubular probes. He fired again. Someone was screaming, pulse-fire revealed Spiro staggering to one side. It wasn't him making that noise because one of the worm-things was pushing its way into him through his mouth. A window shattered and there came further screaming from outside.

Silence.

Then a voice, calm and modulated.

"Absolutely correct of course," it said.

"Who are you?" Reynold asked, backing up through the darkness. A hard hook caught his heel and he went over, then a cold and solid tongue slammed between his palm and his pulse-gun and just flipped the weapon away into the darkness.

"I am your case worker," the voice replied.

"You tried to stop us," he said.

"Yes, I tried to obtain your location. Had you given it the satellite strike would have taken you out a moment later. This was also why I planted that locator in the leg of one of Jepson's men – just to focus attention away from me for a while."

"You're the one that killed our last unit here – the one that planted the device."

"Unfortunately not – they were taken out by satellite strike, hence the reason we did not obtain the location of the tactical nuclear device. Had it been me, everything would have been known."

Reynold thought about the holes through his comrades' heads, through their augs and the holes even through Kirin's laptop. Something had been eating the information out of them even as it killed them. Mind-reaming was the reason Separatists never wanted to be caught alive, but as far as Reynold knew that would happen in a white-tiled cell deep in the bowels of some ECS facility, not like this.

"What the hell are you?"

The lights came on

"Courts do not sit in judgement," said the fat boy, standing naked before Reynold. "When you detonated that device it only confirmed your death sentence, all that remained was execution of that sentence. However, everyone here possessed vital knowledge of others in the Separatist organisation and of other atrocities committed by it – mental evidence requiring deep forensic analysis."

Fat boy's skin looked greyish, corpse-like, but only after a moment did Reynold realised it was turning metallic. The fat boy leant forwards a little. "I am the Brockle. I am the forensic AI sent to gather and analyse that evidence, and incidentally kill you."

Now fat boy's skin had taken on a transparency, revealing that he was just made of knots of flat segmented worms, some of which were already dropping to the floor, others in the process of unravelling. Reynold scrabbled across the carpet towards his gun as a cold metallic wave washed over him. Delicate tubular drills began boring into his head, into his mind. In agony he hoped for another wave called death to swamp him and, though it came physically, his consciousness did not fade. It remained, somewhere, in some no space, while a cold meticulous intelligence took it apart piece by piece.

Thirstlands

Nick Wood

One thing I knew for sure; the rains were late here too.

I scanned the ridge of grey rock towering off to my left – there was no vast, unified surge of water pouring over the edge as I remembered only five years ago – just sparse, thin water curtains dropping from the escarpment into the sludgy green river over a hundred metres below me. Gone was the towering spray of vapour above, no water-cloud sweeping overhead. Deep in the wooded Batoko Gorge, the sluggish river struggled on through the trees. Good old Queen Vic – although she was long dust, her namesake waterfall here in Zambia was drying quickly too – this was no longer 'Mosi-oa-Tunya' either, no 'Smoke-That-Thunders'.

'Record,' I said reluctantly, closing my right eye simultaneously to activate my neural cam. *Du Preez is going to hate this.*

A black-uniformed guard with an AK strapped across his shoulder stood nearby, clicking on his digital palm-slate. The payment request bleeped in my cochlea; with a muttered command, I sent the amount in Chinese *yuan* from the Office account in my head.

No, Du Preez is going to go absolutely mad, absolutely bedonered about this.

The guard moved on, accosting a young black man with an antiquated mobile phone cam. There were only five other people circling the viewing platform; none jostling for a view. I licked my lips, ever thirsty as usual.

<Is that all it is now? What a fokkin' waste of time and money!>

Hell, I had no idea the Boss had joined me, watching

through my eyes like a mind-parasite, tickling my cochlea with his electronic croak.

So I closed my eyes. In the reddish darkness of my interior eyelids I could make out a green light flicking on the right, virtually projected by Cyril 'the Rig's' neural cybernetics. The Office was online, the bloody Boss in.

But there was still only a dull red glow behind my left eye-lid. *Where are you, Lizette? What are you doing right now...and are you okay? You must know I hate having to leave you; but I've got to pay the bills, especially the damn water.*

<So what happened about the fokkin' rain forecast and the Vic` Falls deluge that we flew you out for?>

"Blown away, I think, gone."

I spat the words out with resentment, each one drying my mouth further. Eyes closed, a faint tingle of water from the 'Falls sprayed onto my cheeks – a tantalising tickle onto my dry protruding tongue. I pulled my tongue in before the sun could burn it into biltong steak. The water from my hip-flask sizzled sweetly for a brief moment as I swigged greedily, but then the ever-present tongue-throat ache was back.

Always thirsty, I took a final frustrated gulp and opened my eyes. I stretched my arms and fingers across the wooden railings of the viewing platform, but I couldn't feel any more faint spray. The sky was becoming darker blue – still clear, the bloating red sun dropping onto the horizon.

No, there was no 'smoke that thunders', no constantly roiling crash of water anymore – all that's left is an anaemic spattering of water, me, and a few other tourists scanning the ridge for a riverine surge that would never come.

Beyond, the surrounding green GM bio-fuel fields stretch to the horizon, leeching the river. Over the horizon, in slums on the outskirts of Livingstone, I'd heard there were crowds of desperate thirsty, probably starving, people gathering to watch their food shipped overseas as bio-fuels for SUVs and military tanks. I had taken the long way round to avoid the sight, so I don't know if that's the case for sure – or if it's yet another web-myth. I'm not sure if even Cyril could tell me; I'd heard FuelCorps had censored the overhead sats. Anyway, there's no market for video clips of *that* sort of thing anymore, not even from the last of the official news agencies.

<Hell man, I'm off to ask Bongani how we can jack up your visuals on your clips to see if we can get any of our online Avatar subscribers to pay for them. Not even our Chinese Stanley will want to meet Livingstone with the crappy shots you got there. Du Preez out.>

Ach ja, shit, and the Boss too, of course. I winced at the sharpness of his tone in my ear. I had no energy to reply – he never waits for one anyhow – and swigged another guilty sip.

There was a bleep in my cochlea – a *wifi* neural kit was requesting contact. I ignored it; it wasn't Lizette.

"Hey – have you got the latest C-20 model?"

I looked at a man in the khaki Smart safari-suit, skin reddened by the sun, despite the generous smears of what looked like factor 100 white sun-block. His accent was vaguely Pan-European, the wispy greying hair underneath his dripping pith helmet disguising its original colour. He grinned at me and tapped his head. I've had the latest C-20 model inserted, no need for vocal commands, it's all thought operated."

"Mine's an old C-12 model," I said, scanning past him, along the escarpment and eastwards to the vast maize fields below, which looked as if they were encircling and attacking the shrinking strip of green riverine bush and trees. Perhaps I'd edit the clip later; momentarily too embarrassed to audibly cut my shoot.

The man went on talking, breathing hot meat and beer onto me and I wondered briefly whether he'd heroically Safari-Shot drugged meat before eating it: "My Rig's compatible with the latest web-designs from China and is wired into the optic nerve for six-factor zoom capability."

"That's good to hear, I'm afraid mine just does a job."

It was then that I saw them, scattered on the edge of the trees, as if they'd died seeking cover from encroaching razor-wire. I knew the Boss would kill me, but I had to keep filming –

it was the biggest elephant graveyard I'd ever seen and it had been months since *anyone* had last seen an elephant. Huge piles of bones, like stranded and stripped hull-wrecks of ships, some of them arching their white curves in neatly laid out patches – as if their death had been calm, deliberate and careful to acknowledge an individual, elephantine space for dying.

Jan du Preez may only want Live Game – me, I take what I can get.

The man turned to follow my gaze and grumbled with disappointment: "Bugger – just bloody bones, I thought you'd seen some *real* wildlife for a change. Did you know the C-20 also has full amygdala-hippocampal wiring that allows synchronous ninety three percent recall of emotion?"

"Really?" I looked back at him. For the past few years it felt as if my own feelings were desiccating; the barest husks of what they had been – what must it be like to pull out old video clips saturated with the original feelings, rich and raw with young emotional blood? It's been over two decades since Lizette and I had watched hand-held video-clips of us and baby Mark, now three years gone to an accountancy career in Oz. Three years on from the hijacking that left him without a car outside our gates, but crying with gratitude he was alive, physically unharmed. Three years since I've been too scared to walk outside the house but weirdly okay to travel to so many other places. It's been only two years though, since Du Preez contributed to the Rig in my head – to 'Cyril', who has helped to sharpen and hold my most recent memories.

Still, I've been thirsty ever since. I'm sure they buggered up my thirst centre at the same time they did the Rig neurosurgery – but the insurance disclaimers had been twelve pages long, the surgeons in denial.

The man opened his mouth again; sweat dripped off the end of his nose, as if his Smart Suit struggled to adequately regulate his temperature. I couldn't resist a brief smile at the sight, but turned away, not wishing to say goodbye. Maybe old feelings should be left alone after all, left to dry and wither like fallen leaves.

"Command – cut!" I muttered.

So his Rig was better (bigger) than mine…big bloody deal. He's not an African, just an effete tourist in a harsh land his skin can't deal with, filtering it through his foreign money, fancy implants and clever clothes.

…And me…?

Red blinked behind both my eyelids when I shut my eyes, so I let Cyril randomly cycle a babble of blogs over me as I headed back to the car-park, the public toilet, and the chilly airport hotel, before the early morning flight home.

Home... and Liz.

*

The last kay home is always the longest, so I tried to coax more speed out of the car's electrics. The time, though, seemed to drag on for an eternity, inching past corrugated iron shacks. There were people milling on the right of the road on the approach into Dingane Stad – mainly men, concentrated near a bridge overpass, no doubt jostling in hope to be picked up by passing bakkies or trucks for a desperate day's work.

One old man near the road held out pale palms to me – but I've always avoided paternalistic gifts and dependency; this is Africa. I kept my windshields up, my doors locked.

The fields on the hill were brittle brown and eaten to dust by scraggly herds of cattle, watched by boys with sticks in hands, with shoulder-strapped and cocked Chinese P.L.A. T-74's, that looked in danger of blowing off their legs.

No, still definitely no rains here either – shit man, we're lucky we have our secret back-up, Lizette; a hedge against the soaring costs of privatised water

My eyes blinked heavily with the alternating early morning sunlight and the spidery-web shadows of overhead pirate cables snaking down from Council Electric grids and pylons into the shacks along the roadside. The cables will be cut by officials come sunset tonight and will have sprung-back magically by tomorrow morning. Crazy, man, absolutely bedonered, holding an impoverished community to electric ransom, when there's so much sun for free.

My car was on auto as it turned into the long and bumpy drive past neighbouring sugar-cane fields up to our small-holding, an old disused farmhouse we'd bought at a financial stretch called 'Cope's Folly'...in search of a 'simpler' semi-rural lifestyle. Hah.

I closed my eyes and sent yet another desperate message, almost a plea: <*I'm home, Lizette.*>

The red light under my left lid continued to ache for moments.

And then flickered green: <*About bledy time, Mister Graham bledy Mason.*>

Relief flooded me. *So she's still pissed off with me. That's something, at least.*

The black electrified gates swung open to the car's emitted password.

Liz was waiting, arms crossed, gum-booted and dishevelled in loose and dirty clothes, glowering. There was a barrow of carrots next to her – a good looking bunch, so no doubt due to go to the neighbouring township Co-op, as she's done ever since we moved here and she started growing food.

We pecked cheeks warily, eye contact tentative, and I'm awkward with a complex mix of feelings. Lizette's a big-boned woman, dark of skin, with wild woolly hair that she shoves back with a red Alice-band. Her black hair was greying quickly now, which she almost flaunts with a twist of her band – her brown eyes are lovely, I gave her a furtive glance, even when she's angry. But the anger seemed to have dimmed, she was almost...anxious?

It's not like her to be fearful – she still drives herself alone into the township when I'm away, despite what I always tell her about the dangers. Nah, I must be wrong. She can't be nervous, not Lizzie.

She wheeled the barrow off to pack the carrots away in the shed. I stepped inside and through to the hot sunken lounge, with its big AG ('almost green') Aircon against the far wall. My presence tripped the air-conditioner switch with a 'click';

whirring on. The web-portal was tucked away discreetly in the corner as she'd insisted when I'd had it installed for her, but the controls were on red, as if constantly locked, unused. But she'd sent me that response just before I arrived – and a new decorative screen-saver spiralled, a fuzzy grainy floating picture, hard to make out as I walked through to the kitchen to make cheese sandwiches for us and to grab a drink of water.

She was waiting on the single chair when I came back and she took the plate with thanks, putting it on the side table, as if not hungry. I sat on the couch opposite. She looked at the floor. *Oh no man, was this going to be another rehash of the argument we'd had before I'd left? 'Why can't you demand to stay on local assignments, you've never been able to stand up to Du Preez, blah, blah, blah…'*

"It looks like the garden's been productive despite the lack of rain," I said, breaking the silence, but putting my cheese sandwich down, suddenly not hungry myself.

She looked up at me and smiled. "Yes, our solar well-pump has helped, although I've been careful not to let the well drop below three quarters."

I smiled back, relieved to see her relax. "A bloody God-send that was, you calling in the surveyor – you've always had damn good intuition, Lizzie."

She grimaced and stood up, pacing restlessly over to the web-portal. *What the hell did I say? Must be the swear words – she hated me swearing, never gets used to it, keen Church-goer and all – 'bledy' was the worst of it from her and even that had only arrived these past few years.*

Her dark eyes brimmed with tears when she turned to face me. She leaned against the thin computer screen and the floating screen-saver froze and sharpened beneath the touch of her fingers. It was a picture of a little barefooted black girl in a broken yellow grimy dress, looking up at the screen, face taut with pain… And it looked like it had been snapped from the CCTV on our outside gate.

"Her name's Thandi," Lizette said, "She came here yesterday morning after you left – her tongue was so thick she couldn't drink. She was dying of thirst, Graham. Dying, man, vrek, out on her little feet, true's God. I didn't know things were this bad! She's just seven years old, Graham, but I had to dribble the water down her throat; her tongue was almost choking her."

"So you gave her tap water, or water from the fridge," I said, standing up.

She shook her head: "Nee, Graham, I gave her water from our emergency supply and called the village Traditional Leader to tell him about it and to find her mom – there are others like her, just down the bledy road, man. So I told T.L. Dumisane and said we could spare them ongoing three-quarters of our well supply…"

"Ach shit man, Lizzie, you didn't, did you - that's *ours*! Why the hell didn't you ask me first? You've had free access to my head for three years now. And why didn't you return my calls or let me know you were okay at least?"

"It's hardly free," she snorted, "I can only hear what you *choose* to tell me – and what would *you* have done and said, Mister Graham Mason?" She stood up tall and focused, as if suddenly sure of herself.

I hesitated, but just for a moment: "I'd have given her water from the fridge and told you to keep quiet about the well – you know we have to keep this a secret for our own safety, otherwise we'll be the target of every Water-Bandit and tsotsi in Kwazulu-Natal!"

"See, I knew you'd say that and I hate arguing when I can't see your face. I knew calling you would end up in a fight – I'm sorry I ended up saying nothing and worrying you, but I had to make this decision on my own. Dumisane is a good man, hy sal niks se nie… and there's no way I can live here with children dying just down the road…no ffff…." She clamped her mouth with her hand and took a breath before releasing it and finishing through clenched teeth: 'No… way!"

Lizette *never* swears – and only reverts to Afrikaans when she's absolutely distraught – she seemed to crumple slightly, clutching at herself, sobbing. The little yellow-dressed girl fuzzed over and spiralled randomly across the screen. Of course… she'd always wanted a little girl too.

My anger emptied into a desperate sense of helplessness. I hovered for moments and then stepped forward to coax her to turn towards the screen. I could send her comforting emoti-messages from LoveandPeace Dotcom that should help soothe and calm her.

Her eyes froze me though – her dark, lovely, lined but frighteningly fierce eyes. I knew then with some weird certainty that if I tried touching her, turning her towards the computer screen, she would scream, hit and kick me towards the outside door and gate. Beyond that, I could see that there was no returning in her eyes.

My arms hung in frigid confusion as tears streamed from her blazing eyes.

Shit, what else was there to do? I could only reach out to hold her, awkwardly wrapping my arms around her taut, trembling body.

Her arms were rigid, almost pushing at me for moments but then she seemed to suddenly let go and the sobs strangled in her throat; her hair was thick and tickly in my face; my own eyes stinging from a sudden bite of emotion. I could smell the coconut fragrance in her hair and remembered it had been her favourite shampoo when we'd first met almost thirty years ago. Hell man, it must be *years* since we'd last really held each other.

Since Mark had left.

"Come," she said, pushing me away but then taking my hand in hers, my shirt sleeve wiping her wet face.

She pulled me forwards.

Oh…right…so she's not taking me out to see how the veggie patch has grown.

Dear God, I'd almost forgotten how much of a woman she was.

And, in the end – despite my constant thirst – I wasn't nearly as dry as I feared I might be, either.

*

I left her sleeping.

Face relaxed, serene, dark hair thickly splashed over an oversized yellow pillow, she lay on her back, a soft snore issuing from her nose. It hurt to watch her and I felt strangely guilty to stare - weird man, we'd been together so long - so I rolled over quietly and pulled on trousers and shirt, making my way through to the front door.

The door flickered and dallied while it de-armed, so I toyed with the idea of getting a drink of water from the kitchen... No, a dry mouth never killed anyone in the short term. I scanned the weapon rack behind the door, eventually inserting a taser-rod into my belt, before clicking the electric gate open in the outside wall.

The dry mid-afternoon heat carried little of the past summer humidity in the air. I breathed a set of ten deep breaths to quell my panic and then stepped with jellied legs through the gate, clicking it closed behind me.

As the gate clanged shut, I noted a red sports car parked beneath an ancient oak across the road, its driver in shadow. No time to re-open the gate – it would just expose the house and Lizzie. So I deactivated the fence charge, rammed the hand-panel deep into my trouser pocket and backed against the gate, hauling out the taser. Shit, I should have gone for the gun instead.

The car door opened and a young black woman stood up, her arms akimbo, hands empty – dressed in workmanlike blue overalls, duffle-bag strapped over her shoulders, hair cropped squarely close to her head: "Kunjani, Mister Mason, I'm here about your water."

They certainly hadn't wasted any time; things *must* be pretty desperate in the township.

"Ngiyaphila, unjani wena?" I replied, easing the taser into my belt.

"I am well too," she smiled with a slight twist to her mouth; I wondered whether she toyed with the idea of testing my paltry isiZulu – but thankfully her next words were in English: "I'm Busisiwe Mchunu, a hydro-geologist for the FreeFlow

Corporation. However, I reserve room for a little private freelance work in the services of my community; strictly off the record, you understand."

"Oh," I said, with an African handshake of palm, thumbs grip, palm again: "Graham Mason, pleased to meet you – and of course I understand." *Wow, strong grip.*

"I'm here to survey the underground water on your land – of course, *before* the white man, all of this land was ours anyway."

Oh," I said, "Is that a…veiled threat?"

She chuckled: "Don't be so paranoid, Mister Mason, we amaZulu don't veil our threats. It's just an historical observation. Your wife looks out for us, so we've looked out for you."

"Hello!" Lizette leant against the inside of the gate, back in grubby track-pants and shirt. "Who're you?"

"I'm Chief Dumisane's water rep, Mizz Basson," said Busisiwe, walking across: "Just call me Busisiwe."

"Pleased to meet you, Busisiwe, I'm Lizette". They shook hands through the gate.

Lizette smiled as I gave her the controls. She rattled off a fluent phrase of what sounded like welcoming isiZulu for Busisiwe, who responded with obvious delight. I could tell they'd probably get on like a shack on fire.

"I'm just going for a walk," I told them.

Lizette looked surprised as the gate opened: "Be careful, Graham."

Yes, I do remember this was the path on which Mark was robbed and stabbed in the face; I have replayed his scarred face so many times in my head. But I know I need to do this, if I can.

It's a short walk, but every step felt heavy, my legs stiff in anticipation of someone leaping out at me from behind the tall stalks of sugar-cane densely spearing both sides of the foot-path. The path bent sharply to the right as it had when I'd last walked it with Lizette four years ago, dipping down into the valley with an expansive view of the city, skyscrapers strutting their stuff against the clear sky; no fires today.

There, beside the path, lay the cracked and uneven boulder

Lizzie and I had rested on, after we'd agreed to buy the small holding. My bum warmed as I sat down, the disarmed taser-rod stabbing into the small of my back. Around the city lay blackened Midland hill-tops, informally marking the southern perimeter of the Umgeni Valley. Dingane Stad, 'Sleepy Hollow' as it had once been known, or Pietermaritzburg by the white Afrikaners.

'Switch off.' The Rig fell absolutely silent, no lights blinked inside my eyelids, just the red constant heat of the mid-morning sun filtering through my eyelid blood-vessels.

It'd been two years since I'd been absolutely alone. Two years since the implant and I'd last been quiet in my head, cut off from the electric pulse of the world. Here, there were no hovering voices, no Cyril, just my own solitary thoughts.

My shirt trickled with sweat and with my thumb I killed the black Matabele ant biting my shin It gave off an acidic stink as it died and I stood up quickly, but there was no nearby swarm, no nest hiding under the rock.

This is a hard place to be, but all I know right now is that this is where I want to die... this is where I want to lay down my bones, just like the elephants. Why? I have no bloody idea. Maybe it's to do with the light on the hills, or perhaps just the bite and smell of an ant. The thoughts circled my brain, trapped and private, no place to go.

Still, as I walked the path home, my steps felt somehow lighter, looser, but never quite tension free.

'Switch on,' I said, as if re-arming myself for the world.

<Hey, where the hell you been? You must upload your video-clips from Vic' Falls for the day!>

That bastard Du Preez. I glanced at my watch, it was after four. *<Work's over, I'll do it tomorrow.>*

<You'll do it now! Jeez man, I've heard of sleeping on the job, but you just took the bledy cake on that one earlier with your wife.>

Shit, I must have forgotten to switch off, swept up in the day's events and he had just...watched?

<Did you?> I asked.

No answer, but he must know what I was asking. *<Damn*

you, Du Preez, cut Office.>

I stopped to take several slow and deep breaths, thirsty as hell.

Around the last bend, Lizette and Busisiwe were standing in the shade by Busisiwe's car and turned to me as I approached.

Lizette shook her head.

I looked at Busisiwe. "It's a shallow fresh-water aquifer," she said. "It's also pretty small – I don't think it will last long, unless we get more rainfall."

Lizette looked at me.

This is Africa, I wanted to tell her, doing this may salve our conscience in the short term, but will solve nothing in the long term.

I could tell in her eyes she knew what I was thinking, even without the direct link with Cyril that I'd pressed her so long to get, in the hope that it might bring us closer. I could also see resignation and uncertainty – for us; and all we had tried to build – and, despite this morning, I could also see a fear of the end for us in her eyes.

I opened my mouth, knowing my next words could finish everything.

I turned to look at Busisiwe. "Okay," I said, "We'll help."

"Ngiyabonga," she said.

Lizette put her arm through mine. Skin on skin will do me.

I'll take this moment. I couldn't be sure how long it would last. All I knew for certain was that I wasn't ready for some endings and that the rains were late. *Bloody weird, but I'm not* quite *so thirsty anymore either.*

Long may this last too.